THE BEAR AND THE THISTLE

A Novel

TITANHEART NOVELS BY ROSS D JENKINS

Dragonhead Keep

The Bear and the Thistle

Champion of the Faerie (Available December 2011)

For updated information regarding titles, availability and release dates, please visit www.titanheart.ca

The Bear and the Thistle

A Titanheart Tale

By Ross D Jenkins

Titanheart Publications

This is a work of fiction. All the characters and events portrayed in this novel are purely fictitious.

THE BEAR AND THE THISTLE

By Ross D Jenkins

First Edition Printed 11 JUN 2011

Published by Titanheart Publications (www.titanheart.ca)

ISBN: 978-0-9866877-4-7

Printed by Createspace.com

Cover Art by Brazen Edwards-Hager. For more information please visit www.brazendesignstudio.ca

With thanks to Shelaugh, Koreen,

the Edmonton Writer's Group, and the

Edmonton Sci Fi Appreciation Society

for their friendship and support

Author's Note

This novel, *The Bear and the Thistle*, is a conundrum. I really don't know if this novel is a success or a failure. On the one hand, it is a good book (although I admit to being somewhat biased on the subject). I am happy with it, in and of itself. I think that I have crafted an exciting novel with interesting twists and turns and good characters. As part of the big picture, I have expanded upon plot seeds that I planted in *Dragonhead Keep* as well as beginning several new ones. I have expanded the world of Anshara without sounding too much like an encyclopaedia entry (I hope), and developed all of my major characters. I have (again, I hope) intrigued the reader so that he or she wonders what will happen next and made them anticipate the next novel. On all of these fronts, B&T is a success; and yet, it is also a failure.

The failure lies not in the novel itself, but in the mission statement that I made when I first created the Titanheart universe. In essence, TH novels are intended to be short, fast, easy reads. By keeping them short, I can keep them small and thus more affordable to you, the reader. The 'fast' applies more to me as an author more than you. This series is intended to be the exact opposite of the many giant, epic fantasy series out there, such as those written by Terry Goodkind, Robert Jordan (and now Brent Sanderson), and George R.R. Martin. In essence, I feel that you should not have to wait three to five years between books. My plan is to write between one and two novels a year, with six to nine months between each. Certainly *Dragonhead Keep* took that long, and yet *The Bear and the Thistle* is almost twice as long as DK, and took almost eighteen months to fiinsh.

I tried to make it shorter, I really did. Following the James Cameron adage of 'when in doubt, remove a subplot', I tried to prune away my side stories, but every time I did I realized that I was damaging the novel as a whole. I tried to rethink it and make it shorter, but every time I did so it seemed to get bigger. I tried to cut down on my character arcs, but couldn't do so without weakening my plots. It seems trite, but the book honestly would not let me shorten it.

And so I face this conundrum. I am happy with the book I wrote, and yet it defies the core of how I wish to present the Titanheart Universe. I honestly have no idea what this means for future books. Do I make them longer and larger, thus reducing my publishing schedule to less than one title a year, or deliberately keep them short and stifle my creativity? I don't know, and thus I pass the question on to you. Let me know what you think. Read this novel. Read *Dragonhead Keep* (if you have not done so already) and contact me either in person or via my website, at www.titanheart.ca.

Yours in Frustration,

RDJ

22 March 2011

PREFACE

The most common criticism of these chronicles is that what I write cannot possibly be history, for it reads like fiction. They do not say this to my face, of course, for I am their king and an old man besides. Either on their own would inspire those with soft hearts to not say what they think, but both combined means that I am forever protected within a cushion of well-intentioned lies. Fortunately, I have grandchildren who enjoy spy-work.

My answer to the criticism that no one has proved brave enough to actually say to me is to ask the question 'what is history?' I can take an argument between two people that happened not even an hour before, ask each of them what transpired and get two different answers. All of us have experienced some version of this and thus I get my answer: this is the history I choose to record, the version that I believe, compiled from anecdotes told to me by those who experienced it. If I compile it in a format that is less dry than others, well, I am a king and a grandfather. I have earned the right to my eccentricities.

The Bear and the Thistle marks the second of my chronicles of the Knights of Anduilon. As with my previous work, Dragonhead Keep, the choice to place this work in the sequence that I have is a personal one. Many see the actions of Illyria and her Companions during the Anderite Crisis as the one that would define them. Certainly it is the best documented of their earlier exploits, but—as I have explained in my previous forward—I find their decision to act more important than the actions themselves. Thus, this work is second.

I am by no means implying that what I chronicle here is not important or valorous. Indeed, it is both. While the Knights of Anduilon proved themselves martially at Dragonhead Keep, the events with the Bears and Thistles of Karalon faced them off against a more dangerous foe: politicians. Whether in the end they proved themselves the victors or losers against the intrigues of the Karalinian court, I leave to the judgement of others.

Baldwin V, 43rd High King of Anduilon

CHAPTER ONE

"The wellness of life on the Titan-Worlds is linked indelibly to the dreams of the titans, and those dreams are linked inexorably to the flow of the Lifestream. When it flows true, all below is temperate and fair. Plants grow fuller, animals larger, and the denizens of the many worlds rejoice. When its waters falter, as they inevitably do, famine, ill-weather, and despair always follow.

"Each of the Makers created their worlds and the beings that inhabit them to face this challenge in different ways. In Nintara did Gidim create his children to be strong, so that all would be free to fight for what it theirs. In Erisard did Lalassu create her faeries to create harmony wherever they travelled. In Endilsar did Maskim create his giants hardy enough to withstand any hardship their world could suffer, and in Anshara did Emuranna create the line of kings, whose very souls were enchanted to endure hardship so that their subjects did not have to."

—Ancient Histories of the Middle Waters

Theramus had never ridden on a horse.

It wasn't from a lack of interest or opportunity. He admired the animals for both their strength and long-legged, elegant beauty. Men had ridden, perched on their mighty backs, throughout Ansharan history and many, many poems and odes had been written praising the perfect union of man and animal. Riding across a grassy plain faster than anything else afoot looked very freeing and he wished that he could walk the same path as those around him.

Alas, he was far too large to ever join them in their play and thus could only ever watch as his wards and companions raced across the plain for the sheer joy of it. He was a Noss, a giant whose ancestors had once lived on the Titan-World of Endilsar. Though he and his brethren towered head and shoulders over the mightiest of humans, in their own land they had been the smallest of their kind.

Giants ruled by strength and his people had been abused terribly for countless centuries before some courageous few had dared to leave. Outcast by their own people and hunted by their cruel overlords, they fled Endilsar by gatestone and trekked for countless days and nights before finding refuge in the land of men. Impressed by the kindness and honour of the people they found there, Theramus's ancestors had sworn themselves into service, this time by choice. For as long as the men of Anshara continued to be worthy of their devotion, the Noss would do their utmost to aid them.

So it was, more than fifteen centuries after the founding of the Noss, the 'Brothers united in Purpose', that Theramus strove to serve the children of Man. It did not matter that the High Kingdom was no more. It did not matter that, six centuries after its fall, men themselves had forgotten what they had once been. Theramus did not serve a specific man; he served the *idea* of Man, the potential for greatness that they were capable of. He served the hope that, one day, the Dark Age of misery and selfishness that covered Anshara like a pall would be lifted, and their land would be great once more.

The true power of the Noss was belief, and Theramus believed in this cause with all of his soul. *It shall be so.*

Four horses swept across the grassy plain and Theramus could hear childlike peals of laughter following in their wake. He could not help but smile. It was so rare to hear honest laughter anymore. It always seemed to be one of the first casualties in the constant war that was life in the Five Kingdoms of Anshara.

The horseman in the lead was not one of his. Sir Gennald Hanley, knight of Karalon, was already sworn into vassalage to the lord of the northern marches. He was a decent enough man and an excellent equestrian, but there was something about his manner that Theramus did not approve of. By all accounts he was a skilled and brave warrior, but there was a darkness within him. He did not *shine*, and his actions would not improve this world.

The woman riding immediately behind Sir Gennald was another matter entirely. Her name was Illyria Exiprion, and Theramus knew that there was nothing that she could not do. She was the niece of the king of Nemora and bore the Mark of the Hawk upon her shoulder. The x-shaped 'crownmark' identified her as one of the select few chosen from birth by her Maker, the goddess Emuranna, to be eligible for the crown of Nemora and perform the sacred duties required of all the kings and queens in Anshara: to Join with the Land. It was by this action, acting as conduits between the physical and spiritual worlds and holding them together by the power of their wills, that continued prosperity was ensured. This bond was ancient as Anshara itself and an awesome responsibility to those so chosen.

It would normally be forbidden for a crownmarked heir to wander freely across the land, but the laws of inheritance among the royal families were unusual. Despite his century and a half of life, Theramus still did not fully understand them. Only a select few among the royal family bore the crownmarks and, of those, only the youngest were capable of Joining. The king of Nemora, Kefeus, had sired a son and thus Illyria, despite being a Child of the Mark, was now barred from inheriting the Nemoran throne. Her sole remaining responsibility to her kingdom was bearing children to ensure that the Mark of the Hawk lived on. It was that responsibility that Illyria had rejected in order to fulfil a greater purpose.

Illyria, like the others riding with her, as well as Theramus himself, had all sworn an oath of protection and named herself a Knight of Anduilon. It was, to Theramus's knowledge, the only organization of its type in the world. While other knightly orders were dedicated to the service of their lords and their crowns, the

Knights of Anduilon had dedicated themselves to the service of the High King. Alas, that post had been vacant for more than six centuries now and so, in his absence, they decided instead to serve his ideals. They would not limit themselves to one region or one kingdom. There was no border at which they stopped doing their duty; no dilemma to which they would shrug their shoulders and say 'this does not concern me.'

It was a laudable but difficult—if not impossible—path to trod, but Illyria had not hesitated before setting herself upon it, and Theramus had immediately placed himself by her side. Her courage was a shining beacon and Theramus would give his life to ensure that it was never extinguished.

He would not be alone in this. Ever-present at Illyria's side was her half-brother, Balien. The two shared the same mother, the Nemoran king's crownmarked sister, but he had been fathered by her second husband: a mysterious stranger named Britheon. Lacking a crownmark and of mixed blood, Balien did not share his sister's favour in the royal court. He was a quiet, enigmatic man who gave out few insights to his character save his skill at arms and his devotion to his sister. Balien and Illyria had trained at arms together from a very young age and fought with a lethal symmetry that was both amazing and inspiring to behold.

Beside Balien and Illyria was Theramus's third ward, a young Reshai woman named Sephana. 'Reshai' was a cruel word from the Djido language meaning 'by-blow'. Anshara had suffered under the cruel occupation of the snakemen for over a century, and the race of shunned half-breeds—mostly men, but with snake-like tails and patterns of striped scales against their dark coloured skin—were the unfortunate result. Despite her unfortunate origins, Sephana had overcome cruelty, slavery, and abandonment to arrive where she was today. That she stood proudly with her scales and tail visible against a world that hated her for existing, made her one of the bravest people that Theramus knew.

Willem Jannery, lord of the northern march, sat beside Theramus on the grass. He was fit and able for his age, but a hard life defending Karalon's borders had lined his face and greyed his hair. He watched the four laughing, galloping men and women and sighed. "Oh, to have the energy of the young. Just watching them makes me tired."

Theramus chuckled. Giantkind did not age as humans did. He had a century of life on the weathered nobleman and would probably live five more decades before the frailty of age overtook him. "I find I envy their innocence and enthusiasm more than their health. The young experience life more fully than we do. They savour it more."

"Mayhap." Jannery squinted at the four horses and riders running in the distance. "I wouldn't mind trading all my experience for the ability to ride all day, fight a battle and still be able to stay up all night celebrating." He gave a bark of laughter. "I fear any one of those three is enough to do me in these days."

Theramus nodded.

Jannery looked over at the third man of their company. "And you, sir wizard. You of an age with those young bucks and does out there. Why do you not ride out in their company and celebrate life?"

"Eh?" Eldoth, a leanly built man in his life's prime, looked up from the book in which he had been writing. "A waste of time. They tire themselves and their horses needlessly. Besides, I have work to do." He returned his attention to his leather-bound notebook.

Theramus frowned but said nothing. Eldoth 'the Red' was a self declared wizard—the first wielder of magic seen in Anshara since the High Kingdom's fall— and was the fifth and final member of the Knights of Anduilon. The man's knowledge and abilities made him uniquely valuable, and the fledgling order would have been greatly diminished without him, but Theramus did not like him. He was undeniably intelligent and skilled, but was also arrogant, rude, boastful, and contemptuous of anyone who did not share his views of intellectual and magical superiority.

Most damning, he was rude and hurtful to Sephana, for which Theramus could not forgive him. She and the wizard both hailed from the jungle kingdom of Akkilon and had, in fact, been briefly married to each other. Theirs had been a relationship of convenience and pretence and had not ended well. While both claimed to have forgiven and moved past their shared history, his constant barbs and the hidden pain in her eyes belied their words.

"You should not dismiss their enthusiasm so easily," Theramus said as mildly as possible. He was attempting to be cordial. "The day will come when you can no longer enjoy what you so easily dismiss. There is nothing worse than regretting that which you could easily have done, but did not."

Eldoth glanced up from his journal. "I will allow myself time to relax when I have mastered this ring of magic." Dismissing them, he returned to his reading.

Theramus looked and saw that Illyria and the others were almost upon them. Both riders and horses looked pleasantly winded after their brief exercise. He was glad that they had found an outlet for their abundance of youthful energy. Travelling at the speed of Noss, he knew, was frustrating for everyone.

"Lady Illyria, you have become an excellent rider," Sir Gennald said to Illyria as their small company slowed to a trot. It was not by accident that they were slightly apart from her friends and companions. "I would never know that you have only been riding a month. You are easily the equal of any knight in Karalon." His face glowed with exertion and his brilliant smile made his rugged, handsome features come even more alive.

It was blatant lie, but Illyria found herself returning his smile without thinking. "You flatter me shamelessly, Sir," she said, laughing, "but I thank you, nonetheless." She had to look away before she became lost in his warm, grey eyes. Luckily, she was an inexperienced enough rider that she could do so without being obvious. The last thing her dignity needed was for her to keel headfirst off her horse in front of the very attractive, very charming, and very *available* Karalinian knight.

If possible, he had become even more handsome since their first meeting. He was three years older than her, twenty eight to her twenty five, with just the right amount of experience in his features to keep from looking boyish. His jaw was square, his shoulders broad, and his hair the colour of honey. Even without his armour, as he was at the moment, Gennald was every inch the perfect knight. In a different, kinder world, he was exactly the sort of person she would have enjoyed receiving court from.

The world, however, was *not* kind, and Sir Gennald was merely her escort and travelling companion. He and his liege, March-Lord Jannery, were accompanying Illyria and her companions to the Karalinian capital of New Aukaster. The Knights of Anduilon were a fledgling order and it was critically important for them to receive the recognition of at least one of the four remaining kings of Anshara. Since the likelihood of her uncle granting her such a boon was as likely as a hummingbird outwrestling a bear, meeting with Lionar Usard, the king of Karalon, was her obvious next step.

Given that she and her fellow knights had narrowly prevented the Northmarch from being overrun by A'Cha beastmen, March-Lord Jannery had insisted on vouching for their intentions and introducing them to the royal court. Sir Gennald, his First Knight, had asked to accompany the 'heroes of Dragonhead Keep' (as the people of Northhaven were starting to call them), and she had been unable to refuse.

No, that wasn't right. Gennald was handsome, charming, and never passed up a moment to complement her. Refusing had never even entered her mind. The two of them were from different worlds and could never be, but he was pleasant company.

"Did you not have your own horse in your elf kingdom, My Lady?" he asked, mild confusion on his face. "Weren't your ancestors the ones to introduce us to horseback riding? Lethia, your kinswoman, is supposed to be an superb rider."

And, just like that, the mood was broken. Illyria hid her annoyed frown. "I am not an elf, Gennald, as I have told you before." She had, several times in fact, and each time he had steadfastly refused to believe her. "Elves do not exist, and Lethia is not my kinswoman. She is a fictional character from a series of stories from before the Great War. I am merely a member of the royal family of Nemora, and we are all normal men and women."

It was an annoying persistent rumour that seemed to follow she and her brother wherever they went. Elf tales seemed to have spread across the length of Anshara like a virulent plague and, at some point, they had become confused with fact. That the two lead characters in these stories, Albaraan and Lethia, were superficially similar to her and her brother made the comparisons even more persistent, and no amount of denials seemed to have any effect.

Sir Gennald, not being a (complete) idiot, realized his gaffe. "Yes, you have, and I am sorry, but, Illyria, you are not normal. I don't think you realize how extraordinary you are. Everything about you: your weapons, how you dress, the things you know, your elegance, is so different from anything I have ever seen. Forgive me if I confuse you with someone that embodies grace, skill and beauty."

She meant to stay angry, but his words, as trite as they were, made her smile.

"It's quite frustrating, actually." He continued, frowning with exaggerated insincerity. "In stories, knights are always called upon to chase after damsels on their runaway steeds. Your disturbing competence is preventing me from displaying my knightly qualities."

She laughed, her irritation forgotten. "I won't apologise for that. I have no doubts as to your quality, Sir, and have faith that you will find another way to reveal them to me."

"And how would you like me to reveal myself, My Lady?"

It was one of his most ribald flirtations yet. Etiquette told her to deflect his statement, but instead she gave him a coy smile. "Modesty prevents me from giving you my honest answer."

For a moment they just stared at one another, until her horse's restless shuffling broke the spell. Gennald chuckled and she found herself laughing as well. "Perhaps, later, I can persuade you to be less modest."

She could feel herself blushing. Gennald smiled (a smile that was, she noted, not coy in the least) and rode off before she was forced to give him another lie. Moments later, another horse came along her right side, and she knew without looking that it was Balien, her fellow 'elf'. "Feeling better, Lyri?"

She broad smile she gave her brother was from much more than her ride. "I am. I am gaining a new appreciation for horse-riding."

He smiled back but it didn't reach his eyes. "It's very freeing. You can just forget everything else in the world."

She didn't get to reply before they arrived back at the group. Gennald wasted no time dismounting from his horse—an action that, she couldn't help but notice, pulled his pants pleasantly tight in all of the right places—and checking its tack and saddle. He had been riding since he had been eight years old, he had told her, and he cared for his mount with a casual assuredness that she couldn't help but appreciate. She slid off her own saddle in an attempt to mimic him.

Beside her, Balien did the same. She glanced over at her brother. He was just as handsome as Gennald in his own way: slightly taller, slightly thinner, more graceful certainly, and with dark features that he had inherited from his father. He still wore his rough Derwyn leather coat, despite Lord Jannery's repeated offers to replace it with something finer. His eyes were dark and focussed on someplace that she suspected was not in this world.

She rested her hand on his shoulder. "Are *you* all right?" Balien permitted few others to fuss over him. As his older sister, she was allowed. Barely.

He smiled. This one was warmer than the last. "I am." He just shrugged when she asked him what was wrong. "I'm not sure. Something feels off."

Illyria frowned. Britheon may have been Balien's sire, but she considered him the father of her heart. He had received similar foreboding feelings throughout his life, the last of which he had received only two days before his death. She had learned to trust her brother's instincts.

"I'll keep my eyes open," she promised and he nodded, distracted.

Behind her, Sephana reined in her horse and whooped. "That was great!" she exulted before bounding easily from her saddle. Illyria was surprised that someone with such a large tail—it had scales like a snake's, was as wide around her waist and would drag on the ground if she let it—could sit so comfortably on a saddle, but Sephana had only snorted when Illyria has asked her about it. "I can't believe I've gone my whole life without doing that. That was amazing!"

Theramus admonished her to care for her mount before Illyria had the chance. As the girl checked over her tack and cooed her approval to her mount, Eldoth stood and walked over to her, his gait stiff. Illyria led her horse away from them in a vain attempt to give them some privacy. It was impossible, but better than nothing.

"That was a thoroughly pointless waste of energy," the wizard scolded.

Illyria couldn't see the angry look that Sephana cast at him, but she knew her well enough to know that it was there. "It was fun, Eldoth. It doesn't need to make sense."

Illyria sighed. The constant bickering between those two was the single most unpleasant thing in her life right now. She didn't know what had happened to sour their short marriage four years ago, but neither had forgiven the other for it. Illyria had asked them both—no, she had *ordered* them—to put their history behind them and they had, for all of a week, but now it seemed that every statement they made was just a prelude to yet another fight. It was getting wearying.

"If you fell, or the horse tripped you'd break your neck," he accused. "I'm sure your merriment would have buoyed you over after you lived out the rest of your life as a paralysed cripple."

Illyria barely heard Sephana's reply. "I don't want to talk about this, Eldoth. I have to water my horse."

Illyria glanced at Eldoth, who stared at Sephana's retreating form with surprise and disappointment. When he saw Illyria looking at him his face tightened into its customary sneer, and he turned away.

Illyria shared a confused and alarmed glance with Balien. The dynamic between the divorced couple seemed to be changing yet again. She only hoped that the two of them settled it before Illyria and Balien tied them to their horses and gagged them.

Sephana knew that everyone was staring at her and she didn't care. She hadn't wanted to create the whole stupid scene with Eldoth in the first place. If she had her way she wouldn't talk to him or even be in the same room with him ever again. He was the one who was always coming over and saying something stupid.

Illyria had told them both that they had to forgive each other if they wanted to be members of the Knights of Anduilon. Sephana had wanted to say no, that she would never be able to get over what had happened between the two of them, but the price of refusal was too high. She was an ex-slave Reshai who had done horrible, unforgivable things and had been cast out from her own people, and she had been asked to become a knight. It was an opportunity that would never come again and so Sephana had promised: yes, she would forgive Eldoth. She would do anything she had to be worthy of the honour that Illyria had bestowed upon her.

She didn't hate Eldoth. She never had. Yes, he was arrogant and annoying and, yes, he could get under her skin in five words or less. Mostly, she was ashamed of herself for how she always seemed to act near him and, lately, she was afraid of him.

He had taken his incredible intelligence and applied it to some forgotten book and taught himself wizardry, five centuries after the last human magic user had been wiped out. It was an amazing feat and she should have been incredibly proud of him, but then she had seen him kill Draxul.

Before the two of them had met again, Eldoth had been taken prisoner by an evil Djido wizard named Veeshar. (Yes, the Djido were all supposed to be dead and gone; it was a long story) Veeshar had captured Eldoth and enslaved him, and he had used a frightening lizardman warrior named Draxul to do the guarding.

Sephana and Balien had freed Eldoth and, later, the three of them along with Illyria, Theramus and fifty Nemoran soldiers had gone back. By cruel luck,

Sephana had been alone with Eldoth when they had encountered Draxul again, and she had been witness to when her former husband had gotten his revenge.

The sounds of Draxul's horrific screams still echoed in her nightmares. She hadn't thought she could feel pity for something so evil, but what Eldoth had done to it had been beyond horrible. He had burned it to death from the inside out. As far as Sephana could understand, he had made the creature's bones catch fire *while it was still alive*. It had taken two minutes for its flesh to burn and cook from the inside out. It was the most horrible thing that Sephana had ever seen, and Eldoth had not only caused it, but he had watched it while wearing a cruel smile.

She didn't know who he was anymore. Had he always been that cruel and she had never seen it, or was the magic he was learning somehow destroying his soul? If it was his magic, that meant that as time went on and he learned more, that he would *get worse*.

She didn't want to argue with someone who could do that, and she didn't want to banter. She'd walk away from him when he tried to talk. She was better than that. She was knight.

What's her problem?

Eldoth stared as Sephana led her horse away. The curls of her dark, teak coloured hair seemed to mock him as they bounced and rocked with her every stride. All he'd wanted to do was talk. He noticed Illyria look at him reproachfully and scowled. The elven princess was entirely too judgemental for his liking. They all were.

None of them understood him. They were soldiers, not scholars, and certainly not magicians. None of them fully understood the difficulty or the importance of what he was trying to accomplish. He was teaching himself an entirely new skill set for which he had absolutely no frame of reference.

The Djido had done their utmost to destroy every trace of wizardry in the final years of the Great War. Using their slave armies as well as their own formidable magic, they had destroyed every tower of wizardry, and other place of learning, as well as hunted down and killed all of the remaining wizards. That last act of spite, like a child's breaking of a toy forbidden to him, had been the single most damaging part of the centuries long conflict. By destroying its wizards, the Djido had destroyed Anduilon. Its body had lived on for a few generations, but its mind and heart had been killed when the last wizarding tower had been ground to dust under the Djido's vindictive heel.

It made Eldoth's task all the more difficult. All he had to learn from were the occasional scraps left behind. The Djido had been thorough in their destruction but not complete. Eldoth still found the occasional scroll or manual hidden in rubble or tucked unknowingly in family libraries. He had taught himself Renfel, the language of magic, but his work was frustratingly incomplete. Piecing together ancient, damaged works in a language he didn't fully understand was only part of the challenge of his work. He then had to use those fragmented, incomplete interpretations to teach himself the skills that they discussed; skills for which he had no basis for comparison in this dark, uncivilized world.

Imprisonment and its related unpleasantness aside, his experiences in Durnshold Castle—the so-called 'Dragonhead Keep'—had been most enlightening. He had learned a great deal from his disastrous encounters with Veeshar, as well as examining the keep itself. It formed the basis of his current work. He had already doubled his knowledge of the 'orange' college of magic—the college of matter—and he was confident that, given more time, he could master the fundamentals of indigo magic as well. (He had hoped to gain insights into the especially difficult college of mentalism—blue magic—but, alas, the Seal of Perceptus had been lost.) The next time he faced another wizard in magical combat the results would be different.

Around him the others prepared themselves for more riding. Eldoth concealed his groan. Sephana and the others had taken easily to riding, but Eldoth was having a harder time of it. Their horses were a gift from Willem Jannery and were the finest to be found in Northhaven. He was not fool enough to refuse such a gift, but parts of him—in particular, the muscles in his thighs and rear—wished that he had.

He put away his journal and laid one hand on his mount's large, muscular shoulder. Finding his centre, Eldoth extended his perceptions beyond his body, through his hand and into the animal. He could not detect its emotional state—that would be an act of blue magic—but he could perceive how it felt, physically. It was healthy, rested, and fed but there was discomfort in the skin of its back under the saddle. *I didn't comb it out last night*, he realized. *Its hair is matting under the saddle.* That would make his ride more difficult, but there was nothing to do about it now. Reminding himself to perform the onerous but necessary task tonight, he placed one foot in the stirrup and attempted to lift himself into saddle, but the beast sidestepped as he did so. Eldoth had no choice but to awkwardly hop along with it in an attempt to remain upright as the horse continued to stroll.

He was very aware that everyone around him was already mounted and watching him with various degrees of disdain. It was Balien who came to his rescue, dismounting fluidly and holding Eldoth's horse still until he was finally, awkwardly, able to complete mounting. Face flushed in humiliation, he gave Balien a curt nod of thanks before setting out. He rushed into the lead position, unwilling to let anyone see his face, which he knew was as red as his jacket.

He had not even ridden one hundred feet before coming to a halt. Sir Gennald reined in next to him. "What is it?"

The Bear and the Thistle

Eldoth pointed wordlessly ahead of him to the thick, dark cloud of smoke that hung in the air. Faintly in the distance he could hear screaming and the clash of steel.

Next to him, Illyria and Balien halted their horses. They exchanged a brief, silent look before quickly dismounting.

"Arm yourselves and do it quickly," Illyria commanded tersely as she shrugged into her green and yellow Ilthanaran tunic. "We ride into battle."

CHAPTER TWO

"Be without fear in the face of your enemies. Be brave and upright so as to be worthy of Emuranna's Grace. Do what is right always, even if it leads to your death. Safeguard the helpless and do no wrong."

—Chivalric Oath of the Knights of Anduilon

"I'll stay with the servants and the baggage," Gennald's lord said to him. March-Lord Jannery was unarmed and wore only riding clothes. No one had expected to see combat this far into the Karalinian heartland.

Gennald nodded and looked anxiously at where his riding companions, the self-declared 'Knights of Anduilon' were quickly readying themselves for battle. As he watched, Illyria intertwined her leg with bottom half of her bow and strung it with fast, experienced hands. He looked back at Lord Jannery. "My Lord, will you be all right? May I...?"

He nodded. "Yes, yes, of course. Go with them. Keep them safe."

"Yes, My Lord." Sir Gennald examined his own weapons. He was not decked out for war, not this far away from the march. He had brought his chain, but it was bundled away and would take far too long to put on. He still had his sword and shield and had brought a light lance, but it was more a pennon pole than a weapon. He doubted it would survive a strike against anyone larger than a teenage girl. His tunic was thick leather and better than no protection at all, but not by much. It would have to do.

A righteous knight is never without defence. He is always protected by Emuranna. So it said in the Code of Chivalry and he believed it. He treasured Emuranna's Grace but saw no harm in reinforcing that with a thick set of mail. Just because he was knight did not mean that he was a fool.

He rode up alongside Illyria, who was in the process of fastening her belt with its attached quiver and scabbard. Despite the severity of the situation, he could not help but notice the beguiling way her head moved as she shrugged her hair aside and how her tunic and pants adhered to her lithe figure. It was hard to accept the idea of a woman calling herself a knight and actively putting herself into harm's way. Illyria had proved herself skilled, capable, and determined, but his every instinct rebelled at the thought of her marching into danger.

He could never say such a thing aloud, not after his lord had publicly praised their courage and endorsed their claims of knighthood. Gennald would never contradict or undermine the word of his lord, not while he called himself a knight.

The fact that saying so would bring hurt into Illyria's attention stealing eyes made him even more loathe to speak it.

He could see determination in the 'knight's' faces. They truly thought that their actions and claims made them into knights, despite five centuries of tradition to the contrary. He could not deny that Illyria was the most capable woman he had ever seen. She didn't have the strength of a veteran footman, but she made up her weakness with her skill and the quality of her weapons. Her bow, a relic of the Golden Age, could drop a dogman twice her size in one shot, and handled it with the hands of a master. None of that changed the fact that she was a beautiful, graceful and elegant creature who had no place on the battlefield.

She remounted her horse with only a hint of a new rider's awkwardness. "How far away is it?" she asked with a commander's air.

Gennald judged the column of smoke on the horizon. "A half-mile, maybe. We're coming up on the Kaylin River valley. I'd bet money its coming from Westbridge."

"Then we should get going." She glanced at the giant, Theramus. "Do you think you can make it?"

He smiled grimly. Even with her on horseback, his head was still even with her shoulder. "It is a short enough distance. I will only be minutes behind you." He was already stripping off any extraneous clothing and gear, not that the muscle-bound giant ever wore much.

"We'll wait for you." Illyria glanced around at her companions and included Gennald as well. Everyone, even the wizard, was girded for battle. "Is everyone else ready?" she asked with the casual assurance of one used to having their orders obeyed. Gennald found himself nodding along with the others. "Then let's go."

Her horse galloped off in the direction of the smoke and sounds of violence, and the other Knights of Anduilon followed closely behind her. Sir Gennald, torn, followed. The Code of Chivalry, which before had always guided his actions, did not tell him what to do when the woman he wanted to protect chose instead not to be protected.

It was obvious where the town that Sir Gennald called Westbridge received its name. In ages past a single, massive bridge—far larger than any Illyria had ever seen—had spanned the width of the Kaylin River with height enough in its centre to allow the tallest of ships to pass under it. There was a massive ramp on the near shore of the wide river that rose twenty yards above the water and a corresponding twin on its other side. If the bridge had been whole, she had no doubt that it would have spanned half of a mile from end to end.

Time and war had destroyed the ancient wonder of engineering as well as the city that had surrounded it. Other than the ramps on each side, only massively tall heartstone towers, holes in their centres through which people had once travelled, remained. Most of the stone buildings that had lined the steep river valley were now collapsed or in ruins. Maybe one structure in ten was habitable, and any walled defences there may had once existed were long since destroyed.

Illyria, her fellow knights—that statement still sounded odd to her ears—and Sir Gennald looked down on the town. It was indeed the source of smoke and violence. At least six residences were on fire and groups of armed men were making their way through the narrow stone streets herding the peasantry before them like cattle. Their intention seemed to be to lead everyone and their possessions down to the town's docks where a long, narrow ship was docked. It had a large, square sail, many oars, and a raised prow carved in the likeness of a dragon. While most of the dragon was painted in a variety of colours, its left forelimb, she noted, was jet black.

Beside her, Gennald hissed. "A dragon ship."

"Why in Emuranna's name are they here?" Eldoth asked. He looked oddly frightened.

"Is that your name for the coastal raiders?" Illyria asked. "They are in Nemora as well."

Gennald looked at her oddly. "You haven't heard of the Dragonfleet?"

"They're taking slaves," Balien told them, pointing down to where a line of people, chained into a coffle, were being led up the gangplank. "Children."

Disgust welled in her stomach like bile. "Not while I breathe." This was why she had become a knight: to defend the innocent. "They outnumber us, but we have surprise, and we can use the layout of the streets to our advantage." She glanced at her brother. "How many do you think? Thirty?"

"If each oar has two rowers then there's forty of them. Maybe more." He eyed his sister cautiously. "Those are long odds, Lyri."

"Not if the townsfolk get involved." Balien was right, as always. Attacking seven to one odds was suicide, but there were hundreds of townspeople gathered on the dock. They were cowed with fear now, but surely they would rise to action if given the proper example. A plan began to form in her mind. "We have to cut off their retreat. Sephana, Eldoth, follow the ramp to the riverbank and work your way around to their ship. Try not to get noticed. Do what you can to disable their vessel and free their prisoners." She glanced at the others. "Balien, Gennald, wait for Theramus to arrive, then charge down the main road to the docks. Make as much noise as you can."

"Where will you be?" Balien asked. Gennald, beside him, looked hesitant.

"In that tower." She pointed to a reasonably intact three story building part way down the side of the valley. "I should have a complete view from there and be able to support you."

The others nodded and began to check their gear. "My day was feeling incomplete somehow, but now that I am charging into certain death everything is right once more," Eldoth groused. He said nothing other than his perfunctory complaint, which Illyria took for consent.

Gennald put his hand on her arm. "Illyria, we can't do this. They're Dragonfleet."

He looked very upset, almost like he was in physical pain. "What does it matter who they are?" she asked him, incredulous. "What they're doing is wrong. I don't understand why—"

Something swooped through the air towards them. She didn't know what it was, but it was larger than any bird, man shaped (if men had wings, anyway) and flying directly towards them. Illyria reacted instinctively, fitting an arrow pulled from her hip quiver to her bow, pulling it back to her ear and then loosing it towards her target in a single, smooth motion. The clothyard arrow flew from her bow almost faster than sight and lodged itself in the shoulder of her target, which cried out and fell.

Illyria had begun learning archery when she had been a young child and by the age of sixteen had been regarded as one of the finest shots in Ilthanara. She had continued to hone her skill in the nine years following until the act of sighting, drawing and loosing was as natural to her as breathing. If she had been using a regular bow with a regular arrow she might still have been able to make the shot she had, but such speculations were meaningless. She did not use a regular bow, she used Heartseeker, and with it she could launch an arrow harder, farther and greater accuracy than the strongest of men.

Gennald bit out a curse. "Dammit, Illyria, you've doomed us all. They're *Dragonfleet*."

She turned to face him. "What are you talking about? They're slavers and we're knights. We have to take action against them. What does their name matter?"

His shook his sadly. "This isn't just some random ship of raiders. This is a ship of the Dragonfleet. We have treaty with them and pay them tribute. We cannot take up arms against them by royal decree. That's why no one down there is fighting back."

Illyria stared. "Your king treated with *slavers?*"

"But they've broken that treaty," Balien pointed out and Illyria glared at him. He didn't sound upset about this revelation at all. "The people below should be within their rights to defend themselves if attacked."

15

Ross D Jenkins

Gennald rolled his eyes. "Neither of you have any idea what you're talking about. The Dragonfleet is powerful and...*vengeful*. If their admirals learn that we've defied them, even one of them, they'll come back in force and they'll kill everyone. It's what they do."

"But why would they attack if you pay them tribute?" Balien asked.

Gennald grimaced. "They don't always need a reason, but, in this case, they have one. We couldn't pay all of last year's tribute. An attack like this, this far inland, it's likely a reminder."

Illyria felt ill, and not for attacking that flying creature. She refused to apologise for that. No, what sickened her was that anyone or anything could force a sovereign leader of Anshara into accepting the depredations of slavers. The kings of Anshara had been granted the power and responsibility to rule their land by Emuranna herself, the Maker of all humankind.

"So you expect us to do nothing?"

A group of four men came into sight before he could answer. They carried long, curved swords with guards that wrapped around the front of the hilt and small, round shields. They had steel helms that covered their eyes and wore mail shirts made of interlocking metal scales. "All of you drop your weapons!" the one in the lead commanded. "You're all coming with us."

The second man, larger and broader than the others, pointed his sword at Illyria. "You with the bow. You shot my friend." He grinned. "Maybe after the captain cuts off your hands I'll get what's left."

Sephana watched the exchange between her friends and the Dragonfleet raiders nervously. She'd never seen any in person, but she knew of them. Probably anyone who hadn't grown up in a remote forest kingdom like Illyria and her brother had heard of the slave-taking Dragonfleet. Oddly, they didn't frighten her.

Two months ago, she would have been terrified, but she was a different person now. Where then, she would have seen men in armour with swords and run, now she just tried to figure out the best way to defeat them.

They all stood frozen as the group of raiders approached. There only four of them. Counting Eldoth (and she wasn't sure if she wanted to), the raiders were outnumbered. The two groups were matched in numbers even without counting her pain in the ass ex-husband, and Sephana was pretty sure she could handle herself if attacked.

To anyone who didn't know them, Eldoth was just a man in a red coat, and she was a skinny girl with a tail. She knew that she wasn't exactly tall (Illyria, the next shortest in the group, had a good six inches on her) and didn't carry any weapons larger than her dagger, and if that made people overlook her then that was their mistake. More than one person had underestimated Dawn's First Crescent and died because of it.

Dawn's First Crescent was her dagger, and it was unlike any weapon that anyone—even Theramus—had ever seen. It was a pretty name for a pretty weapon; as pretty as an ancient, indestructible, magical knife could be, anyway. She'd found it inside a wizard's tower deep underground. (She had no clue how a four level, trap-ridden labyrinth could possibly be called a 'tower', but that was another issue altogether) She didn't know why it had been there or who had placed it, but as soon as she had picked it up she had known how to use it.

Armed with her unique weapon and her special instinct that had come with it, she was pretty sure that a single Dragonfleet raider wasn't going to be a problem; assuming it came to violence (and she was pretty sure that it would). There was no way Balien was going to put up with anyone threatening to mutilate his sister or whatever other disgusting thing the big raider was implying, and even less chance of Illyria tolerating it.

She was quite surprised, then, when the first one to act was Sir Gennald.

Gennald didn't know why he did it. It was stupid, impulsive, in defiance of treaty and, arguably, in violation of the Code of Chivalry. Certainly if Lord Jannery was here he would order Gennald to do nothing. And yet...

That Dragonfleet thug had threatened Illyria. He'd threatened to *cut off her hands*. Every argument, every piece of logic, every royal declaration suddenly disappeared into a red haze of anger. Even before he knew that he was doing it, Gennald had drawn his sword, closed the distance between himself and the four raiders, and attacked.

He could see the surprise in the nearest man's eye as he hastily blocked Gennald's attack and countered with his curved sword. Gennald deflected the blow on his own shield but could not retaliate because the raider next to him also attacked.

Gennald suddenly realized that, because his hasty, impulsive action, he was outnumbered four to one. *If my final act is to die for Illyria's honour, then so be it!* He renewed his attack.

The raider on his right gasped and fell, an arrow as long as his leg having gone *through* his shield and into his chest. The man on his left turned and parried frantically as Balien's longsword came at him, seemingly from five directions at once. He managed to prevent the sword from cutting him, but did not see Balien's foot hooking his own and sending him sprawling. He hadn't even come to rest on the ground before his heart had been pierced by Balien's follow up attack.

Gennald used the distraction to knock his own opponent's weapon aside and plunge his broadsword into the man's breast. He turned to face the fourth Dragonfleet raider. The man's sword was raised to his shoulder, but before he could slash it across Gennald's chest something caught his wrist and jerked him off balance. Gennald spared the briefest of glances to see what had caused that and saw Sephana, the curly haired snake girl, holding one end of the thin weighted chain. The chain was attached to, of all things, a large dagger.

He wasted no time slashing his sword across the unbalanced raider's throat.

Theramus controlled his breathing as he ran towards Illyria and his other wards. He seldom thanked Maskim for giving him bottomless endurance and strength, but at this moment he named his ancestor's Maker with reverent thanks. He could not possibly have followed five galloping horses with enough energy left to fight in any other way.

He was hundreds of yards away when he saw the flying creature commonly called a 'percher' swoop near to Illyria and receive an arrow for its troubles. He was almost close enough to hear his companion's words as they argued with Sir Gennald and then confront the four soldiers wearing the distinctive scale armour of Dragonfleet marines. By the time he finally joined them they were confirming their battle strategy.

"...we're in this now, whether we want to be or not," Sir Gennald told them grimly. "We have to kill them all and destroy their ship. There can be no evidence that they were ever here at all, not if we want to come through this alive."

Illyria saw Theramus approach and nodded to him. "The plan stays the same. Theramus, you're with Gennald and Balien. Sephana, Eldoth: that ship *cannot* escape. Do whatever you have to." She looked them all in the eye, every inch of her the commander he knew her to be. They all nodded. "Emuranna grant us victory."

The words were barely out of her mouth before Sephana poked Eldoth in the shoulder and motioned him towards the entrance ramp of the collapsed bridge. Illyria herself was unobtrusively making her way down to a multi story building part way down the valley's slope.

Gennald turned to Balien. "Does she always act so rashly? How do you stand it?"

The corner of Balien's lip curled. "Now you know how I feel."

"We are engaging a Dragonfleet longship?" Theramus asked Balien. "Is that wise? The consequences from this could be severe."

"That decision has been taken from us," the dark-haired swordsman said flatly. "They're nearly in position. It's time." He vaulted into his saddle.

"Time for what?" Theramus asked. "What is our strategy?"

"We charge." Sir Gennald, already mounted, held his lance in one hand and a brass horn in the other. "Right down their throats." Taking a deep breath, he blew into it and a deep, resonant note emerged.

Below them, on the wharf, hundreds of heads turned to see the two armed horsemen poised at the top of the hill. Sir Gennald spurred his horse with a cry and began to run down the steep street, Balien only seconds behind him.

Theramus sighed and readied his battle axe. In human hands it would have been considered a polearm. *It seems my running for today has yet to come to an end.* He followed the two men down the hill and into battle.

Illyria scaled the side of the house easily. Gennald's horn had caught everyone's attention and she wanted to be in a position to aid the brave efforts of her brother and the handsome, reckless knight who accompanied him. She watched with half an eye as the two of them trampled through a group of four raiders foolish enough to try and stop them.

There were twenty-some soldiers in the wharf area. Most were human, but she saw a few flashes of fur or strange coloured skin in amongst them. Standing among them, bellowing loudly, was a tall, broad creature with long horns emerging from its head. At first she thought the horns were some sort of helmet—it was wearing elaborate armour to enhance its stature—but soon realized that the massive horns that the powerful bull's head emerged from was no affectation. It towered head and shoulders above the other raiders and carried an axe with a head that was three feet across if it was an inch.

She fitted and an arrow into her bow and was targeting it into the bull's eye (a horrible pun, and yet appropriate) when she caught sight of movement in the corner of her vision. She was barely able to duck before the winged creature she had shot earlier—though not well enough, obviously—swooped into sight and hurled a spinning blade towards her head.

She cursed and loosed her shaft at the flying creature instead, but her shot was hasty, and it dodged behind a chimney.

It seemed that her companions were on their own until she dealt with this creature. She hoped that they would be all right.

CHAPTER THREE

"Loeking and his 'Dragonfleet' came at the very worst time of the Great War. The armies of the High King, already weakened from fighting against the Nintaran Invasions and fully committed to repelling the newly arrived Djido threat, couldn't react fast enough or hard enough to seriously challenge the sudden arrival of his raiding ships. By the time it was realized how great a threat Loeking was, he was dug into Anshara like a tick and there was no getting rid of him. The Dragonfleet was here to stay."

—The Rise and Fall of Loeking the Maimed, *Author Unknown*

Sephana peered over the edge of the green heartstone tower that had, once upon a time, acted as a support pillar for a huge stone bridge spanning the river. The huge tower—it went up at least fifty yards over her head, maybe twice that—now sat on the edge of a ramp to nowhere. A very *tall* ramp to nowhere. They had to be at least twenty yards over the river, and it was straight down the whole way.

"Nope," she reported to Eldoth, who was already breathing hard from the short run to get here. "We're not getting down that way."

The wizard eyed the distance between them and the vessel docked below. Straight line, it was probably two hundred yards. "I could ignite it from here," he said, "but I doubt that such a fire would destroy the vessel."

She scowled at him. "Not to mention that there are innocent kids aboard." He could be such an *ass* sometimes.

"Then how do you propose we get there?" He demanded. "I am not jumping into the river. We don't know how deep it is."

She chewed her inside of her cheek. For some reason it always helped her think. "We'll have to go down the side." Realistically, it was the only way down and they both knew it. They'd just been hoping for an alternative. The side of the ramp was steep and full of sharp, jutting rocks.

Looking down from the top of the ramp, it wasn't *that* bad. She was pretty sure she could navigate her way down without hurting herself, but Eldoth was another matter.

In the distance she heard the high, pure musical call of a brass horn and saw Gennald and Balien galloping down the main street. Illyria was climbing into place on the top of a tall building. They were running out of time. If she and Eldoth couldn't get behind the Dragonfleet raiders and onto their boat, then their frontal charge was going to be suicide.

"Come on. We have to go."

Eldoth looked down the steep slope and grimaced. "If we must."

Sephana held Dawn's First Crescent handle first and flicked her wrist. The mushroom shaped pommel detached from the rest of the blade and fell to the ground, attached by a chain no thicker than a length of twine. Her hand, wrapped in a glove made of fine mesh very similar to the chain, applied a small amount of pressure in just the right way and the pommel retracted back into the dagger handle. Another subtle press stopped it but kept the solid pommel hurling through the air. She caught the airborne object easily and handed it to Eldoth. "Take this. I'll lower you down."

He examined her for a moment, his face grave, before nodding and taking it. Bracing her legs and wrapping her free arm around a ruined pillar, Sephana began to extend the chain and lower Eldoth safely down the slope.

It seemed ludicrous that a woman her size could lower a man almost twice her weight by a chain no thicker than a string, but Sephana had stopped marvelling over things like that. The chain, like the rest of the blade, was made of Ansharite and was, as far as she could tell, completely indestructible. She was pretty sure that she could use it to carry an elephant if she had to. When wearing the glove (which she always did) and holding Dawn's First Crescent, she had found that she could hold a ridiculous amount of weight without losing her grip (although, really, an elephant was probably too much). Holding Eldoth, with her body braced and arm anchoring her, was no problem.

Eldoth reached the chain's limit—about ten yards—and found a projecting rock to lean against. Sephana retracted her chain and, not letting herself think about it, stepped over the edge.

It wasn't quite a sheer drop, but it was close. Certainly, looking at it from below, she would call the slab of jagged stone an 'angled wall' before she called it a ramp. She wasn't quite falling, but she couldn't really call the movement of her feet down the steep stone 'running' either.

Don't think about it. Just do it. She would not think about how many pieces her body would break into if she couldn't break her fall. She would not mentally count the number of broken bones she would receive if she slammed into the rock Eldoth was standing on. *Don't think. Trust your instincts.*

Without pondering 'why', Sephana gathered her feet under her and leapt. Falling for real now, she flung her dagger's weighted pommel to the side and, at the same time, extended the inch long blades that hid inside it. They were razor sharp and could easily cut flesh, but also transformed the pommel into a grappling hook.

It caught in a small crevice that Sephana had only been peripherally aware of and she immediately began to retract the chain and used it to slow her fall. Less than a second later she was standing next to Eldoth half way down the slope.

"That was reckless...stupid...imbecilic!" His face was red as he spluttered with rage. "What would have happened if you'd missed your throw? How can you possibly justify such behaviour?"

She smiled sweetly, which she knew would anger him even more. He was so easy sometimes. "We don't have time to argue about this, *mother*. I think one more time will get us down. Are you ready?" She offered him the pommel.

Brown eyes blazing with anger, Eldoth snatched it from her hands.

Sir Gennald resisted the urge to charge. It was natural for a cavalryman to want to crush his enemies beneath his mount's steel-shod hooves. The thrill of power one had astride a well-trained horse was almost overwhelming, especially when the enemy was one as long hated as the damned Dragonfleet.

He was but one man, however, and could not afford to act impulsively. A single mounted knight charging into numerous foes was likely to be overwhelmed and dragged from his horse. If Balien had been a greater rider, then perhaps Gennald would have risked it, but the elven warrior, while many things, was not a cavalryman.

Indeed, Balien had already dismounted and was fighting with his longsword to great effect. Gennald had never seen a weapon quite like Balien's—long enough to be a greatsword, but light enough to wield one handed—nor seen one used in such a way. Balien carried it like a staff as often as not, and used the wide crossguard to catch blades, feet, and necks with equal facility.

At his side, with the faithfulness of a hound, was the giant, Theramus. He carried a short handled halberd in both hands and cleared a swath around him with every mighty swing. Dragonfleet raiders swarmed them in an a vain attempt to overwhelm the two warriors and failed in every attempt. Gennald was content to manoeuvre himself and his warhorse around them like a bee around a hive and lay about him with sword and hoof to any head foolish enough to enter his reach.

The bull-headed giant that Gennald guessed to be their leader had yet to enter the fray. He held his humungous axe aloft with one hand and bellowed orders to all around him. The town's citizenry remained under guard and were threatened with painful death if they chose to enter the fray.

Please, Emuranna, let Illyria be all right. It was maddening that he could not see her or know how she was fairing. There was a distinct lack of Dragonfleet corpses riddled with leg-length arrows, though it was possible she was busy elsewhere.

"Archers!" the giant bellowed and Gennald cursed. Balien and Theramus were mixed in with the infantry and made poor targets, but a lone man on horseback was much more inviting. He saw the six men with bows take position on the deck of the ship and made for the nearest side street.

Balien and Gennald would be fine for the moment; they'd have to be. Emuranna, it seemed, had given him the sign he needed. He galloped off behind cover in search of beautiful elven archers.

Eldoth did his utmost to ignore the way his wet clothing clung uncomfortably as he held to the end of Sephana's dagger. He could not argue with the logic of entering the river and approaching the ship from the far side, nor with Sephana's plan of scaling the side of the vessel and using her fascinating magical dagger to pull him up to the deck.

He was no athlete and made no claim to be. There were any number of better things to do than run around sweating and grunting, and thus he had always refrained. Why heave uselessly at a rock when an examination and subsequent proper application of force could perform the same job with a tenth of the effort?

Since becoming a knight, however, he had discovered a critical flaw in his logic. There were times—such as in the midst of combat or scaling the sides of ships—when there was simply no substitute for physical prowess, and a lifetime pursuing scholarly pursuits had left him severely lacking in those areas.

Therefore, despite his humiliation, he was unable to refuse Sephana when she offered to use her unique combination of grace and magic to facilitate his entry onto the vessel. She would mock him, he knew, and he would grudgingly accept it and then afterward both of them could resume their task.

He pulled himself over the deck rail with less finesse than he would have liked and fell dripping to the wooden deck. The smell of salt, sweat, offal and wet fur assailed his nose. *This vessel smells as horrible as the rest.* He cast the unpleasant memory aside. Now was not the time to dwell on the past.

"Graceful," Sephana whispered in his ear.

"Silence," he growled. "What is the situation? Where are the captives?"

"Over there," she pointed. "Chained to the mast." She pointed to a coffle of ten-odd children between the ages of ten and fourteen huddled in a circle in the centre of the ship. "There's six archers, three little black-haired things carrying knives, and a mean looking A'Cha with an eyepatch."

Eldoth observed their opponents as Sephana pointed them out. All of them were, thankfully, absorbed with events on shore.

"Do you have a plan?" he asked. Strategy was not one of his strengths, and she would criticise any plan he devised mercilessly.

Her eyes narrowed and she chewed her cheek in a manner he had found adorable once, before he had hated her. "The kids are only attached to the mast by a single chain. I'll sneak up, free them, and get them clear. Then, you can burn everyone else to ash."

He raised an eyebrow. "I thought you found that sort of thing cruel and disgusting."

She looked away. "Not all of the time. Are you ready or what?"

"I am."

Illyria tried to bring an arrow to bear, but the winged creature kicked it aside. Both Heartseeker and her arrow slid away from her across the rooftop. The creature had no weapons save a bandoleer of its queer star-shaped throwing knives but it didn't seem to need them. Its legs were immensely strong and it had long grasping toes like a raptor's. It had already scored two blows against her and she could feel blood flowing freely down her leg and stomach from where it had struck.

I'm doing this all wrong. Because it bore no arms against her, she had instinctively shied away from using her sword, but the foolishness of that decision was now apparent. The creature jumped into the air, using a quick beat of its wings carry it even higher before bringing the heel of its foot down on her like an axe.

Illyria rolled away from the attack and used the motion to draw her sword. Its name was Maiden's Fang. While not a magical relic like Heartseeker, it had been forged by the greatest blademasters in Ilthanara specifically for her strength and reach. She was not as skilled at fencing as her brother, but she was sure that she was good enough to cut the feet of this damned winged...thing.

It did not oblige her and instead took to the air. It arms flashed and two of its throwing blades hurtled towards her. She was able to deflect the first but not the second and felt a lancing pain in her shoulder. The steelsilk of her tunic stopped most of the blow, but not all.

The creature was too fast and her location on the top of the roof gave it too much advantage. Sheathing her sword, Illyria ran across the roof, picked up her bow, and dove over the edge.

The damn chain was nailed to the mast and, as hard as Sephana pulled, it stubbornly refused to move. If she had a crowbar, or Theramus's axe, she probably could have pried it out, but not with a seven inch knife blade. The kids watched her with wide eyes, fear radiating from their bodies.

She tried again. Any second now, one of the slavers might look back and see what she was doing, and then everything would go to pieces. Eldoth, being Eldoth, would torch everything in sight, and she didn't trust him to not include her or the children in his magical bonfire.

Did her not minding him burning people to death so long as they were bad make her a hypocrite? Was there any difference between that and what he had done to Draxul? *Stop thinking about that. You don't have time to waste.*

Prying wasn't doing her any good. Her knife was sharp and certainly harder than the iron used on the chain. Maybe she could cut through it. Not wasting any more time pondering, Sephana set her knife against the u-shaped staple and began to saw.

Huh. It's working. It wasn't cutting quickly, but the sharp, thin blade of Dawn's First Crescent was definitely making its way through the softer iron. All she needed now was a little more time...

"Hey!"

Sephana felt the heavy footstep on the deck behind her even as the children began to scream. She turned just in time to see a large, orange-furred arm reach for her. The arm belonged to a tall, broad A'Cha, and she was barely able to duck out of its way.

Sometimes called beastmen (in Nemora) or dogmen (here in Karalon), A'Cha infested almost every mountain range in Anshara. They were fast, savage, and muscular, but not very brave. If they couldn't get you in a swift, overwhelming ambush, they usually ran away. They also didn't carry weapons often, having been given large, sharp claws and teeth by their Maker in Nintara.

Lucky her, this one seemed to be different. He wore a scaled shirt like all the Dragonfleet raiders seemed to, carried a large curved knife in one hand, and had a leather patch over one eye. He kicked at her with a snarl and Sephana managed to scramble out of its way, but then tripped on one of the children's chains and was sent sprawling.

Great. That's just great.

"Sephana!" There was a ripping, roaring sound from the rear of the boat and blue light erupted. She'd heard that sound before and knew where the light came from. Eldoth stood near the railing, hands extended, and another bolt of cerulean lightning leapt from his hands. The A'Cha, fur blackened from where the first bolt had struck, leapt behind an oar bench.

Sephana ran back to the mast and resumed sawing.

Sir Gennald reached out with his free hand, grabbed Illyria's wrist and pulled her behind him onto his saddle. Her shoulder was bleeding but it didn't seem to be affecting her. "Have you seen it?"

"Seen what?" Gennald asked as he turned his horse around.

"That winged thing. It chased me off the roof. I'm hoping I'll have a better chance for it here in the streets."

He shook his head. "I haven't."

The two of them emerged at the far side of the dock. Balien and Theramus were still fighting off five times their number in raiders. There was yelling, roaring, and sounds of screaming from the deck of the ship, while, on the dock, the bull-headed captain was still waved his axe around and yelled.

"If you raise a single hand, I will order all of your children slain!" it thundered to the collective townspeople. It pointed with its massive axe towards a stock pen, where eight soldiers stood guard over what had to be at least thirty children of all ages.

"We have to free them," Illyria said into Gennald's ear.

"I agree." He stopped his horse. "Stay here where it's safe and wait for me."

She looked at him flatly, but still slid off the horse's side. "I'll stay here and cover your attack. You don't need to protect me, Gennald."

"As you wish." As long as she stayed out of danger, he didn't care what she did.

Anger flashed in her eyes, making them look violet in the afternoon light, before she turned and drew an arrow. "Stay clear of my arrow's path when you charge. I don't want to hit you by mistake." She might have muttered something else (something about 'not hitting him on purpose,' maybe?), but he didn't catch it.

He lowered his lance and spurred his horse into a gallop, curving slightly to his left as he did so. One arrow flashed past his knee, embedding itself in the chest of a raider, and then another before he reached the stock pen. His target dove out of the way before Gennald could spear him.

The bull headed giant charged with a deafening roar. The axe it carried was huge, its blade as large as Gennald's shield, and Gennald knew that one hit from it would mean his death. He pulled his horse up into a rear before the giant's swing could behead it. His mount lashed out with its forehooves, delivering blows strong enough stave in a man's skull, but they only glanced off the giant's ornate steel helm. Gennald wheeled away before it could attack again.

Two more of the children's guards had fallen to Illyria's arrows, and a third held his weapon menacingly against a young girl, but an arrow shaft appeared in his head before he could inflict any harm.

Keeping his distance from the giant, Gennald approached the gathered townsfolk.

"I understand your fear, but the Dragonfleet cannot harm you if they are all dead!" he said to them. "We can make it seem as if they were never here, but only if we kill them all. Protect your children. Protect yourselves. Fight!"

The crowd *roared*.

Eldoth could have engulfed the whole deck in flames but dared not. So long as Sephana and the children remained in its centre there was little he could do other than keep the ten enemy soldiers at bay with his lightning. Lightning was fast and accurate but did little damage, at least not with the small bolts he was casting. He was unable to create anything greater at his current level of mastery.

While the magical college of energy—more colloquially referred to as 'red' magic—was Eldoth's college of expertise, he was not, to his chagrin, a master. There were five rings of mastery in any school of magic and only the holders of the top two rings could be granted the title of 'wizard'. He was, by his own estimate, only a third ring master of red magic: skilled enough to hurl both fire and lightning, but unable to casually kill with them.

Sephana finally severed the chain on the mast and led the children towards the rear of the vessel. "Do it, Eldoth!"

He would have. The spell was prepared in his mind, but as he raised his hands to cast it, something grabbed his neck from behind. Any thoughts of magic transformed into terror as tiny, sharpened claws began to dig into his throat.

Suddenly there was no one to fight. Balien and Theramus had slain at least fifteen Dragonfleet marines between them, but there were least that same number remaining. Gennald had yelled something in the distance and then an angry, homicidal wave of vengeful townsfolk had overrun the invaders. He smiled, happy that—even though they had needed some urging—the people of Westbridge had taken control of their fate.

There were screams at the dock, near the gangway to the ship and Theramus saw the vessel's captain, a large bull-headed Shadderach, singlehandedly holding thirty people at bay. It's weapon—an absurdly large axe that had to weigh in excess of thirty pounds—was red with blood.

"Balien," Theramus called out and pointed to the standoff. "We are needed."

Balien, who had been looking around trying to spot his sister, nodded in agreement. "Sephana and Eldoth are still busy on the ship, too." They made for the dock.

"To aid them, we must first deal with their commander." Despite his half mile run and several minutes of combat, Theramus was not yet short of breath.

If Balien was intimidated by the Shadderach, he showed no sign of it. "That axe looks too big to wield properly, even for someone so large."

"His weapons and armour both look to be designed for intimidation rather than practicality," Theramus agreed.

"More for the slaughter," the Shadderach boomed, catching sight of Theramus. It pushed past the sea of commoners if they didn't exist and raised its axe. "Do not think your size causes me fear, giant. I have slain Dahona before."

Theramus held his own axe to his chest like a spear, point out, and once again began to run.

"I am not Dahona," he bellowed just before they clashed. "I am Noss!"

Sephana heard Eldoth gasp and lurch backwards. There was something on his back, one of the small, hairy black things she'd seen before. It was about the size of a six year old, but the sharp claws digging into Eldoth's neck were decidedly unchildlike.

If she didn't act right away, it would rip out his throat, and, as much as she disliked her ex-husband, she didn't want him dead. *At least not yet.* "Run to the back and don't stop," she told the children and ran towards Eldoth.

I only have one chance at this. I can't screw up. It was hard, but she forced herself not to think and instead followed the urgings of the strange intuition that she had received along with her strange magical dagger.

She jumped onto the ship's rail, flicked her wrist and extended Dawn's First Crescent's pommel. Not thinking why or how, she spun in place on the narrow stretch of wood, allowing the now spiked weight to build up speed as it circled her head. Dropping downward and catching herself with her free hand, she guided the now hurtling weapon unerringly into the exposed back of the creature. It cried out in pain and released Eldoth, falling over the side and into the river.

There were two more of the black furry creatures scampering along the rail. Sephana lost herself to her new instinct, rolling forward on the rail and vaulting *over* Eldoth to place herself between him and the other two creatures. "Do it now, Prime," she called out in a voice not wholly her own. "Burn them."

Illyria saw it, clinging to the side of a building like some sort of bat. She kept the winged raider in the corner of her vision, not wanting it to know she was aware of it, and casually pulled an arrow from her hip quiver. All she needed was a distraction, something that would occupy its attention for a moment and allow her to loose.

She almost missed that moment when the deck of the ship suddenly exploded in flame. The sudden wave of noise, heat, and light caught everyone's attention and Illyria, despite half expecting it, was barely able to gather her wits enough to turn, nock, and loose.

Even aided by Eldoth's distraction, she barely struck her target. Only the enhanced speed and power granted to her by her weapon allowed her to strike her mark and, even then, she only hit its wing. From the way it fell, she knew it hadn't been slain.

Secure in the abilities of her fellow knights (and Gennald, too), Illyria drew another arrow and went on the hunt.

Eldoth was aware that Sephana was somewhere off to his side, fighting off those small, repulsive rat things and, despite that, had no fear. Despite their occasional animus (though perhaps *frequent* animus would be a phrasing it better), he had complete confidence in her ability. Sephana was, to put it simply, *magnificent*.

Even if he did want to throttle her half of the time.

Confident in his safety and that of the child captives, he was now free to engulf the remainder of the ship with fire. There were at least seven raiders still on board. The A'Cha might have escaped over the side, but the archers, he was sure, had been consumed by flames.

Their death cries bothered him slightly. He, more than most people, had every reason to wish the Dragonfleet ill. They used human lives as currency, inflicted death and misery wherever they travelled, and ruled through strength and terror. Despite all that, death by burning was cruel, and he did not consider himself a cruel man. He was pragmatic, yes, but did not delight in the pain of others. He wielded fire because he was good at it and it made an effective weapon, but he did not enjoy its use, especially in light of his recent mistakes.

The huge weapon arced through the air but Theramus ducked it easily. The Shadderach, despite its imposing appearance, was only a mediocre fighter. Without the edge of intimidation granted by its size and paraphernalia, it had few merits.

The wharf was mostly clear of raiders. The angry townsfolk had achieved their vengeance and now stood in a wide ring around the ship's commander and Theramus. Balien had run off to deal with an A'Cha that had leapt from the burning ship. The Shadderach swung its outsized axe again, missed, and stopped in its tracks to breathe heavily.

"Enough of this." Theramus advanced, feinting with his halberd, but, when the bull-headed creature tried to parry, dropped it and grabbed the haft of his opponent's weapon. The Shadderach tried to wrench it away, but Theramus's grip was unyielding. Standing next to it he was able to confirm his suspicions: massive horns and impressive armour notwithstanding, it was both smaller and weaker than him.

With a grunt, Theramus jerked the outlandish weapon to one side and then another. The Shadderach was pulled along like a puppet on a string. Theramus then spun both weapon and creature around in a large circle until it lost its grip. Mooing in fear, it flew through the air, stumbled upon landing and then fell. The townspeople retreated before it like frost before the sun.

Theramus brought his new weapon to bear. It really was absurdly heavy and ungainly. He would never choose to use such a thing against anything more mobile than a tree but decided, just this once, to make an exception. The Shadderach hadn't even regained its feet when it saw its own weapon speeding towards its head. It died screaming.

Illyria cursed as, with another jumping kick, her opponent knocked her bow out of her hands *again*. Its one arm hung uselessly at its side and its wing was stuck in at half extension, but both of its legs and its talons seemed to be working just fine.

Drawing Maiden's Fang, she advanced towards it and slashed repeatedly but it managed, somehow, to evade her.

Illyria pressed her attack. There was nowhere it could run, and all of its allies had been killed. Victory was a foregone conclusion. All that was left, now, was pride.

Behind her, she saw Sir Gennald approaching on horseback. Illyria attacked the semi-winged creature again and again, keeping it focussed on her and its back to Gennald and his lowered lance. It only realized its error at the last second and turned just in time to see the weapon that slew it.

Gennald's eyes swept over her with an intensity that took Illyria's breath away. His whole body glowed with exertion, and she could not recall having ever finding a man so attractive. "My Lady, are you well?"

She gave him a wide and inviting smile. "Well enough. And you, Sir Gennald?"

Their eyes locked and she felt heat equal to her own sweep over her. "There is nothing that can ail me now that I know you are safe."

Illyria's mouth went dry. She suddenly wanted to throw herself into his arms. If he hadn't been mounted on his horse, she would have so without thinking. She wanted to run her fingers through his hair and taste the sweat shining on his brow. She wanted...she wanted...

She turned away. It was too much. She had never felt anything so intense, not even the freeing passion of battle. As much as she felt like a coward for doing it, she had to retreat in the face of this unexpected primal attraction.

Blinking and clearing her throat, it took all her effort to still her features. When she turned back to Gennald, her face was calm. "It seems we are victorious, then," she said.

She studied his face and could not help but note and appreciate the slight layer of late-day stubble that dusted his jaw. "Victory," he echoed.

The wharf was only a hundred yards away, but Gennald still held out his hand for her to mount behind him. Propriety and common sense both told her not to, but Illyria accepted his offer anyway. His grip was strong and hard as he pulled her behind him onto his saddle. He smelled just as good as he looked and felt even better.

CHAPTER FOUR

"For a man of common birth, there was no higher star to aim for than becoming a burgess. Not quite a noble, but more than a peasant, they formed the backbone of their lord's authority. For many burgesses, the modest income that the post provided was the only way for them to afford the arms and armour that knights were required to possess. These landless knights, knights yeomen, had to work very hard to juggle the twin obligations of service thus created."

—Karalon and the Age of Chivalry, *Koren Penham*

Sephana watched, along with everyone else, as a group of townsmen (*Westbridgites? Westbridgians?*) secured the dragon-headed ship to the nearest of the two bridge pilings in the middle of the river. The ship was piled high with the corpses and armour of the dead.

The last two men left the ship and paddled to their dock. Illyria nodded to Eldoth, who merely narrowed his eyes. The vessel, hastily soaked with whatever pitch and oil they could find, burst into flames and disappeared beneath the surface water less than a minute later. Its inky black smoke marred the blue sky like a clumsy, off-colour brush stroke. Rather than cheering at the death and destruction of their Dragonfleet oppressors, the townsfolk of Westbridge just watched in fearful silence.

Would it be enough? There were no survivors among the raiders, and no one had kept as much as a helmet or sword for fear of discovery. Sephana could see burn damage on a few buildings, but people were already hard at work repairing them. At the end of one day, maybe two, it would be as if the raiders had never been here. If they were all very lucky, the rest of the fleet would think that the ship fell to some random misadventure and not defiance.

"Emuranna's name, Gennald, what were you thinking?" March-Lord Jannery had arrived in town with the servant train shortly after the end of fight and had wasted no time interrogating his knight. "We could be executed for this. If the Dragonfleet finds out, they'll demand the whole town be put to the sword, and the king won't lift a finger to stop them."

Gennald had the face of a man who knew that he should have been sorry, but wasn't. "They'll never find out, My Lord, I swear it. These people know well enough to never speak of anything."

Lord Jannery sighed. "Done is done, I suppose. All any of us can do now is hope that that we survive whatever storm this may cause."

"I apologise for putting everyone in this difficult situation, My Lord," Illyria told him, her head bowed. "It was my ignorance that began everything. The Dragonfleet is not known in Nemora, and I attacked without full knowledge of the situation."

The older man looked knowingly between Illyria and his knight. "Ah, I understand now. As I said: done is done, but heed me when I say that for all of our sakes this event can never be spoken of. The Peer's Court in New Aukaster is a pit of self-serving vipers. Information like this can and will be used against us if it becomes known."

Sir Gennald bowed. "Yes, My Lord."

"Thank you, My Lord," Illyria said with her usual politeness.

He nodded. "I had hoped to cross the river and make another ten miles before evening came, but these events have cast that into the fire." He looked pointedly at his knight. "See to our accommodations. I must talk to the burgess about all of this."

Gennald bowed his head. "Yes, My Lord."

The March-Lord walked off, leaving Illyria and Sir Gennald alone in each other's company. Sephana was suddenly acutely aware of how much her presence wasn't needed here.

"Illyria, would you join me by the dock?" His voice was rough. Sephana noted that that, for the first time she could remember, he hadn't called her 'lady'. She ducked behind a post, wanting to give them their privacy but also afraid that any motion would bring attention to herself.

If Illyria objected to the familiar form of address, she didn't show it. "Why by the dock, My Lord?"

He stepped in closer and lowered his voice. Sephana could barely make out his words. "I would see you alone, My Lady. My words are not for curious ears."

Sephana did her very best to become invisible.

She watched Illyria's eyes turn as large as saucers. "I...you...we..." Sephana was surprised. She'd never seen Illyria at a loss for words before. "I must...please, excuse me, My Lord." She left at as fast as was possible without running.

Gennald followed her departure with his eyes, both surprised and amused, until his eyes fell on Sephana, who smiled sheepishly. He walked over. "So, you saw all of that?"

"Not on purpose."

He snorted. "You and your friends are as thick as thieves, anyway. I'm sure she would have told you soon enough."

Sephana shook her head. "Not about things like this." She hesitated, unsure if she wanted to say anything on this subject. Goddess knew that few enough of her own relationships had ever ended well. Her hellish marriage to Eldoth and current awkwardness with him was evidence enough of that.

Vivid memories of dark hair, laughing eyes, and burnt stew rose unwelcome to the surface of her mind. She pushed it aside. "This is none of my business, but would you mind some advice?"

Irritation flickered across his face. "You are going to tell me that a yeoman knight like myself has no place pursuing an elven princess, yes?"

"No!" Did he really think that she, of all people, would have a problem with being poor? "Nothing like that all. It's just, well, Illyria always looks like she knows what she's doing, but that doesn't mean that she does," Sephana explained. "She's been...sheltered."

His brow crinkled in confusion. "You mean in her elven kingdom?"

"If you ever want to get anywhere with her, don't call her that. Ever." She sighed. "Look, you need to take it easy with her. She was engaged until a month ago. This thing between the two of you, it's really new to her."

She saw dim comprehension in his eyes. "I would never have guessed. She never said..."

Sephana held up her hand. "She wouldn't, but she is." Illyria may have been older, but when it came to men, Sephana was definitely more experienced.

He nodded. "Thank you, Lady Sephana. You're a good friend to her."

She laughed. "Trust me, I'm not a lady."

"Some advice, Sephana, in return for the service you gave me: you claim the title of knight, and in Karalon that makes you noble." His face became serious. "If you have any hope of being recognised as such, you must learn to behave like one" He bowed slightly. "Now, if you will excuse me, *My Lady*, I must see to our accommodations for tonight." He left her standing alone on the dock.

Sephana scowled at Gennald's words. She was *not* a lady. As much as she might want it to be true, it didn't change her past and what she had done. There had been other things in her history that were never spoken of, or—if she had her way—even thought of ever again.

Theramus found Balien at the top of the bridge ramp overlooking the river, tending his sword. All of the town and the surrounding river valley were visible in the distance.

"You fought well," Theramus said by way of greeting.

"And you, as well," the younger man replied. Balien was a difficult man to define. He had been raised among nobility but had been told constantly that he was not one of them. Even his last name 'con-Exipiter' meant that he was only half-blooded. Any offspring he might sire, if Theramus recalled the rules of Ilthanaran genealogy correctly, would not be allowed to share their father's name or be recognised by the court. The noble families of Ilthanara were very protective of their bloodlines.

They were fools.

It was his not place, nor that of his fellow Noss, to judge the past actions of the royal families of Nemora. He had not been alive at the time of their controversial decision to recluse themselves in the impenetrable Ilthwood forest and leave the rest of their kingdom to burn. He could not say whether their decision to protect their noble bloodlines and wealth of knowledge while their citizens were slain was correct or not. What he did know was that no Noss had accompanied them into their self-imposed exile. Whether that decision was a condemnation by disapproving Noss or the choice of the king of that time was lost forever to history.

Even if Illyria and Balien's ancestors had been at fault, he would never have held the two of them responsible for the failings of their forebears. He had been alive for six human generations and had spent three of those wandering across Anshara. He had watched young boys become men, fathers, and then grandfathers. He had seen firsthand that there was no benefit in blaming the son for the sins of the father. Balien and Illyria were no more at fault for the actions of the ancient Ilthanarans than Sephana shared her ancestor's sin for giving birth to snake-blooded half-breeds, or Eldoth for being descended from a people who had willingly embraced Djido occupation.

What the Ilthanaran peers did not know, in their arrogance, was who Balien's father really was. Theramus himself could not guarantee it, but he had strong suspicions. 'Britheon' was an unassuming name from the mountain people of eastern Karalon and meant little, but there were other things about Balien, things that he claimed he had learned from his father, that raised Theramus's suspicions. His sword and the style in which he used it were unique among the Ansharan people. Some of his phrases of speech reminded Theramus of someone he had known almost thirty years ago. That man's name had been Baldwin and he had been the last of a very long, very special line of people. Theramus had thought Baldwin's line lost forever, but was now unsure.

He did not know if Balien was Baldwin's heir, but, if he was, then his safety was paramount to Anshara's future. For that reason, as well as his personal liking of the young man, Theramus had made him his very special project. Balien would not die as long as Theramus lived. It would not be so.

The man in question was eying Theramus warily. "It has been decided to stay here for the night," Theramus said. "Sir Gennald has arranged for our lodging. Dinner will be served in an hour."

Balien nodded and was silent for a moment. "We swore to always do what is right. It was part of our oath," he said, "and yet, in our first act as knights, we do something that can never spoken of."

"Emuranna understands." Theramus hesitated. The question he was about to ask was impertinent, but, for many reasons, he needed to know. "Forgive my asking, but, in light of Illyria and Gennald, I am curious: why have I never seen you undertake any romantic dalliances? You are handsome enough by the standards of your kind."

Balien looked at him oddly. "Why haven't you?"

"I am Noss. We do not practice marriage as men do." Theramus smiled wistfully. "Our females would never allow it."

"As a moral man, I cannot not allow myself to," Balien said. "Any women worthy of romancing is also worthy of marriage and security. I cannot, so I do not."

"It is not right to cut yourself off from happiness," Theramus protested.

"There are different kinds of happiness." Balien said nothing as his eyes watched the horizon. "My mother and father loved each other deeply. When I think of happiness, I think of what they had together. I won't get married for less."

"You are the last of your father's line," Theramus counselled, disliking the need for subterfuge. "It would be a tragedy if his greatest gifts to you were not passed down."

Balien laughed without humour. "I put little value on bloodline. My father's greatest gifts were the lessons he imparted, and his legacy will be the actions Illyria and I perform in his memory."

Theramus nodded. He would press no further. "I am sure that, if he was still alive, he would be very proud of both of you." He paused. "And what of Illyria? What will become of her flirtation with Sir Gennald?"

"Whatever she wants it to," Balien said before standing and putting a stop to the conversation. "Her choices are her own."

Illyria did her best not to wince or flinch as Sephana passed needle and thread through the flesh of her thigh, stitching up the long, deep scratch left by the 'percher's' talon. Both she and Balien were fair hands at wound closure, but neither could stitch as finely or quickly as Sephana and her small, nimble fingers.

They chatted amiably as Sephana worked. Though they had known each other for more than a year, they had never really communicated beyond small talk until recently. Whether the barrier between then was due to Sephana holding herself aloof or Illyria's lack of trust was largely irrelevant; everything had changed after the events of Dragonhead Keep, and Illyria was glad of it.

"So, you and Gennald," Sephana said with a coy smile as she packed moss over the injury and carefully wrapped a bandage around Illyria's thigh. "Is there anything happening between you two?"

"I...what? No!" Just the mention of his name made Illyria blush. Their last conversation was seared in her mind. The way he had said the word 'alone' still made her shiver. "I don't know what you're talking about. Gennald and I are just acquaintances, friends. We're friends." She couldn't meet Sephana's eyes as she said it.

Sephana looked at her through knowing eyes. "Are you sure that's all you are? I saw your eyes."

Illyria cursed the quirk of birthright that had given her the most peculiar trait in her family: hue changing eyes. Her eyes changed colour depending on what she felt: brown when she was happy, hazel when she was sad, blue if she was frightened, and violet if she was angry. They only turned the colour that Sephana had seen, green, when Illyria was experiencing a very different emotion.

A giggle escaped her lips, horrifying her. *I am a Child of the Mark and descended from royalty. I was taught decorum by the queen of Ilthanara. I do not giggle.*

"I...he...we..." The ability to form a complete sentence had escaped her. She took a deep breath, aware of the large smile that seemed to have grafted itself to her face. "I rode on his horse, that was all. He..." she couldn't believe that she was saying this out loud. "He smelled really good, I admit it, but nothing happened." As much as she might have wanted it to. "Nothing is *going to* happen."

Sephana just raised her eyebrow.

Words began to pour from her lips like a stream in spring. "I mean, yes, he's very attractive. He has a very nice..." she wanted to say rear end, but couldn't, not even to Sephana. "...*chin,* but anything between us is impossible. We both know that."

"You like his chin, huh?" Sephana asked wryly. She stood up. "I'm done. See if you can still put your pants on over that bandage."

She could, even if it was fairly tight over the wound. She'd have to borrow a pair of Balien's pants to wear until it healed.

"Good. Now lay down and let me work on the one on your chest."

Illyria shrugged off her robe and lay back, not wincing as Sephana began working her needle and thread quickly and carefully along the (thankfully) shallow wound. It was foolish, considering the life she had chosen for herself, but Illyria still had her vanity. She didn't own any clothing in which this particular wound would ever show, but it was nice to know that if someone were to ever see it...whenever that might be...that it wouldn't mar her overmuch.

"He is pretty cute," Sephana admitted, "and he does have a nice...chin." She smirked and Illyria could not help but burst into more laughter. Sephana joined in and in that moment Illyria had never appreciated her company more. "But are you sure you're just friends? It didn't look that way to me. It looked like you wanted to tear his clothes off."

Illyria's face was flaming now. "We're friends; nothing more." She aware that it had not been a denial. "He's sworn to Lord Jannery and lives in the Northmarch. We're only in Karalon long enough to gain an audience with the king. We can only *be* friends." The idea of parting struck her with the force of an arrow, especially after what his eyes and words had promised earlier. "No matter what we might want."

"You need to tell him that," Sephana counselled, wise somehow despite her youth, "before one of you gets hurt or does something stupid."

Being stupid had never sounded so appealing before. "You're right, I should." She didn't want to give Gennald the wrong impression, nor did she want a repeat of what had happened with Alwyn, a Nemoran prince who had become infatuated with her.

But Gennald was different than Alwyn in so many ways. The prince of Derwyn had fancied that he loved her and wanted her to marry him, but Illyria had felt nothing towards him in return. He was a nice enough fellow and attractive enough, but he didn't ...*draw* her...the way that Gennald did. Alwyn had never made her smile just by looking at her. Her blood had never run hot and cold at the same time at the mere thought of him. Most certainly, she had never had to hold herself back from kissing Alwyn as she had with Gennald just an hour ago.

It was the first meal that they'd eaten in over a week that hadn't been made over a camp fire, and Sephana was determined to enjoy it. Eldoth was acting strange, even for him. She'd caught him staring at her no less than five times during the meal—roast goose, dilled carrots and some sort of oaty pancake—but it hadn't been his normal stare of mixed bitterness and condescension. No, he was looking at her like she was some sort of puzzle he hadn't solved yet. She could handle his dislike of her. In fact, she preferred it to whatever *this* was.

Illyria, seated beside her, ate with a dainty grace that Sephana envied. She kept her eyes fixed on her food but sooner or later always seemed to find some reason to speak to or look at Gennald. The knight was being more discreet but not too much so. It was Balien, of all people, who broke the silence. "Lord Jannery, if you wouldn't mind, would you tell me more about this treaty your king has with the Dragonfleet. Neither my sister or I have heard of it before."

"You mean that there is some piece of knowledge unknown to elfkind?" Jannery said with a smile. "I thought your great libraries told of everything."

Both Illyria's and Balien's faces both tightened at the mention of the word 'elf'. "Our libraries haven't been updated in six centuries, My Lord, and neither my brother or I are scholars," Illyria said with the smallest brush stroke of annoyance. "We make no claim to universal knowledge."

Lord Jannery chuckled. "You'd never know it by my observation." He sobered. "Right: the Dragonfleet. You do know of them, yes?"

"Only that they raid from the sea and that their preferred prize seems to be young children. They are called either 'coastal raiders' or 'sea people' in Nemora. Their names are cursed universally"

"Yes, well, they are all that and more," Jannery said, scowling. "About a century ago, in King Edarn's reign, their raids got to be horrible. It got to be so that there wasn't a town within fifty miles of the sea that hadn't been sacked by them, and Emuranna only knows how many of our youth ended up taken from our land, chained in their holds. I remember my grandfather saying that every man who could ride a horse and hold a sword was called to Aukaster and knighted on the spot."

He smiled in reminiscence. "They say that there were so many horsemen patrolling the coast that you couldn't even see the grass beneath them. They called it 'The Year of the Broken Lance.' There were so many battles. We burned over a hundred ships that year, according to royal record, but took a horrible beating for it." He scowled. "Hundreds of knights were killed, maybe as many as thousands, not to mention half the coastal towns razed. It was horrible."

"Then, just after SummersEnd—which until then had always been the end of the raiding season—a massive fleet was sighted off shore. No one can agree on how many ships there were: some say dozens, some say hundreds, but they landed as big an army as anyone had ever seen and raised a white flag. Demanded to parley with the king himself.

"He came, of course. No one knows exactly what they said, but they impressed King Edarn enough that he signed a treaty with them. It was either that or we grind ourselves to powder fighting them off. Anyway, this treaty set terms. Lord Jannery grimaced. "Five hundred children between the ages of eight and twelve per year, *every* year, or their attacks would begin again."

Illyria gasped.

"Don't worry, My Lady. He didn't. King or no, we would have thrown him into the sea if he had agreed to such a thing. The fleeters graciously agreed to accept other things instead of slaves: five thousand pounds of wheat or one hundred pounds of gold per child. That was the price of our kingdom's future and what the king agreed to." He shrugged. "We've been giving them most of our wheat harvest ever since."

"You son, Davin, he mentioned a wheat blight last year," Balien said to him. "And Sir Gennald told us that you missed last year's tribute."

"No. Last year we had a week long rain storm just before the reaping. Almost the entire crop rotted on the stalk, but the end result was the same."

"So there is no wheat blight?"

"Oh, the blight exists for certain. We don't grow much wheat up on the Northmarch—it's all oats and mountain barley—but you ridden past the same fields that I have. Half of this year's crop has been infected by some sort of rust that stunts its growth. And, if that didn't damage the crop badly enough, spring planting was pushed back by almost a month because of late snows. We'll be lucky to pay even a third of our tribute this year."

"And this is the cause of the dispute Davin was so concerned about?" Illyria asked. "The conflict between the Golden Bears and the Anderites?"

Jannery scowled. Sephana, like everyone else, knew that the March-Lord's son did not share his father's politics. That division between father and son had almost allowed the Northmarch to be overrun.

"I don't care what those vultures say. King Lionar is a good man," Jannery said. "He'd die before he let something like this happen. If these blights and bad weather have any cause, it's not with him. Anyone who wants to replace him with prince Ander is a damn traitor!"

Illyria and Balien exchanged worried glances. Sephana didn't really understand it all. She knew that the 'Golden Bears' was the name given to those who supported King Lionar while the Anderites instead supported his eldest son, but she didn't really get why.

"Nonetheless, you must admit that this second bad crop is a cause for concern," Illyria said carefully. "Surely missing another tribute will affect everyone."

"Of course it does. That's why everyone in this kingdom has been taxed until their eyes bled. It's why I was so eager to trade with prince Alwyn, my future son in law. Selling that Nemoran cotton of his is the only thing keeping me out of debt."

The rest of the conversation may as well have been the squawking of Myna birds as far as Sephana was concerned. Ancient history and economics made her brain hurt, and Eldoth's constant staring was getting way too creepy. She pushed her chair away from the table. "It's getting late. I'm going to tend my horse and then go to bed."

Illyria stood as well, trying to hide her glance to Gennald and failing. Badly. "We should all retire. It has been a very strenuous day."

"Don't do anything that might break your stitches," Sephana teased.

Illyria gave her a look that was part knowing smile and part feigned ignorance. "I...thank you. I will. I mean, I won't."

Despite her admonition, Illyria was far too restless to sleep. Walking the streets of Westbridge calmed her somewhat, but dark and cold ultimately forced her to retreat to the inn. The common room had been empty, to both her relief and frustration, and she finally gave up. Whatever it was that she was expecting to happen (although she wasn't entirely sure what that was) wasn't. Unable to think and beginning to feel foolish, she finally began to make her way to her room.

Gennald stood in the shadowed hallway, obviously waiting, and a shiver of excitement went through her. *This* was what she had wanted to happen. If it had been anyone else, finding someone loitering outside her door would have been annoying, or even alarming, but it was *Gennald*, and he was doing it for her. It made her feel...warm.

The wisdom of Sephana's advice rang as true now as when she had first said it. Their situation was impossible, and it made absolutely no sense to begin anything with him. She would tell him that, right here and now.

Really, she would.

Gennald walked up to her, his broad shoulders taking up most of the hallway and his tunic stretched tightly across his chest. His skin shone like marble in the candlelight and his eyes, grey like a cloudy day, were visible only as twin glitters in the shadowed plains of his face.

"Illyria," he said, the growl of his voice making her shiver.

She stopped in front of him, close enough to touch him if she so wanted to. 'This is a mistake'. That was what she was going to say. 'Nothing between us can ever be'.

"You broke treaty with the Dragonfleet for me," she found herself saying aloud, even as her mind wondered where the words were coming from. "You defied your lord. Thank you."

He reached out to her with large, strong hands and pulled her close enough to him that their chests almost touched. "I would fight Anshar himself for you." It was barely a whisper.

She placed her hands on his broad, firm chest and looked up into his eyes. His hands, still cupping her elbows, pulled her even closer. Illyria closed her eyes and raised her face, knowing what was going to happen and excited about it, even as her rational mind protested.

She didn't care about that right now. She didn't want to think. All she wanted to do, right now, with no one watching her, was experience something she'd never had but always wanted.

Loud, echoing footsteps sounded on the stairs behind her and Illyria leapt away from Gennald as if scalded. Her hands smoothed clothing that wasn't rumpled and pushed back hair not out of place. She turned, knowing her face was flushed red and that her eyes, if anyone could see them, were as green as a forest's heart.

It was Balien in the company of Lord Jannery. Her brother's face was typically expressionless while Jannery's grimaced with embarrassment.

"I was...that is...I should...goodnight." she managed to stammer out before fleeing into her room and slamming it behind her.

Coward.

CHAPTER FIVE

"Two elves, brother and sister, left their forest home, saw that the world was broken, and decided to fix it."

—The Crown Cycle, *Lord Florian*

"I am not an elf!"

—*Comment commonly attributed to Illyria Exiprion*

Gennald stroked the nose of his horse and crooned nonsense syllables to the noble, powerful animal. It disliked boats and the ferry ride across the Kaylin, as brief as it was, had unsettled it. The horse was a treasured gift from Lord Jannery himself, given to him on the day he had successfully passed his trials and been accepted as a knight of Karalon. That, as well as his sword and mail (given to him by his father on the same occasion) were his most precious possessions.

As a knight-yeoman, they were his only important possessions. The Hanleys had served the lords of the Northmarch for the last four generations and had been well rewarded for it. His father was the burgess of Ruthcroft—as high an honour as the Jannery's could provide. He was, for all intents, a nobleman, but without title or right to inherit. That small difference, with the rights and privileges that accompanied it, was huge.

There were landed knights aplenty in Karalon's heartland, but Gennald and his father were not counted among their number. There were no Hanleys in the Peer's Court, nor would there ever be. The permanent granting of lands could only be done by the agreement of a majority of nobles, and Gennald knew too well that they would never do so for the servant of a March-Lord. Gennald's only assets were what he wore and the protection of his lord. Those were no small things, and Gennald had treasured them above all else; until he had met Illyria.

He had found her attractive from the beginning—oh, yes—and had delighted in her company, but he had always been able to keep his thoughts in check. No matter how pretty she was or how much he enjoyed her company, she was a crownmarked princess and he a mere yeoman. They could never be, and so he had contented himself with friendship.

Then they had gone into battle together, and his world had been forever altered. When he had seen her in action in the streets of Westbridge, so beautiful, so brave, so *alive*, he had known that somehow, in some way, he had to have her.

She felt that way as well; he could see it in her eyes. It was difficult for him to reconcile the images of the reckless warrior and the shy virgin, as Sephana suggested she was, but, given the way that Illyria had run from him last night, he had to grant at least some truth to it.

It only made him want her more.

Illyria watched as Lord Jannery's baggage train assembled itself. The people of Eastbridge were examining everyone with unabashed curiosity. They had seen everything that had happened yesterday. It had only been luck that the raiders had come ashore on the west bank of the river. If they had decided otherwise, Illyria and her knights wouldn't have been able to do anything other than watch in horror as they made off with the town's future.

Had it been fortune or misfortune that had delivered the Knights of Anduilon to the scene of the Dragonfleet's raid? She did not know.

Lord Jannery was speaking to the burgess of the town, and she saw a purse changing hands. It filled Illyria with uneasiness. She didn't like being party to events that involved bribery to ensure silence. It sullied everything she did, and yet she could not deny the need.

What we did—the lives we saved—was right and good. It has to be.

She mounted her horse and directed it towards where Gennald and the others gathered, acutely aware that many eyes followed her. She had become long accustomed to it. Her fine Ilthanaran clothing and the company she kept never failed to draw attention, but for some reason her watchers felt more accusing today.

When she mentioned this to her companions, Gennald just chuckled. "It's because they've never seen a woman wearing pants riding a horse before." Sephana muttered something too quietly for Illyria to make out. "Karalinian ladies ride side saddle or in carriages."

"Illyria doesn't even own a dress," Sephana said.

Illyria found herself blushing for what felt like the tenth time today. "I do, actually," she said, all too aware of Gennald's eyes on her. "I just have few opportunities to wear it often."

Gennald smiled. "I'd like to see that. I'm sure you will look lovely in it."

She was saved from finding an answer that by Lord Jannery's arrival. "Everything is in readiness. Their silence has been ensured."

Gennald nodded, and between one heartbeat and the next transformed from handsome courtier to commander of men. "Then I shall give the order to move out." He nodded to the others. "Sirs, ladies, excuse me."

Illyria couldn't help but watch him as he rode off.

The Bear and the Thistle

Eldoth was still looking at her funny. Sephana twitched her reins and her horse started walking closer to his. She still wasn't a very good rider, but, she noted with a smile, she was better than her self-proclaimed 'wizard' of an ex-husband.

Her actions snapped him out of whatever contemplation he had been in and he looked at her oddly—well, *more* oddly—but made no protest as she steered them out of earshot.

"What's going on?" she asked. They had passed the stage of requiring chitchat years ago. "You've been looking at me like that all day. Is there some magical secret tangled in my hair?"

"I was?" He looked startled, but she couldn't tell if he was lying or not.

She rolled her eyes. "Yes, you were. It's creepy. Stop it."

He had the grace to look embarrassed. "I'm sorry."

Sephana blinked, surprised.

"It's just that, well—" He broke off and looked at her again with unabashed curiosity. She wiped at her face with her free hand, still not sure that there wasn't something on her forehead. "You called me 'Prime.' "

"I did what?"

His face lit up and his words started to come out faster and faster like they always did when he was explaining some new idea. "On the ship, during the fight, when you fought off those three rat men—"

"Oh, you mean when something the size of a six year-old tried to rip out your throat and I saved your life?"

He grimaced at the memory. The parallel red gouges were still visible on his neck behind his beard. "Yes, then. You said 'do it now, Prime. Burn them.' " He looked at her shrewdly. "Both those words and how you said them were very unusual for you."

"What? No I didn't." Her memories of the battle, especially that part, were fairly weak, although she wasn't going to tell him that. It was the downside of not thinking.

"You did. I heard you quite clearly."

Sephana snorted. "Right. Because you're listening powers are at their best when you're throat is getting ripped out."

His eyes flared in irritation. "Don't be contrary just because I am the one bearing this message."

"I'm not. I'm 'being contrary' because you're just making things up. What is your problem?"

His face, she was satisfied to note, was quickly turning the same shade as his coat. "At the moment, stubborn, pig-headed women who *refuse to listen*. Sephana, this concerns me. Saying things that you don't have memory of could be a symptom of a greater problem."

She hesitated. He sounded sincere, but then she remembered who she was talking to. "And what stupid thing would I have to do to help diagnose this problem, huh? What are you up to, Eldoth? Are you trying to make a fool out of me or get my clothes off? I can never tell which it is with you."

He bristled. "It is difficult to make you seem an even greater fool than you already are." He flicked his eyes over her disdainfully. "As for the latter: I have already received that dubious honour and am in no great hurry to repeat it."

Her mouth opened in anger but nothing came out. "Zulum take you, Eldoth," she was finally able to spit as she wheeled her horse around. "Don't talk to me, don't look at me, don't even *breathe* near me. Do I make myself clear?"

"As rain water," he said. "I apologise for being concerned. It will never happen again, I assure you."

Nothing happened that day. After the violence and carnage they had endured in Westbridge, the sheer mundanity of travelling seemed surreal. As they neared the shore of Vinander Lake, source of the Kaylin River, Theramus noted a lone horseman on the road ahead of them. He was a knight by his arms and armour, and a wealthy one, too. Even from this distance the quality of his equipment and fine breeding of his horse were obvious. His shield and surcoat were vividly white and his crest was a rampant bear bearing a sword and shield. A golden crown adorned the bear's head.

The knight stopped his horse, removed his helm, and waved his free arm above his head. In front of Theramus, Jannery mirrored the gesture and when the other knight gestured to the ground in front of him, Jannery mirrored that as well. They were ritualized greetings between knights, Theramus knew, cordial ones. Knights on less friendly terms would not have removed their helms, or dared move their sword hands far from their weapons.

"Is he a friend?" Illyria asked Jannery.

"Of sorts," Jannery began riding towards the unknown knight. "He's a templar. No one, not even a landed noble, refuses a templar's invitation to parley."

"What is a templar?" Illyria asked. "I'm not familiar with that term."

"He's a temple knight," Jannery told her, "from the Holy Order of the Sacred Valley."

Illyria nodded her comprehension. "They defend your holy places. Do they live with the priests in the campus, or outside it?"

He looked at her oddly. "He is a priest, My Lady. All of the templars are."

Illyria looked shocked. "Your priests are knights? They bear arms?"

"It's hard to be a knight without them," Jannery replied dryly. "Do your elf priests follow a different tradition?"

"Very different." Such was Illyria's shock that she gave no reaction to the word 'elf'. "There are no weapons allowed in our Sacred Grove at all. Our priests take vows against violence."

"I envy the peace you must have in your elf kingdom, that such a thing is possible." His voice was mild, but Theramus could hear the sting beneath it.

Illyria must have heard it as well. "It was not meant as a criticism, My Lord. I make no claim that any of my people's customs are in any way superior. I was merely noting the difference."

Jannery made no reply. Instead he looked off in the distance and swore.

Theramus followed his gaze. A mile down the road, past the waiting temple knight, was a carriage accompanied by ten mounted knights. Their surcoats and the caparisons of their mounts were emblazoned in parti-colour red and blue, though their crest was far too small to make out.

Jannery apparently did not need a crest to know who the riders were. "Attenham."

Illyria looked over in curiosity.

"Redding Attenham, Count of Deremshire," he explained. "His lands lie to the south, up this valley."

Behind him, Theramus heard Sephana gasp. "Is—is that that the road to the Wightland Valley?"

Jannery turned in his saddle. "Yes. Have you heard of it?"

Sephana shook her head. She was as pale as her skin allowed her to be. "Only stories."

The temple knight—Theramus had heard of this order of knightly priests, though he had never seen one before today—made the same gestures of greeting and invitation to the approaching carriage. The lead knight returned them after briefly consulting with someone inside the carriage.

"There's no getting out of this now, not after accepting a templar's invitation. Damn." Jannery sighed. "Templars do not technically outrank landed nobles," he said in answer to Illyria's unspoken question, "but the reality of it is more complicated. Templars answer only to their grandmaster, and the Grandmaster answers only to the king." He indicated with his chin. "Do you see the golden sword and crown on his crest, and the black borders on his surcoat? That means that he's a Knight-Master, one of the most powerful men in the kingdom. Even a duke would think twice before giving him offence."

"And why would you risk such a thing?" Theramus asked.

Jannery grimaced. "It's not the templar that bothers me; it's his company. I have to share a parley and make polite small talk with the man who wants to overthrow my king. Count Attenham leads the Anderites."

Illyria watched as her host and his....that was to say, *Gennald*, stiffened as they approached the temple knight, who stood idly next to his horse. He was a handsome enough man, with dark hair lightly dusted with grey. He wasn't as attractive as Gennald, but...

Illyria stopped her train of thought so hard that its traces shook. What was she doing, considering the handsomeness of a *priest?*

Despite her discomfort at the idea of an armed priest, she still intended to give the man every respect. His was a sacred duty, granted to him by a magical bloodline almost as exclusive as that of the king he served. Her breeding allowed nothing less than perfect behaviour.

Both Lord Jannery and Gennald dismounted and fell to one knee with one hand steadying their sword and the other touching the ground. Illyria motioned to her fellow knights to imitate the motion. She could not help but perform her act of obeisance in the Ilthanaran style, drilled into her by countless hours of deportment training. She dropped down both knees, placed both hands over her heart and bowed her head. "Wise Father," she murmured while the two Karalmen said "Master" in respectful tones.

"Willem, Gennald, it's good to see you both," he said with casual familiarity. He looked over Illyria's shoulder and stiffened. She didn't need to see where his gaze pointed to know that he was looking at Sephana. "Bear. Come!"

A huge dog with long, russet hair ran to his side. Even if she had not seen the leather harness that it wore, its size, health and training made it obvious that it was a hound warden. It was a different breed than she was used to seeing, but she had no doubt that it was as ferocious and deadly as its Nemoran counterpart.

"Wise Father, I assure you that we are no danger to you," she said to the suspicious-faced priest. The heavy-set dog outweighed her and Sephana by a substantial margin, and was probably almost as heavy as Balien. Pound for pound, it was stronger than any of them except perhaps Theramus and she had no doubt that its strong jaw could break bone—if it chose to attack. As much as her hand itched to hold her knife handle, she didn't dare; not in front of a priest. She continued to speak in calm, even tones. "None of us are corrupted, despite how we may appear."

Could she kill a temple dog? Even if it was attacking her friends? She hoped to ever find the answer to that.

"What's with the dog?" she heard Sephana whisper to Balien.

"It's a Hound Warden," he answered her in a low voice. "Bred from birth to hunt the evil and the corrupt."

Sephana paused. "But we're not evil."

They were all still on their knees, but Illyria was sure that everyone was as tensed for action as she was.

"The guilty always profess their innocence the loudest," the priest said in an even voice, "but none can hid their nature from a Hound of Karalon." He knelt next to the dog and removed its muzzle. "Bear: search!"

The dog advanced cautiously, sniffing first at Lord Jannery and then Gennald.

"Do not run from him, or he will chase you down," the knight/priest warned.

The dog neared Illyria and gave her a cursory smell. It was even larger close up and its breath smelled of blood. While all dogs had acute senses, those of a Hound Warden were supernatural. Where other animals smelled for sweat, musk, and blood, these dogs, specially blessed by Emuranna, could smell possession. If any of them were possessed by a spirit—including a simple disease spirit—it would know, and if the spirit was Corrupt, or especially malevolent, it would attack. From this close, she doubted that any of them save Theramus would be able to stop it before it ripped their throats.

Luckily for all of them, being Reshai had nothing to do with possession. Any creature born in Anshara was considered 'natural' to a temple dog's nose, and they had nothing to fear.

The dog—Bear, the priest had named it—sniffed Theramus and then Eldoth before it reached the last of their number. When it got near Sephana, it growled.

Sephana gulped. She was pretty sure that her head would fit inside that dog's mouth with no problems. With her luck, it had a taste for snakemeat, too. Could she evade it if it attacked her? Her instinct said yes. In fact, it said to attack now, shove her dagger's pommel down its throat and trigger it's blades. The urge was so overwhelming that she actually had to squeeze down on her wrist with her knife hand in order not to.

The temple knight strode over and looked down at her over sternly crossed arms. "A spirit's brushed you," he said darkly.

"It...what?" The dog's eyes were a intense, deep shade of green—like an emerald—and were fixed on her intently. It was alert, but didn't seem like it was going to attack. Much.

"Bear! Heel!"

The massive, shaggy dog bolted for its master's side and sat eagerly. Its tail thumping at the ground. The priest knelt and replaced its muzzle. "A spirit brushed you, and recently, too. That's what Bear smells, but there is no evil in you. Rise." That last comment was addressed to everyone.

"Oh, good," Sephana muttered as she got to her feet. "That's a relief." Both Gennald and the priest shot her dark looks, but she didn't care. She crossed her arms and glared right back.

The priest's gaze swept over their whole company. "I am curious, Willem, about how you find yourself in such peculiar company." His words were superficially friendly, but strengthened with iron-hard authority. It was a demand, not a request, and everyone knew it.

"I am curious about that myself," said a new voice. They all turned to see a well dressed nobleman stepping out of very expensive looking carriage. His doublet bore the same colours as the crest painted onto the carriage's side: red, blue and gold. His hair was the colour of old wash water and his face was rat-like. Even if she hadn't known who he was, Sephana wouldn't have liked him. As it was, it just made him easier to loathe.

"Greetings, Master Sheltan." He sketched a fast, rough bow. "I am honoured to share parley with you."

"Count Attenham," the priest said with a frown, nodding his greeting. "It is always a pleasure to break fast with such an honoured peer of Karalon."

"No, master, the pleasure is mine." Attenham glanced over at Sephana and the rest of Jannery's party. "I must ask, though, whether that pleasure should extend to such mixed company. Far be it for me to tell you what is acceptable behaviour in the marches, My Lord Jannery, but we have standards of decorum here in civilized lands. Nobles do *not* share company with circus folk; not on my land."

"This is the king's road," Jannery growled, "and the leader of the Anderites is in no place to lecture me on the company that I keep. I, at least, do not consort with murderers."

Illyria could see that things were going to get unpleasant very quickly.

She stepped up to the priest (*knight-master* seemed such a harsh title for one of Emuranna's Chosen) and bowed before either Lord Jannery or the newly arrived Count Attenham could escalate the situation. "Allow me to introduce myself, Wise Father: I am Illyria Exiprion, Child of the Mark of Nemora and niece to King Kefeus of Ilthanara. This is my brother, Balien con-Exipiter, as well as my companions: Sephana of Akkilon, Eldoth the Red and Theramus of the Noss. It is our greatest honour to meet you."

The priest looked surprised but, to his credit, nodded graciously. "Greetings, My Lady, and to your companions as well. How does such a...diverse...group come to travel with a Peer of Karalon?"

"They are my vouchsafed guests, Knight-Master, and under my protection," Lord Jannery said, staring pointedly at Count Attenham. "The Knights of Anduilon are heroes of the Northmarch, and are journeying in my company to speak to the king. You do not know it yet, but you owe them your thanks. Their brave actions have saved untold thousands of lives."

Illyria had never appreciated Lord Jannery's loyal nature as much as she did now. Her fellow knight's actions had indeed saved countless lives and halted a foreign invasion, but they had also earned them a invaluable ally. When he had told her that all he had was hers after the battle of Dragonhead Keep, she had replied by asking only for his endorsement. He had protested at the time that it was not enough, and had generously gifted them with five of his best horses, but she stood by her decision and considered his words a prize greater than gold or rubies.

Perhaps, though, he could have stated them with greater diplomacy.

Knight-Master Sheltan's face hardened at Lord Jannery's words and Count Attenham's showed disbelief. "Knights...of Anduilon. Really? I am unfamiliar with such an order."

Nothing to do but step in front of the target. "We are newly formed, Wise Father," Illyria told the priest and ignoring the count's poorly concealed snort. "It is why we seek an audience with King Lionar: to get his endorsement."

Attenham spoke up. "Knights? How can you claim to be knights when a snakespawn is standing in your midst? You would bring such a hideous thing before my king? And demand recognition?"

Jannery bristled. "Mind your words, Attenham. As I have said: I have vouched for them, and they are under my protection. To insult them is to insult me."

Attenham smiled thinly. "Is that so? I shall have to remember that for future occasions."

"Call me that again," Sephana demanded, stepping in front of the count, her hand on her dagger. "Call me that again and see what happens."

"Snakespawn," he repeated. Illyria managed to place herself bodily between them, and just in time, too. Sephana would have hurled herself at him had Illyria not intervened.

The priest—Master Sheltan—spoke up angrily. "Act your station, sir! This is a parley and you are a noble."

"Nobody calls me that!" Sephana snapped. Her eyes were blazing. "No one. I don't care what he is."

"That's enough," Illyria cautioned as she physically held the lighter girl in check. "We can't afford any problems now."

"No man ever strikes another under parley," Master Sheltan said. He glared at Lord Jannery. "You claim these people to be knights? They act like ruffians."

His last statement caused Sephana to still as if Theramus had stood on her. "Sorry."

"I fear we have gotten off to a ill start, Wise Father," Illyria said. "Please, forgive our poor behaviour. It is inexcusable."

He looked slightly mollified. "She was not unprovoked." He glanced at Count Attenham. "Neither is without blame."

Anger glittered in Attenham's eyes. "I would never insult a noble so, Master Sheltan, in parley or otherwise, and maintain that I have not. I do not recognise that thing as anything more than an abomination of nature."

"And yet she has been vouched for by Lord Jannery, a respected Peer of the Realm," Master Sheltan's voice was steel. "You will respect her as you respect him."

Attenham bristled, then turned to Lord Jannery, whose face was dark and stormy. "I apologize, My Lord, for mistaking your guests for uncultured freaks of nature."

The air became thick with angry silence.

"Perhaps it would be best if we withdraw," Illyria said with exaggerated politeness. She bowed her head to Master Sheltan and the count as well. "My Lords."

"I shall join you," Lord Jannery growled. "I see little benefit in remaining in the current company."

"If you could wait a moment before departing, Lord Jannery," the Knight-Master interrupted smoothly. "I have not mentioned why I called this parley."

It was difficult for Gennald to hear any irritation in his voice, but there was no doubt that it was there. Gennald felt horribly embarrassed for his lord. Both Sephana's and Count Attenham's behaviour was deplorable, especially before one of the most powerful men in the kingdom. Knight-Master Atterly was a high ranking member of the Karalinian priesthood, and it was whispered that he was first in line to take over the office of Grandmaster when its current title-holder retired.

Sephana's behaviour was slightly more forgivable, given her foreign and base upbringing, but Count Attenham's was not. And not because it was his lord's—and therefore *his*—honour that had been impugned. It was just one more example that Redding Attenham was undeserving of his title.

Gennald had only met the count a few times and had never actually spoken with him—he was only a knight yeoman of indistinguishable birth, after all, while Attenham was a Peer of the Realm—but he did not like what little he had seen. He knew somewhat of the count's background: he has been some second cousin to the previous count and had gained his title under questionable circumstances, he was ostentatious with his displays of wealth (which seemed to be in excess of his income), and wielded an inappropriate amount of influence for his rank. That he was also the most vocal opponent for the overthrow and murder of King Lionar only made it that much easier to despise him.

"And what reason is that, Master Sheltan?" Lord Jannery asked.

"I received a most disturbing message this morning, from a resident of the town of Eastbridge," the templar said, frowning. "He had run through the night, almost killing himself, and was barely able to pass on his message before collapsing in exhaustion. He said that Dragonfleet raiders had attacked, but had been repulsed by an odd group of strangers, leaving no survivors. I am distressed by this, it should go without saying, especially so close to this year's tribute presentation." He glanced at Lord Jannery and Illyria's group of mismatched knights. "You ride from that direction. I am eager to hear of any news you may have about this."

All of them froze. The nickering of Master Sheltan's horse seemed deafening in the sudden silence.

"We left Eastbridge just this morning, Master, and saw no evidence of such a thing." Lord Jannery said.

"Really?" Count Attenham asked, his voice just as bland. "Your ragtag collection of circus showfolk didn't see an odd group of strangers? How unobservant of you."

Master Sheltan interrogated Lord Jannery with his eyes. Finally, the priest nodded and turned away. "I am glad to hear that such a rumour is unfounded, for all our sakes."

Attenham's eyes narrowed. "The town of Eastbridge lies within just within my county. It would be remiss of me not to investigate such a chilling rumour." He bowed. "Excuse me, Master, Lord." His lips tightened into a faint sneer. "Knights."

No one said anything until the count had returned to his carriage and ridden off. "Will he find anything?" Master Sheltan asked, his eyes knowing.

Lord Jannery chose his words carefully. "We saw no evidence of any Dragonfleet raider when we left this morning. We looked quite thoroughly."

Master Sheltan nodded. "Then I will inquire no further." He glanced at Illyria and her knights. "My warden has detected no evil among you, so I must take you at Lord Jannery's word. If he names you knights and heroes, then I will treat you as such."

Illyria nodded in acknowledgement. "My thanks, Wise Father. I am aware that our company must appear...unusual to you."

Gennald has barely able to swallow his snort of laughter. *Unusual?* Attenham—damn him—had struck in the black when he had called them 'circus folk'. Without seeing them in action, dressed as they were, no one could be blamed for mistaking them for a freak show. His lord was doing them a great service, vouching for them as he was.

"Wise father, forgive my asking," Illyria continued, "but why is a...knight—" Her hesitation with the word was faint, but noticeable—"of your importance venturing beyond the borders of your sacred valley so close to SummersEnd? The moon has just begun its blossoming."

Master Sheltan eyed her curiously. "You sound familiar with the sacred duties, My Lady."

"All Children of the Mark receive spiritual training, Wise Father."

"She and her brother are elves, master," Gennald found himself interjecting.

Illyria gave him a look that was both irritated and resigned.

"Is that so?" Master Sheltan looked intrigued and Gennald regretted ever opening his mouth. "I have never met an elf before. Are you a related to Princess Lethia?"

"Elves don't exist," Illyria explained. "They're fictional, and Lethia is just a character from a story. Sir Gennald is mistaken. My brother and I are from Ilthanara, the hidden city where the Nemoran royal family lives. I began training as a priestess in our own sacred forest when I was twelve. Given what I have heard concerning King Lionar's previous Joinings, I am surprised to see you away from your temple. I would think that you would be there, preparing for SummersEnd. The weeks leading up to a Joining are critical."

"You're not an elf. That saddens me." He made a non-committal grunt. "But you are correct, My Lady: this time leading up to the king's Joining is indeed critical, but the grandmaster has decided that it is more important to discover the nature of this land's affliction. My fellow knights and I are scouring all of Karalon for the source of this wheat rust. Whatever infects our land," he gestured to encompass everything around him, "is not natural and it is out there, somewhere. My entire order took questing vows. We will not rest until we find it and destroy it. Only then will our land be healed."

"If all of the templars are off searching for the cause of this evil, then you must not believe that King Lionar is to blame," Lord Jannery said. "You must tell this to Duke Raebyrne. It will kick the stuffing out of the Anderite movement."

Master Sheltan shook his head sadly. "We serve the temple, Willem. We are forbidden to interfere with politics. You know this."

Gennald's lord nodded. "So you keep saying. You may be forbidden to speak of it, but I am not. I am seeing the duke tomorrow. He must know of this."

"Do as you must, Willem." He turned to gather his horse's reins. "Lady Illyria, I am sure there is an entertaining story behind your presence here and your association with Lord Jannery, but I am afraid that my quest does not permit me time to hear it." He mounted. "My Lord Jannery, knights. Emuranna guide you and protect you."

"And you, master Sheltan," Lord Jannery replied, nodding.

"Bear, come!" Knight Master Sheltan, resplendent in his expensive mail and surcoat, rode off; his well-named hound warden trotting faithfully off his right foot.

"He's on a quest to find evil things, and he thought I was one of them," Sephana muttered, her arms crossed and her face dark. "That's just great."

"Who are they?" a feminine voice asked.

Redding Attenham, Count of Deremshire, settled himself into the seat of his carriage. "A group of freaks and outlanders. They called themselves 'The Knights of Anduilon'." He snorted. " 'Knights', with no crest, no lord, and, obviously, no standards. They're no danger to us."

The carriage's other passenger raised a delicate eyebrow. "I wouldn't be so quick to dismiss them, My Lord. They have a Noss in their company. They don't give their allegiance to just anyone." She wore a dark, exquisitely made dress that had cost him a small fortune, and looked beautiful in it. "Our plans are too close to fruition, My Lord, for us to take light of anything." Her tone was mild. If anyone had seen them or overheard them, they would appear to be nothing more than a peer of the realm engaged in conversation with his young, pampered mistress.

"My Lady Myria, I assure you: they are pursuing an audience with the king. If they show up looking as they do and speak to him as they spoke to me, they will be laughed out of the capital with their tails between their legs. They are a danger only to themselves."

Myria leaned forward, her eyes—a beguiling shade of hazel—leapt from the shadows to pierce his own. "Do not talk to me like a fool when there is no audience to play to, My Lord. You *will* set your agents to discover who and what these so-called knights are. Our plans are not so far along that we can blithely ignore potential complications."

Leaning forward as she was and looking like she did, Redding should have been distracted by her tremendous beauty, but he wasn't. When they had first met, two years ago, he had made the mistake of dismissing her as yet another pretty, disposable face, but Myria wasted no time disabusing him of that notion. While some distant part of him did acknowledge her attractiveness, he did not allow it to effect him. It was impossible for him to be attracted to anyone that frightened him as deeply and thoroughly as the woman who currently sat across from him.

He had learned through painful experience that there was only one thing to say when she gave him a direct order: "Yes, of course. I'll see to it right away."

She nodded, satisfied and peered through the curtains to the road beyond. She looked at Redding with a frown. "Why are we going east?"

He smiled, happy that, just for this one small moment, he knew something that she did not. "I heard tell of an interesting incident in the town of Eastbridge. If there is even a kernel of truth to it, it could mean disaster to the Golden Bears."

She settled back in her seat, openly curious. "Tell me."

CHAPTER SIX

> " 'So I understand why the nobles loyal to the king are called the Golden Bears: because a
> gold bear is part of their crest, but I don't get why the other faction are called the Anderites.
> Shouldn't they be named after the thistle? It is the other part of their symbol.' "
>
> " 'What's the other colour in the Karalinian crest?' "
>
> " 'Blue.' "
>
> " 'And what would that make their faction's name?' "
>
> " '...the Blue Thistles. You're right. That would be stupid.' "
>
> —anonymous conversation between two soldiers

The road was lined with birches and aspens, their leaves golden. Karalon's forests were pretty enough, but nothing here compared to her memory of the vast panorama of autumn in the Ilthwood, with its endless varieties of oaks and maples. When the trees of her homeland celebrated the end of the season they exploded into breathtaking riots of red, orange, yellow and purple. Compared to that, autumn here could only ever be called 'pretty'.

Beyond the trees, on their left, was a much more impressive sight: Lake Vinander. It was, quite simply, the largest, grandest lake Illyria had ever seen. It was large enough that only the tips of the towering Karnem Mountains, more than one hundred miles to the north, made her believe that she was not standing on the edge of the ocean.

Theramus, wise in all things, had told her that it was the largest lake in the kingdom and she believed him, but he had also said that there were much larger bodies of water in the kingdom of Tirim. She found that much harder to believe. Such things just did not exist in Nemora, especially in the Ilthwood. It was just one more reminder of how much her life had changed.

It galled her that something so easily recognised by everyone as the Dragonfleet had been unknown to her. Before yesterday, she would never have believed that an organization could exist that was large enough to bully a kingdom into submission. The thought was so foreign to her that, even when she had seen the fear in Gennald's eyes, she had attributed it to something else.

Gennald.

She turned to look at him. By some unknown method of divination, he sensed her eyes on him and looked over, smiling broadly. Thankful that she was riding, and therefore that her suddenly weak knees could not betray her, she smiled back and ignored the fluttering in her stomach.

No man had ever affected her like this. She had never felt herself become so...unnerved...by a mere glance or a smile. No one else had ever inspired child-like giggling like she had done yesterday with Sephana.

Certainly she had wanted to kiss him last night.

It wasn't like she was some chaste priestess. She *had* kissed a man before. When she had been a teenager she had formalized her engagement to Turius Kaythart with a lengthy embrace in front of the whole court, and had practiced with him no few times before the announcement. In the years that had followed, they had kissed and done somewhat more several times. He had been very passionate on the last night before she had left, and, if not for her desire to remain pure for her wedding, would have given him her virtue.

She had never felt as desperate for Turius, with his sloppy, insistent kisses and probing hands, as she had with Gennald. He frightened her as much as he excited her, and part of her had been relieved when they had been interrupted.

I'm twenty five years old. I've negotiated with kings, faced off against Djido sorcerers, and slain dragon-lizards, she scolded herself. *I will not allow myself to become a fool over something so trivial!*

There were, after all, more compelling matters at hand. Purging all thoughts of Gennald and his strong hands, she thought back to the stilted conversation she had witnessed between her host and the count of Deremshire.

"You and the count, you have history?" she asked Lord Jannery.

"Not so much as you think," he replied, his gaze focussed somewhere to the north. "I dislike him. Cankers like Attenham are everything that is wrong with this kingdom. They stink like bonerot and infect everyone they come in contact with. Last year he was a snake, whispering behind the king's back about his fitness to rule, and not even a year later he is the head of a faction that would cast Lionar to the wolves."

"You are a good man, My Lord. I do not believe you would give your loyalty lightly."

He laughed, but it held little humour. "You flatter an old warhorse, My Lady. I am a poor excuse for a noble and I know it. In my heart, I am a soldier and a knight, like young Gennald there. It is difficult for me not to speak my mind. Your man, Theramus, he is the same." he pointed with his chin at the blue-skinned giant who was walking along side Sephana.

"Theramus is not mine, not in the Karalinian sense," Illyria corrected. "We are equals in our company. Companions."

Willem snorted. "You may give speeches about equality and being comrades in arms until WatersEnd, My Lady, but my eyes see what they see: they're yours, all of them." He eyed her sidelong. "Gennald would be yours as well, if you let him."

"My Lord, I—" She found herself flushing yet again. "Sir Gennald and I...we are friends and travelling companions, that is all."

He just grunted. "I've been after him to marry for years now. He is honoured and respected in Northhaven. He has no property, of course; he's a yeoman, but I'd grant him a borough in a heartbeat if he asked for it."

Marriage. The very word sent icicles down Illyria's spine. "I cannot marry, My Lord, I am en..." She had almost said 'engaged' before she catching herself. It had always been the excuse she had hidden behind when a man made overtures towards her. She had been engaged to Turius for so long that saying it had become habit, and, worse, so had thinking it. She had never seriously considered any romantic offers since leaving the Ilthwood. She had not wanted to betray her vow, and thus she had said 'no' to many attractive and charming men more times then she could count. It had gotten to the point where, she now realized, she didn't even know how to say 'yes'.

There was no reason for her to say 'no' now, other than habit. She had broken her engagement, and she was free to do...whatever she wanted. That did not include marriage by any stretch of the imagination, not with her knighthood less than month old, but as for anything short of that, well, what was the harm in it? She could think of none, beyond her own fears, and she was choosing here and now not to be afraid.

Her sudden smile felt wide enough to split her face in two, and she knew that if she dwelled on her decision and the ramifications of it, that she would be a useless twit for the rest of the day. She needed something to distract her, something not Gennald, and wracked her brain trying to recall what she and Lord Jannery had been discussing. It took a moment, and when the thought came she clung to it like a drowning child to a log.

"Can you explain this granting of boroughs, My Lord?" she asked, as if there had just not been an awkward lull in the conversation. "Is it not the same as giving land?"

"Not at all. Land gifts are permanent and those who are given them become nobles. Their heirs inherit both land and title, and it continues so in perpetuity. Only the king can grant land but, since the signing of the Great Charter, he has needed the approval of the Council of Peers."

"I'm sorry, who?"

"The Peers are the assembled nobles of Karalon. I am among their number, of course, but I have little power within it. As a march-lord, I defend vast swathes of land, but own very little. Most counts hold more sway than me, and a few of the stronger barons as well. We form like-minded groups, when the situations warrant it, but I am seldom directly involved with any of them. My true place is in the Northmarch, keeping the dogmen in check."

"The Golden Bears and the Anderites are two of these 'like-minded groups,'" Illyria guessed.

"Yes. They formed once it was realized that we wouldn't be able to meet last year's tribute. The Anderites want Lionar to step down, and for his son Ander to replace him, while the Golden Bears oppose it. It was to oppose a no-confidence motion that I left Northhaven in such a hurry last month." He grimaced. "I fell, and was unable to complete my journey, but luckily the motion was overturned anyway. You'd be addressing a new king if they had not."

Illyria was shocked. "The council, it has that much power? It can overrule the king?"

"Only in some matters, and only with cause."

"I...see." It bothered her: a king not being sovereign in his own land. "And a borough, it is administered by a burgess?"

"Yes. They act on their lord's behalf, and represent him. They administer justice, collect taxes, levy militias, and the like. I have dozens of burgesses under me, more than most nobles, but I see it as the least I can do for them."

"I don't understand, My Lord."

Jannery sighed. "A knight is a nobleman, by definition. If he was not one before, the act of knighting makes him so. It is the cornerstone of chivalry. A man of any birth can, at his lord's discretion, become knighted if he is found deserving. There are dozens of stories in our histories of noble families being founded that way."

"But noblemen must own land," Illyria said. "You said that as well."

"Yes. All knights are noble, and all nobles own land. Therefore it is a lord's responsibility, upon knighting someone, to grant him land. My own family was ennobled that way, and granted lands in the Northmarch to defend."

"I sense that there is more to this story, and that it is sad. The Year of Broken Lances. You said that hundreds of men were knighted."

"You are correct. Hundreds of new nobles, each granted land and titles for their bravery and their service." He scowled. "Each of them betrayed."

"By who?"

"The Council of Peers. They rebelled against the crown; surrounded New Aukaster with knights and wouldn't let even a speck of food into the capital until the king agreed to annul all his new noble appointments."

Illyria listened in silence, horrified.

"He lasted for months and told them all to kiss Zulum's ass on their way to the underworld, but the people of New Aukaster were starving. He eventually gave in for their sake, and signed the piece of paper that they forced him to. The 'Great Charter', they call it, signed by the king and every noble in the kingdom. It gives the Council the authority to overrule his decisions by a majority vote." He shrugged. "Some call it a travesty, others the dawn of a new age. I'm still not sure which it is."

"It is not my place to judge, My Lord," Illyria said, still mulling over what she had learned.

"Gennald's great-grandfather was knighted in the Year of Broken Lances," Lord Jannery said. "He was worthy of his knighting by all accounts, and of the barony given to him in reward. He held that title for less than two years before being stripped of it. My family has supported his since that time, granting them boroughs and taking them in as knights-yeomen. Gennald has refused all my attempts to reward him thus."

"Why would he not do so?" Illyria asked. "It seems a great honour."

"Because then he couldn't be my First Knight." There was pride in his voice. "Burgesses spend two thirds of the year in their borough. As my First, Sir Gennald is the head of all military forces in the Northmarch. He doesn't want to give that up, which is flattering, but it makes it damn hard for me to reward him."

"I see, My Lord. Thank you." Illyria's mind was whirling. This new revelation was both welcome and not. She could not help but admire Gennald for his devotion and with that admiration came a deeper, more intellectual attraction.

A dark thought intruded. "My Lord, what will happen if Count Attenham discovers what we did in Eastbridge? Have my actions made you party to treason?"

He shook his head. "Don't think of such things. It is everyone's best interest to keep this secret, and no one on these shores will lament the death of slavers. Even if Attenham does bully some witness into talking, we saw to it that no evidence remains. The king will never convict a nobleman of treason on mere hearsay, and you are under my protection."

"I dislike lying, even to a man of his ilk."

"This is a lie that will save all of our lives," he warned. "None of us like having to treat and pay tribute to the damned Dragonfleet, but they'd wreak havoc across the whole kingdom if we denied them now." He looked away. "And there's the matter of the hostage."

"What hostage?"

He looked like he was going to be sick. "We missed most of our tribute last year, if you recall."

"Yes. There were heavy rains at harvest time."

"Yes, well, the king met with their admiral and apologised. He gave them all the gold he could raise and promised that we would pay a penalty this year to make up the difference." He spat. "My king, grovelling to a piece of raider scum like he was a common debtor. It makes my blood boil. Anyway, their admiral agreed to it, but he demanded surety."

"A hostage," Illyria deduced. "Who was it?"

Anger and despair warred on his face. "Princess Elisanna, his brother's daughter. She's a sweet young thing, not even eighteen, and he had to give her up to them like some piece of livestock. Emuranna only knows what she's had to endure this last year, or if she's still alive."

Illyria felt sick to her stomach. "I would hate myself if my impulsive actions put her return at risk."

He shook his head vehemently. "No. Done is done. Besides...I don't know if I could have stood by while they took a hold full of children right in front of me. You did the right thing, Illyria. Damn me for a traitor if anyone hears me say it, but you did."

Sephana smelled it before she saw it and wrinkled her nose in a vain attempt to ward off the scent. "Ugh. Did we pass by a cess-pit or something?"

Theramus shook his head. "No, we approach the city of New Aukaster. Its sewers are sadly lacking."

"What happened to Old Aukaster?" she asked, vainly holding her hand over her nose. "Did they stink it to death?" As jokes went, it was pretty tame, but it stunk too much for her to think of anything better.

The trail opened up into a clearing. Such was their height that the entire countryside was visible for miles. A small, unattractive city sat on the west side of a small bay abutting a narrow valley. Theramus pointed to a large, grey expanse of gravel and rock across the bay. "It was destroyed by the Djido during the Great War."

"Nothing grows there, not even weeds," Eldoth said from behind them, bringing his horse in line with hers. She glared silent death at him but he didn't notice. "I searched it when I first arrived here for magical artefacts. I believe that it's haunted."

"That's...not funny." She stared at the drab, colourless field that had once had hosted buildings, markets, and palaces that was now a tomb for the unquiet dead. "The new city is right next to it. Why make it so close to all of that death? Why remind themselves?"

Theramus pointed beyond New Aukaster to the narrow valley beyond. "The Sacred Valley of Olsarum lies beyond there."

"That's where that priest came from, right?"

Illyria rode up alongside them in the company of Sir Gennald. Her cheeks were flushed. "Yes. It's where the king joins with the land," she said. "There is no place more sacred in Karalon."

Theramus nodded. "The king at the time chose to remain close to it. If I recall correctly, they also chose to remain near the ruins of the old city to remind them of their enemy's cruelty."

"It still stinks," she grumbled. "I escaped Akkilon so that I wouldn't have to smell the inside of a cess-pit all day."

"There were no more wizards or scholars by that time," Eldoth told her. "The builders did not understand the need for sewers."

"That's great," she said with false cheer. "How long do we have to stay here?"

"Long enough to gain an audience with the king and convince him of our sincerity," Illyria said. "Kings don't make hasty decisions. I'm anticipating weeks." Her gaze flickered to Gennald.

"You will have my hospitality, of course, for as long as it takes," Lord Jannery said, Joining them. "I owe all of you that much, and more."

They started down the hill towards the ugly blight of a city. A realization hit Sephana and she gasped.

"What is it?" Balien asked.

"I'm going into a city for the first time, you know, as myself." She gestured towards per headscales and tail, both plainly visible. "The last time anyone saw me like this in Karalon they tried to burn me at the stake."

"We won't let that happen."

"It's easy to forget what I am when I'm with all of you," she said, suddenly fascinated by the stitching on her saddle.

"You're a knight now, Sephana. That *is* who you are."

It was worse than she thought it would be. It wasn't the smell (although that wasn't exactly *good*), but the staring, whispering, and pointing that everyone had to endure because of her was terrible. Even growing up as the only Reshai with a full tail in the slave plantations of Akkilon hadn't been this bad. There, surrounded by 'her kind', at least they'd known what she was. They had hated and shunned her, but they hadn't held knives fearfully as she passed by, shielded their children from her with their bodies or blamed her with their eyes for the destruction of their kingdom five centuries past.

They wouldn't even have made it through the gate without Lord Jannery. She'd seen the first guard's eyes bulge when he saw her tail laid across her horse's rump.

She'd stupidly, defiantly, brushed her hair away from her earpit, looked him right in the face, and demanded if he had a problem.

Thirty seconds later, when four frightened men were levelling spears at her, she'd wished she had never stopped wearing her headscarf. Two minutes of Theramus's bluster, Illyria's cool diplomacy, and Lord Jannery's iron-hard authority later, they'd finally been admitted into New Aukaster. She'd hidden her tail under a blanket and covered her headscales with her hair, but the damage had already been done.

Rumour of what she was had raced ahead of them, and every eye on the street had been fixed on her. The tight, crowded streets—combined with the stink of being in a place where emptying a chamber-pot into the street was considered acceptable—filled with people staring at her was stifling. She didn't like people staring at her at the best of times, but just having to take it as she sat on her horse, being groped by hundreds upon hundreds of angry, frightened eyes, was much, much worse.

The winding, twisting ride to Lord Jannery's manor (which was, thankfully, uphill and upwind of the rest of the city) was one of the longest trips of her life. By the time they finally arrived she just wanted to curl up in a corner and cry.

Theramus ducked to fit through the low doorway. It was inconvenient, but he had been living in Man's world for several decades now. He was used to not fitting.

"Perhaps I should stay in the garden," he suggested to the house matron after viewing the selection of available rooms.

The woman, somewhat past her life's prime, managed to look scandalized despite her obvious nervousness. "I'll not have it said that My Lord made his guests sleep outside! We'll be getting early frosts soon."

"I am giantkind. I am not bothered by the cold," he assured her, "and none of this furniture can accommodate me."

She wrung her hands. "It's not proper."

"I insist."

"Well, then, I suppose My Lord will be all right with it." She looked relieved despite her bluster.

He would have been happier staying in the stable—and had done so many times over his decades of life—but Lord Jannery's urban residence did not have one. Property was too expensive here, especially for a comparatively poor border lord.

The house was fair enough. As Sephana had frequently pointed out, post-war architecture in Karalon favoured the functional over the ornamental, and this place followed that trend. But it was also a noble's residence, which meant that it was large enough to receive visitors.

He had just finished erecting the tent against the back wall when Illyria approached him. "There are no rooms to your liking?"

"None that fit. This will suffice for the duration of our stay."

She smiled. "Lord Jannery has sent word to a friend in the palace. He is hoping to call an emergency council session tomorrow in which to introduce us. If only the Golden Bears are aware of it and not the Anderites, it will hopefully make things easier for us."

"Especially with Count Attenham, their leader, not yet in the city." Theramus frowned. "I dislike politics. Have you given thought about what we will do once the king recognises us?"

"*If* he recognises us," Illyria corrected. "He was a boor about it, but Count Attenham made a good point: we do resemble a circus act, and our story is very unusual. Even with Lord Jannery's endorsement we might find ourselves thrown out of court. King Lionar has troubles aplenty right now."

"Yes. The Dragonfleet tribute, the grain blight, all of this business with the Golden Bears. The crown must be weighing heavy on his brow right now."

Illyria stilled, then began to smile broadly. "Thank you, Theramus. You've just given me an idea."

My needs are purely intellectual, Eldoth repeated as he entered the rear walled garden currently host to the Knights of Anduilon's largest member. *That is my only motive, nothing more.*

He knew that the ensuing conversation was going to be difficult. There was no love lost between Theramus and himself, and even less regarding the subject he wished to discuss. They were of different worlds and only had one thing in common. The opinions they held on that shared interest were very, very different.

The commonality in question, Sephana, stalked past him out of the garden. On the list of insulting things she had done to him, frigid silence was common, but mild. Still, it left him oddly unsettled.

Theramus stood in the centre of the garden, his arms folded across his ridiculously large and muscular chest. His eyes, troubled and sad, were fixed on the door Eldoth was passing through and a large frown dominated his expression. At Eldoth's approach he grimaced momentarily. "Hello, Eldoth," he said with false politeness. "Are you settling in without trouble?"

"I have had better accommodations and worse," he replied with a shrug. He hadn't come here to exchange pleasantries. "They are private, which I appreciate."

"Ah. That is well."

"She seemed upset," he found himself saying.

Theramus knew who he was referring to. "She is troubled by the reactions of the people on the street." He held up a warning finger the size of a cudgel. "There is nothing you can say to her now that would improve her mood, so I suggest you leave her be."

"Why would I ever willingly begin a conversation with her?" Eldoth replied automatically, regretting the words as soon as they left his mouth. Not only were they blatantly untrue, which both of them knew (he had lost count of the number of times this last month he had badgered her into an argument) but it also did nothing to make the giant more inclined to share information with him.

"You need to make a greater effort to get along with her," Theramus warned.

Eldoth nodded obsequiously. "Yes, yes, I do. Much of behaviour towards my ex-wife is...reflexive."

"Change your reflexes," Theramus said flatly. "It is one of the greatest gifts given to Man, the ability to change their nature. I would also suggest that you refrain from referring to her in those words. She is no longer that person, nor are you."

It rankled Eldoth to have to endure advice on a subject so personal to him, but he also knew that sharing that sentiment would garner him no assistance. "Thank you, I will consider your words." He was surprised how civil he sounded.

Theramus's eyes narrowed. "Is there something you wished to discuss?"

"Yes, there is, if you don't mind." Eldoth moved a chair opposite Theramus as he thought about the best way to phrase his request. *Best to appeal to his vanity.* It was how Sephana had first gained his attention, after all. "You are very learned," he began.

"I am well travelled," Theramus corrected.

"Yes, but you have also read books," Eldoth amended, his voice disgustingly ingratiating. "Many things you know, particularly of events before the Great War, could not have been garnered through mere travel."

"My people are long lived," Theramus admitted. "Our lore has not been diluted by age as your has. We have many books, but I had little patience for them when I was younger."

Eldoth looked up eagerly. "But the lost library of the Noss exists, and you have seen it?"

The giant folded his very large, very blue arms across his chest. "You have done little to impress me as being worthy enough to trust with that knowledge."

It stung and it must have been visible in his expression, for Theramus softened. "What is it that you wish to know?"

He cleared his throat to hide his excitement. "What do know about the word 'prime'? " Despite Sephana's opinion to the contrary, he was certain of what he had heard.

"It means 'first'," Theramus said, surprised. "Surely you know this."

It took all his effort to not say something sarcastic. "Yes, of course. I meant as a form of address."

The giant gave him a level, assessing, look. "As you may know, it is the way of my people to serve others. We continued to do so after we left Endilsar, the difference being that this time we chose those who were worthy."

Eldoth did, in fact, know this, but he was loathe to interrupt the single time Theramus had chosen to impart any of his precious knowledge to him.

"There are those, however, who took that level of service higher than the most others," the giant continued. "They became more than servants. They became guardians and mentors to those they felt especially worthy. They were called Wardens, and the person that a warden entrusted was called his Prime." He looked at Eldoth inquiringly. "Where did you hear of this?"

"A journal entry," Eldoth lied. "Tell me, did the Noss become Wardens to many wizards?"

His large head shook in the negative. "The High Wizards were insistent upon protecting and policing their own. Their relationship with us was..." He smiled faintly. "It was rather like the one between you and I, actually."

"I see," Eldoth said, unsure if he had been insulted or not. He stood. "Thank you."

Theramus came to his feet and loomed above Eldoth. "This lack of trust you give me, this inability to tell me the truth regarding why you make this inquiry, this is why my people never served the High Wizards. We did not deem them worthy."

Eldoth left before he said anything that would damage their relationship further.

Dinner was subdued. The house matron not been told of their arrival and their meal—while hot and filling—had been made in haste and was fairly plain. Sephana was dirty and tired. While everyone else had been able to take advantage of the public baths (even Theramus), she hadn't dared. Walking in the streets of New Aukaster had been bad enough; there was no way she was going to step naked into a pool of water where everyone could see all her scales.

She just wanted to hide. Lord Jannery had given her a small but well furnished room complete with feather-stuffed bed. She hadn't even wanted to come down, but Balien had badgered her until she had finally agreed to join him. It was just oat gruel with salted fish and turnips (with a side of steadfast apology from the scandalized chef), but satisfying. She'd never tell Balien, but she was glad she had left her room.

Eldoth was staring at her again, but she ignored him. She was just ladling a second helping of watery stew into her trencher when Illyria entered the room. Sephana almost dropped her bowl. Illyria was wearing a dress. It was Karalinian in style, which meant it was fairly modest, with a front-laced crimson kirtle and bone white under-dress. It looked nice on her, though it was still wrinkled from being packed.

"My Lord," Illyria murmured as she sat, tucking her skirts under her while her eyes surveyed the table. "Will Sir Gennald not be joining us?"

"He is out on business and has not yet returned."

"I see." She didn't do a very good job of hiding her disappointment.

Sephana tried to think of something to say that would give Illyria a chance to recover. "So is Prince Ander really that bad?"

Lord Jannery frowned. "What do you mean, 'bad'?"

She suddenly regretted opening her mouth. Now everyone was looking at her. "I mean, isn't everything about whether or not he takes his father's throne? Would letting Ander take over really be that bad? He's not, like, crazy or anything, is he?"

"The boy is...no, I do not think he would make a bad king, although others disagree with me," Jannery admitted. "He's young, scarcely older than you, My Lady, but Karalon has had younger kings. And queens," he added.

Too young? Sephana wasn't too young for anything. She was twenty-one. She had already fallen in love and gotten married (although not in that order, and certainly not with the same person), been to three different kingdoms and become a knight.

"Ander's worthiness is not the issue," Illyria said, more herself now. "Am I correct, My Lord?" Jannery nodded. "It is the matter in which he takes the throne. When a king or queen is crowned, they undergo a ritual that links their soul to the health of their kingdom. This connection is unbreakable."

"So...for Ander to become king..." Sephana began.

"...then Lionar must first die," Jannery finished, his face grim.

Oh.

"Kings have died for their kingdom in that way before," he continued. "It is not without precedent, though it has not happened in centuries." He stopped. "It is not my place, you understand, to criticise the decisions of my liege. I am lord of the Northmarch, but I am also vassal to Duke Raebyrne, the leader of the Golden Bears."

It was chance that Sephana didn't have anything in her mouth. She probably would have either choked on it or spit everything across the table. What name had he said?

No one seemed to notice her open mouthed surprise. "But there are actions taken by the Golden Bears that you disapprove of?" Illyria asked.

Lord Jannery see-sawed his hand back and forth. "Disapprove is a strong word. It is not a tactic I would have undertaken if the decision had been mine."

"I understand, My Lord," Illyria said. "Your oath as a vassal remains intact. What would you not have done?"

"Having Lionar kill himself was one of the first things the Anderites demanded," Jannery continued. "The harvest had been ruined, Lionar was sick, the weather was terrible; kings have died for less, but something about it didn't sit right, so rumours were spread." He looked away. "Slander, really. We claimed that Lionar couldn't step down, because Ander wasn't worthy of the throne. Stories were created, whispers passed in dark corners, about how Ander was emotionally unstable, or was plotting against his father." His face was stony, but Sephana could see the shame and disapproval that lay beneath.

"It was the only weapon we could use," he insisted, even though his heart wasn't in it. "It was a play for time, for supporters, to find the truth of what was behind all of this, or for Lionar to regain his health, and it worked. We've overturned three motions for Ander to replace him." He trailed off.

"But it isn't a tactic you would have chosen," Illyria said into the silence.

"No. I don't know what else I would have, but...no."

Sephana was barely aware of the conversation. Duke Raebyrne; that was the name he had said. She was sure of it, as much as she didn't want to be. She didn't even excuse herself, just got up and left the table.

Gennald's duty had never seemed so onerous before. Any other time, carrying sealed messages between his master and the leader of the Golden Bears would have been a privilege, but not today. Today he just wanted to deliver his sealed correspondence and have it done with.

Thoughts of Illyria consumed him: how her golden hair flowed when she rode. The suppleness of her body beneath her form-fitting elven garb. The way her eyes changed colour from brown to green when he was near. The sultry sound of her voice when she said his name, and the way her lips begged to be kissed when she pursed them. It had been maddening these last two days. Travelling in close company as they were, with his lord and her brother observing their every action, made anything more than idle flirtation impossible.

The code of chivalry disallowed the very thing he wished for. A knight did not enter into a relationship with a woman that he did not intend to marry. That a woman like Illyria: elven, possessed of grace and beauty, and, more importantly, royal, would ever deign to marry a yeoman knight and great-grandson of a disentitled noble was beyond imagining. This was all madness, and she far too high a target for him to ever attain. She would be gone in a week or three anyway, off on her impossible mission to unite the Five Kingdoms of Anshara. He should...

Damn chivalry, and damn reason. He was a man, she was a woman, he wanted this, and, most importantly, she did as well. He could see it in her eyes, her sidelong glances, and the words she did not say. Her every glance and touch towards him made him dare to dream. He was brave in battle and had faced daunting odds there. Entering into a relationship with Illyria would be just as great an act of courage, and he could not call himself a man if he did not try.

He had arrived at this decision before they had entered New Aukaster and became embroiled in all of Sephana's needless drama. Before they had arrived at Lord Jannery's manor, Gennald had the makings of a plan. He had told Mrs. Shanford to house Illyria in the largest, grandest quarters in the manor. The guest suite was not only the most private room in the house and located next to his own, but it had an attached sitting room and was ideal for...entertaining.

It was late in the season, but he had still found a few late blooming flowers for purchase from a vendor. Those, and some fresh honey-cakes he had found, were sure to be enough to gain him access to her room after dinner. Once inside, he was confident that matters would take care of themselves.

To Gennald's chagrin, the first person he saw as he held his flowers and smiled his lecher's grin was Balien. Illyria's brother. The man didn't *look* dangerous. In truth Gennald had always thought Balien more fair than handsome, but he had also seen Balien in combat. Unassuming features aside, there was no one he would want to face in battle less than the dark haired elf and the strange sword that he wielded with a master's hand. Even the giant, Theramus, would be a better pick.

Controlling his expression, he nodded in greeting as he passed by. "Balien."

He just nodded in return. He had seen Gennald's grin and the flowers he carried. He wasn't an idiot. He had to know what Gennald's intentions were, and yet he did nothing. Damning himself for a fool even as he did it, Gennald stopped and turned. "You're not angry with me?"

No clarification was needed. Balien just shook his head. "No. I wish you well of it."

Gennald gaped. "But...she's your sister!"

"Yes, and she is an adult who can make her own choices. I trust her judgement. She doesn't need my approval or my protection for who she gets involved with."

Gennald just stared. "I...you... You should be beating my head in, or threatening to cut off my jewels with a rusty knife. You're her brother. Protecting her is your duty."

"If that's what you think, then you don't know either of us very well."

"But..." This was his problem: the huge festering canker that lay beneath his every interaction with the beguiling, wilful, and *stubborn* elven princess. "How can you not want to protect her?" he whispered, his words twisted by anguish. "How can you let her do the things she does when all you want to do is lock her up safe in a fortress while beating to death any man who would even *think* to harm her? How do you do that, Balien?"

The man who should have been thrashing him instead lay his hand on Gennald's shoulder. "Of course I want her to be safe, but I also want her happy, If you honestly think that she would ever accept being cloistered like a storybook princess while you slew her dragons for her, then you will *never* understand her."

"Doesn't it frustrate you?"

Balien chuckled. "Every day." He stooped and picked up a stray flower that had escaped Gennald's grasp. "Here, you'll need this."

Gennald took the flower and tucked it into his meagre bouquet. He turned to leave, but stopped. "You're really all right with this?"

"Would you prefer it if I threatened reprisal should you hurt her?"

Gennald had to smile. "It would, actually."

Balien's eyes narrowed and Gennald quailed before what he saw there. "Consider it said."

Why had Gennald never thought that he didn't look dangerous?

Illyria tried to focus on the words on the page before her, uncomfortable in her seldom worn gown. The madness that had possessed her to wear it had passed (not to mention that Gennald hadn't even been there to see her in it), and now she needed to concentrate on important matters. The Knights of Anduilon needed the recognition of the Karalinian king. She knew the games of nobility enough to know that nothing was ever given out for free. She would not let herself make any more foolish mistakes due to her ignorance. What she needed to determine was what the king needed.

That quest for knowledge had brought her to Lord Jannery's study with its meagre library, but now that she was here she found herself unable to concentrate. Images of handsome, self-sacrificing knights kept sneaking into her mind.

"Lady Illyria?"

She looked up at the sound of Gennald's voice; her automatic smile widening when she saw the fistful of wild flowers in his hand.

"Sir Gennald," she purred, standing and smoothing out the skirts she was once again happy to be wearing. "Are those for me?"

He gave them to her and she held them to her nose. They were pretty. "If I could have, I'd have given you thistles," he said gravely. "They'd go well with your eyes."

"Thistles?" she smiled quizzically, not understanding.

"They are part of our national crest. They represent beauty, strength of character and strong feelings." His eyes met hers. "They suit you perfectly."

Warmth flooded through her. She'd never look at the thorny flower the same way again. "Thank you." Her voice was low and rough.

His eyes caressed her body. "You look lovely tonight."

"Thank you," she repeated with a smile.

Beside her, Lord Jannery cleared his throat and stood. "I will leave you to your privacy."

"My Lord, no," she protested, propriety warring with desire. "This is your room."

Gennald held out his arm. "My Lord, with your permission, we'll withdraw."

She hesitated. She knew where they would go if she took his arm and what would happen. She waited for her internal voices to object and found only silence. Not waiting any longer, she wrapped her hand around his the strong muscles of his arm. Heat radiated from his body.

Lord Jannery was smiling widely. "Yes, of course. I will see you both in the morning."

They communicated only in glances as they walked down the hallway to her door. She turned to him at the door's threshold, watching him from under her eyelashes. She still had a chance to douse this. She could politely bid him goodnight, and perhaps allow him to kiss her hand or cheek. Certainly her etiquette training told her to do just that, but those thoughts died stillborn when she saw his gaze flick down to her lips and his head begin to lean down. *Etiquette and propriety bedamned. I'm tired of saying 'no'.* Heart hammering, not allowing herself time to talk herself out it, Illyria raised her head just in time to catch his mouth on hers.

It was wonderful.

She had wanted this for weeks. Longer. Every glance, denied moment, innocent touch, and flattering comment shared since their meeting had been amassing to right here and right now. Lips and tongues met and became acquainted in a manner that was both too gentle and not gentle enough for what she wanted.

When they parted, both were flushed and breathing hard. Titans would have been unable to separate their gazes.

Illyria smiled widely and, feeling incredibly bold, entwined her arms around his neck and pulled his face down to hers. They kissed again, deeper and harder this time. She moaned into his mouth when he wrapped his arms around her and pressed his body into hers.

Gennald really was an excellent kisser: strong and confident, but not overly insistent or probing. They broke again, and she opened her eyes to look into his, closer to her now than they had ever been. It was her last chance to retreat and end this, but that thought didn't stay with her for even a second as she stretched up to meet his lips while her hand reached blindly for her door handle. She had been given an entire suite to stay in, with a sitting room and a large fireplace.

Going into a bedroom with Gennald would have been too much, too fast, but the idea of idling on a couch with him before a fire was perfect. She found the door latch and pulled it open, half pulling, half following Gennald as they stumbled across the threshold. She heard a gasp behind her.

Tearing her lips from Gennald's, Illyria turned to see Sephana, eyes red from crying, sitting on that very same couch with shock and embarrassment on her face. "I sorry. I'll go."

Sephana, who was always so hard, had sought out Illyria for comfort. They hadn't even been friends a month before. Even though it meant a very different evening than what she had planned, Illyria didn't hesitate before leaving Gennald's arms and catching her. "No. Stay. Gennald was just leaving." The look she sent him was both an apology and a command.

Five different expressions crossed his face inside a second. Finally, his face a polite mask, he bowed to both women. "So I was. Lady Sephana, Lady Illyria. I will withdraw." He turned and walked away awkwardly. Illyria picked up her forgotten bouquet and set it on a side table.

"I am so sorry," Sephana said, her expression stricken. "You really didn't have to do that."

"It's all right." Illyria put her arm around the smaller woman. Despite her protests, Sephana didn't resist very hard as Illyria guided her to the couch. "I've known you longer."

She took Sephana in her arms and rubbed her hands soothingly down her back as the girl resumed crying. "It will be all right," she assured her. "Everything will be fine."

Sephana felt horrible. Those two had been building towards that moment like a pair of charging elephants for a whole month, and she had just stepped between them like a growling tiger.

"It's not too late," she said once her tears had stopped. "I can still get him."

"No," Illyria said gently. "Tell me what's wrong."

Her face was filled with so much kindness that Sephana had to look away. "It's stupid."

"Tell me." Gentle hands stroked her hair.

"I..." Fresh tears coursed down her cheeks. "It's just bad memories, that's all."

"You were in Karalon before, were you not?" Illyria asked. "This is where you first met Theramus."

Sephana's eyes became lost in the dancing flames. "Yes, almost two years ago. I'd been in Karalon for a more than a year by then. This is where I came after I ran away from Eldoth."

"What did you do?"

She shrugged. "A little bit of everything. Mostly I was the maid to a woman that I crossed the Karakks with. It wasn't a great life, but it was better than what I had left." She turned suddenly to Illyria, her eyes wide. "I don't mean Eldoth. He wasn't that bad. I mean, I didn't run *from* him—"

Illyria nodded. "You don't have to explain. Were you pretending to be human?"

"Yes, but my patrons knew. We were all refugees. Not many Karalmen were willing to work for them, so they had to take what they could get."

"So why the tears?"

Sephana couldn't help but smile. "A man. What else?"

"What was his name?"

"Edrik. He was a knight."

"Oh." Sephana barely heard Illyria say it. "Did...did he break your heart?"

She shook her head. "Not the way you mean. He died. I mean, he was killed. Saving me."

"Oh, Sephana." She felt Illyria's arms wrap around her and sank into the embrace. It felt good.

The words, once they started, refused to stop. "My headscarf fell off one day when I went to the market. When they found out what I was they tried to burn me at the stake. Edrik rescued me, but he was killed during the escape."

"I'm sorry," Illyria murmured.

"I...I thought I was over it. I mean, it was years ago, but with everything that happened..." She buried her face in Illyria's shoulder.

"The crowd today?"

"Everything. The trees, and the food, and how people dress. Everything reminds me of what happened." Her voice hardened. "Attenham..."

Illyria stiffened. "Count Attenham? What about him?"

Sephana just shook her head. She'd already said more than she had planned to. "Nothing. Really." She coughed into her hand and blinked away the last of her tears. "So...you're wearing a dress," she said, scrambling to find another subject.

Illyria coloured. "It was the only thing I had that didn't smell like horse."

Sephana had to laugh. "I'm sure that's exactly why you wore it. Did Gennald say he liked it?"

Illyria smiled coyly. "Not with words."

They both laughed. Sephana's guilt returned a hundredfold. "I am so, so sorry. I have the worst timing ever."

Illyria shrugged a shoulder. "They'll be other nights."

They both stared into the fire for a while.

"Thank you," Sephana said. "What you did...thank you. It means a lot."

Illyria smiled and squeezed Sephana's hand. Her eyes were a warm shade of brown. "You're welcome. Any time."

CHAPTER SEVEN

Dear Davin:

Thank you for your letter voicing your concern for me. Despite the cruel rumours you may have heard, I am indeed in good health and of sound mind. While I am, of course, concerned for my father's well-being, it has in no way affected my mind, body, or spirit. I remain, as I always have, ready to take my place on the Throne of Ur should the circumstances demand it. I pray daily to Emuranna that they do not.

Yes, Davin, I do recall your visit to the royal palace last year and think back on it with fondness. We are of a generation, you and I, and will be instrumental in shaping the future of Karalon together. We must stand united against those would do us ill and try to destroy the kingdom that we both hold so dear.

It is that subject that I must bring up now, and I do so with a heavy heart. Your father has made his loyalties to the 'Golden Bears' clear in court, and they are the ones, as you know, who have levelled their unkind allegations against me and my fitness. Your father is known across Karalon as being a good and honourable man, and I would like to believe that he has not been party to my slandering. It is my belief that those actions were undertaken by the leader of the Golden Bears, Duke Raebyrne, without the knowledge of his faction.

I would consider it a favour to me and act of friendship between us if you would attempt to convince your father of the wrongness of the Duke's actions, and persuade him to voice this opinion in court. I do not ask this lightly. I am reluctant to pit father against son (in much the same way that I am forced to against my own father), but I feel that the need is great and the cause just.

I have received council and the support in these troubled days from Redding Attenham, the count of Deremshire. Redding has been a strong shoulder and voice of reason for me since these troubles began, and I encourage you to write to him of any concerns and questions you may have. He is a good man, and I consider him my friend, as I do you.

Together we can save this kingdom, my friend, if only we have the courage and determination to see it through.

Yours in friendship,

Ander Usard

—Understanding the Anderite Crisis, *Kade of Langdon*

Illyria and her fellow Knights of Anduilon followed Lord Jannery and Sir Gennald into the Golden Palace of Ur. Retainers in blue and gold livery smoothly opened the doors, allowing them to pass through without slowing their stride. An older man in similar livery but with a crimson sash waited inside and bowed to Lord Jannery.

"Welcome, My Lord. I am afraid that there has been a complication." He fell into step beside Lord Jannery. Illyria and the others, not knowing the castle, could only follow.

"There are always complications," Jannery groused. "How bad is it?"

"The Anderites have learned of this morning's meeting and are here in force. The matter you wished to present to the king will be very public." The man glanced at Illyria and her companions. "These are the guests you are presenting?"

"Yes." Lord Jannery nodded but did not stop. "Forgive me. This is Genallen Stolton, viceroy to the king and ally of the Golden Bears. Genallen, these are the Knights of Anduilon. I vouch for their conduct within the palace."

The man stopped. "Knights...of Anduilon?"

Lord Jannery laid a consoling hand on the man's shoulder. "All will be explained, my friend. I assure you: they are worthy of the title."

Illyria stepped forward. "A star shines upon our meeting, My Lord. I am Illyria Exiprion, and these are my companions. If Lord Jannery is your friend then I name you mine as well. Thank you for the assistance you have given us in his name."

He paused and gave them a longer, slower look. "Well met, Lady. I await your tale eagerly." He face clouded. "I only wish that I could give you a better opportunity to do so. Count Attenham and his Anderites are there to stir up trouble, mark me."

"There's no point asking how they learned of this meeting," Lord Jannery grumbled. "These walls bleed secrets. Nothing to do except bully through it, now."

Illyria exchanged a glance with her brother. "Count Attenham is here?"

"I'm afraid so," the viceroy replied. "Have you met him?"

"Briefly." *He must have run his horses to death, given the start we had on him.*

They resumed walking.

Lord Jannery frowned. "This complicates things. I don't want the Anderites to see them before they are introduced. Every minute will just give them more ammunition."

"They cannot enter once the chamber doors are sealed," the viceroy replied.

"I am aware. Take them to the south gallery. It's out of the Anderite's line of vision, at least."

Their travels had taken them down a long, stone corridor to a wing of the castle of much more recent construction. Two elegantly dressed halberdiers guarded a pair of ornate, metal-banded doors. Above their heads were a pair of rich blue pennants bearing a rampant bear standing between branches of thick-leaved thistles: the arms of Karalon. Both bear and thistles were exquisitely rendered in bright gold thread.

"I must take my seat with my peers," Lord Jannery said to Illyria. "The viceroy will lead you to your seats when it is time." He turned to Sir Gennald. "Stay with them."

"Yes, My Lord."

He gave her an encouraging smile before passing through into the council chamber.

Illyria was tired. The memory of kissing Gennald had kept her awake long after Sephana had left. A large part of her had wanted to sneak down the hallway to Gennald's room and ask to be invited in. She was certain he had been as awake as she. Propriety, in the end, had restrained her. She had yet to speak to him this morning and didn't know what to say when she did.

It would have to wait until after this crucial meeting. She was about to address a king. The melodramas of her personal affairs amounted to very little in comparison.

The viceroy popped his head into the room and motioned to them. "Come. It is time."

Sephana stood in a shadowed alcove along one side of the Chamber of Peers. It was very Karalinian in style, which was to say: severe. She didn't know if the people here were offended by decoration or were too busy being serious to have the time. Maybe all their vows and webs of allegiances took up all their energy and they just didn't know how. She found that more sad then the fact that no one in the city knew what a sewer was.

She worried the end of her hair with her fingers. Her hair was thick, curly, and hard to manage. She'd worn it under a headscarf for the last two years, the only way she'd found that allowed her to conceal her headscales and earpits. Since declaring herself a Knight of Anduilon, she'd tried a few different styles, but after the events in the street yesterday had chosen to wear it loose instead. It was harder to manage this way, but it also concealed more.

Of course, what a person could or could not see on her head was pretty meaningless; her tail was clearly visible (and it itched, too, but it seemed wrong to scratch it right now). Compared to that, it didn't matter how nice her clothes were or what her hairstyle was. She was clearly not human.

She recalled what that lying cheat, Count Attenham, had called them a few days ago: circus performers. She hated to admit it, but he was right. Illyria was by far the most presentable of all of them, but she was wearing the same tunic and cape that she did when she was tracking or fighting. Admittedly, her clothing was Ilthanaran, and whatever magic the 'elves' had used to make it was still in effect. Its colours were as rich and its hems as unfrayed today as they had when Sephana had met her. Balien wore a beige cloak that matched his sister's (and, boy, did he look great in it) but the rest of his clothing—while clean and whole—was, well, common. Eldoth looked like Eldoth. Other than his beard being freshly trimmed and his hair brushed clean; he looked like he always did, which was to say: weird.

Theramus's clothing mattered as little as her own did: he was obviously, overwhelmingly, alien.

How was anyone going to take them seriously?

Sir Gennald, in contrast, looked every inch a knight. His mail gleamed and his black and yellow surcoat was spotless. What were any of them, compared to that?

So far, being in the Peers' Court was pretty boring. She had the distinct and rare privilege of watching the richest, most powerful men in Karalon argue and bicker like children. One particular unlucky sap had the unfortunate job of reading out what had happened in the previous meeting while everyone else either booed or applauded everything he said. At least they all seemed to be too occupied yelling at each other to notice her or her friends, which was just as well.

The court chamber was a large, well-lit, white stone chamber. There were two lines of richly varnished tables on opposite sides of a wide, centre aisle. At the far end of the room, on a raised dais, was a large, ornately carved throne. The throne was occupied by one of the best dressed, most haggard men she had ever seen.

It had to be the king. His name was Lionar Usard, and the picture of him on the coins of the realm was that of a handsome man somewhere in his forties, but the person hunched over the throne barely resembled him. His clothing was oversized and his hair—more grey than black—hung drab and flat. His face was both pale and flushed, if such a thing were possible, etched deeply with lines of exhaustion.

Both rows of tables were filled with richly dressed nobles actively scowling at their counterparts across the aisle. The Golden Bears and the Anderites, she guessed, but as to which side was which she had no idea. One of them was standing and yelling accusations at the opposing faction when a man with a large, filigreed neck piece, sitting by himself off to the side of the throne, slammed the butt of an ornate staff against the stone floor.

"That is enough, Lord Dowell!" he shouted. "I have declared the matter closed. Curb your tongue, or I will have you ejected from this chamber!"

"Duke Raebyrne, the current Lord Speaker of the Council," she heard Sir Gennald whisper to Illyria. "He's a good man, and as loyal to the king as they come. Win his support, and all the Golden Bears will fall in behind him."

Sephana froze at the mention of the Duke's name. *As if I didn't have enough ghosts to haunt me today.*

A familiar voice spoke up. "My Lord Speaker, is it time for new business?" She recognised the back of his head: it was Count Attenham in all his ratty glory, somehow already back in the city after snooping around Eastbridge.

The Speaker nodded. "It is, but I warn you, Count: if you or any one of your precious 'Anderites' mention one word about the king's fitness, I will close this session immediately."

Across the aisle from him, Lord Jannery, cut off before being able to speak, frowned.

Attenham nodded. "Of course, My Lord, but may I remind you that the position of Speaker is without bias or prejudice. You are not a Golden Bear while you hold that staff."

"Do not presume to lecture me, Count," the Speaker commanded. "If you have new business, I suggest you get on with it."

Attenham stood and Sephana held her breath. Had he discovered anything? She agreed with Illyria that what they had done against the Dragonfleet was morally right, but it was still illegal. If he had any proof of what had happened, they'd be arrested on the spot.

Or, at least, they'd try. Sephana had already experienced the kind of 'justice' that Reshai received from Karalmen. She wasn't sure that she was ready to die to avoid imprisonment, but she did know that she wouldn't go quietly.

From his place in the centre of the Anderite faction, Attenham bowed. "Thank you, My Lord Speaker. I do, indeed. I, of course, make no aspersions against the crown and its ability to enforce justice, but I must report, again, that the plague of outlawry affecting my land, and the land of many others, remains unchecked." He paused dramatically. "I regret to inform you that my shipment of the taxes intended for the Dragonfleet tribute has been stolen."

The room erupted. Sephana, still hidden from view, let out a ragged breath. They were safe.

She saw the king raise his head and speak, but she couldn't make out his words over the furore. The speaker, Duke Raebyrne, did, and slammed his staff against the floor several times. "Silence! The king speaks." He glared at the entire room. "This is the Peer's Court, not a jousting field. Act your stations, all of you."

She could barely hear King Lionar's whispered question. "How much was taken?"

Count Attenham hung his head. "Alas, your majesty, all of it. Twenty thousand gold crowns, raised from my county at great difficulty. I thank you for the escort you sent me, but it wasn't enough. They were ambushed in the Deremwood Forest, in the Wightland Valley, and I have heard similar reports from many of the fine nobles in this room." He paused. "While I am sure that there is no connection between the king's fitness and the impotence of his marshals to enforce justice, I cannot help but point out that, if we had not been afflicted with another failed harvest, such a tax would remain unnecessary. Outlaws seldom steal wheat."

His last statement was made amidst another chorus of nods and cheers from his side of the chamber and angry mutterings and cat-calls from the other. Duke Raebyrne beat his staff futilely against the stone floor, trying vainly to silence them.

"We need that gold to pay the tribute," announced one of the Golden Bears. "If we're short, and they begin raiding, it will be on your head!" The nobles surrounding him nodded their agreement.

"I gave my tax money into the possession of the king's knights," Attenham countered. "The responsibility to replace it is his, not mine. I have a signed writ to that effect."

"I wouldn't use your writ to wipe my ass!" someone yelled. "You aren't going to use a piece of paper to get out of paying what you owe."

"And where do you propose I *get* this money?" Attenham asked over the cheers and boos. "This is the third emergency tax that the king has demanded this year alone. I've already taxed my peasants to the bone. *There's nothing left.*"

"I've seen your manor house. There's enough gold and silver there on your tables and walls to pay at least half what you owe." The Golden Bear looked to his fellows for support. "I say we go down there and get it." Half the room nodded in agreement. "We'll tear down his walls if we have to."

The other half did not. "Any man trying to gain access to My Lord Attenham's manor will find his head decorating a spike outside the gate," an Anderite noble declared. "I pledge a hundred of my knights to the defence of his manor."

"You'll need them," a Golden Bear growled. "We have more than a thousand men between all of us."

After that, it got worse.

The weakened stronghold of decorum fell in a cacophony of frustrations and threats: "Any man who backs Attenham is a traitor. It's no crime to kill traitors."; "I'll surrender my lands to the dogmen before I give the crown one more coin."; "If we can't get enough gold and the Dragonfleet demands children, I'll make sure that yours are at the front of the line."

They were one very small step away from coming to blows. *So this is what a country tearing itself apart looks like*, Sephana thought numbly. She couldn't decide if it was more sad, funny, or pathetic. Beyond all of it, looking frail upon his throne, King Lionar mouthed words that no one could hear.

The duke, his face red with anger, beat the tip of his staff into the floor hard enough to make sparks. "That is enough, all of you! You are nobles. Behave that way!" Sullen and angry, the room fell into a dark, angry silence. "Hold your tongues. The king speaks."

A palsied hand rose and pointed towards beyond the Anderites to where Sephana, Illyria, and the others stood. "Who are they?" the king's reedy voice wheezed.

Theramus was dismayed at what he saw. Not only were the so called 'nobles' of Karalon acting in opposition to their name, but he had not realized Lionar's health was so far gone. He understood now the origin of the whole Anderite movement, and was not sure that it was not justified. The king and the land were one, both in illness and in health.

Willem Jannery stood. "Your majesty," he said with a bow. "I have come not only to show my continuing support for you, but to report of a near disaster in the north and introduce you to the heroes who prevented it."

The haggard king mumbled something and motioned with his hand.

"His majesty thanks you for your support and asks for you to continue, March-Lord Jannery," the speaker said.

Jannery motioned to Sir Gennald, who led everyone to the centre of the chamber. Many eyes weighed them, which bothered Theramus little. Eldoth, however, was fidgeting and Sephana looked especially ill at ease. Illyria and Balien appeared unaffected by the scrutiny.

"My Lord Speaker, I must protest," Count Attenham said. "I have met these so called 'heroes' and they are not worthy to stand in this hall. One of them, that girl—" he pointed at Sephana "—has a snake tail."

"I personally vouch for them, Attenham, and you will soon hear why."

The king mumbled something again. "The king would hear your report, Lord Jannery, and is content with your assurances. Your guests may stay." Speaker Raebyrne glowered at the Anderites. "I will tolerate no interruptions, My Lords. Lord Jannery has the floor and will give his report without disruption. Am I clear?" He did not wait for a response. "You may begin."

"Yes, My Lord Speaker. Thank you."

He told the events surrounding what people in the north were already beginning to call 'Dragonhead Keep', of how the Interloping Djido wizard Veeshar had allied with a grey-skinned desert warlord and brought a score of monstrous 'dragon lizards' with him. Veeshar had used his magic to ensorcel the minds of the defenders of Durnshold Castle and held it until the Nintaran leader, Olamm-Ta, could bring his forces to bear. Jannery did not flinch in his own negligent role in the events that followed, how his sudden departure had left his teen-age son in command, and how the boy had bungled the matter. He told of how Illyria and her companions, acting as escorts to a Nemoran trade caravan, had taken it upon themselves to investigate the matter and, when Jannery's son, Davin, had proved unequal to the task, had led a group of Nemoran volunteers to liberate the keep and prevent an invasion of the Karalinian interior.

Gasps of disbelief, angry mutters, and open scoffing could be heard from both sides of the council chamber as he continued, but—after a few warning glares from the Speaker—no one interrupted him.

"I know this sounds incredulous, My Lords, but I offer proof." He nodded to Sir Gennald, who retrieved an object from within a sack: the fearsome skull of a dragon lizard. They had been terrifying to face on the battlefield and only the inherent weakness of the magic used to force their obedience had allowed them to be defeated.

The skull was two feet long, weighed more than twenty pounds, and was dominated by a massive mouth filled with deadly curved teeth. It was appropriately fearsome to behold and the assembled lords of Karalon stared at it with wide eyes.

Attenham stood abruptly. "My Lords, I must protest. This skull is obviously a fabrication and this whole piece of theatre is an elaborate excuse to cover the fact that Lord Jannery cannot pay his tribute tax!"

"But I have paid it, My Lord, in full," Jannery said, a smug expression on his face. "I delivered it to the exchequer myself just this morning."

Attenham visibly faltered. "You...did?"

"Lord Attenham, I expressly forbid you from making exactly this kind of interruption," the Speaker declared. His eyes, though, remained fixed on the dragon lizard skull making its way around the chamber. "Your point, however, is not without merit. This tale...defies belief."

A lord from the Golden Bear side of the chamber stood. "My Lord Speaker? I can verify Lord Jannery's story, at least partly."

"Then please do so, Baron Packard."

The baron nodded. "Yes, My Lord. As you may know, my lands lie alongside Lord Jannery's and my manor on the road to Durnston."

The speaker nodded. "Yes. Go on."

"I was in residence when My Lord Jannery arrived. He had fallen from his horse and twisted his ankle. I was seeing to his hospitality when it came to my attention that several refugees from Durnston had arrived at the town of Sukhold. They all told the same story: that scaled demons had taken over the town and were occupying the keep. They begged me to send aid and help their families."

"I see. And what did you do, My Lord?"

"At Lord Jannery's request I gathered as many men as I could, put them under the command of my First Knight, and sent them north. My men returned a week later and while they didn't see this battle lord Jannery speaks of, they did see its aftermath."

"And what did they see?"

"Dozens of heads like that one." He pointed to the dragon lizard skull. "They were all on stakes on both sides of the road to the keep. He also saw foreign soldiers working with Lord Jannery's men to clean up the mess. There were dogmen corpses being laid in piles, My Lord Speaker, hundreds of them, and dozens of those grey men, too." He squared his shoulders. "My First is a good man, My Lord Speaker: steadfast and loyal. If he said he saw these things, I believe him."

In front of Theramus, Jannery caught the eyes of the baron who had supported him and nodded his thanks.

On this throne, the king began to cough. Everyone stopped to watch as his deep, hacking coughs continued and a nurse, who had been waiting unobtrusively at the side of the chamber, rushed up and administered a tonic. When his coughs finally subsided, he murmured something and the speaker turned back to Willem Jannery.

"Thank you for your report, March-Lord. I speak for my king and, I think, all the lords in this room, at our relief that our northern border is once more secure. Also, congratulations at your daughter's engagement to this Nemoran prince and for securing a trade agreement with them. Such an arrangement can only benefit us all."

Jannery bowed low. "Thank you, My Lord Speaker, your Majesty. It could not have been done without the brave people standing behind me. My Lords, may I present to you the heroes of the Northmarch: the Knights of Anduilon."

There was silence.

Illyria stepped forward. "My Lords, your Majesty, I know that our claim may appear outrageous, but I beg you to hold off any outrage until you have heard us. Our appearance is unconventional, I know, but my fellow knights and I are worthy of this title. We ask only this opportunity to prove it to you."

The speaker—Duke Raebyrne, Jannery had named him—narrowed his eyes. "And you are?"

Illyria bowed in the Ilthanaran style: bending at the waist, kissing her cupped hands and raising them in offering as she straightened. "Forgive me, My Lord Speaker. Peers of Karalon, your Majesty: I am Illyria Exiprion, Child of the Mark and niece to Kefeus Sheldrion, King of Ilthanara. This my brother, Balien, as well as Theramus of the Noss, Sephana, and Eldoth the Red, a wizard." She had asked them how they had wanted to be introduced and Sephana hadn't been able to think of anything. "We have sworn oaths of obedience and fidelity to Emuranna and vowed to restore the ideals of the High Kingdom to Anshara. We name ourselves the Knights of Anduilon and would consider ourselves privileged if you would recognise us as such."

The nobles muttered quietly to themselves but made no outright objections. The king gazed at them from surprisingly sharp eyes, but it was the speaker's expression that worried her the most. "Is part of this recognition clemency for past crimes?" he asked, an edge to his voice.

The question and its tone gave Illyria pause. Did he know of Westbridge? "No, My Lord."

"Oh, really?"

He obviously had more to say, but was forestalled by the king's thin voice from behind him. "I would speak to these Knights of Anduilon." He coughed wetly. "Have them approach me."

The speaker left his chair and knelt before the throne, whispering something. Lionar shook his head. Raebyrne spoke again, more firmly, and the king's reply was vehement enough to carry across the chamber. "Have them approach me!" he rasped before descending into another fit of coughing.

The speaker stood stiffly. "The *Knights of Anduilon* will approach the throne," he intoned formally while, on either side of him, peals of muttering rolled through the chamber.

Illyria glanced at the others and, with a nod, they advanced. Raebyrne gestured for them to kneel, but stepped up to Illyria before they could do so. "He is saving his strength for SummersEnd," he whispered. "Do anything to weaken him, and I will remove you from this kingdom with my bare hands!"

"We will be respectful, My Lord." The duke grunted before giving a final nod and retaking his seat. Illyria dropped to one knee and fixed her gaze at his feet, giving the kingdom's most sacred and important man the respect he was due. "Your majesty," she intoned. The other's followed her cue.

At his gesture she raised her eyes. He looked worse from close up, but also sharper. There was intelligence in his eyes, as well as fear and desperation.

"Who are you, girl?" he wheezed. "Are you crownmarked, as you say?"

"Yes, sire. I bear the Mark of the Hawk, but I am no longer eligible for the crown."

He examined her intently. "You are an elf."

Illyria bit back on the curse that wanted to escape her lips. *Even here I cannot escape that label!* She did her best to keep her voice level. "Yes, sire, as is my brother."

"Your uncle, the elf king, he allows you to serve like this?"

Her eyes dropped. "I gave him no choice, sire. I believe in this cause very strongly."

He gave a brief smile. "Why knighthood. Why...Anduilon?"

"Because, sire, there is no one else."

"Humph." He turned to Theramus. "You are Noss."

"Yes," the blue giant rumbled in his deep, resonant voice.

"Your people served the High King."

He straightened as much as his position allowed him. "No, we serve him still."

"It must be hard, being the only one of your kind in this land. Why?"

"They are worthy of my service, and their cause is just."

The king slumped further into his throne. His eyes raked over Balien and Eldoth, but he said nothing. Lastly, he looked at Sephana.

"What are you, girl?"

What. Not *who*.

Illyria was very proud of the way Sephana kept her voice even. "I am a Reshai, sire."

The king's eyes narrowed. "We have Reshai in this city. They do not look like you."

"We are part Djido, sire. Our ancestors were forced upon by their captors during the Great War. Most Reshai hide their scales behind cloth to hide their shame."

"But you do not."

"I am not ashamed of who I am."

His gaze flicked down. "I have never seen one of you with a tail."

The tail in question twitched. "We are all born with them, sire, but almost all are severed at birth. I was raised apart from the clans. My mother chose not to uphold that particular tradition."

"Hmm." He locked his eyes with hers and Sephana met his gaze squarely. "And are you in league with the Djido?"

"No!" Her immediate, indignant reply was loud enough to be heard from at the back of the chamber. She took a deep breath, then continued in a quieter tone. "I am not, sire, nor are any of the Reshai I know. My loyalties are to my companions and to Anduilon."

The king coughed: a horrible, racking deep chest cough. "I have seen enough."

This was the moment Illyria had been waiting for. "Use us, sire."

He wiped his mouth with a blood-flecked cloth. "Use you? How?"

She looked squarely into his rheumy eyes. "As you see fit, sire. We are weapons. Point us towards your enemies. Let us prove our worth to you."

He laughed thinly. "I am surrounded by enemies. They compete for the privilege of defeating me."

"There is an expression sometimes used among my people, sire: 'Two birds can be struck with one arrow, if one is skilled or desperate enough.' I can do nothing for your health or your connection to the land, but these outlaws and the tribute they have stolen, that we can solve for you."

The sudden strength in his eyes was worthy of his name and title. "Five of you can succeed where my greatest knights have failed?"

"I do not insult your knights or their courage, sire, but we have access to both the magics and lore of the High Kingdom, as well as..." The words wanted to stick in her throat, but she forced them out anyway. "...*elven* training and woodcraft."

He hesitated and she forged ahead. "All I ask for, sire, is the chance for us to prove ourselves to you. Let us help you, please. It costs you nothing."

"It has been my experience that so called 'free' gifts are seldom so. What is it that you want, Illyria Exiprion?"

"Your blessing, sire, and recognition for our order."

He laughed hollowly. "I think you overvalue my influence." He waved them away with a weak gesture. "Stand aside. I must address the nobility."

Sir Gennald stood in uncomfortable silence, taking no action other than watching the throne with dread anticipation. The assembled Peers, both Golden Bear and Anderite, did so as well. The chamber was as silent as Gennald could remember it being.

No one could hear what was being said other than one loud outburst made by Sephana. Even Duke Raebyrne, seated at the base of the dais, seemed unable to overhear the hushed conversation if the frustration on his face was any indicator.

Gennald's eyes were drawn to Illyria like a lodestone was to iron, though he could see little of her other than her long, blonde hair and the length of her beige elven cloak. He wanted to be angry at her for what had happened last night (or, more precisely, what had *not* happened), but could not.

Oh, he was frustrated, most certainly. Not even his difficult teenage years, when he had not known how to wear the mantle of manhood that Emuranna had pressed upon him, had never frustrated him as much as walking away from Illyria as she rushed to console her weepy little Reshai friend. He could (and did) damn the strange and unfathomable bonds of feminine solidarity, but he could not remain angry at Illyria. It would be like blaming a puppy for wetting the floor, or a baby for crying.

What did it say about him that here in the Council of Peers—in the presence of his king and surrounded by nobles who wished his lord ill—his eyes and mind remained fixed on a woman, and not just a conventional woman but one who carried a sword and made the absurd claim that she and her friends were knights?

There was movement on the throne and Speaker Raebyrne came to his feet quickly. "Silence! The king speaks."

Some of Illyria's group didn't seem to know what to do, but when the woman herself, so full of her damnably attractive noble bearing and assurance, stood at the side of the throne, the rest followed suit. The king, still heartbreakingly frail, spoke as loudly as his condition allowed him.

"The matter of the recognition of the Knights of Anduilon is too grave to be decided here. I have taken it under deliberation." He wasn't much louder than a normal man's speaking volume, but the effort made his body shake. "In the meantime, I am declaring them my special investigators into this plague of outlawry. They proceed with my full authority and you will give them your co operation." He stopped to cough.

Angry murmurs spread throughout both sides of the council chamber. The Speaker finally had to strike his staff to silence them.

"As to the other matter, that of my fitness to rule, I will give you all this oath:" There was only silence now. "I will take this matter from your hands. My next Joining with the land happens in ten days time, on the second day of SummersEnd. I swear to you all now, with Emuranna as my witness, that if you do not see the moon full and clear on that night, that I will fall upon my sword."

If the king had anything more to say no one heard it. There was in an instant, loud, protest from the side of the Golden Bears and smiling cheers from the side of the Anderites. Duke Raebyrne's repeated shouts for civility went unheard. It took a horrible coughing fit from the king, far worse than the previous ones, to silence the room. Gennald could only watch along with the Peers of Karalon as his liege motioned to Illyria with a quavering hand and whispered something into her ear.

King Lionar's physician rushed to his side and after a quick examination, motioned two burly attendants to his side. The king was quickly whisked from the chamber leaving eddies of gossip in his wake. Behind them, speaker Raebyrne shouted to a room of deaf ears that the council session had been closed.

CHAPTER EIGHT

" 'Duke Raebyrne is asking to be the next Speaker? He has the right, I suppose, but why? No one ever requests that position, except maybe for some of the newer barons, and they only do it for the novelty of having the power to tell their betters to sit down and shut up. But a duke? Never.' "

—*comment attributed to Genallen Stolton, Viceroy of the Golden Palace of Ur*

A knight in a red, yellow and blue surcoat stepped in front of them and bowed before they could leave the palace. "My Lord Jannery, his Grace, Duke Raebyrne, requests a moment of your time."

"Yes. Of course." Jannery looked at Gennald. "Wait for me here."

"Yes, My Lord."

He nodded to Theramus and the others, "Excuse me."

They stood in antechamber off of the Peer's Court. The various nobles from within, Golden Bears and Anderites both, cast veiled glances as they whispered amongst themselves. None had ventured as far as actually speaking with them, save for the duke's messenger.

"Courts are the same the world over," Theramus rumbled as quietly as he could. "They are all wondering how to turn our arrival to their advantage."

"Of course they are," Illyria said. "It is why I wanted to address the king directly. We'd have been having whispered conversations for weeks otherwise."

"I hope we can deliver on the promise you made," Balien commented.

"I'm sorry you had to learn about it like that," Her words were directed to all of them, not just her brother. "It was the only way I could think of to gain his trust."

Sephana shrugged. "Isn't that the kind of thing we're supposed to be doing anyway? I mean, we're knights, right?"

"I should have discussed it with you first," Illyria said, apology in her voice. "I would have, if it hadn't happened so quickly."

"I am content to follow your initiative," Theramus assured her.

"You promised him magic and knowledge from the age of the High Kingdom," Eldoth criticized. "That is somewhat of an exaggeration."

Sephana rolled her eyes. "Aren't you always bragging that you're the greatest wizard in five hundred years?"

"Not to a king!" he protested. "And I never said that I possess ancient magic. They'll be expecting me to build bridges or something equally beyond my abilities."

Sephana snorted. "Some wizard you are. Can't even build a bridge."

"I'll throw you off of one if you aren't silent."

"Stop it, both of you," Illyria scolded. "We're in a palace."

"What did the king say to you, Lyri, at the end?" Balien asked.

"He was hard to make out. 'There is evil in my house,' I think. He wanted to say more but his coughing became too severe."

"Is he really going to kill himself?" Sephana asked.

"Not if we can help it," Illyria said. "I agree with Lord Jannery: there is more to all of this than Lionar's health. I do not think passing the crown to his son will solve Karalon's problems."

"We can't solve every problem," Balien said. "We've committed ourselves to hunting outlaws. A desperate man can aim for two targets, but only a fool tries for three."

She shrugged. "Even fools are lucky sometimes. We have ten days until SummersEnd. Anything can happen."

"It might take us ten days just to get there," Balien warned. "Where is the Wightland Valley?"

"Two days from here," Sephana said. "One, if you ride you really hard, but it's in Deremford: Count Attenham's land. He said that he'd arrest us if he ever saw us there."

"We have the king's personal permission to investigate this matter," Illyria pointed out. "A Count might outrank a March-Lord, but the king outranks them both."

Sephana looked like she wanted to say more, but didn't.

"When will you be departing on your quest, My Lady?" Gennald asked. He had been cold and distant towards her all morning. It hurt, though she knew why he was angry. She wasn't sure, given this new development, that she would have an opportunity to properly apologise.

"Sooner is better," Balien advised. "We could leave this afternoon."

He was right. Time was of the essence, but it was not practicality that commanded her thoughts now. She recalled the taste of Gennald's lips and the feel of his hands. "Tomorrow morning," she found herself saying before her rational mind could stop her. "First light will be early enough."

She thought that she saw a flicker of warmth on Gennald's face. Balien nodded, his face inscrutable. "I'll handle our provisions."

She could not help blushing. She wasn't fooling anyone.

Someone cleared their throat. Illyria turned to see a pretty blonde girl curtsying. Illyria recalled seeing her before: she was a nurse and had helped tend to King Lionar when his condition had overcome him.

"Excuse me. I...I come from the royal chambers. His majesty told me to give this to you." She held out a folded sheet of parchment.

Balien smiled warmly at the girl as he took the paper. "Our thanks. How fares the king?"

The nurse smiled shyly. Balien often had that affect on women. It was something about his eyes. "He is recovering. He took a tonic for his cough." She paused. "He refused to rest until he had written that note. I had to swear to deliver it myself before he would retire."

His smile was wider than Illyria could recall it being in months. "You have fulfilled your errand. You may return to his majesty and assure him it was delivered."

She curtsied once more. "Thank you, My Lords." She glanced across to Illyria and Sephana. "And ladies, too. Excuse me."

Balien's gaze followed her as she left.

"She's cute," Sephana observed with a smile. "You should go talk to her."

"Perhaps." His eyes rested on the door that she had exited from.

Illyria smiled, happy to see her brother so. She opened the letter, held shut by the royal seal. The writing was untidy, but legible. *The Bearers of this letter, the Knights of Anduilon, pursue their activities with my authority and approval. To deny them is to deny me. L.U.*

She handed it to her brother, who read it and raised both eye brows. The caution in his eyes needed no translation.

Sephana took it and read it before handing it to Eldoth. "We only have this authority for the next ten days," he pointed out. "If the king dies, so too does any power granted us."

"We still leave at first light?" Balien asked, his face non-judgemental.

Guilt flared through Illyria. She knew that she should order their immediate departure, but even as her mind thought one thing her lips said something else. "Yes. First light."

Lord Jannery returned and Gennald bowed. "My Lord."

Lord Jannery nodded in acknowledgement. "Let us begone. These politics stink worse than a corpse."

Everyone fell into step. "Is all well, My Lord?"

"As well as it can be in a kingdom where half of its nobles cheer the idea of the death of its sovereign."

They made their to the front of the palace and waited as attendants brought their horses. While most nobles in Karalon would have taken a carriage, Lord Jannery had insisted on riding his own mount.

"Was your meeting with the duke confidential, My Lord?" Illyria asked. "Did he perhaps say anything that might aid our quest?"

Her quest. Illyria, the woman he had held in his arms so briefly last night, called herself a knight and claimed to have a quest. She had private conferences with his king and inspired letters making her immune to authority. By this time tomorrow she would be en route to a bandit infested forest and a day after that would be on their trail.

The idea almost made him ill, but he didn't know which part.

Their horses were brought out and they mounted. Even the bent-footed wizard managed to get into his saddle without making an idiot of himself.

"Nothing secret was said," Lord Jannery said once they were free of the palace grounds. "His Grace was curious, that's all. I assured him that, despite not being sworn to me, that you had my complete faith and were beyond reproach."

"You are very kind," Illyria said.

"Kind, nothing. You've earned it, all of you. We said nothing that would be of any aid to you, I am afraid. Duke Raebyrne is the king's staunchest supporter. He has sworn to never harm me, my family, or those in my service. He has no involvement with these outlaws, I'd bet my life on it."

"His grace is fortunate to have such loyal allies," Illyria said.

"No more fortunate than I, My Lady."

They talked more, but Gennald took no notice of it. He could see nothing beyond golden hair, courtly poise, and shapely limbs as she expertly controlled her mount.

I defied my king for her. Non-interference with Dragonfleet activities had been the first decree from King Lionar's mouth upon reaching the throne, as it had for the king before him, and so on for a hundred years. Gennald had broken a century old commandment for the sake of that elven princess and knew that, in the same situation, would do so again.

Did that make him less of a knight, or more of one? A knight swore to protect the honour of all women, as well as defending the innocent and the helpless. It was a cornerstone of the chivalric oath, but so was a knight's obedience of his lord and his king. What did a knight do when to obey one oath he had to break another?

"Your face looks so serious, Sir Knight," Illyria said, her face an exaggerated parody of solemnity while her eyes danced with mischief. At some point she had ended her conversation with Lord Jannery and steered her mount near his. Illyria glanced at him from the corner of her eye, a hint of her beautiful smile brightening her face. "What deep, serious thoughts are you thinking about right now?"

He smiled, his dark thoughts vanishing. How could he not when presented with such radiance? "The king, what else?" he lied. "I had not thought his health so far gone."

Her face softened in compassion, and it was hard not to kiss her. She reached across and covered his hand with her own. The strength of her grip shouldn't have surprised him, and yet it did; every time. "We have ten days. We'll find the truth of it."

She *is seeking to comfort* me?

When she gazed at him through her lashes, her eyes were as green as a forest. "Starting tomorrow, we'll give every effort to save him and solve this mystery."

Gennald knew an invitation when he heard one. He bored his eyes into hers, letting a hint of the fire that she ignited within him show. "Then that leaves us with tonight, My Lady. This time I will brook no interruptions."

She said nothing, only smiled coyly over her shoulder as she rode away.

Redding's steward entered the room and bowed, one hand holding a perfumed kerchief to his face. "My Lord, Prince Ander has just arrived upstairs."

The largest problem with mentoring a crown prince was that he did things on his own schedule. When Prince Ander wanted to see you, he saw you; and when he wanted to leave, he left. There was little that a mere count could do about it. The rewards were worth it (or, at least, they would be), but riding under the lead of a needy, spoiled brat was trying in the mean time.

"Offer him the usual refreshments and see him to my study, but give me time to ready myself first." He turned away from his new 'guest' and wiped a floral-scented cloth across his hands and neck. He had almost inured himself to the awful stink in his hidden basement chamber, but knew that those around him had not. Normally, he bathed and scrubbed himself raw after his sessions down here, but with Ander's sporadic appearances being what they were, he would have to settle for quick wipedown and a change of clothes.

He barely made it up the stairs and through the hidden door into his study before the prince arrived. He was still buttoning his doublet closed when the steward opened up the door and admitted him.

"Who are the Knights of Anduilon?" Ander demanded before Redding could speak.

Lionar's eldest son was tall and lean like his father. They both had the Usard nose, but Anders' features were softened by his mother's fine cheeks and jaw. It made him look dainty, almost effeminate. That, and his pale skin, made Redding's efforts to make the prince look strong and resolute difficult. At least he had finally cut his hair, and was wearing the riding attire that Redding had suggested. It made him look vital.

Redding put on his most encouraging smile. "Your Highness—Ander—please, calm yourself. They are no one; an attempt to distract us from what is really going on. It's a pathetic act of theatre done by desperate men. It only shows how desperate the Golden Bears have become."

"They're supposed to be heroes," Ander said quietly. "I heard a song about them. It says they've slain dragons."

A song? He'd have to make sure that it was silenced before the day's end. He'd thought that these 'Knights of Anduilon' were nothing but an embarrassing joke, but, making the entrance they had in the Peer's Court and having been endorsed by Willem Jannery—known for his honesty and integrity—he was starting to revise his opinion.

"Don't believe songs you hear in taverns, your highness, and don't believe in heroes. They don't exist."

"Do you really think so?" Ander looked heartbroken.

What kind of idealistic pap has he been fed in that palace? Best to begin undoing that damage now. "These 'Knights of Anduilon' may give the appearance of doing good deeds for their own sake, but I guarantee you that it is an act that they put on to get what they want. Mark my words, Ander: they have an agenda, and this is just a ploy to them."

"I don't want to believe you," Ander said, pouting.

Redding ground his teeth. When the Golden Bears had begun their campaign of slandering the prince's fitness, he had thought it a beautiful, hand-wrapped gift. The prince had gone from favoured son to pariah almost overnight, and Redding had happily stepped in to become the prince's steadfast friend. No one was closer to Ander's confidence than himself, and there was no doubt who he would name royal advisor once he took the throne.

He was beginning to see, though, that even the loveliest of thistles still had thorns and that the prettiest of leaves could hide the most reeking piles of dung. He hadn't realized that Ander was such an annoying idealist.

"Believe this, Highness: nobody willingly does anything that doesn't benefit them. No one; not heroes and not kings." He put his hand on Ander's shoulder. "You have a good heart, Ander. It does you credit, but the Golden Bears will use it against you if you let them. You need to be able to look past the lies people give you and see the truth, or you will never be a good king."

Ander smiled. "Then it is just as well I have you to advise me, isn't it?"

Redding smiled. "It is indeed, Highness."

Eldoth sat cross-legged on his bed and concentrated. The stack of small rocks before him obediently rose into the air. He allowed himself a small smile of satisfaction. There was a gentle knock on his door, but even that didn't reduce his focus.

"Enter." Intent as he was, he didn't really think about who would wish to speak with him or why. Certainly none of his fellow knights bothered with overtures of friendship anymore. When he saw the door open and his ex-wife enter he lost control not only of the pebbles—which fell to the bed with a clatter—but his globe of magelight as well. Luckily the candles that the manor servants had brought still provided a modicum of illumination.

Four years of separation had done nothing to diminish her appearance. At seventeen, Sephana had been a half blossomed flower: attractive, but not yet fully formed. Half-bloomed or not, her charms had been enough to lure him into offering to share his meagre food and shelter with her, as well as proposing marriage. That her seduction had been an act and she had later betrayed him utterly did nothing to diminish her appearance (and, truthfully, her Reshai features had only ever added spice as far as that was concerned).

At twenty-one, she was fully developed in every sense of the word. She wore more clothing here than in Akkilon (sadly), but her longer pants, full sleeves, and vest did nothing to reduce the effect of her long, curly hair, round hips and shapely legs. It was almost enough to make him forget that she was a lying, cheating, vengeful little witch.

Almost.

"That was impressive," Sephana said, gesturing to the pebbles now lying in front of his lap. "You couldn't do that before, could you?"

He stared at her for a moment, surprised that she had neither mocked or insulted him. "No" he replied in kind, "I have only recently reached this point after studying the runes of enchantment at Durnshold. I estimate that I have reached the equivalent of the second ring of mastery in the college of Matter."

"Oh, that's good." She seemed oddly subdued.

He waited for her to make her inevitable verbal barb and mentally prepared a few of his own to return, but she did nothing, just stood in his doorway anxiously. "Why are you here?" he asked. "It is not like you to make idle chatter."

She shrugged, shifting her weight from foot to foot. "I...I just feel like talking, I guess."

He doubted that, but something about her tone concerned him. "Come in then. Have a seat."

"Thanks." She closed the door and sat on the corner of his bed. Her eyes were dark in the candlelight.

"Is there anything in particular you wanted to discuss?" he asked after an awkward moment of silence. "You could insult me if you wish."

She smiled wanly. "You haven't done anything stupid yet."

Now he was definitely worried. "Sephana, what is troubling you?"

She opened her mouth to speak and then stopped. "Why do you have to burn people to death?"

"Excuse me?"

"On the boat, against those archers." Her eyes were accusing. "You burned them to death."

"You told me to," he blurted, still not understanding what was happening.

Anger blended with confusion and scorn on her face. "What? I would never do that. Why are you making things up again?"

He sighed. Their moment of civility had passed and they were now back to familiar territory. "I have an excellent recollection of the event in question, and you most certainly did. That, however, is irrelevant. What does it matter how I killed them? They were Dragonfleet raiders engaged in the act of child slavery. They had to be slain."

She still looked confused. "But...why *that* way?"

His temper flared. "Are you under the presumption that because you use steel to kill you are in some way better than me?" His voice was acid. "Would you prefer I bludgeoned people to death with scented cushions? I could smother them in lace doilies if you felt it was more humane."

"I...no..." She shook her head. "That's not what I'm talking about."

"Then what are you talking about? You're speaking drivel."

That set her off. Eldoth concealed a smile. "Drivel? You are such an ass."

"That is entirely possible, but I am at least making sense in my annoying, assish manner." His smile was too large to hide now. "I would ask you to either say what you intended when you first came in here, or leave me to my studying. I don't have time to interpret your emotional histrionics."

"Emotional?" Her face clouded in fury, as he had known that it would. This was going to be entertaining. "I came here to apologize, you pretentious jackass, for the argument we had yesterday, but you can forget that. Interpret this, you smug, condescending pile of dung: I was there when you killed Draxul and I saw your face when you did it. You didn't just kill him; you tortured him for fun, and if I ever see you do that again, I'll kill you."

Eldoth's jaw dropped. He saw fury and disgust in her eyes and knew her words to be sincere. *She had seen...* Before he could process her words any further she launched to her feet and stormed from the room. "I...what? No. Wait!"

He might have followed her if he had been able to get his legs to work.

Nervousness warred with desire as Gennald gently knocked on the door to Illyria's room. The few seconds it took for her to approach the door were some of the longest in his life.

He carried a basket of honeyberry wine and sweets with him. A gentleman always brought a gift for his lady, but his duties (as well as his slack coin-purse) had prevented him getting anything more befitting for an elven princess. Besides, she was due to leave in the morning and had no room to spare for trinkets.

When she finally did open the door, he found it impossible to breathe. Her hair had been brushed out until it shone, her face was clean and radiated youthful beauty. She wasn't wearing her green elven tunic, just a white, short sleeved undershirt that was only partially laced up. She had on a pair of loose, low slung lounging pants and beneath that her feet were bare.

She smiled and looked at him with green eyes as she leaned against the door frame. She was wearing nothing beneath her shirt. "Sir Gennald," she purred. "I'm glad you came." She held out her hand. "Would you like to come in?"

"Yes, I would," he replied hoarsely. "Very much." He took her hand and let her pull him inside.

Illyria could barely think. It had never been like this before, with Turius. She had always felt like prey with him, like she was something to be consumed or a prize to be won. Aside from the thrill of the illicit and fulfilling a sense of obligation, she had never really enjoyed it. She had been a fool, thinking that she had experienced everything about kissing.

Being with Gennald was infinitely more enjoyable. He was more experienced, confidant, sure in his touch, and not frantic at all. She wanted to melt.

She didn't know how long they had been on her couch, their lips, tongues, and bodies entwined. She wouldn't have been surprised to find they had been there together for only a minute, or if dawn was just breaking. She could do this with Gennald forever.

Exploring hands slid over body parts, lingering in some places and not in others. Her eyes long since closed, she saw Gennald through the palms of her hands. He was beautiful. The broad expanse of his chest, the muscular smoothness of his back, the barely contained power of his shoulders; all of them felt wonderful and perfect. They both still wore all of their clothing, though most of their ties had been loosened or undone. Gennald's delicious, talented lips had migrated from her face down to her neck and from there to the bare skin of her shoulder. She was fairly sure that this shirt would need mending before she could wear it again.

Assuming that she ever wore it again. She might just keep it as a keepsake, just as it was.

She had thrilled at the feeling of his lips pressing against her crownmark, something no man other than her brother had ever seen. His lips were following down where his hands had already travelled when Gennald suddenly froze. She could feel through her hands as his whole body tensed.

Illyria opened her eyes. "What's wrong," she asked in a husky voice that was not her own. "Why did you stop?"

Even as she asked, she knew. His lips had found the bandage she still wore over the wound she had received in the fight against the Dragonfleet. It had given her minor discomfort so far, but she was beyond the point of feeling any pain.

He pulled away from her, his hair tousled, lips bruised, face glowing orange in the firelight. "Illyria, don't go."

She blinked, forcing herself to comprehend words that made absolutely no sense to her. "Don't go where? What do you mean?"

He held both of her hands in his own. "Don't go into the forest. Please. Stay here and let me go in your stead."

She examined his face closely, sure that he was joking but seeing no sign of mirth. "What are you talking about?" She still couldn't think, her body reeling from the echoes of his hands and mouth.

"The thought of you out there, in danger; it drives me mad." His face was the epitome of earnestness. "Please, for me: stay."

His words began to penetrate and the fire within her was suddenly extinguished, replaced by a sickening feeling of betrayal. She pushed herself away from him and wrapped her arms tightly around herself.

"What you ask is impossible and inappropriate, Sir Gennald," she informed him, icily cool. "I have sworn a vow to this purpose, as you well know. Do not presume to place yourself between myself and my mission."

The Bear and the Thistle

He exploded off the couch, cursing as he paced back and forth. "How do you do this, Illyria? How do you place yourself so blithely in danger?"

"How do you?" She eyed him coolly, though part of her wanted to cry.

"It's not the same, dammit. I'm a knight. You're a—" he cut himself off.

"What am I, Gennald?" Illyria stood slowly, part of her feeling foolish having this argument in half worn sleepwear. "Choose your next words very carefully."

He scowled. "I'm sorry. That's not what I meant."

"No, that's exactly what you meant," she accused. "I swore the same oaths as you, Gennald, and have as much claim to the title. We serve different masters, but we are the same." She lowered her eyes. "At least I thought we were."

She was unmoved by the expression of anguish on his face. "I said it badly, Illyria. I'm sorry. My words were unthinking and stupid. Please, forgive me."

"I think you should go, Gennald." It was both the hardest and easiest thing she had ever said.

"Again: I'm sorry. I saw the bandage on your chest and I went...crazy. Illyria please: don't do this. It won't happen again, I swear."

She walked around the couch to the door, which she held open for him. "Goodnight, Gennald."

He walked to the door but stopped when he reached her. "Illyria, please. I do respect you, and what you are. Really, I do."

She said nothing and after a moment he sighed and left the room. After he had gone and the door had been secured she allowed herself to feel the lethal combination of emotions she had been holding at bay. Betrayal, humiliation, thwarted desire, and naked pain bombarded her all at once. Clutching her chest and blinking away tears, she sat and stared into the fire.

I am a knight and a Child of the Mark. I will not cry over a man that is not worthy of me. I will not!

Getting angry felt much more appropriate. Her eyes fell on the basket of food and drink that Gennald and brought and left on the side table.

Sephana was supposed to be sleeping. First light was far closer than she would like, and, as much as she knew that she should be resting, she couldn't. Finally giving up, she opened the door to her room and crept out. A single candle lit the hallway and everything was quiet (which meant that things with Illyria and Gennald were either going very well, or very, very badly). She padded down the hall in her bare feet, still not exactly sure what she wanted to do now that she was up. Finally deciding to go to the solar at the end of the hall, she stopped in surprise when she saw that Balien was already there.

99

Clad only an undershirt and pants, he was lit only by a single stroke of moonlight. It made his face look silver. She sat opposite him and gave him a silent smile of greeting. He nodded in reply. Neither said anything.

As usual, she was the one to finally break the silence. "It's all real, isn't it?"

Balien just cocked his head.

"The king and the land," she continued, "and them being linked. It's real, isn't it?"

"Of course." He didn't scoff or look at her like she was an idiot, unlike *some* people she knew. "Why did you think it wasn't?"

"Even as an outcast slave, I heard the stories, but they didn't really mean anything to me." She shrugged. "I mean, I lived in a sweetgrass plantation. I never saw any kings or priests or anyone like that. And then the king was overthrown. He was killed by his nephew, and the reason he gave was that the old king had 'lost his connection to the land' and that he was doing it for Akkilon."

"Maybe it was true," Balien said.

"Maybe, but I didn't see any strange weather, or failed harvests or anything. Nothing like what's going on here. When I heard about the Golden Bears and the Anderites, I figured that was just the excuse you gave. If you want to be new king, you say that the old one lost his connection to the land and you kill him." She looked at Balien, or, at least, the sliver of his face that was visible. "But it's real. The king really is sick, and it really is making the wheat not grow."

"It is. That's why kings are important."

Sephana smiled. "And that's why everyone in your family is such a jerk to you: because you don't have a crownmark. You can never Join with the Land."

He shrugged one shoulder. "It's more complicated than that, but yes. Essentially."

She gnawed on the inside of her cheek. "What do we do about that? How do we heal a whole kingdom?"

His answer was cut off by the sound of a door opening. They both looked down the hallway in time to see Gennald striding angrily down the hall. He stopped when he saw them, his face a cloudy thunderstorm, but said nothing before stomping into his room and slamming the door.

I guess that answers that question. Balien stood quickly, concern obvious on his face, but Sephana put a hand on Balien's arm. "She doesn't want to talk to you right now."

He frowned. "I'm her brother."

Sephana laughed. "No, right now you're a man, and that means you're the enemy. Let me talk to her first."

He hesitated before nodding. "Tell her that I'm still up if she wants to talk."

"I will."

She knocked gently before opening the door. Illyria hadn't heard her. She was kneeling next to the fireplace in her sleeping clothes. An upended basket lay next to her and the room reeked of burning food. As Sephana watched, Illyria shredded a loaf of bread into pieces and began to tossing them angrily into the flames.

"Hi," she said from a few paces away. Illyria's whole body tensed before she saw who it was. Her expression was clearly angry, but softened immediately. Twin streams of tears reflected like molten gold in the firelight.

"Hi," she replied, her voice rough.

Sephana knelt beside her next to the fire. "Men are jerks," she announced.

As she had hoped, it made Illyria laugh. "I can think of a few exceptions, but otherwise, yes."

In a strange mirroring of the previous night, the two shared laughing stories of the stupidity of the male gender. Sephana was about to ask what ass-faced thing Gennald had done when three armed, black-masked men burst into the room.

CHAPTER NINE

" 'Minstrels would paint some terrible, dramatic picture of blackshields. If you listened to them, you'd think that every masterless knight out there is the victim of a tragic romance or has been unjustly accused of a crime. It's horse droppings, all of it. They're mercenaries and brigands, the lot of them, and unworthy of Emuranna's service.'

" 'Damn minstrels.' "

— Anonymous

Gennald woke to the sound of hammering. For the briefest of moments he thought that perhaps Illyria had changed her mind and come grovelling to his door, but as he emerged fully into wakefulness he realized his folly. Not only was there little chance of her backing down so easily on a matter of honour, but it was an entirely different kind of hammering. Not only was it far too loud to be made by a fist, but the sound was definitely that of metal on metal. Someone was nailing a spike into the door.

He leapt from his bed and tried to open the thick, wooden door. The latch lifted, but the door itself was stuck in place. He heaved at it with his shoulder to no avail. He didn't know why or by who, but he was trapped within his room.

He could hear more spikes being hammered out in the hallway, as well as the shouts of several men and an angry bellow from out in the courtyard. He cursed and threw himself against the door, but once again it didn't budge. Illyria was out there, and so was his lord. He had to defend them against this new, sudden danger. He had to.

He was desperately afraid for both of them, but couldn't say which fear was greater.

Illyria bolted to her feet and whirled at the noise, uncaring about her state of undress. There were three men, all dressed in black. While two of them wore swords, they were wielding short, heavy cudgels while the third held a drawstring sack.

They want us alive. That will make things easier.

She darted to the fireplace and seized the iron fire poker. "Hold them off," she ordered Sephana, tossing her the makeshift weapon. She didn't wait for acknowledgement before turning and running to her room. They were outnumbered and, from the sounds of it, there were more out in the hall. She needed naked steel.

Theramus gave a loud bellow and slammed his shoulder into the door. As he feared, whoever had invaded Jannery's house had barred the rear door in addition to spiking it shut. The manor had been built with defence in mind, and all outside doors were made from thick wood bolstered with iron bands. The windows were slitted and impossible for even Sephana to pass through.

He ran to his tent and retrieved his current weapon, the modified halberd he had taken from Durnshold. Yes, it was an axe, but meant for cleaving heads, not chopping wood. Its head would snap clean off if he used improperly. Ironically, the heavy, unwieldy weapon that the Dragonfleet captain had carried would have been ideal here.

Still, a comparatively fragile halberd was better than no weapon at all. Planting his feet carefully and measuring the weight of his swing, he issued a silent apology to the master of the house and swung

Sephana awkwardly blocked the powerful cudgel strike from one of her three opponents, twisting and retreating as she did so to prevent either one of his fellows from getting behind her. It would only take one hit to her unprotected back, or getting her head bagged, to end this fight in a hurry.

I wish I had Dawn's First Crescent!

Illyria didn't announce her presence with any sort of yell. She was suddenly just *there,* and one of the three men threatening them lay unconscious at her feet. She still wore her loose undershirt and sleeping pants and her hair flew loosely around her head. She looked like some seductive vision except for the two feet of shining, curved sword blade in her hands, held with utmost confidence.

The man bearing the cudgel dropped it with a curse and drew his own sword. Illyria attacked him in a blinding fury, his frantic parries not letting him get in even the smallest of counterstrikes.

Sephana used Illyria's distracting arrival to confront the remaining man, the one with the sack. She swung the poker two-handedly into the side of his knee and, when he fell cursing and swearing, again at the side of his head.

Illyria had backed her opponent across the room, almost to the door. He was so focussed on keeping Maiden's Fang from him that he did not see Sephana behind him until her poker slammed into his back. When he turned, clutching at his wound, Illyria slammed the pommel of her sword into his jaw.

"The snake girl's not in her room!" another black clad man said as he rushed in. He lurched to a stop just past the threshold.

Illyria and Sephana both turned, weapons ready, surrounded by their fallen opponents. "That's because she's here."

Eldoth held his hand against the door and closed his eyes, concentrating beyond his normal senses. Yes, the door was jammed shut but that presented little obstacle to him. He had been practicing and meditating on the manipulation of solid matter through magic—the 'orange' college of study. A month ago, he had been limited to the most rudimentary of tasks: straightening bent cutlery or removing impurities from small measures of water.

Magic was very strict in its limitations. The orange college only applied to matter that had never been alive and, unfortunately, almost all of the things around him fell into that category. Cloth, leather, and wood were considered to be 'flesh', or close enough to it, and thus beyond his current level of manipulation.

The stone walls that currently surrounded and imprisoned him were non-living, of course, but existed in such quantity as to be immune to his meagre abilities. A third ring master could perhaps crumble a foot thick stone wall, but not a second. Not in any reasonable amount of time, anyway.

The item that held his door shut, however, was a steel spike, and the door itself was banded at top and bottom with iron. Both were definitely of a size to be within his abilities. He could escape this room at his ease, but there were several men outside and they were undoubtedly armed. Eldoth had already learned, to his chagrin, that, magic or no, he came out poorly in physical conflicts.

To minimize that possibility, he had to act carefully. Timing was everything.

There was some sort of disturbance beyond. Good. Distraction would aid him. He heard a voice from just beyond his door yelling something. 'Get the women' he thought. Deep, unreasoning anger filled Eldoth, though he could not for the life of him say why. It was almost enough to ruin his focus, but he managed to retain just enough of his calm to concentrate on the steel spike.

He motioned upward with his hand and knew that, outside the door, that the spike holding the door shut had shot upward like a crossbow bolt and whoever was next to it yelped in surprise. *I hope I drove it through your brain, you lack-witted thug!*

Hand motions weren't necessary when performing magic, but it had become his habit. Just as a woodsman lined up his axe to his target despite thousands of successful splittings, so too did Eldoth mime the actions he wanted to perform. It was easier and aided concentration, but was not necessary. He could—and had—cast spells while completely motionless.

Not giving whoever was beyond the door a chance to recover, Eldoth pushed out with both hands. Neither made contact with the wooden door, but it still leapt open as if kicked by a horse. He heard a satisfying 'thud' as it impacted with someone followed by the crash as whoever it was stuck the ground.

"What in—" a black clad thug exclaimed as he turned and saw Eldoth. He was closer than he would have liked, but Eldoth had prepared for this possibility. The pile of pebbles at his feet—the same ones he had been practicing on every spare moment for the last month—projected themselves into his face and chest. He doubted that they were fast enough to kill but, as Eldoth had discovered through painful trial and error, they still hurt like the blazes.

The thug clutched his face and screamed. Eldoth smiled.

Theramus frowned at his lack of progress. The door was very well constructed and had thus far withstood his efforts. His wards lay within, in what peril he did not know, while he remained without.

If we all survive this craven attack, I will fashion a weapon better suited to my strengths. These adapted human weapons continue to betray me.

Frustrated, he gave a bellow and slammed into the door with all of his strength. It withstood him, if only barely.

"Sir Giant! Theramus!" hissed a voice to his left.

Theramus turned and saw the lord of this manor, Jannery, motioning to him from around the corner. Knowing that further attacks against the door were useless, he went over to the older human.

"How did you escape the men within?" he asked. "Where are the others? Are they injured?"

"I know my manor better than these brutes," he explained. He wore a night shirt but carried his broadsword. "They locked me within my chambers but did not know of a servant's stair into the kitchens. I made my way from there to the cellars to here."

"There is another way inside?"

He led Theramus around the side of the manor house to a large stand of shrubbery. "it will be a tight fit for you. Even I must crouch to enter."

"Show me."

Illyria and Sephana, clad only in their night clothes, confronted seven armed men in the narrow hallway. From what Illyria could see, every door except for Sephana's and her own had been spiked shut. They would receive no aid from their companions.

"It was us you that came for, was it not?" she taunted down the length of the hall. "I invite you to try."

Sephana, still holding the fire poker, fidgeted nervously. "Are you sure you want to be saying things like that? I don't think these guys will be as easy as the last ones."

Illyria kept her eyes levelled down the corridor. "We cannot show them any fear. They can only face us one at a time in this hall. We only have to hold them off long enough for the others to free themselves."

There was a particularly loud yell followed by a heavy slam and then silence. Someone striking at their door from within (Gennald?) could be heard in the comparative silence.

One of the men raised his sword and pointed at them. "Get the women!" They began to slowly, cautiously, advance.

There was a loud bang and the man who had given the order to attack recoiled and swore. Without warning, the door slammed open, catching the surprised man in the face. Even as he fell, another turned to the commotion before screaming and falling while clutching at his face. A second later Eldoth stepped into the hall.

There were four men between him and Illyria. He raised his hands up and suddenly Sephana was grabbing Illyria and pulling her back into her room. Even before they had hit the ground, bright blue, acrid smelling lightning arced down the corridor and struck where they had been just been standing.

"Stupid, crazy, ass-faced wizard," Sephana muttered as she got to her feet. The lightning continued to twist and writhe though the hallway. "We're still here, you stupid idiot!"

He must have heard her. A moment later, the bright, crackling light stopped and left only silence. Illyria recalled the last time Eldoth had used his magical lightning. It had been potent enough to injure and stun, but not to kill. She darted down the corridor, which was dark with metallic smelling smoke. Four men were either writhing on the floor, panting on their knees or, for the closest man, leaning against the wall. It was easy for Illyria to knock his sword from his stunned fingers and club him across the head with her sword hilt.

What she was doing was dangerous. They were greatly outnumbered and there was no guarantee that any man she knocked out would stay that way. She was, in essence, leaving her back unprotected and she would never have done so in a time of war.

But she was not at war, and these were men, not the scalykind from Ijisar or Nintaran interlopers. Yes, they had invaded Jannery's house and attacked her, but their weapons had been cudgels and sacks. If they had burst into her room intending her death, she didn't doubt that they would have succeeded.

The question, then, was 'why', and she could not get that answer from a corpse.

Between herself and Sephana, the other lightning stunned men were quickly disabled. Eldoth was caught between looking very pleased with himself and being concerned for Sephana.

"You're...all right?" He asked. He was *not* immune, Illyria noted, to the fact that she wore only a sleeveless sleeping shift.

Sephana scowled and pushed him into the wall. "No thanks to you, idiot. You almost fried us."

The sound of banging came from Gennald's door. "Illyria? Is that you?"

She turned to his door at the same time that Eldoth's open door, which had been blocking them from the rest of the hallway, slammed into the wizard and Sephana and sent them both sprawling. On the other side of it was one of the three men they had immobilized. He raised his sword with a snarl and Illyria was forced to forget about the people still trapped within their rooms. Gennald, Lord Jannery, and her brother were safe for the moment.

Illyria stepped forward and met steel with steel.

Theramus crouched behind the kitchen door and watched the five men in the main hall. They had full length battle spears levelled at the door he had been unable to break through and glanced at each other nervously.

"Do you think he's still there?" one asked nervously.

"I don't know. He's been quiet for too long."

A third shook his head. "I can't believe he almost broke through that door. Four men and a battering ram couldn't hit that hard."

Part of him was amused that five men had been tasked to counter him, but had to admire their choice of armaments. If he indeed come through that door and faced five spears in tight formation, he doubted he could have defeated them easily, even with his halberd.

However, he was not. He had contorted himself through the hidden entrance into the kitchens and now crouched, hidden, on their flank. He did not have his weapon with him, but he would not need it. "I fear your furniture will not survive this," he warned Jannery, who crouched next to him.

"I don't care about that. Get rid of them."

Theramus did just that. He burst out of the kitchen, rending the door doing so, and grabbed nearest the piece of furniture, a table. He swung it with a loud battle cry, catching the two nearest spearmen across their chests and hurling them into the wall. The others were not able to bring their spears to bear before Theramus, holding the table crosswise, slammed into all three of them.

"Behind you!"

Theramus turned in time to see another swordsman, previously hidden, rushing towards him. Jannery, hale for his age but still past his prime, confronted him. Theramus rushed towards them but the intruder knocked the old lord aside before he interceded.

The unknown assailant raised his sword to strike his fallen opponent. Theramus was still too far away. "Jonten, no!" one of the other's yelled. "Not him!"

The attacker hesitated and that was all the time Theramus needed. His punch caught the man high in the chest and sent him crashing across the room.

There was violence happening upstairs. He could hear it, followed by the sound of someone running. He was barely able to see another black garbed man— unarmed—run to the front door and yank it open. The intruder's escape attempt was thwarted when, instead of a clear path for flight, he found Balien instead. Clad only in a pair of sleeping pants but also carrying his signature sword, he brought the heavy crossguard up and struck the fleeing man in the face.

He had not even finished hitting the ground before Illyria, also in her sleeping garb and carrying her sword, ran nimbly down the stairs. Sephana, carrying her green Ansharite dagger, was close behind her. Illyria looked around and took in the unconscious men, broken furniture, as well as the presence of Theramus and Jannery.

She gave the latter a deferential nod. "My Lord, I am glad to see that you are well. I believe that the house is now secure."

All too aware how the captured men were eying her (and not wanting to have to slap Eldoth again), Sephana quickly threw on some clothing and grabbed a cloak to cover Illyria. She was thanked with a smile. Beside her, Gennald scowled fiercely and glared at the eighteen men—some with broken bones, some just bruised— bound and secured in the manor's great hall. Their hoods and been pulled back and their masks removed. Other than being beaten, they looked very ordinary.

"Blackshields," Lord Jannery spat. "An army of blackshields invaded my house and attacked my guests. *My house!* Why?"

No one knew yet. They had had admitted to being hired by a mysterious patron, but nothing else.

Illyria's brow wrinkled in confusion. "What is a blackshield?"

"A disgraced knight," Gennald growled. He wouldn't meet her eyes. "They have no lord, no code, and no honour."

The Bear and the Thistle

Balien tapped his sister on the shoulder and motioned for her to join him and Lord Jannery out of earshot of the prisoners. Sephana followed. "This was too well organized. Too precise. They knew what rooms we were all in. They knew that Theramus was in the garden and prepared from him specifically. Also, the front door wasn't forced."

"Someone gave them information and aided them," Illyria deduced. "Someone in this household."

"One of my servants? The people I house under my own roof?" Lord Jannery was livid. "Sir Gennald, assemble the staff."

Gennald couldn't decide which was greater: his fury or his humiliation. The house of his liege lord had been invaded, and not by a lone thief but almost a score of armed soldiers. To make matters worse, when events had turned violent, he had proved himself utterly, completely useless. Even Balien had managed to climb out his window and attack their flank. Gennald had stayed trapped inside his room unable to protect his lord or the woman that he—that was to say, unable to protect his Lord or Illyria. Lord Jannery had rescued himself while Illyria had defeated almost half of their number wearing only her undershirt. The same shirt that, one hour previously, he had unlaced and pulled open so that he could see her—

Stop! That kind of thinking will get you nowhere.

The hope for another chance to prove himself as both man and knight buoyed him while he gathered the servants and staff of the manor. They had been locked in their quarters while all of the violence had happened, a spike hammered into the door to the basement.

"One of you has betrayed me," Lord Jannery began. "One of you has cast my trust into the midden pit and spat upon my loyalty to you. Yes, my loyalty to you. The oath of fealty you took upon entering my service does bind you to me, but me to you as well. You give me your loyalty and service and I, in turn, provide food, shelter, protection as well as my vow to always treat you fairly. That is the ancient bond between servants and masters and has remained unchanged since the days of the High Kingdom. I have never asked more of you than you can give. I have never been a tyrant to you, and yet on this night my trust has been betrayed."

None of the nine people standing before him would meet his eye. Gennald stood behind his lord and surveyed them. They were frightened, nervous, and somewhat bewildered, but whether that was from their lord's words or the trauma of having their home attacked, he could not say.

"One of you told those blackshield scum who was in this house and in what room. That same person also provided either a key to allow them entry, or left the door unlocked for them." He stopped and looked at all of them. "Tell me now who

109

did this and why, and I shall be lenient. If I discover the identity of who betrayed me by any other means, you will feel my wrath." They remained silent. "Speak!"

One of the newest labourers, Aran, was looking fit to burst. He looked anxious, but not guilty. Gennald stepped up to him. "Do you know who it was?"

The young man—barely more than a boy, really—screwed up his face and, after a second, nodded.

"Who?"

"I saw...I saw Derry at the front door, after everyone else had gone to bed. She unbarred it."

Dereanna—Derry—had tended the garden here for the last fifteen years. Lord Jannery stepped up to her, close enough for them to kiss if the situation had been very, very different. "Is it true?" His voice was low and dangerous. "Did you leave the door open? Did you allow criminals into my home?"

She looked like she was going to deny it but then sighed and set her shoulders. She met her lord's eye. "Yes, My Lord."

"But *why?*" his face was twisted as if in pain.

"She's snakespawn, My Lord." There was no need to say who 'she' was. "It isn't right: her being treated like she's better than the rest of us, tail hanging out where everyone can see it. It's a snake trick, My Lord. She's bewitched you, my word on it."

"It's not your place to decide!" She looked away. "I gave her my trust. I gave her my word that she would be safe under my roof, and now you have made me a liar." He glared at her. "Get out of my house. I'll lay no charges out of respect for your service, but you are no longer a part of my household. I'll not set eyes on you again." The woman, only a few years younger than Lord Jannery, nodded and walked out the door with only the clothes on her back.

"Is there anyone else among you who also thinks so?" Jannery demanded. "Do any of you think that this woman, granted leave *by the king himself,* is a Djido spy? Do any more of you think that my will has been taken from me? If so, then get out now. You are not welcome in my service."

Two more people: Kurinna, the upstairs maid, and Jomm, the assistant cook, also stepped forward.

Lord Jannery looked sad and old. "See them out, Sir Gennald. The rest of you, please: clean up this mess."

Illyria kept her features impassive as she came near Gennald. Barely disguised pain and fury burned in his eyes. An uncharitable part of her was glad that he suffered, though how much of his anguish was for her and how much for his lord she did not know.

Most of her fury towards him had been engulfed in the fever of battle. For those few minutes she had been engaged in mortal combat, she had gleefully set aside the aftermath of her throbbing physical need, the implications of her promise to the king, and the many dangers faced by Karalon. For those few moments, she had simply acted and reacted as the situation demanded. It was very freeing, and part of her wished that everything could be as simple as that: to succeed or fail based on the merits of one's skill and instinct.

She strode beyond him to where Lord Jannery paced his great room before his prisoners.

"What will you do with them, My Lord?"

His jaw was tighter than a trap and his blue eyes blazed fire. "In this house, my word is law, but I cannot break the king's peace. They are prisoners now; I can't kill them, as much as I want to. They have taken no lives, thanks to your fast action, and destroyed none of my property." He frowned. "There is no crime in being a blackshield, though by rights there should be, so the worst I can do is seize their arms and throw them in prison."

"We were their target, My Lord, not you. Their intent was to capture us, obviously at the behest of their master."

"Who they won't reveal, damn them. Its unusual loyalty for men so spineless."

One of the prisoners, one of the ones Illyria had defeated, bristled with anger.

"It is our intention to leave at once, My Lord, before anyone learns of this attack's failure. We would ask that you not report this until after we have left the city."

"Of course." His face fell. "I am sorry, Illyria. I have failed you as a host. As guests in my home you are under my protection. This, what happened, is inexcusable. I should have had more men. I should have been more prepared."

Illyria could not help but colour at the thought of what one his men—in fact, the leader of his men, if any more had been present—had been doing just an hour before the attack.

"Do not blame yourself, or Sir Gennald, My Lord," she assured him. "You were betrayed. This circumstance could not have been foreseen."

He scowled. "I know you mean well, My Lady, but you do not understand Karalinian ways. I am your host; you are under my care. There is no excuse."

"I'm sorry, My Lord." She didn't know what else to say.

Gennald stepped up and knelt before Lord Jannery. "My Lord, I beg you: let me make amends for my part in this shame."

The lord contemplated his vassal. "I do not ask for your penance, Sir Gennald. We are both to blame."

Gennald raised his head. "Let me go with them, My Lord, please. Let me offer them protection in your name during their trials ahead. This attack has failed, but you know that there will be more."

Illyria stiffened. More time with Gennald? The part of her that wanted to see no more of him than his backside warred with the part that wanted to bury herself in his embrace. "My Lord, this is not necessary."

Gennald glared at her, anger only one of several emotions present on his face, before turning back to Lord Jannery. "My Lord, please. It is a matter of honour." He took a deep breath. "I have never asked for anything from you, My Lord. Please: give me this."

Jannery gazed down into Gennald's imploring face, his expression grave, before finally nodding. "If you wish it."

Illyria was partly dismayed and partly elated. "My Lord, what of your safety? Who will protect you?"

He surveyed the room, looking every one of his fifty years. "My home has been betrayed from within. I would not feel safe here even with a hundred men. Duke Raebyrne has offered me assistance. I will be safe enough under his protection."

Gennald was still kneeling. "My Lord, thank you. I swear by Emuranna and my king that I will not let you down."

Lord Jannery's face softened and he lay a hand on Gennald's shoulder. "I know. Rise, my friend, and begin your quest."

He rose. "I will, My Lord." He turned to Illyria, his expression satisfied. "My Lady, I beg you to forgive my earlier statements. I was not myself."

Illyria had her doubts about that. She stepped close to him, unable to ignore the breadth of his chest and his sharp, masculine scent. "Is it honour that guides you, Gennald, or something else?"

For the briefest moment he looked at her with such hunger and passion that she thought her knees would give out. A moment later, however, his features became covered by a cold, hard mask. "My Lady, you insult me. I am a knight."

She watched him stalk out of the room and sighed. This was going to complicate things.

The Bear and the Thistle

CHAPTER TEN

" 'What? Magic has no colour that can be seen. We name the colours of magic so, but they are just names. Renthalin named them after the colours of the spectrum out of deference to Sheethu, but that is a human convention. I am sure the Djido have their own names for the different colleges, just as fairies do.'

" 'Seeing magic in colours. How absurd.' "

—Eldoth

Gennald tried for the fifth time (or was it the sixth?) to talk to Illyria, and, for the fifth (or sixth) time, she responded with the same gesture: passing her hand down across her mouth like she was wiping something off of her lips.

It was 'Forest Speech'—or, at least, that was what Sephana called it—a gesture-based form of silent speaking used by elven hunters. Illyria and Balien were masters of it (of course), and Sephana had picked up a fair bit in their travels together. Gennald knew a total of three gestures: 'hold in place', 'resume walking' and, the one with which he was the most familiar: 'no talking'.

They were hunting. They had ridden hard out of New Aukaster and reached the crossroads that led into Wightland Valley shortly after dawn. All of their horses were exhausted, but none fatally so, and they had made it to the location of Attenham's ambushed tax caravan by early afternoon. It had been a grim sight.

The ambush, which had occurred two days before, had been savage. More than twenty men had been killed and the few survivors had spent little time seeing to their fallen dead. Scavengers, of both the two and four legged variety, had stripped the bodies of most of their flesh and belongings. Eldoth and Theramus—both ill-suited to woodcraft—had stayed behind to bury the bodies while the rest of them had departed on foot to track the treasure-laden outlaws.

He was unsure if he shouldn't have stayed behind to help tend the fallen knights. While he doubted the giant and the wizard would inflict any further disrespect to them, they deserved to be laid to rest by a knight. A *real* knight. Balien and Illyria were doing all of the tracking, anyway. For all of his (silent) disapproval of Illyria's companions and their claims, he could no fault their skill. The training and forest sense of the elven siblings was beyond parallel. Gennald and Sephana were there for...what? Moral support, he supposed.

He was unable to even do that, since Illyria wasn't allowing any of them to talk.

No, that was a lie and he knew it. No doubt Sephana and Balien knew it as well. For all of Gennald's protest of slighted honour and knightly duty, there was only one real reason why he had begged his lord to release him from his duty, and it annoyed him to no end that she wasn't allowing him to speak to her.

He had erred badly, he knew this. Last night was supposed to have ended very differently for the two of them. She had been willing and eager in his arms and Gennald knew that, if he hadn't opened his stupid mouth at the worst possible time, they would have resolved a month's worth of teasing and flirting in the way that only men and women were able.

Not to mention that if he had been in Illyria's room instead of his own when the Blackshields attacked, it would have been Sephana locked up helpless in her room instead of him. He wouldn't have been trapped impotently behind a locked door while a motley collection of elves, scaly servant girls and judgemental giants performed what should have been his knightly duty. Again.

Yes, his ill-thought statement made in the heat of passion had ended most unfortunately indeed, (but, really, what man could look upon an injury to such a beautiful woman and *not* do his utmost to ensure it never happened again?) but he would make right his wrong. Illyria would forgive him eventually and he would have a chance to display his true quality to her. He would feel her lips upon his again and, when presented with any of her injuries and scars, he would *keep his damned mouth shut.*

In front of him, Illyria froze and held her hand up to her shoulder. 'Hold in place'. He couldn't see or hear anything that made this particular patch of forest different from any other, but that didn't matter. Illyria's senses were as keen as the sharpest dagger, and, in the several hours that they had been searching, both she and her brother had each called several halts, all with cause.

She pointed at the ground and Balien nodded. She knelt and began gingerly moving some twigs while Balien followed some invisible path with his eyes. Gennald could not help but admire the elegant lines of her back and neck, as well as be captivated by how her brow furrowed as she concentrated. He recalled the whimpering gasp she had given when he had pressed his lips into the hollow of her throat and the feeling of warm, soft flesh beneath his hands when he had slid his hands under her shirt. His eyes caressed the narrow curve of her waist and the rounded swell of her hips. He pictured himself undoing the laces at the side of her pants and sliding his hands beneath...

Sephana hit him in the shoulder and glared. He had the grace to be embarrassed. They were alone in unfamiliar territory, on a mission critical to the kingdom. This was not the time and place to undress Illyria with his eyes, and yet, he could not help it. She affected him in a way that no other woman ever had.

In front of him, the object of his desire cleared something off the ground and shuffled to the side. She pointed down in front of her, and Gennald saw a fine string suspended across the trail. Beside her, Balien moved some shrubbery aside to reveal a rough wooden frame to which a multitude of sharpened stakes had been lashed. A horsehair spring, like that used in a catapult, joined it to a nearby tree.

The nature of the trap was obvious and Gennald could not help but shiver as his mind's eye saw those sharpened stakes perforating Illyria's perfect body. *I will not moon over her like an adolescent boy, not here. Not with such obvious dangers before us.*

He was a knight. It was time he started acting like one.

Eldoth sat cross-legged in the centre of the clearing, staring at the stone that lay before him. He focussed beyond the fatigue caused by a day of hard riding on only a few hours of sleep and the ache caused by helping dig a mass grave. Hardships of the flesh were meaningless to him. He extended his senses, feeling how they were connected to each other and picturing ways that he could manipulate them. He closed his eyes, removing extraneous sensory stimuli, and focussed his will. He did not need his eyes to tell him that the irregularly shaped stone, roughly the size of his head, now held a cubical shape.

Success!

Eldoth smiled and reached for his journal to record his findings, but found himself unable to put pen to paper. Sephana's words from the previous evening or, more precisely her *tone,* echoed within his mind. Her argument was ridiculous. Dead was dead, and his flames were the most efficient means available of dealing with groups of opponents, yet the obvious pain in her voice was something for which there was no counterargument.

He supposed that it was possible to use other forms of his magic. In last night's attack on the house he had used a handful of gravel to disable a man. Bludgeoning seemed a rather...inelegant...means of attack, but there were obvious benefits. He could disable a target, rather than cause permanent burns. It was silent and emitted no light, which might cause problems in dark conditions. Also, he was in no danger of creating any fires this way, and there were fewer chances of inadvertently hitting the wrong target. Plus, it would be good practice for him, manipulating matter under combat conditions.

Yes, those were all very good reasons to begin using rocks as weapons in combat. He was absolutely *not* doing this for Sephana. Not at all.

Having resolved the issue, he was finally able to record his finding without distraction. Across from him, Theramus also sat. The imposing giant held a small knife—well, small for a giant—and was using it to strip a long, thick tree trunk of its twigs and branches.

Ross D Jenkins

The two hadn't spoken much beyond logistical necessities, not since the giant's scathing condemnation the day before. There was not a magical quandary large enough that would necessitate Eldoth's asking him for advice any time soon, and it was equally apparent from the giant's attitude that he had no need of Eldoth's skills or knowledge.

He watched Theramus lay a thin sheet of bronze in the coals of the fire. Eldoth looked at the sheet, the pole that Theramus was whittling smooth, and the smithing hammer that lay by his knee.

"That fire will not heat the metal enough for shaping," he said into the silence, not certain why he did so. Theramus looked up at him, brown eyes searching. "You intend to bend it around the end of your pole, yes? Make into a cap of some sort?"

After a moment, Theramus nodded. "A hotter fire would be ideal, but I can make do with this. The sheet is thin."

Eldoth hesitated before speaking. "I may be able to assist you, if you would like." It was boredom that inspired the offer, he told himself. Certainly there was nothing else for them to do while they waited for the others to return.

Theramus tried to hide his look of surprise but failed. Nonetheless he gestured towards the flames. "Please."

Eldoth knelt before the fire and extended his senses. The radiating energy was plainly visible to his magical 'eye', and it was fairly simple for him to magnify it. It wanted to flare, to expend itself in a massive fireball, but Eldoth contained it and focussed its output as if through a lens. In the fire pit, the flames brightened, dimmed, and then turned blue. As they both watched the thin sheet of metal began to glow around its edges. "This is actually good practice for me," Eldoth said through his concentration. "I seldom get the opportunity to exert myself in such a focussed manner."

Theramus reached for some tongs. "You are doing very well. It is almost ready."

Eldoth waved him off. "May I?" The giant gave a gesture of acquiescence. Eldoth made a lifting motion with both of his hands and the sheet of metal floated into the air. The fire, without his will to sustain it, died immediately. "Hold your pole up," he instructed.

Theramus held the smoothed end of the wooden pole near the floating bronze. Eldoth cupped and turned his hands, extending his will into the glowing, heated metal. The sheet wrapped around the wood as if it were paper. Theramus turned it slowly as Eldoth focussed, the two working in silent accord to bind the two objects.

Hot bronze was very easy to manipulate, he discovered. Metal was harder to shape with magic than stone—something about its refined nature—but he had never focussed his will upon metal that was glowing hot. It made perfect sense:

116

smiths heated metal so that it was soft enough to shape but he had simply never thought of it before. It was quite annoying, really.

No distractions, he chided himself. *Focus.*

He ran his hand over where the metal joined, his palm almost touching the hot surface. Gritting his teeth, allowing himself to perceive nothing but the metal before him, he forced the edges together and willed them to merge so that there was no visible seam. Gesturing with both hands, he thinned the sheet slightly enough so that he could create an end cap and joined it seamlessly to the rest of it.

When it was done he sighed and sank back onto his heels, surprised by how much the act had drained him. Theramus examined the metalwork closely, running his fingers—Eldoth recalled that a giant's skin was extremely heat resistant—over the smooth metal.

"This is excellent work. Thank you."

It was, quite possibly, the most civil conversation the two had ever shared.

"You're welcome."

Theramus retrieved another bronze sheet from his bag and reversed his pole. It was a staff, Eldoth realized, scaled for its enormous wielder. "After a rest, would you care to assist me with this part as well?"

Eldoth guzzled from his water skin and nodded cordially. "Yes, of course."

Illyria waited until Balien had braced a sturdy branch against the swinging arm of the fence trap before she motioned Gennald and Sephana to advance.

Even with her back turned, she could feel Gennald's eyes sweep over her. As hard as she tried to focus on the job at hand, she could not help but be aware on some small level that he was there and that he still desired her.

She still desired him, too. Despite her anger over how he had ruined what should have been a perfect night, she still wanted him. It was unnerving, really, how much her hunger seemed to override her common sense. She could—and should—have refused him when he had asked to accompany her. His claims of dishonour notwithstanding, he was still leaving his lord defenceless. He had been blinded by his humiliation and she should have refused for his sake, or at least argued more vehemently, but she hadn't.

They probably didn't have to be as silent as they were—the trail they followed was days old—but it gave her the excuse she needed not to hear his plea for forgiveness. She was going to forgive him, she already knew that. She knew that it was petty, but she wanted him to suffer, no matter how minutely, for the pain he had put her through. A day or two of enforced silence was an ideal punishment.

They passed safely through the fence trap—it had been well laid; its designer had been a master forester—and into a clearing. The ponies had been relieved of their burden here and led back to the road while a group of men, making multiple trips, had carried the stolen tax money towards the hills.

/The ponies mean nothing. We should follow the men,/ Balien's fingers said in Forest Talk. She nodded her agreement and indicated the need for a short break. He nodded and passed the message onto Sephana before crouching down and digging his water skin out of his pack.

He glanced at Gennald—who looked just dishevelled and sweaty enough to make him more handsome than usual—and asked her a question with his fingers. */Are you all right?/*

She gave him a quick, almost rude, reply. */Later./* Forest Talk wasn't designed for chitchat. While it was possible to carry on a conversation using it, it wasn't easy. It was made for passing on critical information between hunters when speech was impossible. Questions like 'where is the enemy?' and 'how many are there?' could be answered fairly simply, but discussing feelings and the ups and downs of your love life was more difficult.

/Stay focussed. Danger close,/ his fingers said, but his smile and warm brown eyes made his true message clear: *be careful. I love you.*

She smiled. */Message received. Situation clear/* she signed, but they both knew that she really meant: *I love you, too. Don't worry, I'll be fine.*

Theramus and Eldoth talked for an entire hour. Certainly it was a record for them both.

Mostly, Theramus just listened, something that many humans were surprisingly bad at. In his experience, most men were so caught up within their own thoughts and prejudices that they were unable to realize that other's attitudes might be different from their own. They were surprised when someone held a different opinion, or saw things from a different perspective. Just as often as that, even if they knew that others held different opinions, it did not occur to them that they were valid. It was, Theramus thought, humanity's single greatest flaw.

No one had listened to Eldoth in a very long time.

Admittedly, he did not make it easy to like him. He had formed shields of arrogance and disdain too thick for casual overtures of friendship to penetrate. Theramus certainly had not. The venomous sarcasm he used against Sephana, and the vindictive glee he took in causing her pain had hardened Theramus's heart against the young wizard. If Eldoth had not made the overture of aiding him in the creation of his new quarter staff, it was likely that Theramus would not have tried to find out who he really was.

The man's talent was impressive. He had accomplished in minutes what would have taken Theramus hours of heating, pounding, and nailing; and his application of the second bronze sheet was even more impressive. He hadn't even needed a fire. He had just stared at the sheet of metal until it glowed, gestured, and it had been done.

After that, he had been as happy as Theramus had ever seen him. He had gone on about energy and matter, speaking so fast that Theramus could barely make out his words, to say nothing of comprehending them. Apparently the ability to heat an object directly was an entirely different process than applying a flame to it, and opened countless possibilities towards future research. Theramus did not fully understand what he meant, but he was happy for the wizard.

All that being said, Theramus still did not know—having gotten to know him somewhat—how much he *liked* Eldoth. He had the greatest of human flaws in abundance. He had no tolerance for those without his knowledge or intelligence and no patience to hear points of view that did not mesh with his own. He was also unable to see what was blatantly obvious to anyone who had ever watched him interact with Sephana.

Theramus had spent the last ten minutes listening to the wizard expound on what he had deduced about the political structure and aims of the High Wizards. Considering the amount of information he had to base his theories off of, some of his guesses were surprisingly accurate.

"I would imagine the libraries of your secret city contain much more accurate information, however," he said with an unsubtly raised eyebrow.

"There is no secret city," Theramus answered. He had said it enough times for it to be rote.

Eldoth snorted. "Come now. You told me that your people have ancient libraries. Where would those be if not in some secret location? Call it a fortress, or a monastery if you wish, but do not lie and say it does not exist."

Theramus rankled. Eldoth had promise, and his intellect was indeed impressive, but he had *not* earned the right to address Theramus so. "I merely said that we have many books. You are the one who assumed they were centrally located." It was both true and not. "The stories of a secret Noss city are just that: stories."

" This lack of trust you give me, this inability to tell me the truth," Eldoth said mockingly, "*This* is why people do not seek you out for your wisdom. They know that you will not deem them worthy.' " Theramus recognised his own words being echoed back to him.

If it were possible for a sneer to draw blood, Theramus would have been haemorrhaging into the dirt.

"The Noss do not serve you, human," Theramus snapped. There was something in Eldoth that brought out the worst in him. "You are in no position to make demands of us."

" *'Human'*, am I now?" Eldoth snarled. "How dare you sit in judgement and decide what knowledge I am worthy of, *Noss*. You may quibble about what form your depository takes, but you do not deny its existence. This is information that people *need*. How many have died of disease over the centuries, in Karalon alone, because no one knew how to build a simple sewer? How much of the squalor in this world could have been avoided if you and your kind deigned to descend from your mountains and *help us?"*

"Do you not think that has not occurred to us?" Theramus stood angrily, knowing even as he did it that it gave him an unfair advantage. "Do you not think that it was..." he trailed off as he saw the wizard physically quail before him. He realized that his fists were clenched angrily and that his posture was very aggressive.

This had never been his intention. Taking a deep breath, he relaxed his fists. "I am sorry," he said in a much quieter tone. "My behaviour is inexcusable. I should not have raised my voice to you."

Hate glittered in the wizard's eyes. "You think you are being wise and benevolent, but really you are sanctimonious and judgemental. What have I not done that would make me worthy of you, oh great and mighty Noss? What does my darling ex-wife possess that makes her so special?"

"She cares for others besides herself," Theramus said. "She is brave and noble, and willing to sacrifice for greater things. What have you sacrificed, Eldoth? What bravery have you shown?"

"Did I not join your band of knights and swear the same oath as you?" Eldoth demanded, yelling now. "I will not perform like a trained animal in order to prove myself to you, but know that I intend to save this world from itself just as surely as you. My weapons will be knowledge and wizardry instead of brute force, and I will do this without your judgement and sermonizing."

Sephana stopped as Illyria made a series of hurried signals that she didn't fully understand. 'Something something' *'enemy'*, 'something else, something else' *'unseen'*. When she and Balien gestured for everyone to get off the trail and hide, Sephana figured out the rest: someone was coming down the trail towards them.

They crouched behind a moss covered tree trunk while Balien expertly erased any sign of the their presence. It didn't take long before Sephana could hear them. There were four or five men talking casually, obviously thinking that they were in no danger this far into the forest. Illyria and Balien both had their bows out, but no arrows nocked.

She tugged on Balien's sleeve and held her arms out in enquiry. (It wasn't Forest Talk but she was pretty sure he understood her anyway). He gave her a two-handed reply that she couldn't understand before bending towards her and murmuring very quietly into her cupped ear. "We're going to follow them and see where they lead us. It will serve us better than engaging them or taking prisoners."

She nodded and relayed the message to Gennald in the same fashion. He had been fingering his sword but grudgingly let go and nodded. Making as little noise as possible, the four of them settled down to wait.

Sephana straightened abruptly. The trap! The one with the frame of sharpened stakes that they had disarmed and bypassed: it was uncovered and anyone going down the trail would be sure to notice it.

She closed her eyes and listened to the voices in the distance. They were still around the bend and out of sight. If Sephana made it back to the trail, she was pretty sure she could make it back to the trap, cover it, and hide before they got there. She pulled out Dawn's First Crescent.

Balien grabbed her wrist, his expression curious and concerned. She tried to answer him quickly in Forest Talk but knew by the look on his face that she had flubbed it up. She tried to mime what she intended but again could not make herself understood. Finally, all too aware that her chance to act was slipping away, she hissed her intentions at him.

Both he and Illyria were making the sign for 'stand still' but she didn't 'listen'. Her strange instinct told her that she could do this. All she had to do was not think.

Almost of its own volition, her hand swung the weighted pommel of her dagger over a branch and applied just the right amount of pressure to the proper part of her mailed glove. The chain retracted with incredible strength, pulling her up into the air and away from the hiding place. *Can't have any tracks leading back to everyone else.*

She rode the dagger up into the air, retracted the pommel chain at the apex of her flight, and half rolled in mid air so that she landed on the hard packed trail cleanly and silently. It was at times like this that she loved being Reshai. With her thick, muscular tail acting as a counter balance, she had complete control over herself when she was in the air. No one she had ever met was able to flip, jump and roll as well as she could, and Dawn's First Crescent let her use her talents to their utmost.

The outlaws were still around a bend and out of sight. She darted down the trail, as silent as only someone truly shunned could be, and made her way over a small rise without being spotted. It only took a minute for her to get back to a place it had taken a half hour of careful creeping to clear out of. The tripline was clearly visible on the forest floor and she scattered leaves and twigs over it, making sure to note its location and not do anything stupid.

She could hear the voices approaching her as she tried to silently replace the concealing branches around the frame without being heard. It seemed like every time she brushed something that its rustles and snaps were as loud as thunderclaps (though still quieter than her heart beating in her ears).

The voices got too close. The frame was only partly hidden, but it would have to do. She ducked behind a pigeon berry bush not even ten feet from the edge of the trail that she hoped that it would be enough to conceal her. She peeked through the bush towards the trail, wondering how they could not be in sight yet considering how well she could hear them, when something caught her eye. The branch that Balien had used to immobilize the swinging motion of the frame was in plain sight.

Instinct took over. She had pulled her dagger out of its sheathe and loosed the pommel before her conscious mind even realized what she was doing. She spun the pommel at the end of its fine chain and cast it out. It had not even fully caught the branch before she extended the bladed hooks and started pulling.

It didn't move. Sephana frowned, instinct fading as it penetrated just how close she was to the approaching outlaws and how desperate the situation was. She pulled again. The stick moved but did not break and, worse, the entire frame shook gently with the movement.

Desperate now, She retracted the chain fully into her dagger pommel. Surely the same strength that could pull her into the air could free a stubborn branch. It didn't come free as much as it snapped. Balien had secured the trap very securely indeed and the sudden pull did more than free the branch. It triggered the trap.

The wooden frame swung into the path with a loud snap and whirr. Against the relative silence of the forest, the sound was deafening, and, if that was not bad enough, the trap had a rope attached to the end of the frame that she hadn't noticed. It had easily a dozen old pots, bowls and ewers tied to it and they made a cacophony of ringing clangs audible for probably a quarter mile. Theramus and Eldoth had probably heard it back at the camp.

Gennald didn't know what the metallic crashing noise was, but he knew that it signified something bad. He heard pelting feet along the trail and knew that the outlaws that they had intended to follow were retreating back the way they came.

He couldn't let them get away. Gennald surged to his feet and could see several men in front of him, running. One of them saw him, stopped and raised his bow. Even as he released his arrow, another arrow, twice as long as his, sprouted in his chest. Gennald threw himself to the ground and the shot flew wide.

"Ambush!" one of the outlaws shouted. It was quickly echoed by the others as they ran. Gennald scrambled to his feet, and stumbled through the bush to the worn path. They weren't that far ahead. He could still catch them.

"No!" he heard from behind him, but he ignored it and surged forward. After weeks of frustrating inactivity he was finally able to do something. He had spent the entirety of the Durnshold invasion locked in a cell and had been similarly imprisoned during last night's blackshield raid. Then, of course, there was a different kind of inactivity caused by two successive nights of being denied his place in Illyria's arms. He had energy enough for ten men.

He felt no fatigue as he surged down the pathway, the outlaws just visible in the distant bush. The blood pounding in his ears dismissed all outside distractions and his vision dimmed to a grey haze. He was a knight, in pursuit of those who had thwarted the king's justice. In Emuranna's name he would not fail.

Something grabbed him from behind. It wasn't strong enough to stop him and he would have pulled loose except for something entangling his leg. Whatever had his arm grabbed his chest as well and he tumbled to the ground. Such was his speed that he rolled over twice, still entangled with his opponent, before stopping. Finding himself on top, surrounded by bushes, he pulled back his fist to strike only to find Illyria laying below him.

Her face was flushed, her chest was heaving and her eyes were a bright, sapphire blue. Their faces were only inches apart and he forgot who he was chasing and why. They just lay there, staring at each other.

"The..the path is trapped," she breathed. "We can't chase them, not like that."

They were the first words she had said to him in hours. He had been staring at her lips, remembering how they had tasted. It took a moment for her words to penetrate and then he remembered the springing stake trap, they had passed by. The image of it catching him up—or worse, her—made him shiver. "Oh, right. Thank you."

Neither of them moved. They just lay there, staring at each other. The fire of the chase changed into a different kind of heat. He lowered his mouth to hers, only to have her turn her head and land instead on her jaw. He tasted salt.

"We should get back to the others," she said with difficulty and began to get to her feet.

He could have kept her there. The hunger within him wanted to. He was strong, and if he pressed it,he didn't think she would resist over much, but the knight within him said 'no'. He had wanted to be in this position with her for weeks now, yes, but they were miles from safety and two of their number were unaccounted for. There were better times and places for romance.

When will that be? His frustration asked. *How long must I wait for it, and will I have the strength to endure until then?*

He didn't know, not any of it, and prayed that Emuranna would give him those answers.

Ross D Jenkins

He stood and held out his hand, but she did not take it. They both stood on the path, covered in leaves and twigs and not able to meet each other's eyes. Balien and Sephana came into view, weapons out, but both relaxed their guard when they saw that Gennald and Illyria were unharmed. Balien's expression as he took in both of them and their appearance was disapproving while Sephana's was wracked with guilt.

"I'm so sorry. This is all my fault."

Illyria still had no words. Balien shook his head. "It's no one's fault. We all forgot to reconceal the trap. You were right to try and there's no blame for failing at an impossible task."

"But they got away."

"We have a fresh trail to track," Illyria assured her. "We'll have to be wary for more traps and ambushes, but we know that they are here." She placed a hand on the Reshai girl's shoulder. "We'll find them."

Sephana didn't look convinced.

"There may also be answers to be found on the body of the one Illyria killed," Gennald told her. "It was a minor setback, that's all."

The words sounded hollow to his ears. Half a day of tracking and all they had was a dead body and a group of outlaws now alerted to their presence. The next few days were going to be long indeed.

124

The Bear and the Thistle

CHAPTER ELEVEN

"Then spake Aldus, last in the line of High Kings: 'O, Lethia, for on my heart hath fallen despair, till I know not what I am, nor whence I am, nor whether I be King. And well for thee, saying in my darkest hour, when all the purport of my throne hath failed. King I am, whatsoever be their cry, and one last act of kinghood shall thou see yet, ere I pass.'

"And uttering this the King made at the Dark Colossus: and then did it smote Aldus hard on the helm which many a blow had beaten thin, and was he laid low.

"So all day long the noise of battle rolled among the mountains by the broken city of kingly splendour until the all of the High King's Champions had fallen around their lord, Aldus Whitecrown. Then beautiful Lethia uplifted him and bore him to the borders of Erendor and then did she lay one last kiss upon his brow, and did her tears stir into him life.

"Then spake High King Aldus to his lady love: 'The sequel of today unsolders all the goodest fellowship of kings and knights whereof this world holds record. I think that we shall never more, at any future time, delight our souls with talk of great deeds, as in the days that were. I perish by this people that I made.'

"Then spake beautiful Lethia: 'My King, king everywhere! And so the dead have kings, there also I will worship thee as king. Yet in Erendor is there life everlasting, and there will you still live and and share my love for thee.'

Then spake Aldus. 'And what of my people, dear lady? How shall fare they, brave souls that they are, while we reside in the land of the elves?'

Then spake Lethia, most beautiful and beloved of all the elves: 'They shall live for hope, my king and my love, for in a day to come, when thy body and thy spirit be whole, thou shalt return, and then will Anshara be whole and the Djido cast out, and will the land be healed.'

"Then did Lethia bear Aldus, last High King of Anduilon, into Erendor and there do they live still, until the day of their inevitable return."

— *excerpt from the* Aldurian Cycle

Eldoth missed his coat. It had been designed and tailored to his exact specifications and made at great expense from the highest grade of silk. He had survived many ordeals while wearing that coat. It was *comfortable*. It was no exaggeration to say that, after his stele and his research journal, it was his most prized possession. He never let on how much he liked it, as Sephana would mock him endlessly if she knew, but that did not diminish his affection.

Unfortunately, its brilliant crimson colouring was considered inappropriate to the task of skulking through the forest, and he had been forced to relinquish it. The cloak he wore in its stead—dull woollen grey and stinking—was a poor substitute.

It was just one of the many unpleasant things he had been forced to endure these last three days, which also included being covered in grime, craving any food item that wasn't a dried oatcake, and being imprisoned behind a concealing screen

125

with Theramus and Gennald. Any one of those things alone would have made him unhappy, but combined with and added to the denial of his beloved silk coat, made it truly insufferable.

A contingent of knights had arrived at the ambush site early on the second day, under strict orders by the king to give the Knights of Anduilon every possible assistance. As they were twenty knights in full armour, with spare mounts and squires to assist them, they would have been utterly useless in the network of interconnecting trails of the Lower Deremwood forest. Illyria assigned them to marching loudly up and down the main road in the hope of flushing out their quarry while she waited quietly nearby. She also assigned them to watch all of their horses, which enabled Eldoth and Theramus to join them.

Unfortunately, being considered quieter that an armoured, mounted knight did not mean that he was quiet enough to follow Balien and Illyria through the forest. That Sephana had passed that muster while he had not was something he did not want to contemplate. While those three had been off creeping through the underbrush, Eldoth and the others had been restricted to hiding and waiting for the call to action.

As frustrating as this inactivity had been, it had allowed him to develop an unexpected new skill. Eldoth could not state it for certain, but he believed that he had learned how to deflect arrows. They were mostly made of wood and feathers, and thus beyond his ability to manipulate, but most all arrows were tipped with metal heads. As deadly as they were, they were quite small and easy to manipulate with his current level of orange magic. Once the theory had been developed, he had experimented with thrown rocks and daggers before moving onto softly fired arrows and then full powered shots from Balien's and Illyria's powerful Ilthanaran bows.

If he was properly focussed, an arrow loosed from a regular bow could be deflected at any distance, while a shot from Balien's much stronger bow had to come from more than twenty yards away. Any closer, and the arrow flew too fast for him to react in time. Illyria's bow—enhanced by ancient magic—propelled its missiles too fast for him to react to at any of the ranges they had tested.

It was a tricky skill to master and Eldoth was proud of his ability to do so, but it did not erase the fact that it was only practical *when people were shooting arrows at him*. It meant that he was purposefully putting himself in harm's way and risking injury or death. Yes, he could deflect arrows (as many as five at a time) if he concentrated, but he had been in mortal combat before. That degree of concentration was difficult to maintain, and was done so at the expense of other things such as the avoidance of difficult terrain or knowing that a slavering thunder lizard was charging towards him.

His latest contemplation was interrupted by the sound of movement from beyond the screen. Signs and countersigns were given, and it was determined that is was indeed Sephana and the others returning. All it took was one look at their faces and Eldoth knew that the boring wait of the last three days was over. The enemy had been found, and he had a sinking feeling that he was about to put his new found ability to the test.

Illyria had been on worse hunts. Four days of stalking before spotting the target was difficult, but both she and Balien had undergone greater hardships during their Ranger trials. Armed only with a dagger, she had tracked her target—a white-striped puma—for nearly three weeks before felling it while her brother had taken two weeks to hunt and kill a black bear. While tracking forest-savvy outlaws was not without its challenges, it was well within her abilities.

She was enjoying this hunt. She was good at this, and while focussed on the tasks of tracking, stalking, and observing she could ignore the other, less controllable problems that surrounded her: her family's reaction to her becoming a knight; poor, sick king Lionar and the future of his reign; and of course, the constant frustrating, alluring presence of Sir Gennald.

Part of her had hoped that he would join the column of knights tasked to assist her and that same part had also been happy that he had not. They had not said more than ten words to each other in days, but actual speech had not been necessary. She knew that he was sorry for what he had said and wanted to make amends. She also knew that he wanted her with at least part of the same intensity as she wanted him. It frightened her how much she yearned for his touch; how much she could recall the sensation of his lips on her face and neck. If she spent any time alone with him she knew that she wouldn't be able to hold herself back.

That, more than any desire to root out these outlaws, was what inspired her to seek them out while he remained behind at their base camp.

Balien knew, of course. She was unable to hide secrets from him, nor he from her; not that either one of them would ever think to. Her love and trust for her brother were absolute. While she had come to appreciate and rely on Sephana, Theramus, and even Eldoth as of late, her connection to them would only ever be a fragment in comparison.

She followed Balien into the seemingly invisible enclosure that hid their camp and its occupants from the surrounding forest. It was small, all the more so because of how much room Theramus occupied. Eldoth sat in one corner, lost in this thoughts as usual, but she only had eyes for Gennald.

He was as dishevelled as only a person confined to a small space for three days could, but still managed to be irresistibly handsome. Somehow the stubble, unkempt hair and dirt on his face only made him more attractive. His grey eyes met hers unerringly and everything else fell away.

Nothing had changed. Despite keeping herself away from him for most of the day, their mutual ardour burned brighter than the largest bonfire. If they were alone, if there were no outlaws, if she allowed herself to succumb to him, she'd be in his arms right now and licking the salt from his cheek.

Sephana's tail flicked her leg and Illyria blinked. She and Gennald were *not* alone. The outlaws *had* been sighted, and she could not allow herself to be weak, not here and now. Her fellow knights were depending on her, and the fate of a kingdom relied on their action. She had to be strong.

Being strong had never been this hard before.

She made the hand motions in Forest Talk that they all knew by now. *Enemy sighted. Make ready.*\ While Gennald, Theramus and Eldoth scrambled to make ready, Illyria and the others made a hasty meal of stale oatcake, tough jerky, and flat tasting water. They would need all their strength for the coming confrontation.

Sephana watched as Balien peered up the hill and made what looked like a see-saw motion with both his hands. *Enemy sighted. No movement,*\ his motions said.

She wasn't so sure that was a good thing. The outpost they had discovered was at the top of a steep hill with only one approach. The outlaws had bows. There wasn't much cover between them and where the Knights of Anduilon (and Gennald, too) were hidden. She knew the plan, but she didn't like it. It meant depending on Eldoth, and he didn't look very thrilled by the prospect either.

Everyone else was crouched beneath a hillock, ready to go. She knew her part in the plan. Illyria had come up with it on her first glance at the outpost and the terrain leading up to it. A big part of any of Illyria's plans was misdirection and speed. That usually meant big, noisy distractions and quiet, fast flanking. Theramus was the best at being big and noisy and Eldoth, for all of his many, many faults, was pretty good at it too. With Gennald in his chainmail with them, it would be hard to make anything easier to notice.

Sephana, because of her Djido blood, was almost always the flanker. She was the fastest of all of them on foot, and was pretty quiet when she wanted to be. Now that she had Dawn's First Crescent, she was more than capable of handling herself. She'd taken on Dragonfleet raiders, rooms full of armed knights, and the occasional tattooed lizardman. Three or four outlaws would be no problem.

It was one of the first times she had done this that she didn't feel scared. Finally, she was pulling her weight. Finally, she was being a knight in deed as well as name.

Eldoth, his hands steepled in front of his chest as he concentrated, nodded his readiness. Sephana sprang to her feet and sprinted away from the group. Her route was far from direct, but it kept her out of sight of the ridge except for a few clear spots. There was a forty foot sheer cliff to scale—the reason why her path wasn't guarded—but that wouldn't be a problem for her.

Her biggest worry was that Eldoth would screw up and get one of her friends shot.

Gennald felt horribly exposed. They were jogging up an exposed path to a raised fortification defended by archers, and their plan hinged on a grumpy wizard and a girl no larger than a thirteen year old. He had no part in this plan beyond looking imposing, and standing next to Theramus, he couldn't even do that.

Why was he even here?

Illyria and her brother stood on either side of Eldoth, murmuring directions to him and steering him around any hazards in his path. Gennald looked up and saw a darting black shape fly towards them from the top of the hill. He gritted his teeth and held tightly onto his shield. This was it: the first arrow of many to come their way. This was when they discovered whether Eldoth's alleged magic could do what he claimed, or if they all became bleeding, arrow-ridden corpses.

Out of the corner of his eye he saw the wizard twitch a finger and watched as the arrow jerk aside as if pulled by a string. *By Emuranna and the kings of Karalon, it works!*

He felt a little better now, but it was a long, dangerous path to the top of the hill and they were hampered by how fast the wizard could move while concentrating. Half a minute later four more arrows arched up before hurtling down towards them. All four abruptly fell from the sky as if they had struck an invisible barrier.

Gennald's hope slowly began to rise. *This might just work after all.*

All seemed to be going well. They had succeeded in making it a third of the way up the hill and seemed to have drawn all attention of the defenders at its top. Theramus was both surprised and not that Eldoth had been successful, thus far, in shielding them from all incoming missiles. The wizard was quite intelligent and had proved adept in his ability to master new magical abilities. The caps on his new quarter staff were evidence enough of that.

Eldoth's words still rankled. *"I intend to save this world from itself just as surely as you,"* he had said, as well as *"I will not perform like a trained animal in order to prove myself."* What exactly had the wizard done—other than being arrogant and insufferable—to not be worthy of Theramus's respect? By his deeds, Eldoth had saved them all. He had been instrumental in the taking of Dragonhead Keep and had done his part against the Dragonfleet raiders. Certainly their current plan would not have been possible without his unique abilities.

Theramus just disliked him, but perhaps that was not being fair. Eldoth *had* taken the same oath as him, was in the same forest and was facing the same dangers. Theramus could set aside his personal dislike for the moment, so long as Eldoth continued to prove himself.

That matter settled, he did his best to locate Sephana. He glanced along the rocks and gulleys of her route but was unable to see her. He was uncomfortable with this part of Illyria's plan, but could not deny that not only was Sephana the only one who could scale the cliff and cut off the outlaw's escape, but that she had proved herself against more dangerous foes. He had no justifiable reason to object to her involvement.

He could not deny that Sephana held a special place in his heart, larger than those given to his other wards, both past and present. He wanted her to excel, just as he did with Illyria and Balien, but more than the others he wanted for her not to be hurt. She was unique in this world, and alone: an undisfigured Reshai, just as he was a lone Noss, and she, like he, had seen too much sadness.

They were half way up the path now and the rain of arrows continued unabated. There were only four archers; it was all the position needed. They could have defeated ten times their number from any other force. He looked to the side and saw Sephana: she was walking up the side of the cliff as if it were a tiled hallway. Once she reached the top she would be free to block the outlaws' retreat.

"We need to go faster," Balien said.

"By all means do so," Eldoth grated, his steepled hands white from exertion and his eyes focussed on a place beyond mundane perception. "I will do my best not to trip over your arrow ridden corpse when I catch up to you."

Balien made no reply.

"They've seen Sephana. They're running," Illyria reported. Theramus looked to the top of the hill and saw exactly that. The rain of arrows had stopped, and there were no defenders remaining. Illyria, Balien and Gennald all took off up the ridge at a run. Eldoth just stopped, closed his eyes and fell to into a crouch.

Theramus hesitated. "Are you well?"

"I am fine, just...tired. Maintaining that degree of focus on this terrain is quite draining."

"You did very well," Theramus replied, surprised that he meant every word.

Stupid branch.

Sephana was pretty sure she could have snuck right up behind the four archers if she hadn't caught her foot on that one branch. The branch had been laying against a loose rock. The loose rock had been sitting over top of a shale deposit. One errant brush had led to one thing, then another and another. One of the archers had looked over at the noise and seen her before she could hide. Seconds later she was dodging arrow, and they were running away.

If they didn't have bows she could have caught them, but every time she made to follow them, one began shooting at her. It didn't take her long to realize that, by herself and with them knowing the area, she was better off waiting for the others. Illyria and Balien could probably follow their trail, and Eldoth would be there to stop any arrows that might be shot at them.

It still bugged her that she had failed, and because of something so stupid, too. Eldoth wasn't going to let her hear the end of it.

More marching. Wonderful.

Eldoth managed to choke down yet another oatcake and swallow some ill-tasting water before they set out again. While part of him wanted to tell the others that he could heat a cook pot without the aid of a fire, he knew that if he did so they would soon regard him as little more than a stove with legs. More than that, they would want him to prepare meals, and he loathed cooking.

Their attempt to pursue the three fleeing archers after Sephana's club-footed bungling had proved fruitless. The terrain was too dangerous and their foes too canny to allow them to make up any distance. There were too many places to set up ambushes and, they had learned, several concealed traps along the same route.

It had taken them several hours to cross a few miles of rough terrain, and in that time their quarry had evidently led them onto some sort of false trail. They had ended up at a dry creek bed that abutted a long collapsed mineshaft and could go no further. Further painstaking searching by Illyria and Balien had revealed a hidden trail, which they followed, again with due caution. The end result had been several hours of climbing directly up the side of the Silverheart Hills.

"This isn't a hill," Sephana complained when they had stopped near the crest to gather their breath. "It is a mountain. We didn't climb this much crossing the Karnems." She was referring to the mountain range that separated Karalon and Nemora. Eldoth had not yet had the privilege of traversing those particular mountains. He preferred to avoid that sort of thing.

Theramus wasn't even short of breath, damn him. "They are steep, yes, but not high. We have not even climbed one thousand feet."

"Feels like a mountain," she grumbled. Eldoth had to agree. He would have voiced his agreement if doing so would not make him more likely to vomit.

"These hills were rich in silver and lead," Gennald told them. Even wearing a third of his weight in armour, the knight was in better condition than him. "That's what the legends say, anyway. No one has been able to get so much as an ingot out of them since the High Kingdom fell."

"The view is lovely," Illyria mentioned.

Eldoth was normally immune to such splendour, but he had to agree. The entirety of the Wightland valley lay below them, covered almost entirely with trees. Lake Vinander, eighty miles from shore to shore at its widest point, was clearly visible to the north and even the town of Westbridge—or at least its signature bridge columns—could be seen off in the distance.

"Where's New Aukaster?" Sephana asked.

"We can't see it from here," Balien said. "It's beyond the other side of the mountain. Hill, I mean."

Sephana strained to look up. "I think I see something." They followed where she pointed and saw a single large elm tree near the edge of a crag. "That tree looks really out of place up here. Do you think it's hiding something?"

"It's possible," Balien admitted. Eldoth had no opinion on the subject. They marched over to it and examined closely, but in the end determined it to simply be a large, healthy tree.

"But why is it here?" Sephana asked, confused. "Everything around it is a shrub, or moss. Don't you think that it's strange?"

"Somewhere, an Imvir is laughing," Balien said with a shrug.

She looked at him oddly. "That doesn't make any sense."

"Imvir," Illyria explained. "Spirits that live in the Lifestream. They shepherd souls and create life, sometimes for reasons beyond mortal understanding." She gestured at the tree. "They wanted that tree to live, so they made it grow here."

"I have seen many instances of this and similar things all across Anshara," Theramus said. "It is not unusual."

"They say that Imvir have strange senses of humour," Illyria said. "So when you see something like this, or an animal that has no place being where it is, that the Imvir did it as a joke."

"We call them quicklings, here," Gennald said. He had been quiet so far. "But we don't call it a joke. We call it a 'Quickling's Kiss.' "

"Oh," Sephana said, nodding. "I know what a quickling is."

"We're almost at the peak," Illyria said, ending the conversation. "Let's push on."

Eldoth groaned.

It was late afternoon by the time they finally crossed the peak of the Silverheart 'Hills' and began descending down the far side. It was definitely more than an animal trail that they were following; several humans had traversed these same hills in the last month, but Illyria couldn't narrow down the time frame any more than that. If this same trail had been in Nemora, she could have determined their number, what they were laden with, and their skill at woodcraft. Here, in foreign Karalon, surrounded by rough, rocky terrain, she could find only frustrating vagaries.

They were all tired, except for Theramus. Poor Eldoth's face was the same colour as his borrowed cloak and Gennald, for all of his stoic silence—how silly was it that she found such normally sneer-worthy behaviour to be admirable?—was slowing down as well. Sephana's tail was drooping and even Balien was dragging his feet. Illyria was no better.

At least the ground had finally flattened out. They were in a steep, narrow-walled valley less than half a mile across. There was a warm stillness to the air as well as a calming freshness unlike anything Illyria had experienced in Karalon. It reminded her of home, oddly; rather like the magical, ancient Ilthwood forest that her people resided in. Even the trees seemed to be taller and leafier here than anywhere else in the Land of Golden Bears.

Illyria smiled and looked over at her brother. He felt it, too. "This place is magical," Gennald murmured. It seemed wrong to speak any louder.

"We should rest," Illyria said in an equally hushed tone. No one disputed her, and it didn't take them long to find a small clearing next to a quietly chuckling stream. Even the water tasted sweet and they had been resting and chatting for several minutes before she remembered what had brought them here.

She placed her left hand flat against her mouth with her palm facing out. It was Forest Speech for 'no talking' which she followed with /Unfriendly territory. Possible enemies,/ Everyone caught her sign and nodded. It was a small comfort that she had not been the only one lulled into complacency by the serenity of the valley.

The pleasant silence was broken a moment later by the chattering of a flight of birds—a Karalinian variety of swift, she saw—that circled above them for a moment, chattering all the while, before flying off down the valley. The silence that followed in the bird's wake seemed deafening.

Large trees...sweet water...flocks of swifts...Something was wrong.

Illyria glanced around her at the various shrubs and bushes that dotted the forest floor. She hadn't noticed before, but she saw now that clusters of butterflies sat on almost every plant.

She knew where they were.

"Don't touch your weapons, no matter what you do," she warned her fellow knights. "We are in a place of peace."

Everyone exchanged confused glances.

133

"Why are you talking again?" Sephana whispered. "I thought we were being quiet."

"There is no need," Illyria replied, glancing around her. "The outlaws aren't here. We followed a false trail."

"I don't understand," Gennald said. "Where are we?"

Her answer was forestalled by a very large, very angry barking in the distance. Balien met her eyes briefly, understanding brightening his eyes. "We're in Olsarum," he told everyone. "The Sacred Valley of Karalon."

CHAPTER TWELVE

Guests may, upon personal invitation by the monarch or his crownmarked kin, accompany the procession to the Circle of Joining within the Sacred Valley of Olsarum. Any person in the royal procession must abide by the following conditions:

No one is permitted, at any time, to raise their voice even to the level of common speech.

One must bow one's head whenever meeting any member of the priesthood, including all templars, squires, acolytes and lay-priests.

No one is permitted, at any time, to leave the cobbled path between the valley gates, the Circle of Joining and the Campus of Ur. This includes doing so for the purpose of relieving oneself. Entry into the Wardswood is strictly forbidden

No one is permitted, at any time, to damage or pick any flowers, leaves, branches, berries or fruit from within the Sacred Valley.

No contact is permitted, at any time, with any of the wardens of the valley, including all hounds, seeker birds and butterflies. The only allowed exception to this is if said animal initiates contact with you. If this does happen, you must allow it to linger, perch upon you, or relieve itself as it sees fit.

— Appendix to Karalinian Guide to Proper Decorum and Style

Gennald wanted to retch. "Emuranna forgive me. I did not know."

Theramus nodded sadly. "Of course. It makes perfect sense."

"We are forbidden to be here," Gennald whispered, mortified. He glared at no one and everyone, wanting to blame someone for this profane transgression, but unsure who. "By my oath, I *cannot* be here."

"We'll leave before any harm is done," Balien counselled, but Gennald refused to be calmed.

"Any harm? Do you really believe that?" His voice was shrill. "The harmony of the whole kingdom depends on this valley's sanctity. If the king cannot Join with the Land at SummersEnd it will be *our fault*."

"Gennald, peace," Illyria said. "This sanctity is not so easily broken. We have neither shed blood or profaned the Circle of Joining. Your oath has not been violated. Trust me."

He wanted to believe her, he truly did. "You're sure?"

"Yes." She smiled kindly and Gennald felt his heart lurch. If he could have ripped it out of his chest and given it to her, he would have.

"The Seekers have already found us," Balien warned. "And there is at least one hound warden coming."

Indeed, they could all hear loud, angry barks and crashing brush.

"The Seekers are the birds, right?" Sephana asked.

Theramus nodded and held his quarter staff warily. "Yes. They are the eyes and ears of the temple. What they see, the entire valley knows."

"So what do we do now?"

"We cannot shed any blood," Illyria said. "Any violence within the valley will disturb its tranquillity, but shedding blood here is much, much worse. Even a healthy king would have difficulty completing his Joining in such circumstances." It didn't need to be said that poor Lionar was far from healthy.

"Does that 'shedding blood' thing apply to the dogs as well?" Sephana asked.

"Theramus, use your staff. Try to hold it at bay," Illyria ordered. "Whatever any of you do, don't draw your weapons and don't run. Stand your ground no matter what comes."

They were backing warily back towards where they had come, but she knew that flight was futile. The crashing in the underbrush was getting nearer. From the sound she guessed it was only one dog, but if were anywhere near the size of Bear, one would be enough.

A moment later the dog broke into the clearing and, if anything, it was even larger. It wore neither harness nor muzzle and Illyria knew that with no priest near to command it, it would defend this valley to the death.

Theramus stepped forward, the brass-tipped end of his staff lowered at the beautiful, impressive creature. To her relief, it did not attack and instead continued to bark loudly, keeping pace with them as they retreated the valley's edge.

She was just as surprised as anyone else when it caught sight of Balien, stopped barking and instead began wagging its tail.

He looked just as surprised. He advanced towards it cautiously, his hand extended. Illyria fingered her hip quiver nervously. Sanctity or no, she would allow no man or beast to hurt her brother.

He saw her and held up a warning hand. The dog's whole posture had changed. Its hackles had fallen, its legs weren't as stiff and a huge pink tongue appeared in one side of its mouth. It sniffed Balien's hand cursorily before giving it a friendly lick and then pressing its ruff against it. Balien, reflexively, gave the dog's shoulder a scratch before falling to one knee. The dog, its tail wagging eagerly now, pressed its huge body against Balien's chest and tried to lick at his face.

Illyria traded a baffled look with Theramus, but he looked equally dumbstruck.

"Shouldn't it be trying to kill us?" Sephana asked warily.

"Yes," Illyria answered. "Hound wardens are only loyal to each other and the temple priests. Never to anyone else. Never."

Illyria cautiously made her way towards her brother and the imposing dog. It was natural of her to assume that it was a hound warden, but she was no longer sure. Perhaps it was just a dog. A very large dog, but a dog nonetheless.

When she came within three paces of it, it stiffened and its tail stopped wagging. A deep, dangerous growl sounded from within its chest and its bright blue eyes fixed upon her like a hawk's. Balien tried to catch the dog's attention but it ignored him and continued growling. Only when Illyria backed off a few paces did it stop.

"There's a rider coming," Sephana warned. Illyria tore her attention away from the Hound Warden that wasn't and then she heard it: the irregular drum of hoof beats that indicated a cantering horse. A moment later it came into view.

It was a temple knight—a templar—but this one's armour was golden, its tunic blazing white and the rampant bear on its chest bore a golden halo. If Knight-Master Sheltan was one of the highest ranking templars, then there was only one man this could be.

Illyria fell to one knee, averting her eyes. What title had Sheltan given him? Oh, yes, she remembered now. "Please, Grandmaster, please forgive our trespass. We mean no harm."

In Balien's arms, the dog erupted into even more savage barking.

Theramus knelt. This was obviously the High Priest of the Sacred Valley, styled as a knight as they were here. He wondered why he was alone before recalling that all his priests had made questing vows and were off searching the land for spiritual corruption.

"Please, Grandmaster, forgive our trespass. We mean no harm," Illyria said, her eyes averted. Everyone followed her lead and knelt except for Balien, who was on one knee already with the dog that Theramus had previously thought to be a Hound Warden. For it to act this way to Balien but not to the High Priest marked it as an impressive but ultimately mundane creature.

The priest reined in his mount and stared down at them angrily. "Who are you to intrude in this place? This is sacred ground."

The dogs barking increased and Balien, his arms wrapped around its neck, was barely able to hold it in check.

The priest looked over at them and his expression soften. "He likes you, does he? I think you're the first I've ever seen him take a shine to." He looked sternly at the others. "Don't think for a moment that, because a quietborn temple dog likes you, it excuses your trespass. Who are you and why are you here?"

"Wise Father, forgive us," Illyria repeated. "We are agents of the king, in pursuit of criminals. We followed a trail that led us to this grove. We did not mean to trespass and have committed no defilement. With your leave, we will depart before we offend you further."

"Agents of the king? I have heard nothing of this. I recognise a knight among you, but the rest of you are foreigners." His eyes settled on Sephana and his face twisted in anger. "You dare to bring a snakespawn into my grove?"

Grandmaster or no, that kind of behaviour was unacceptable. Theramus's angry reply was pre-empted by Gennald. "Grandmaster, I beg you to forgive us this offence. In Emuranna's name, Lady Illyria speaks the truth." He looked up the priest. "I would die before I put the king's Joining at risk. Please, we will leave if you allow us."

"Forgive you, for this? We shall see. I would know to name of the knight who asks for so unlikely a thing."

"I am Sir Gennald Hanley, My Lord, First Knight of Willem Jannery, Lord of the Northern March. I am on a quest, My Lord, to regain my honour."

"You do your honour no favours," the high priest snapped. "Do you have any proof for your claims? You have the look of criminals to my eyes."

"Wise father, may I explain?" Illyria asked.

He dismounted. "You may, but I have a keen ear for trickery. If you speak false I will know and my punishment will be severe."

The dog, whose growling had subsided, began a new round of angry barks. Only Balien's presence seemed to be restraining him.

The High Priest of Karalon just called me a snakespawn. Sephana tried vainly to blink away the angry tears that threatened to fall onto the ground that everyone claimed was holy and sacred. It looked just like land to her, and the priest just another man. *I'm never going to be accepted for who I am. All everyone will ever see are the snakemen who raped my ancestors.*

Illyria was explaining herself. "I do not speak false, Wise Father," she assured him, presenting the king's letter for his inspection. "As you see, our claims are legitimate, and I assure you that our presence here is in error. We are on the trail of those who have stolen gold for the king intended for the Dragonfleet tribute. They are canny foresters, and led a false trail here that we followed. With your leave, we will depart as we came to continue our pursuit."

He read the letter several times and closely examined its seal. Finally, he returned it, his face softening marginally. "I would not interrupt his majesty's agents on so important a quest. The upcoming tribute weighs heavily on all of us. With SummersEnd approaching, I can take no chances on interfering with the king's upcoming union."

He motioned them to stand. Sephana wasted no time getting as far away from him as she could.

"Wise Father, may I ask you a question?" Illyria asked.

"You may."

"Is the king...well? Is he up to the challenge of the Joining?"

"We must hope that he is, for the sake of us all."

Sephana couldn't keep quiet. "What's with the dog?" The huge animal was still being restrained by Balien.

The so-called Knight-Grandmaster glared at her, but Sephana met his eyes defiantly. He'd called her snakespawn. Respect was earned. "He is quietborn. Not a Hound Warden, just a dog. He is a fine animal, but not friendly. I have never seen him take kindly to a person before today."

There was little to say after that. They gathered their belongings and departed the way they came, escorted by the high priest on his horse and the mysterious dog who would permit only Balien to touch him. He would have accompanied them out of the valley, she was sure, if he had been able to make the climb.

"Do not heed his words," Theramus said to her. "Just because he is a priest does not mean his words have any weight beyond spiritual matters. He is a fool to condemn you so superficially."

She did her best to hide the sullen melancholy that had taken her over. "He treated me better than other Karalmen have," she gave what she hoped looked like a casual shrug. "There wasn't a burning stake in sight. I consider that an improvement."

He was not deceived. "You do not do yourself any favours by allowing wrong behaviour. Injustice must be fought."

"I can't save the whole world, Theramus," she told him bitterly. "Not by myself."

"Is that not what we are, as knights? Is that not part of our quest?"

They spent a thoroughly miserable night midway up the largest of the Silverheart Hills. Eldoth had passed into a place beyond pain—which pleased him—but also beyond thought, which did not. His every movement was mechanical. He did only what he was told when he was told. Even that fact that Sephana took it upon herself to watch over him made no impression. Once they had stopped and eaten yet another cold, tasteless meal, Eldoth staggered to the nearest scrap of shelter, wrapped his borrowed cloak around his body and slept like the dead. When he woke again it was morning and he felt slightly better, but he did not truly regain his senses until once again on flat ground.

"So what now?" Sephana asked as they all choked down still more oatcakes. "Where else can we search?"

"Whatever we do, we must do it soon," Illyria said. "The SummersEnd festival is less than a week away, and all of yesterday was wasted chasing false trails."

"Are we so sure yesterday was a waste of time?" Sephana asked. It was not the first time she had asked it.

"Yes!" Gennald's face was dark with anger. It was not the first time he had answered her. "Sir Lanton is the Knight-Grandmaster of Karalon. He is second only to the king in stature. He is beyond reproach."

"But what about the dog?" She crossed her arms defiantly across her chest. "It hated him. I thought hound wardens were loyal to the priests."

"They are!" Gennald stepped closer to her, his fists clenching. "This one was quietborn. It befriended Balien. No Hound Warden would ever do that. They are loyal only to the priesthood and the crownmarked heirs of Karalon."

"You keep saying 'quietborn' like it means something. What is it?"

"It means that it isn't a Hound Warden, just a dog. It happens sometimes."

"It's common with magical creatures," Illyria added, her voice far calmer than either of theirs. "Not all offspring inherit the abilities of the their forebears. Wardens, priests, and crownmarked royalty all come from magical bloodlines. It's why my people take their lineage so seriously. There were one or two quietborn hounds in every litter in Ilthanara. I imagine it would be the same here." She frowned. "It seems odd that they would let one live to adulthood, though. We always put ours down."

"But what about the tracks?" Sephana continued. "Illyria and Balien both agree that there were already tracks along the whole length of the trail we took."

"It was a false trail! They admit that, too!" He stepped even closer. She looked very small next to him. "I will not stand by and let you impugn the name of a great man just because he called you a bad name!"

"He called me a snakespawn!"

"You are a snakespawn!"

There was a sudden, awkward silence and Gennald blanched. "I mean...that is...as a Reshai, you cannot deny that your ancestors are, well...snakes."

"I know exactly what you meant." Sephana pulled off her mail glove and glared up at him. "I slap you in the face with this, right? That's how one knight signals another that he wants to duel?"

The idea of her thrashing the arrogant knight appealed greatly to Eldoth. He watched the confrontation with interest.

"You're not a knight!" Gennald yelled.

It felt good to finally say it, even though he knew, in this particular company, that it was possibly the worst thing he could say. He'd been biting his tongue for far too long, out of obedience to his lord as well as respect for Illyria, but it had rankled every time.

Now, for better or worse, it was said. The words he'd been holding back for weeks continued to pour out of him. "You're not; none of you are, and every time you say that you are, you insult everyone who has ever born the title."

Sephana was furious, as he'd expected, as was her loyal protector, Theramus. The wizard, Eldoth looked *amused* for some reason (Gennald had always thought him a bent blade) and Balien's expression was as unreadable as always. It was Illyria's expression that he feared the most, and it was bad as he feared. She looked *hurt*.

In front of him, Sephana tightened her hand into a fist. "If that's what you think, then there's nothing stopping me from hitting you."

He laughed. He couldn't help it. She was half his size and he was wearing armour. He doubted he'd even feel it if she struck him. "Are you really that foolish?"

"That's it!" Sephana's hand dropped to her dagger even as Illyria stepped in front of her.

"Stop it, both of you!" Illyria ordered, her eyes a blazing shade of violet. "You'll alert the whole forest that we're here. I know that you're tired and I know that you're frustrated. We all are, but this is when we need to be our best. Time is running short and for the sake of Karalon we cannot make any more mistakes. We *have* to be better than this." She looked steadily at Gennald and Sephana. "You both need to forgive each other and apologise so that we can find the people who really are guilty and punish them."

"I will not," Gennald said between clenched teeth. "I'm done holding my tongue while all of you make mockeries of everything I believe in. It's beyond insulting. I—"

"Gennald!" Her eyes bored into his. "Can I speak to you for a moment? Privately?"

Despite everything, he was unable to deny her. He nodded wordlessly and followed her into the forest.

"I am not apologising," Sephana said to the three men who remained with her. She was literally shaking with rage. "Not after what he said."

"I agree, you should not," Theramus said. "His behaviour is inexcusable."

"This isn't about getting insulted," Balien said, his voice quiet. "You've been called names before; cruel ones, and you've endured it." She opened up her mouth to protest but he overrode her. "I am not saying Gennald is right or that it's fair, but we all know that the world is neither of those things. We *are* knights, and that means we endure all hardships. It's not about pride or avenging insults—no matter who is insulted." He glanced at Theramus. "This is about finding criminals, seeing justice done, and protecting the innocent. If you are a knight in your heart, you will say that you are sorry, accept Sir Gennald's apology, and let us go back to the business of hunting. Being a knight isn't just about fighting, it's about being noble."

"And what if he doesn't apologise?" She knew she sounded petulant, but couldn't help it.

"Then you do it anyway, knowing that you are the better person."

Sephana scowled. "Why do we even need him? We have the king's letter."

"He's a Karalinian nobleman and our authority is tenuous, even with the letter. We're better having him than not."

She looked at him levelly. "That's why he's here? It doesn't have anything to do with his relationship with Illyria?"

Balien didn't answer.

Both kept their silence until they were out of earshot. Gennald's words had struck her like a kick to the stomach and different parts of her wanted to either collapse in tears or beat him within an inch of his life.

Currently she was leaning towards the latter.

"So you felt like this from the very beginning," she said when they were far enough away. "Before we even left the Northmarch, you'd decided that we were some blight on the face of chivalry." She felt tears starting to form in her eyes and willed them to disappear. She was *not* weak. "You thought we were a joke."

"I never thought you were a joke, Illyria," Gennald said, his expression earnest. "Never you."

She snorted. "But you thought my friends were? My brother?"

"I think that you are...misguided."

Anger flared. "So we're children to you, then. Who made you our lord and gave you permission to judge us?"

"Do you really want to get into this now?"

She ignored the part of her that wanted to yell. It would serve no purpose here. "Why didn't you say anything to me about how you felt? We don't have to agree on everything, but I thought we could be honest with each other."

" 'A knight is obedient to his lord,' " Gennald quoted. "Lord Jannery told me to give you and your friends every courtesy. My opinion didn't matter."

"Courtesy?" It came out loudly, despite her intentions. If his previous words had felt like a kick, these struck her like a dagger to the chest. A dull, rusty dagger. "Is that what you were doing when you were with me? Being courteous?"

"You know that isn't true," Gennald stepped in close and locked eyes. Anger emanated from him like a torch. "I broke a royal order for you and raised arms against the Dragonfleet. I've abandoned my lord and followed you into this damned forest. I did it because I love you."

Her anger vanished as if it had never been. "You..." Words escaped her. Thought escaped her. She barely knew how to stand.

"I love you," Gennald repeated. He stepped closer. Staring into her eyes, he took her by her elbows and pulled her against him. Only the discomfort of being pressed against chainmail stopped the moment from being perfect.

He was going to kiss her and she knew she was going to let him, as much the thinking part of her didn't want to. Somehow she found the ability to speak. "I don't know you, Gennald. Everything you have said to me has been a lie."

He leaned in to kiss her and she didn't have the power to stop him. He pressed his lips against hers and it was all she could do to hold herself stiff in his arms. Passion, hot and intense, ignited between them. It would burn her to cinders if she let it. "This," he whispered huskily into her ear. "This is real, Illyria. This is love." He kissed her again, deeply, and she lasted only a moment before surrendering and wrapping her arms around his neck.

His arms slid up her body, squeezing and caressing, and she moaned. It was only when she realized that he was undoing the ties on her tunic that she balked. "Gennald, no," she mumbled around his hungry lips. "We can't."

"Yes, we can," he replied, his fingers tugging impatiently at knots. "I can't wait anymore."

She wanted him to continue. She truly, truly did. Her body had been literally aching for him since their argument that last night in Lord Jannery's manor, but somehow she found the strength to wrap her fingers around his wrists. "We can't. Not here. Not like this."

"I need you, Illyria. I want you." He pressed his body into hers, stepping forward every time she stepped back until the hard, rough trunk of a tree pressed against her back. His hands, still fettered by her grip, began pulling her tunic up over her head.

"My brother is nearby, and there could be outlaws near," she protested, weaker than she would have liked.

"I don't care," he growled as his lips pressed below her ear.

If I don't stop now I won't be able to later. She pulled his wrists away from her body and pushed them against his chest. "No. Gennald, no. Not here."

He tried to kiss her again but she pushed him away. His eyes were ravenous. "Not here, but somewhere else, later?"

"Yes," she breathed, still holding him at arm's length. "Later."

He laughed wickedly and the sound almost mad her legs give way. "I'll hold you to that."

Promising with her eyes what her lips could not say, she continued to hold his warm, strong wrists while vainly trying to control her breathing. "You have to apologise to Sephana."

Her words broke the spell and he turned away with a scowl. "No. I will not allow her to slander the name of a great man."

"Do it for me." Even as she said it, she wished she could take it back.

"What?"

The words, once begun, couldn't be stopped. "Apologise to Sephana, and never bring up that subject again. Please." Her body acted of its own volition, stepping close to him and looking up at him through her lashes, even as her mind cursed her for lowering to such base manipulation. "Do it for me. Do it because I asked you." There was no need to say what his reward would be; they both knew it. He didn't even have to nod for them to both know that he had accepted her terms.

That such bargains had been struck between men and women since the Age of Creation did nothing to lessen her guilt, and yet she made no effort to take back her words. When the two of them shuffled back to camp, she likewise did nothing as both Sephana and Gennald made apologies and acceptances that rivalled each other for their insincerity.

CHAPTER THIRTEEN

"The first night of SummersEnd, on the final day of Gidoss, ninth moon of the year, is given to the people, to celebrate the collection of the harvest. They eat, drink and revel under the light of the full moon for they know that autumn will soon be upon them and, after that, winter, but that is not truly SummersEnd.

"It is the second night if SummersEnd which is truly holy. It is the day between summer and autumn, the time when day and night are equal. It is a holy day, neither Gidoss or Meloss, and the day when Nasheeth, the moon, hangs high in the sky through both day and night as decreed by Anur, in memory of Sheethu, his wife and only love."

—The Holy Days of Anshara, *Sadis of Alashadimm*

Redding hastily dried himself and threw on some clothing, cursing under his breath all the while. Myria had interrupted his bath and dismissed his attendant with a knowing wink. That would have been fine if she really had been his mistress, but all she had done once they were alone was to throw a washcloth at his face and demand an update. The 'as soon as possible, and damn your inconvenience' had been unspoken but strongly implied.

He was getting tired of this. He was a landed noble, a peer of the realm and one of the most powerful men in Karalon. No one ordered him around, no matter how much influence they had. The day would come, sooner rather than later, when he showed Myria who was the master of whom.

Unfortunately, that day was not today. Ander was not yet king and Redding had not yet been named his royal advisor. SummersEnd—and thus Lionar's final failure—was still five days off. He could put up with Myria's insufferable attitude until then.

He re-entered his bedchamber cautiously, his clothing uncomfortable and damp. Myria was undressing, but there was nothing amorous in her actions. As his mistress, she was of course expected to spend her nights in his chamber. It was a cover that allowed her to operate at night in her other guises without suspicion. He had no idea when she actually slept.

"I still stink," he complained, watching as she unselfconsciously stepped out of her dress. He had no idea how she was able to hide so many weapons on her person. "That room's getting worse every day. I've had more baths this month than I have in the last year."

"I've noticed." She stepped into a sturdy pair of black dyed thistle-cloth pants. "Have a servant clean it out if it bothers you."

"The last one I sent in there never came out, and the rest of them refuse to enter."

She shrugged into her shirt. "You only have to put up with it for another few days."

"One of several annoyances I shall be happy to be rid of once Ander is king," Redding said with what he hoped was an innocent smile.

Her eyes narrowed but she said nothing and strapped on her weapon harness. Two wicked, exotic shortswords crossed her chest. "I've received word from Manson: The Knights of Anduilon are making trouble in the Deremwood. I have to deal with it and will be gone for a few days. Tell me everything that's happening."

He didn't think of disobeying. He'd seen her use those swords. "I've magnanimously convinced my fellow Anderites *not* to start a civil war on my behalf...at least not yet, anyway." He grimaced. "Our 'guest' is comfortable in the basement and has agreed to our terms, and Prince Ander has *finally* asked for my aid as a crown councillor once he takes the throne."

"It sounds like you have everything in hand. Keep it that way." Myria opened the window and turned to face him, her eyes dangerous. "We've worked towards this for two years, Redding. Don't do anything foolish."

She vanished into the darkness before he could rebut her. Redding scowled and closed the window before he caught a chill. Autumn was almost upon them.

Damn Myria and her threats, and damn him for being unable to defy her. The only consolation he had was that, as she had said herself, they were almost done. Some of them, however, would be more done than others.

"I don't want to know what happened to Old Wighton" Sephana said quietly to Theramus as they both looked down at the town of New Wighton. "Seriously. Don't tell me."

"It was sacked and destroyed by the Djido during the Great War," Theramus said, his voice a low rumble. "The town was rich with silver mined from the hills and was one of their first targets. This village is a shadow of what its namesake used to be."

Just like everything else in Anshara.

"I told you not to tell me," she grumbled and Theramus smiled. The fact that she could respond to him in that way indicated that she was already in better spirits.

Their morale was the lowest it had ever been in the aftermath of Sephana's and Gennald's near disaster yesterday morning. Theramus was sure that it would have devolved into violence, or that their anger would provoke them into unwise decisions, but cooler heads had prevailed. Instead they had rejoined the main camp and enjoyed hot meals and baths for the first time in almost a week. Gennald had been eager to spend the night there, obviously to spend some time alone with Illyria, but she had insisted otherwise. Their spirits nonetheless buoyed by their brief respite, they had returned to the hunt until they had finally discovered the only outlaw trail that did not terminate at yet another dead end. Instead, it led them to a small village off of the main road: New Wighton.

Gennald had been incensed at the idea of villagers collaborating with outlaws and wanted to put the entire village to the question, but Illyria had disagreed. They would get better results by asking politely than by threatening, she had said, and Gennald had been quickly persuaded.

Sephana had refused to enter the town, saying that if these villagers were like the others she had met, she would not receive a warm reception. Theramus had chosen to stay with her, and thus they were now both watching from the tree line as their fellow knights investigated.

"This is a waste of time," Sephana said. "No one is going to say anything to a group of strangers."

"Then how would you suggest we proceed?"

"There is no good way," she admitted. "This close to the outlaw camp they are all either working with them—in which case they will never admit anything—or they are scared to death."

"If the villagers are being threatened, then they should confide their fears with us. We can help them."

She shook her head. "No one is going to believe us. Two rangers, a knight and a guy in a red coat? I wouldn't."

He knew that she was right, though he did not like it. In his forty years of searching Anshara he had seen the weak intimidated by the strong too many times. "It should not be so," he growled. "This is what is wrong with this world."

"What? Strong-arming?"

"I was not referring to intimidation," he told her. "No, lack of belief. Lack of hope. That is our greatest enemy, and the most difficult to vanquish. These people, they cannot imagine themselves achieving a better world, and that is why they will never see it. They do not believe it possible."

"As you may or may not know, a group of knights escorting a tax caravan were killed five days ago, and the gold was stolen," Illyria said, addressing the thirty odd people gathered in the village square. "This gold was intended to be given as tribute to the Dragonfleet, to ensure that the children of this kingdom are not taken as slaves. These criminals who stole it, they did not just steal from king Lionar, but from all the parents of Karalon. This gold must be recovered, and the men who took it brought to justice. We are not asking you to fight, all we want is information. Anything you can tell us would be greatly appreciated."

No one in the square said anything.

"This is a waste of time," Gennald muttered, standing next to her.

"You don't want any of our money?" A woman asked suspiciously.

"Not that we have any to give," someone in the crowd said in false whisper. "The tax collectors have already taken everything."

"I am not your lord," Illyria told her. "That is not my place and, as you say, you have already given all that you can. We seek those who stole it, not twenty miles north of here. They are headquartered near here, near enough that you might know of them." No one said anything. "It cannot be easy, living so close to dangerous men. If you tell us where they are, we will ensure that they arc never a danger to you again."

"Four of you?" a man scoffed. "What can a woman, two men and one knight do to help us?"

"We are all knights, though not all of us wear armour." Illyria said levelly. *Despite what Gennald thinks.* "We are more dangerous than we appear."

He had not actually apologised to her. It made her angry when she had a chance to think about it, but somehow in Gennald's presence the conversation she needed to have with him never happened. She always became...distracted.

"You all are knights?" the same man asked, openly guffawing. Laughter echoed through the square. "A woman who acts like a man, a pretty boy, and that one too scrawny to hold a sword? You call yourselves knights? What daft lord would ever take you into his service?"

She knew that this would happen, but that did not lessen the moment's sting.

"We are the Knights of Anduilon," she repeated, as much as to Gennald as to the villagers. "We have sworn to uphold justice for all and were given this mission by King Lionar himself. We are vouched for by the Lord of the Northern March and accompanied by his First Knight, as a sign of his trust. We *can* help you," she looked in the faces of the doubters across from her, willing them to feel her sincerity. "But only if you help us."

They still didn't trust her, she could see that and, as frustrating as it was, she couldn't blame them for it.

"I am Sir Gennald Hanley, First Knight of the Northern March," Gennald declared. "You know as well as I what horrors the Dragonfleet have inflicted on our kingdom in years past, and you also know that our king has paid these villains tribute in order to safeguard his people from their evil. You think you are safe, here in your village a hundred miles from the coast, but you are wrong. We cannot give the Dragonfleet the wheat they ask for, and now the gold we would give them in its place has been stolen. That leaves one thing that we can give them to keep them from attacking us, and you know what it is: your children."

There were ugly mutterings at that. Gennald was a good speaker, and he certainly looked dashing enough in his mail and surcoat, but that made him no better a knight than she.

"If the king gives the command to his lords to gather up five hundred children, where do you think they will take them from?" Gennald continued. "Not from their own families, and not from the cities where they live. Think on who your lord is, and think on where he would go to find children who would not be missed. He would get from here, or places like it: small villages off the main roads. You might escape unscathed this year, or even the next, but sooner or later, knights would ride into this village and take your children. Your future, your flesh and blood, taken off in a dragonship's hold never to be seen again and all because you *would not help us*."

Sephana watched as a scruffy, ill kempt villager slipped out of town and moved furtively into the forest. The possibility that he happened to choose this particular moment for a walk—just minutes after Illyria gave her big speech—was a bet she wasn't going to take. She stood silently and prepared to follow him.

"I do not like the idea of you going alone," Theramus whispered.

Sephana glanced at her hunched, disapproving friend and smiled. "You don't do sneaky very well, Big Blue. You know that this has to be just me." She patted his shoulder.

"I know, but I do not have to like it. If you find yourself in danger—any danger at all—simply yell and I will move land and sky to find you."

She gave him a brief, impulsive hug; something she couldn't have done even two months ago. She knew that he loved her—although not in any kind of gross, romantic way—and she felt so privileged for it. It made all of the stares, whispers and occasional kidnapping attempts worth it. She didn't feel ashamed of who she was when she was with him. "I'll be fine," she whispered in his big, cauliflower ear before slipping out of the concealing screen and following the suspicious villager with the silence of, well, a snake.

She did her best to focus on the hunt, and to not think about Illyria and Gennald in the village. She didn't know what she should feel when those two were together. Sure, Gennald had apologised, but his words had carried as much sincerity as a rancid fart. Why was he still with them, other than the obvious, and, more importantly, why was Illyria letting him get away with it?

The more she thought about it, the angrier she got. The best thing to do then, since she couldn't change anything, was to not think about it.

Think about the mission, nothing else. Follow that villager and find out where he goes. It had to be enough. It had to.

Illyria and the others spent a frustrating hour vainly trying to gain the confidence of the villagers of New Wighton, to no avail. No one would admit to the existence of any outlaws, to say nothing of giving up information against them. Gennald's fear inducing speech had caused a few guilty looks, but nothing more. It seemed that Sephana had been right, which Illyria found saddening.

"Excuse me, err, milady?"

Illyria turned. Hidden between two wattle and daub houses was an older, attractive woman with chestnut hair and hazel eyes. She retreated from any curious eyes and motioned for Illyria to follow. Illyria followed her cautiously—it was a perfect place for an ambush—but no dangers presented themselves.

"Are you really hunting outlaws?" the woman asked, her eyes darting.

"We are." Illyria hid her smile of triumph. "We're hoping to find someone brave enough to help us, someone who might know something."

The woman snorted. "I'm no brave one, believe you me."

"There are many kinds of bravery," Illyria assured her. "What's your name?"

"They call me Derra, Derra Heatherwood. My husband's name is Linden and we own the public house." A public house, Illyria had learned, was what Karalmen sometimes called a tavern. Derra's voice quieted to a whisper. "My husband's a good man, Emuranna bless him, but not the sharpest knife in the drawer, if you get my meaning. I think he's gone and got himself involved in something dangerous."

Derra the public house owner's wife proceeded to tell Illyria about how her husband, on hard times like everyone else in the village, had started meeting with mysterious strangers sometime in the last year and that, shortly after, he had begun acting strangely. He started keeping secrets, forbade Derra from entering the brewing shed and going out at all hours of the night, but became snappish and angry when she asked him about it.

He paid his taxes in full and in cash, unlike most of the villagers of New Wighton who could only give goods or services instead.

"He got beaten something fierce this last spring, about a week after those late snows caused the roof on the brewing shed to collapse, but he said he just fell down the stairs going to the cellar." She snorted. "I love the man, but he's a dog-faced idiot if he thinks I'd ever buy such an obvious lie. My father was a drunkard and a brawler, Lady Illyria. I know a beating when I see one."

The older woman clutched Illyria's hands. "Can you protect him, My Lady? My Linden is a good man, I swear by Emuranna that he is, and if he's helping these men that stole the tribute money then it's against his will. He didn't do any wrong, not by his choice." Her words rang with sincerity. "I'll help you catch these outlaws, but only if you swear by the goddess that you won't hurt or arrest my husband."

Illyria could not help but be touched. It was impossible for her not to compare herself to the older woman. Would she be as devoted in a similar circumstance? "Your love for your husband does you much credit, Mrs Heatherwood," she said. "to stand by him so despite what he has done to you."

Derra shrugged. "He can be an idiot, but he's mine and I'd have it no other way. Will you help him?"

Others in the group might disagree with her—Gennald especially—but Illyria could not help but be swayed. "How can I not, after you have pleaded his case passionately?"

"Thank you, My Lady. Thank you." Derra squeezed Illyria's hands again, then gave one more furtive glance to see if they were being observed. Once satisfied that they were alone, she drew Illyria in closer. "You can't tell anyone I told you this. These men, they're dangerous, and they have spies in the village; I am sure of it. He didn't know I was near, or he would never have said it, but I heard my Linden telling one of the men from the forest that he'd have what they wanted on the first night of SummersEnd. He said it'd be 'in the usual place'."

"Where is the usual place?" Illyria asked her, excitement building.

"Linden mentioned about it being safer now, since the roof was rebuilt. It has to be the brewing shack."

Members of the elusive band of outlaws would be in New Wighton on the first night of SummersEnd, two days from now. Finally, after a week of frustrating escapes and dead ends, they had something solid. It took all of Illyria's will not to break out singing.

She settled for smiling instead. "That is very good, Derra. Thank you. For your sake and your husbands, both of you need to stay far away from the public house that night. Can you do that?"

She snorted. "We may be a small village, My Lady, but we know how to do SummersEnd right. Linden's giving ten barrels of his best beer for everyone to drink, and I guarantee you that there won't be a drop left come morning. Mark my words, everyone in the village and from miles around, my husband and I included, will be in the green dancing, drinking, and making fools of ourselves." She glanced around one more time. "I should be getting back before anyone starts asking questions. Thank you again, My Lady. You are as kind as you are beautiful." She turned to leave.

"Derra, can I ask you a personal question?"

"If you wish," Derra answered cautiously. "You've earned the right, I dare say."

"Your husband," Illyria began, already embarrassed. "You love him, that is obvious, but do you *like* him?"

Her eyebrows rose. "Like him? Of course. He's my Lindy."

"Even though he lies from you and keeps secrets?"

Derra scoffed. "Oh, I know he's not perfect, My Lady. I'm just as bad as he, in my own way, but he's worked hard to keep a roof over our head these last twenty years and helped me raise three children. He's a good man, in spite of his being an idiot sometimes, and that's enough for me."

Illyria thought carefully on Derra's words. "Thank you for your frankness."

The older woman's eyes gleamed in mischief. "And who are you in love with, My Lady? The handsome elf lord that is never far from your side?"

Illyria blushed. "That is my brother."

She chuckled. "Oh, if I were twenty years younger... So is it the knight then, the one who's so busy scowling at everyone? He's very handsome."

Illyria could not help but laugh at the description. "Sir Gennald is my companion, that is all." It sounded weak, even to her own ears. She couldn't meet Derra's eyes.

"Companions, hmm?" Derra cackled. It was beyond propriety for her to speak to her so, but Illyria had opened that honey pot all by herself. "The blush on your cheeks tells me its more than that, at least to you."

"Thank you for your cooperation, Mrs. Heatherwood," Illyria rushed out. "I wouldn't want to put you any more at risk. Excuse me."

Knowing chuckles followed her as she left.

"Where were you?" Gennald demanded as Illyria finally reappeared in the village square. "We thought you had been abducted, attacked, or worse."

She didn't seem troubled by his agitation. "We?" she asked, a mischievous smile on her lips and her eyes a warm, rich brown.

It wasn't the response he was expecting. "Err, yes. We were." He looked to Balien standing beside him for support, but the enigmatic elf just raised his eyebrow in a mirror of his sister. "Well, I was worried."

His anger disappeared completely when she leaned forward and kissed him. "Thank you for worrying."

He tried to speak but no words could form. What did one say to that?

She turned to brother. "I think we've finally got the break we needed. At least one of the outlaws will be coming here for supplies on the first night of SummersEnd."

"It's a good lead, if it's true," he agreed. "Do you trust your source?"

"I do."

He nodded. "We should make a more permanent camp then." He gave her and Gennald an approving nod before leaving the square.

Gennald stepped in closer to her, alone with her despite an entire village surrounding them. She looked up through her lashes and smiled invitingly, her eyes lightening to green even as he watched. When he pulled her against him she gave no resistance.

"Three days?" he whispered hoarsely. His body burned where it touched hers. "Nothing is going to happen for three whole days?"

He saw her eyes follow the length of his mouth while her tongue enticingly traced along her lips. "We're hunting, Gennald, just like before: no fires, no talking."

Three days hidden behind a camouflaged screen, close enough to her to touch; it would be either torture or paradise. He leaned his head down, close enough to feel her ragged breath against his throat. "We don't need to talk to be together," he growled just before he kissed her.

He wasn't surprised when, sometime later, she pushed him away. "Not yet," She breathed, "and not in the hide."

She hadn't said 'no', just 'not yet'. "When? Where?" If he wasn't a knight he would have dragged her off to the nearest cottage and made such questions irrelevant.

She rested her forehead against his chest and he eagerly inhaled the smell of her hair. "Not while we hunt. After." She looked up. "I swear, after."

Somehow, he was still able to think. "How do you celebrate SummersEnd in your elf kingdom?"

Her brow furrowed, clearly not expecting this question. "The same as you do. Dancing. Feasting."

"Celebrate it with me, here," he asked. "All strangers are welcome at SummersEnd; they cannot deny us. Your brother can track alone for one night. You won't be needed."

She didn't refuse, which gave him hope.

"It would be best if we had someone inside the village to watch, wouldn't it?" he pressed. "Just in case?"

He could see her starting to weaken. "I want to see you in a dress, Illyria. I want to dance with you and hold you in my arms. I want to have the last dance with you and only you. Don't you want that, too? Doesn't the need for it burn in you like it does in me?"

Her eyes were wide, somewhere between blue and green.

"It does. I do." She broke out into a blinding smile. "We will. Balien will be fine without me for one night." She held up a warning finger. "But nothing can happen until then. Nothing, Gennald. I mean it."

He grinned so broadly that he thought it would split his face. Finally, an end to this exquisite torture was in sight. He only had to wait three more days...trapped next to her, unable to touch and under the angry glares of the others.

"I don't know if I can," he admitted. "I'm not that strong."

Oh, she liked that. "Go back to the main camp and take the others with you. A two person hide would be better anyway. Harder to spot."

Yes, he could do that. Barely. It was going to be the longest three days of his life.

CHAPTER FOURTEEN

" 'Being a Ranger is a hard life, and not for everyone. You'll often find yourself tired, cold, hungry and alone. A Ranger puts his duty first and foremost. He lives in the shadows and doesn't care about glory. His achievements will never be celebrated and his death, should it happen, will likely be unheralded. There is no dishonour in realizing that this is not the life for you.' "

—The customary warning given to would-be Rangers of Ilthanara

Eldoth walked in a trance. He was aware enough of his surroundings not to stumble off the road, but his companion's sporadic attempts at conversation were so much droning his ears.

Illyria and Balien had left New Wighton with them before doubling back and concealing themselves in order to observe both the brewing shed behind the tavern and the path to the tree where the informer had left his message. Secrecy was paramount this close to a populated area but, while Illyria had suggested that the others leave in order to report to the group of knights assigned to them, Eldoth knew the true reason: she did not trust them not to reveal their presence.

Eldoth didn't mind the multi-day make-work project. He had already recently endured a very similar hardship, and, while he could do so again, if there was an alternative—any alternative—he was happy to take it.

The four of them were walking openly down the main forest road. If any outlaw was foolish enough to attack them, not only were they confident that they could handle themselves, but they would welcome the opportunity to capture some prisoners. While he knew that neither he nor Sephana were physically imposing, they were travelling in the company of an eight foot tall, muscle bound giant wielding a ten foot staff as well as an armoured knight. From what Eldoth had gathered about their quarry, they were not stupid and was confident he and his fellow knights would arrive at their destination unmolested.

Or, at least, unmolested by outlaws. How they would fair against their alleged allies was another matter entirely.

Eldoth's contemplation of how he would counter an opposing mage's attempt to limit his magic (a difficult conundrum, considering his limited contact with opposing mages) was interrupted by the sound of approaching hoof beats.

Or, rather, by Sephana squeezing his shoulder painfully once she became aware of them.

Gennald recognised the four horsemen coming towards them and was glad for their company. He disliked marching at the best of times, and the current times were less than stellar. The torture of being apart from Illyria notwithstanding, the cold shoulder he was receiving from the three non-elven 'knights' was positively glacial. The idea of spending a whole day of frigid silence in their company was more than unpleasant. He would have abandoned them and returned to New Aukaster and his Lord but for his promised reward on SummersEnd. For Illyria, he would endure any hardship; even the wrath of her companions.

The approaching knights were all in the service of Count Fordham, a Golden Bear. They had served under him last year in the Northmarch, but, being landed knights, had resented taking orders from a mere yeoman. It amused Gennald that, during their forty days of royal service this year, they now found themselves under the command of a female outlander 'knight' whose claims of nobility could not be proven. Being good knights, they would serve obediently, but he knew that they rankled.

They came to a halt twenty feet away. Gennald took a quick moment to admire their finely-crafted mail and well-tended surcoats. Such luxuries could only ever be a dream for the likes of him, and admiration from afar was as close as he could ever get. Their leader, Sir Wilton, did not remove his helm before lifting his empty hand in greeting. It was how unaligned knights hailed each other, not allies as they were.

He looked down from his horse and gave a curt nod. "Sir Gennald, we did not expect to see you on this road. Is all well?"

"Sir Wilton, greetings," Gennald replied, matching their incivility with his own. "All is well. We have been searching in the forest and are returning to the main camp for resupply. Do you have any news from the capital? How fares the king?"

None of the knights, Gennald noted, greeted or even acknowledged the existence of Theramus or the others. Wilton dropped his hand and showed no signs of dismounting. "The king is unchanged. He prepares for his last days on this world. You should prepare for it as well. Things will be much different under King Ander."

Gennald stiffened. "I did not think there were any Anderites among the king's knights."

Wilton shrugged. "It is obvious which way that flag will fall. Anyone with eyes can see that Lionar is too ill to survive his Joining. Mark my words: Prince Ander will be king before the end of the week, and only a fool wouldn't prepare for it."

"It doesn't matter what happens when Lionar joins with the land," Gennald said stiffly. "Until he does, he is our king and worthy of our loyalty. Obeying him is still your duty."

"Don't lecture me about duty, yeoman. I will obey it to the letter for as long as Lionar lives and waste my time chasing ghosts in these forests if he so orders, but expect things to be different under Ander." His eyes flicked briefly over Eldoth and Sephana. "These charlatans you associate with will be treated much differently. You would do well to distance yourself from them."

"Hey!" Sephana yelled. "We're right here!"

His only reply was a bitter chuckle. "If there is nothing else, Sir Gennald, we must resume our entirely pointless patrol. Good journey."

Gennald bit back his angry reply. "It would save us time if one of you could ride to camp and have one of your squires return with horses."

The knight looked down on him. "It is wrong that a knight should walk. I have one spare horse that I can share with you, Sir Gennald, in remembrance of our shared times in the Northmarch."

Gennald knew that such an offer came with strings. He shouldn't accept. Not only did he not like these three knights, but he did not agree with them. However, he *was* tired of walking, and it wasn't like Sephana could dislike him anymore than she already did. Really, what did he owe any of them? In a week, this Anderite/Golden Bear business would be over in one way or the other. Why not spare himself some discomfort?

"Very well, I accept." Ignoring the look of surprise on Sir Wilton's face and the disappointment on Theramus's, Gennald vaulted onto the free horse and braced himself an afternoon of bland faced lies.

"What a jerk!" Sephana said as she glared at the retreating horsemen.

"Who?" Eldoth asked. "Gennald or the others?"

"All of them."

"Their noble bloodlines do not justify such rude behaviour," Theramus said.

"Their advice remains valid," Eldoth pointed out. "We would be wise to prepare for the possibility that Lionar will fail and his son claims the throne. What will happen to us if that does occur?"

"Our knighthood would not be recognised, certainly," Theramus speculated. "We would likely face arrest."

"They can try," Sephana said.

"We are difficult to imprison," Theramus agreed. "It is more likely that we will be exiled."

Sephana didn't care; not right now. Not paying attention to the others, she pointed herself down the road and resumed walking. They still had half a day of walking ahead of them; five hours with nothing to do but think.

She didn't want to think; not right now. Everything she had seen today, from the houses in the village to the casual disdain of the knights, brought back painful echoes of a time she desperately wanted to forget.

"You're not taking what they say seriously, are you?" It was Eldoth, looking oddly concerned. "They're ignorant buffoons."

"No, it's not that, or maybe it is." She didn't trust his uncharacteristic moment of sincerity. She didn't trust *him*. "I don't want to talk about it."

He nodded but didn't go away. She made it more obvious. "Go away, Eldoth."

"There's a flaw in your logic," he said instead.

Sephana rubbed her hand across her headscales. She knew what he really meant when he said that: he wanted to bring up some earlier argument that he had lost. He'd been mulling it over in his head for Goddess-knows how long and now had a counterargument. What he never seemed to realize was that none of their arguments had never been about logic.

She sighed. "What was the flaw?"

"The night of the blackshield attack, before we left New Aukaster, you stated that I used fire as a weapon because I enjoyed causing pain. I do not. It is simply the most effective weapon in my arsenal."

He wants to get into this now? Fine. If he wanted a fight, she'd give him one.

"Really? I saw your face when you burned Draxul to death. You were grinning like the mummers were in town."

His face darkened. "You are mistaken. That was...far from a pleasurable experience."

"I know what I saw, Eldoth. I know you." Her mind's eye recalled the hideous grin that had twisted his features and the sadistic gleam in his eyes as the dying lizardman had smoked and burned.

"No. There is no logic to retribution."

Sephana had to laugh. "It wasn't about logic. Draxul hurt you and you wanted him to suffer. And you did."

"I admit to being angry," he said after a long pause.

He was giving her a headache. "No, you were furious," she corrected. "And when you get that mad, you get *mean*. You always have. The only difference between then and now is that now you can do something about it."

"I..." he faltered, both confusion and annoyance crossing his features. "I need to consider this," he continued in a weak voice.

Translation: she'd won. At the moment, she didn't care. She quickened her stride, trying to escape everything that was bothering her but knowing that it was impossible. For that, she'd have to leave the kingdom. And change the past while she was at it.

"Would you like to talk about what is troubling you?" Theramus asked, his long legs easily keeping up with her.

"Nothing's bothering me," she lied.

"These last few days have been quite stressful," he rumbled. "All of this covert movement and enforced proximity can be quite frustrating. I have felt it myself."

"It's not that," she paused. "Well, kind of. It's not making anything any better, but that's not what's bugging me."

"Then what is?"

She gestured with her hands to indicate everything around her. "It's that village, this valley, the time of year; they remind me of things."

"Of when you were last in Karalon, before we met."

"Is it that obvious?"

"To one who knows you, yes," he said. "I observed your increasing unease the moment we entered the heartland."

"It's stupid. It shouldn't matter. It happened years ago." She looked up at him. "I'm a different person now. I am!"

"Our past forms the foundation of our present," Theramus said. "we cannot escape it. Acknowledge it, yes, and learn from it, but we cannot forget it."

She blanched. "But I don't want to. My past is just...pain. I hurt myself." She glanced guiltily at Eldoth. "I hurt other people. I don't want to live that again. I can't."

"Such feelings are like disease: they linger, fester and poison everything around them. If you do not accept the errors of your past and come to terms with them, they will infect every aspect of your life until you are incapable of feeling anything else. I have seen it happen, Sephana, too many times, and I do not wish that fate for you."

His words echoed in her mind. He was right; she *was* infected.

"We are your friends, Sephana," Theramus continued, his patience and gentleness like that of a god. "You can share your burdens with us. That is what friendship is, to say nothing of the vows we share and the purpose that unites us. I dislike seeing you in such pain."

"I...I can't." There was no blinking away her tears now; they were streaming openly down her face. "I can't be who you want me to be, Theramus." She couldn't. Not here, not walking down a road with Eldoth listening. "Just let it go, ok. I'll get over this. I just need a bath and a hot meal. I'll be fine."

"As you wish," he said sadly. "My offer remains, but if you do not wish to talk to me, then please talk to someone."

She didn't say anything, just increased her pace until she was too far away to talk.

They walked in silence for a half hour, insignificant compared to the golden splendour of the tree filled valley. Sephana still strode stiff-legged ahead of the rest of them, isolating herself from her friends within her cocoon of bitter memories. If Theramus thought it would do any good, he would have shaken her until the melancholy that afflicted her had no choice but to flee her body.

If only such things were possible. His hands were powerful enough to rend steel, but they could not heal the spirit of one he loved as much as his own children. What was the point of his having knowledge, wisdom, and power if he could not use it to help those who were dear to him?

"His name was Sir Edrik and I loved him," he heard Sephana say quietly. She had slowed until she walked next to him, though her eyes remained fixed forward.

Theramus, afraid to break the spell, said nothing.

"He said he was a knight, but I guess he was a blackshield," she said. "I had only been in Karalon a few months, less than a year after I left Eldoth."

The wizard in question opened his mouth to speak but Theramus shook his head in warning. After a moment, the man subsided.

"I was a servant to one of the Akkilinian noble women that fled the coup. None of the Karalmen liked us, but we had money and that bought us some respect. It also made us targets. The family I was travelling with was robbed by some bandits. Sir Edrik stopped them, then took pity on us and offered his hospitality."

She brushed her hair back, so that her Reshai heritage was plainly visible. "I was still hiding who I was then. He thought I was just a girl. He didn't care that I was a servant; he just liked me, and I liked him. He was a landed knight, related to some duke, but he wasn't a jerk like those guys we just met." She blinked back tears. "I stayed behind when the others left. I took off my headscarf and he didn't care. We loved each other."

Eldoth's face clouded in anger and Theramus gave him a strong look of warning.

"He thought there was something suspicious about all the outlaw activity going on in the Deremwood. They knew too much. But before he could find anything, he was accused of high robbery by Count Attenham—yes, the same one—and became a blackshield, but he was innocent. I *know* he was. The two of us and some of his men fled into the forest. We were in the Upper Deremwood—about fifty miles from here—and we lived in the forests there for almost a year. Edrik was determined to prove that Attenham had framed him and he almost did, but then I screwed up and got him killed.

"I was getting supplies in a little village that might as well have been New Wighton. It had the same buildings, the same people; the same *everything*." He voice dropped to a whisper. "It was spring, I was happy and I got careless. My headscarf fell off, the villagers got scared and I tried to run but there were too many." Her face darkened in hate. "They chained me to a post, stripped me naked and left me hanging there for *two days*. They yelled at me, poked me with sticks and threw every disgusting thing they could find at me. They had a 'trial', if you could call it that, and found me guilty of everything every Djido had ever done."

Theramus was sickened. He had seen similar things and pitied those whose imaginations were so small. What Theramus disliked most of all was how Sephana casually described the cruelties that had been done to her, as if such behaviour was *normal.*

"I was sentenced to death, of course. They would have burned me at the stake if not for Edrik." She swallowed. "He and his men found me and attacked the town just as they were about to torch me. They rescued me, but they didn't know that it was a trap. Count Attenham had found out somehow that Edrik and his 'notorious band of outlaws' consorted with snake women. When he'd heard that I had been caught, he sent his men to the town in secret. I got away—after all, I was just the bait—but Edrik and everyone else were killed. Attenham was hailed as a hero."

Images of Sephana and the knight she had allegedly loved rattled through Eldoth's mind. He didn't know why he was so angry.

"You cooked and cleaned for him?" he asked her. "Willingly?"

"I didn't mind, for him." She shrugged. "You do stupid things when you're in love with someone; things you'd never think of doing for anyone else."

"You always act moronically," he spat out. "Who was the lucky fellow during our marriage?"

"Not you," she growled even as Theramus rushed to intervene.

"You aren't the only woman I was with, either," Eldoth said, needing to hurt her.

"What?" she looked tired and confused. Her scales were dull and her tail dragged in the dust of the road.

"There was a woman I stayed with, during my time in Tirim," he continued. "Her name was Mariska. She cooked and cleaned for me very well, and never complained about it. I found her a refreshing change."

Sephana glanced at him briefly before resuming her stare down the road. "I don't care, Eldoth."

That only served to make him angrier. "She was very beautiful, and performed her other tasks as well, most dutifully."

"I'm glad you found someone to do your laundry for you," she said dully.

"I wasn't referring to laundry," he told her with a leer.

What am I doing? What does any of this matter?

She glared at him. "I know exactly what you were talking about, and *I don't care.* It's not my business what some Tirimar girl with really bad judgement did to you or for you. It's been four years, Eldoth. A lot happened to both of us."

Before he could say anything else—what was he trying to say, anyway?—a large, spade-like hand fell onto his shoulder. "That is enough," Theramus announced even as he physically forced the wizard away. "This is not a conversation that she needs at this time." He stared at Eldoth, his massive mouth and jaw set into a large frown. "If you wish to impress me with your worth, you must first *act* worthy. Getting petty revenge upon Sephana because you feel betrayed does not speak well of you."

"I am *not* getting petty revenge," Eldoth protested. "And she and I have dealt with the matter of her abandoning me."

"That is not the betrayal I speak of," Theramus said.

"I...I was making conversation," Eldoth insisted aloud, knowing that he was lying.

"You may tell that lie to yourself if it gives you comfort, but you will not say it aloud to her. Is that understood?"

Eldoth stopped and glared. "I am not lying, to myself or anyone else."

"As you wish," Theramus replied noncommittally.

Illyria crawled backwards and tapped Balien on the shoulder, indicating that he should replace her in the 'window' of their hiding place. He nodded wordlessly and fox-crawled into the small hole they had made in the copse of bayberry shrubs they had selected as their hide. There was barely enough room for the two of them between the tight, scratchy bushes, but that was for the best: no one would ever think to look for them here. It was tight, uncomfortable, infested with insects, and stank from the animal musk they had dribbled around the outside edges to mask their scent. It would be their home for the next three days.

The Bear and the Thistle

She squirmed into the Balien-sized depression that still held the warmth of his body and stared up at the sky. She would have slept if she could. That was the problem: she had too much time on her hands with nothing to do except think. To a ranger on the watch, thinking was the enemy. Proper observation required focus: to be aware of everything around you without being drawn in by any one thing. It was hard work and mentally draining. No one could keep it up for more than a few hours. She and Balien had switched off countless times over the course of the last day and would do so again until the job was done.

Balien had been on watch twice as long as she had. She just couldn't keep her mind focussed; left to its own devices, her thoughts invariably returned to Gennald: his voice, his smell, the line of his jaw, the way he tasted when they kissed...to say nothing of the promise she had made and where she was going to be in two days. He wanted to share the last dance with her. She didn't know what that meant in Karalon, but in Ilthanara there was a saying: the last dance only ended when with the sun rose the next morning.

The thought of spending the night with Gennald gave her shivers. It also shattered her concentration and brought her period on watch to an abrupt end. As embarrassing as it was to be so useless, it was better than allowing their quarry to escape. Her stepfather, Britheon, had impressed very strongly upon her and Balien that duty always came first. A ranger was only as good as his word, and if said ranger could not perform a job to the best of his (or her) ability, then he should withdraw.

She knew that she was being unfair to Balien. He had bad days, too, sometimes, and, when he did, she was there to support him. He was her brother, and they had worked as closely as two people could for all of their lives. It was a bond that not even her frightening hunger for Gennald could weaken.

The wind picked up and the sound of the leaves rustling made her think of how Gennald's hands had sounded as they slid over her tunic. Illyria closed her eyes and shivered at the mental image. *What am I going to do? I have two more days to wait.*

Two days. She'd be lucky if she could stand watch for ten minutes at a time by then.

CHAPTER FIFTEEN

" 'Knights Errant.' They just started appearing one day, like worms on the ground after a hard rain. They claim no masters and spend their time wandering the countryside searching for things to slay and maidens to rescue, all for the sake of their honour. The Knights of Anduilon were the first, going on about how they served ideals and not men, but they were far from the last. Now, you can't turn around without running into one band or another, each acting more righteous than the last. This kingdom has fallen into disgrace, let me tell you, and it's all their fault. Things were different in my day. Being a knight meant something then."

—Anonymous

Sephana didn't know if it was funny that she was actually happy to return to New Wighton, or sad. The last two days, spent in the company of a score of surly Karalinian knights, had been torture. The only thing preventing them from harming her was the king's edict and Big Blue's glaring bulk. She'd rely on the latter until WatersEnd, but the former might not extend past tomorrow evening. It was the first day of SummersEnd, and the question of Lionar's fitness would be answered, one way or another, tomorrow night.

Even the most loyal of Golden Bears were beginning to doubt their king's fitness and beginning to wonder what would happen if he did fail. Sephana had seen what happened to those who chose the wrong side in a civil war. She had left Akkilon in the company of those who had wisely chosen flight, but many others had been executed.

She had said maybe five words to Gennald, all of them about horses. She still couldn't look at him without getting angry. *'You're not a knight,'* he'd said. No one, not even Eldoth, had hurt her so much in so few words in a very long time. As much as she tried to convince herself that his opinion didn't matter anymore than a horse dropping, she couldn't. She'd shared his company for more than a month. He'd taught her how to ride a horse. He was romantically involved with Illyria. For that, if no other reason, she wanted to find a way to, if not *like* him, then at least not hate him.

He had been ridden out alone early this morning, wearing his finest clothing. Sephana, Eldoth, and Theramus had followed at a more reasonable hour, and had arrived outside the bustling village in early afternoon.

The green outside New Wighton was filled with people erecting tents, tables, and decorations. They all seemed happily ignorant of the perils threatening to befall them and Sephana couldn't help but envy them. She was pretty sure that happiness was going to be in short supply pretty soon.

While she and the others had been training, eating hot food, and sleeping in warm tents, Balien and his sister had been trapped inside a tiny clump of bushes with no comforts at all. The only thing stopping Sephana from being totally wracked with guilt was that they had willingly chosen their task and had told Sephana and the others to go.

One more person wandering around the village today wouldn't be noticed. Still unwilling to betray the location of Balien and Illyria, Sephana walked quietly along the path. She was still out of sight of the village, she hoped, but plainly visible to Balien and Illyria. She loitered at a junction in the path and stared pointedly down towards the creek before making her way down there.

Illyria joined her ten minutes later. She looked soiled and tired, but her expression brightened when she saw the bag that Sephana carried. Sephana had tried to think of what someone who had been hiding in a bush for three days would want and the answer had been clean clothes, a bar of soap, and food as fresh and as warm as she could manage. She was curious which Illyria would use first.

The food won out, but only barely. Illyria hadn't even finished half of the warm gruel before she stripped down and jumped into the water.

Sephana eyed the dirty pile of clothing uneasily. They really did stink. "So was all that watching worth it? Did you find anything?"

Illyria, alternately soaping and dunking her hair, shook her head. "There was plenty of activity in the brewing shed, but nothing unusual considering the festival tonight. No one carried anything strange into or out of it, and no one entered the town from up the mountain."

"Nothing?" Sephana couldn't keep dismay from her voice. "SummersEnd is tonight! The king joins with the land tomorrow. How can we not have anything more than when we started?"

Illyria scrubbed herself down quickly and thoroughly. "We know that the outlaws are operating near here. We've tracked them to within a mile of this village three different times. We just don't know where they go." She frowned. "Or how we keep losing them."

"It feels like nothing," Sephana muttered.

"The meeting I was told about is supposed to happen tonight," Illyria reminded her. "We can't say whether we've succeeded or failed until after the festival."

Sephana frowned. She had to say it. "If tonight is so important, why are you spending it in the village with Gennald?"

Illyria reddened. Her eyes looked for somewhere—anywhere—to settle on that wasn't Sephana's face.

"With the festivities tonight, it's the only time we can observe inside the village without attracting notice." Still not looking at Sephana, she quickly slid into the clean clothes that had been thoughtfully brought for her.

"Really? Because it looks to me like you just want an excuse to dance and hold hands with him."

Illyria didn't reply—what could she say that wouldn't damn her as either a hypocrite or a liar?—and focussed on drying her hair. She couldn't see Sephana through the towel but felt her eyes burn into her just the same.

"Have you spoken with Gennald?" she asked casually a minute later. 'Did he talk about me' was what she had wanted to ask, but it seemed too juvenile to say out loud.

Sephana shrugged and looked away. "Not much."

"He's not a bad person," Illyria defended. It sounded inadequate.

"Hmmm," Sephana said with absolutely no sincerity. Illyria could see her jaw tightening from the effort of keeping mouth shut.

The need to defend Gennald was automatic. "I know you two had some disagreements—"

"He called me a snakespawn!" Sephana snapped, hurt radiating from her eyes. "He said we weren't knights."

Just hearing the words felt like a dagger to the chest. She didn't want to have to defend Gennald's behaviour in this. Sephana was entirely justified, and yet here Illyria was, apologising. "I know that he said that, but..."

"But what?" Sephana demanded. "He's got a cute chin? You like him? I understand that, but these next two days are really important. Why do this now?"

"He's..." She stopped. Those weren't the words she wanted to say. "I love him." It was the first time she'd said it out loud. It wasn't the relief that she'd thought it would be.

Sephana's eyes widened in shock. "Oh."

"I know that tonight makes no sense, I know that. We might be criminals tomorrow. The king might die. I don't know what I'm doing." She was babbling now; she knew she was and yet she was unable to stop. It was like a dam had been unstoppered and a whole spring's melt now poured out her mouth. "I'm scared and I'm excited and...and I want one night. One night for everything to be normal. I know I'm being selfish and that you don't like him and I'm sorry, but can you help me with this? Please?"

She finally ran out of words and just stared at Sephana, beseeching. She'd never needed another woman as a friend as much as she needed Sephana now.

After a long, long moment, Sephana smiled. "Of course."

The Bear and the Thistle

The strains of music from the village were faint but still audible. Sephana had gone off to help Illyria with something, leaving Eldoth alone with Theramus and a half dozen horses. The sun hung low in the sky and, in Eldoth's judgement, the ritual harvesting had probably come to an end. The true festival of SummersEnd, with all of the feasting, dancing, and ritual burning that it entailed, was likely about to begin.

In front of him, Theramus paced.

"Do Noss even celebrate human holidays?" Eldoth asked, as much to break the tedium as for any other reason.

Theramus looked down at him in mild surprise. "Of course. My people have lived on Anshara for more than fifteen centuries and venerate Emuranna just as you do. If anything, we have more to be grateful for, as she gave us sanctuary after we forsook Maskim."

Eldoth was curious. "And how would you be able to tell that?"

Theramus shrugged. "She allows us to exist. We breed true, even after all this time. Interlopers, those races who arrive by gatestone, seldom last more than two or three generations, and those who do usually have weakened blood."

Eldoth leaned forward in interest, his eyes brightening. "That is a fascinating theory. But what of the Djido? They occupied Anshara for centuries."

Theramus sat down facing him. "No Djido remain. Even during the occupation, there were few reports of any being born. They only kept their numbers strong through constant reinforcement from Ijisar. That is why their numbers began to dwindle after the Shieldstone was created and all of the gates were sealed shut."

"Except for the Reshai."

Theramus glared at him. "The Reshai are more human than Djido, and have also bred true for centuries. It obvious that Emuranna does not hold them responsible for the actions of their forefathers." His jaw clenched angrily. "That is why their persecution angers me so. If Emuranna does not punish them for being what they are, then why do her children?"

"But there is a flaw in your logic," Eldoth argued, enjoying this conversation more than any other in months. "What of the Nintarans? They have been here as long as the Djido—longer, in fact—and they breed true as well. In fact, I'd say that they thrive here better than men do. Is their presence also endorsed by Emuranna?"

Theramus hesitated before answering. "That is a common argument in the learning halls of Emilon. I have yet to find an answer that satisfies me."

Eldoth tried to keep his voice sounding casual. "Emilon?"

Theramus closed his eyes momentarily. "The city of the Noss, from where I and all of my kin hale."

"It does exist!" Eldoth exulted. "And there are learning halls, you admitted it. Therefore there must also be libraries, full of books from before the fall of Anduilon!"

"It was a mistake to tell that to you," Theramus said quietly. Well, quietly for him, anyway. "It is forbidden knowledge."

Eldoth was incredulous. "But you possess the accumulated knowledge of the High Kingdom. Even if it is not complete, it is hundreds of times more valuable than gold. You cannot hide it while mankind continues to live in squalor."

Theramus scowled and pushed himself to his feet. "It is not my decision to make, and there are other considerations."

"But we *need* this knowledge," Eldoth insisted, standing as well. He still stood two feet shorter than the giant. "It's ours, and it is a crime to keep it from us."

"No. You *want* this knowledge, to aid you in the study of your magic," Theramus contradicted, looming massively above him, fists clenched. "Your needs are selfish."

It took all of Eldoth's courage not to quail before the being who could kill him with one hand. "My learning magic benefits everyone and, no matter how much you bully me, it will not change the truth."

Theramus took a long, calming breath and relaxed his hands. "It is not my intention to threaten you. I apologise if in my...fervour...that I give that impression." His voice was as gentle as Eldoth had ever heard it. "But this conversation cannot continue. It deals with subjects that I have sworn oaths not to discuss or reveal. I cannot give you the knowledge you seek, Eldoth. I am sorry."

Sephana gave Illyria's appearance a critical once over before finally nodding her approval. It was hard not to be jealous. Illyria's figure was a smooth hourglass, her chest pleasantly full, and her golden hair straight and lustrous: all qualities that Sephana definitely lacked (and Illyria wasn't marred by any ugly patches of scales, or a big tail, either). In spite of all that, though, Sephana found it impossible to resent her.

Maybe it was because her upcoming meeting with Gennald had turned her into brainless idiot.

"Ok, you're ready," she assured Illyria for the third time. "Your hair is brushed, we fixed the dress, you smell like all the berries I gathered and there isn't one speck of dirt on you anywhere."

Illyria bit her lip. "Are you sure?"

It was hard not to scream. Instead she just smiled, not sure if she should be amused or horrified by the transformation that had occurred in front of her. The normally brave, skilled, and deadly Ilthanaran princess that she knew had been replaced by an adolescent teenager.

"Yes," she insisted and, before Illyria could invent yet another excuse, grabbed her by the shoulders and turned her towards New Wighton. "Go. Gennald is waiting for you." She didn't bother with the lie that the two of them were infiltrating the town to observe it from the inside. They both knew exactly what Illyria and Gennald were going to do. She couldn't pretend that she *liked* Gennald, but she could tolerate him for Illyria's sake. Those two had experienced terrible luck recently (for which Sephana knew she was partly to blame), but hopefully tonight would work out better for them. At least one member of the Knights of Anduilon would be happy tonight.

Finally, Illyria squared her shoulders and made her way into the village. Sephana shook her head and gathered up Illyria's belongings. There wasn't much to do now except wait for either Balien or Illyria to bring back word that someone had been spotted. It seemed that she was going to spend SummersEnd in the company of Eldoth, Theramus, and a bunch of horses.

She'd had worse holidays.

She made her way down to the not-so-hidden encampment but stopped when she heard Theramus and Eldoth arguing. *Great.* Just what she didn't want or need right now. There was plenty of forest around. She was pretty sure she could find her own little cubby hole to hide in until something happened.

The villagers had looked askance at Gennald's sudden appearance, but a convenient donation of three gold crowns and a story about a lamed horse had quickly made him a welcome and honoured guest.

"It's good luck to host a stranger on SummersEnd, My Lord," the village leader had assured him. "Are you alone?"

"No," he had replied. "My Lady will be joining me later, once she prepared herself." He hoped that the statement was true. He hadn't seen Illyria in three days. Her decision to join him here had been impulsive and she'd had many opportunities to change her mind. They had arranged to meet at the camp and enter the town together, but Sephana had relayed another message and now he was here, alone, waiting.

He hadn't felt so nervous since he'd been a squire. He was a knight and a leader of men. He'd led mounted charges against armies of dogmen. It was foolish for him to feel this way, and yet he was. He was going to see *her* and, if all went well, finish with his body what his imagination had started two weeks ago.

He didn't think he'd ever wanted anything, not even his knighthood, this much. After all, he'd followed her into this forest on her foolish task. He'd invented a quest just as an excuse to be with her and endured a week in the company of those whose idiotic claims offended his very nature.

"My Lord, may I ask a delicate question?" asked the village leader nervously.

"You may."

"When you were here before, seeking what you were..." the older man wrung his hands nervously. "Did you find anything?"

The outlaws. Gennald chose his words cautiously. "Our search lies elsewhere and will resume after the second day of SummersEnd."

The man let out a sigh of relief. "I am glad to hear that, My Lord. All we want is a simple day of celebration, with no troubles from anyone."

Gennald smiled and clapped him on the back. "I wish that as well. I am here only for the celebration." A lie, but a small one. Certainly Gennald had performed greater affronts against Emuranna and his chivalric code in the last month. If she forgave him those (which he sincerely hoped she did) than she would forgive him this as well.

He was unable to say any more before the sight of Illyria approaching left him dumbstruck.

She was...perfect. She was wearing the same dress that she had on her first night in New Aukaster, and looked far better in it than he recalled. The late summer sun bathed her in its radiance and set her golden hair aglow. By far the most beautiful thing about her was wide, shining smile and eyes, which looked at him and him alone. She looked like a woman in love and she was looking at *him*.

Gennald knew that he could meet Zulum with no regrets, having seen her look at him that way. Well, maybe *one* regret, but he would do his best to remedy that before the end of the evening.

Villagers were stopping and staring as Illyria crossed the green towards him. Gennald was surrounded by silence by the time she finally stood before him. She curtsied gracefully. "Welcome, My Lord," she murmured, her lips promising more.

He bowed courteously and extended his hand. "My Lady. You are as beautiful as Emuranna herself."

She just smiled, her green eyes never leaving his.

"You two are so adorable," squealed an older woman. Someone next to her elbowed her and murmured in her ear and she grimaced. "Forgive me, My Lord and Lady. I meant no insult."

Illyria turned and smiled. "None taken."

The woman relaxed. "You and your lord, are you married? You look very happy together."

"No, we are not, but we are happy together." Only Gennald, incredibly attuned to her body, could see how she stiffened at the question. He thought about how the two of them—young, unmarried and arriving together in a small distant village—must look, and what obvious conclusions the villagers must be making.

He knew that he should be offended on Illyria's behalf, but found that he didn't really care. Did that make him a bad man? A bad knight?

The woman clapped her hands. "Corky! They should be the lords of the festival." The Lord and Lady of Summer, usually a newly married or engaged couple, presided over the SummersEnd festival. A new one was selected every year and being named so was universally seen as a sign of good fortune.

"We're flattered," Illyria said, "but that honour should fall to a local couple. Surely you have already chosen one."

The village leader, who the woman had named 'Corky', shook his head. "No, we insist. Between the blight and all of this business with the king, this year has not been the happiest for us. There have been no new marriages. Our Lords of Summer from last year were set to do it again this year, and everyone knows that's bad luck. You would be doing us all a great service if you accepted."

Illyria looked back at Gennald, who shrugged. The Lord and Lady of Summer were the first to dance and encouraged to kiss and embrace in public. He did not object in the least. "Very well," Illyria said. "We accept."

The woman squealed. "It's Emuranna's will that brought you both here to us today. It's a sign: a sign that all these evils will be vanquished and that next year will be better for us."

It was hard for Gennald to keep his smile on his face. Emuranna hadn't brought them here; his lust had. What kind of event did that portend?

"So which of them is your prime?" Eldoth asked Theramus with annoying insight. "You are a warden, obviously, watching over one or all of them, but which?"

"A warden has only one prime," Theramus answered absently, peering into the bushes.

"Then it must be Sephana," Eldoth concluded. "You watch over her much more than either Balien or Illyria."

She should have returned by now. "Sephana is not my prime. I ceased being a warden decades ago."

"But you were!"

Theramus's jaw tightened. He was revealing more than he meant to and would have to watch his tongue more in the future. "I have never denied it, but, again, you are asking questions that I cannot answer."

"Why?" Frustration filled his voice his voice. "You have the rarest, most precious gift of all: knowledge, and you refuse to share it. I demand to know why."

Demand? "I will say no more." Theramus looked into the forest and frowned. "Where is Sephana? She should have returned by now."

Eldoth shrugged, unconcerned. "Off annoying someone else for a change. Perhaps she is with Balien."

Theramus had heard enough. "Stop concealing your feelings beneath this facade of hurtful behaviour!" Eldoth startled at the sudden outburst. "You are fooling no one and hurting her. Stop it!"

"Concealing? Facade?" A dozen emotions crossed his face. "What in Sheethu's name are you talking about?"

Theramus could see in Eldoth's eyes that he truly did not understand. He shook his head sadly. *Perhaps he is not so intelligent after all.* "Continue with your studies," he said, picking up his staff. "I am going to search for her."

As he left he thought he heard Eldoth mutter something about morons.

Sephana leaned against the trunk mid-way up a large birch tree. She was close enough to hear the merriment from the village green but far enough not to be seen. Her one knee was gathered up to her chest, her tail curled loosely around her hips, while her other foot hung loosely. Sometimes she was proud of her heritage and sometimes she hated it. Her scales were pretty, usually; especially after they had just moulted when they glistened and sparkled like a sunlit stream. Then there was the way they felt when caressed by a lover...

Edrik. She'd been up to whole weeks that she could go without thinking about him, and when she did, as often as not, it was without any of the usual deep, stomach wrenching pain. When she'd become a knight, she'd really thought that she'd put all of that behind her, but then she'd journeyed to New Aukaster and proved herself a liar.

Am I ever going to be over him? Will I ever be able to live my life without being in constant pain?

Being in this village in this valley made it worse, she knew that. Hopefully, it would be better once they found the outlaws and recovered the missing gold. Maybe the new king—if there *was* a new king—would be so impressed by them that he would recognise them anyway.

It seemed like a long shot, but it was possible. It was something to hope for, and right now she needed hope.

Suddenly Sephana found herself laying face first on the ground gasping. Something had her foot—had she been pulled from the tree by it?—and was using it to wrestle her into some sort of hold. She struggled to regain her senses even as her body fought for air.

She rolled onto her back and reached for Dawn's First Crescent at her hip, but it was too late. She saw a brief flash of hazel eyes and dark hair before something struck her face and everything went black.

CHAPTER SIXTEEN

"For every quart of honey, take four quarts of water. Put your water in a clean kettle over the fire and, once it is warm, add the honey. Skim it always until it is very clean, then for every gallon of water, add one pound of blueberries, pigeon berries or some pleasing mix of both. Let them remain in the boiling liquor until they are swollen and soft, take them out and strain all juices and seeds back into the wine. Pour it all through a hair strainer into an empty wooden barrel. Seal the cask for at least thirty days, then open and pour into another barrel, leaving the dregs behind. Add cold, fresh water to the top and seal again. Place the barrel away and do not drink before nine months have passed."

— To Make an Excellent Honeyberry Wine, *Anonymous*

Illyria raised the wooden chalice. "I drink this in honour of Great Sheethu, mother of the gods and sister of the titans, in thanks for her gifts of love and life." She looked over at Gennald and was oblivious to the hundreds of villagers watching her. His eyes, grey like the sea after a storm, never left hers. She took a long drink of the strong, heady wine and passed the cup to her Lord of Summer. Her fingers tingled where they brushed against his.

He looked very handsome, in spite of the woven crown of wildflowers that he wore to signify his role. He raised the cup. "I give thanks to Anur, father of the gods and mightiest of all titans, who created the sun, sky and heavens." He took a deep drink and handed the cup to the village leader, his eyes never leaving hers. "He did what he did for love," he murmured for her ears alone.

Illyria shivered, even as she tried not to remember how the story of Anur and Sheethu ended. Anur had created the cycle of life and death, yes, but he had done so in Sheethu's memory. The Mother of Us All had given her life in the creation of Imusasus, the Wellspring of Souls from which all life derived, and had never lived to share her love with her husband. It was only in Eshumarum, the world beyond death, that the cosmos's first lovers had finally been united.

She hoped that story, and the parts in it that she and Gennald were re-enacting, did not prove prophetic. She did not want love to be her final, eventual reward. She wanted it now, to experience, enjoy, and savour. That wasn't too much to ask for, was it?

"For Anur and Sheethu," murmured the next person down the line as they took their own ritual drink of the potent, flavourful honeyberry wine but Illyria didn't see or care. Her senses only perceived one person and she did her utmost to etch Gennald as he was now into her memory: his sculpted, muscular body, his sharp, musky smell, the rustle of the dried flowers in his hair as he leaned into her, the feel of his strong arms as they wrapped around her.

His taste...

They kissed deeply and intimately, uncaring of the hundred strangers watching them. It was not just for the ritual of SummersEnd that they did this, though it made things easier. Illyria lost herself in the kiss, both aware and not of his body pressing against hers. She could do this forever.

It was only the sound of whistling that brought her out of the moment. Pulling away from Gennald, she could see many villagers grinning and chuckling amongst themselves when not giving loud, two fingered whistles. She could feel her face burning, but refused to be sorry.

"If the Lord and Lady of Summer aren't too busy..."said the village leader with a teasing smile.

"Of course," Illyria murmured, still blushing. She wrapped her hand in Gennald's. She knew the Ilthanaran version of this ceremony, and it didn't seem too different from the Karalinian one. Other than the whistling, maybe. It was an ancient rite, much older than the Great War or the fall of Anduilon. She found the idea that people were still celebrating this same holiday in this same way be reassuring.

"We thank Sheethu and Anur for this great bounty," she said loud enough for everyone in the village to hear. "May it give us food and strength for the times to come."

"So let's eat!" Gennald concluded and everyone laughed. Someone in the back began whistling and the sound was soon repeated.

Illyria was glad of the opportunity and didn't need any more prompting. She and Gennald began another toe-curling kiss and the crowd cheered. She didn't think about outlaws, surveillance or impending civil war. Nothing existed beyond Gennald's arms.

Eldoth scowled while staring at the fire. His hands turned in slow, lazy circles above the burning wood, unaffected by the heat, while the flames spun obediently beneath his outstretched palms. His mind was elsewhere.

What had that muscle-brained giant meant? What concealment? What facade? Whatever Theramus thought he saw, he was wrong. Eldoth felt nothing for his annoying, pest-like ex-wife beyond the requisite concern for a comrade, and even that was an exaggeration. Her tales of woeful love lost meant nothing to him, and neither did the woman herself. He had moved beyond Sephana, her huge, expressive eyes and her lithesome figure. She was in his past—in that way, anyway—and that was that.

He turned his hand palm up and pulled the flame up along with it. Spinning it now with the fingers of his free hand, Eldoth lost himself in the dancing, swirling flames.

All right, yes: he found her attractive. He always had. It was the tool she had used to trick him into marrying her in the first place and he had been young and foolish enough to succumb to it. She had pretended to be obedient and interested in his theories while beguiling him with her slender, sensuous waist and hypnotising, twitching tail. She had remained so until they had passed the period of annulment, and it was only then that she had become the hurtful, shrewish harpy he knew her to truly be. That was when his affection had been transformed into his current bitterness. He had been glad when she had abandoned him. He had gotten his first full night of sleep in a year in his suddenly empty bed, and then his life had changed.

He cupped the flame briefly in both of his hands before pulling them apart. Now two flames danced: one in each palm. He turned both palms outward and spun them in a circle until a ring of fire, existing solely because of his will, hung in the air before him.

Would he ever have become a wizard if she hadn't left him? If he hadn't suddenly had nothing to do other than open the mysterious book that she had given him as a wedding present? Likely not. She would have harried him and tortured him until he tore out his beard in frustration and probably burned the book in an act of spite. He would never have learned his first spell. Never been exposed to the fascinating mysteries of the cosmos.

That, then, was why he no longer hated Sephana. Despite the pain she had caused him—and did, still—he owed her too much. As much as it galled him, he would not be the man he was today without her. There was also the nature of her amazing facility with that fascinating magical dagger of hers. She *had* saved his life on several occasions. Another reason not to hate her.

Crossing his arms across his chest, Eldoth directed the hovering, fuelless ring of fire around the forest clearing but not too close to the tethered horses. Making no motion beyond a slight furrowing of his brow, it collapsed into itself until only a fiery ball remained. Lines extended from its top, bottom and sides until a cross hung before him. Slowly it began to spin.

That, then, was the sum of his current feelings towards Sephana: grudging respect and acknowledgement. While he by no means *liked* her, he could tolerate her. Yes: tolerate. That was a good word.

That giant blue moron has no idea what he is talking about. Happy to have arrived at this conclusion he let the spinning cross of fire vanish into nothingness before turning to rummage into the food bag. It was only by that random, impulsive action that he caught sight of the figure with a bow aimed at him and saw the flash of the arrow as it sped towards him.

The Bear and the Thistle

Illyria danced like a dream.

She didn't know the local dances, but he wasn't too much better. Even the hundred miles between this forest and his native Northmarch was enough for local differences, but they were totally foreign to her. She only had to watch them being done once before she knew them, but even without she was a pleasure to watch. She had the grace of a cat.

It took some begging, but she eventually showed everyone one of her elven dances. It was dainty and beautiful, but took deceptive skill to perform properly; which was just like her. It was impossible to watch her and not want her: every sway of hips, arch of her foot and gesture of her arms seemed to accentuate her grace and beauty. She reminded him of a horse, but she had laughed at him when he had told her that.

"So what reminds me of a horse more," she had asked, her eyes lit with laughter. Both of them had enjoyed more than their fair share of honeyberry wine. "Is it my four legs, the neighing quality of my voice, or my pungent odour?"

"No, no, no," he denied, laughing. "A horse is beautiful to behold, just like you..."

"But in a different way, hopefully."

"In a different way," he confirmed. "But a horse cannot be truly appreciated unless it is moving. A horse and rider moving at full gallop is truly a wonder to behold. Far more beautiful than when they are simply standing there."

She'd raised her eyebrow. "I've heard what they say about knights and their horses. Should I be jealous?"

It wouldn't have been as funny if he had been sober, but her question had made him laugh out loud. "Ha! You aren't the first person to ask, believe me. Non riders don't understand, but that's not what I mean." He looked down at her, all at once serious. "I've always thought you were beautiful, but that was before I saw you dance. You are more beautiful than the Makers, Illyria. I have never seen, ever in my whole life, anything so completely captivating as you."

The merriment had vanished from her features and while he'd watched her eyes turned a colour he hadn't seen before: a shade of brown so dark as to almost be black. "That's the nicest thing anyone's ever said to me."

"I love you, Illyria," he had said as some magical force drew their bodies together.

"I...I love you, too, Gennald," she had breathed out just before their lips met once more.

The crowd had cheered and finger whistled upon catching sight of them, which they had done several times through the evening. They had finally, reluctantly broken apart from each other at which time the cheering had increased. It was good luck for the Lord and Lady of Summer to kiss often, and Gennald was determined to give them as much luck as possible. Illyria had blushed and ducked her head afterwards, as she had every time, before the moment ended. A group of young girls had come up and dragged her off, anxious for her to teach them the basics of elven dancing and she had gone with them laughingly. The look of longing and desire she had cast over her shoulder had left him dumbstruck.

He watched her now, leading a group of giggling girls through a series of sweeping arm motions and complicated balance changes. The effigy burnings were about to begin and already the collection of wooden snakemen, pirates, and dragons were being assembled near the bonfire. After the effigies would be more feasting—honey cakes, puddings and dredge beer—and then the couples dance. Having watched Illyria cavort through the group dances and given the villagers plenty of excuses to whistle, he was quite anxious to finally hold her in his arms.

"Beware, My Lord. Guard your lady well," someone murmured from behind him. Gennald whirled but saw only dancing, drinking, and merry villagers. Gennald's blood ran cold and he was suddenly reminded of why he was supposed to be in the village, and why he and Illyria were in these woods in the first place.

Beware of whom? Guard his lady against what? And with what? He looked around the firelit green, vainly looking for something untoward but finding nothing.

He had told Illyria that he had loved her, and he meant it as much as he could. That meant that she was his lady, her claims of knighthood notwithstanding, and therefore under his protection. This would be no repeat of their last night in his Lord Jannery's manor, with him locked in his room while she fought in her night clothes. He was a knight, armed with Emuranna's grace and filled with her righteous determination. He would defend Illyria with his life's breath.

Until then, he would watch her dance.

Theramus prowled the forest with as much silence as his giant's body allowed him. Something about this evening felt off, and not just because of his argument with Eldoth. He was not accustomed to being challenged, not in his own actions or the beliefs of his people.

He believed; that was his strength and that of his people, and those beliefs were long held. The traditions of the Noss went back fifteen centuries and, in the dark days following the fall of the High Kingdom, had been all that kept them from succumbing to despair. Certainly no other members of the Knights of Anduilon challenged him so. Who was this self-declared wizard that he felt he could question him? It made Theramus angry enough to crush rocks.

And yet, was Eldoth—despite his rudeness and bluster—wholly wrong? Had his people been wrong to hold back their knowledge? Had he? If he had, what was the best way to address it?

It was an important, weighty question, but not one for this moment. At this place and time his charges were potentially in jeopardy. While not his prime (despite what Eldoth insisted), Sephana was very dear to him, and he would never forgive himself if she came to harm through his negligence. It seemed unlikely that anything could happen at SummersEnd, a holy day to all living beings in the Middle Waters, but it was not beyond possibility. Anyone who would steal the Dragonfleet tribute, leaving Karalon no option but to give up its future into slavery, was capable of anything.

Theramus searched the forest for Sephana in vain. His eyes were like an owls; he could see in all but the blackest of nights, of which tonight was not. Nasheeth, the monument placed in the night sky by a grieving Anur in memory of his beloved wife, was at full blossom. As tomorrow was the true day of SummersEnd it would remain there past dawn and through all of the day, falling only at dawn the following morning. Only the blind would be unable to see after dark, so long as the sky remained clear.

Theramus prayed that it would. Tomorrow night the king would attempt to Join with the Land. If he succeeded, the sky would clear and he would live. If it became overcast...

I must not dwell on such thoughts. Lionar will Join with the Land and we will discover the location stolen gold. Karalon will be saved from civil war and foreign extortion. It will be so!

Balien appeared so suddenly that Theramus almost struck him.

"The outlaws are here, and in number," he told Theramus. "Twenty at least, and armed for war."

"They plan to attack the village?" Theramus mused aloud. "That seems unlikely."

"Not the village," Balien disagreed. "Us."

"I do not understand how this came to be, but there will be time for understanding the why later," Theramus growled. "Have you seen Sephana? Is she with you?"

His heart fell when Balien shook his head. "Perhaps she's with Illyria. The others are in danger and we must act quickly."

"I will see to Eldoth." He did not like the wizard, but he was a Knight of Anduilon and, as such, a comrade in arms. He would defend him to the death if need be, though he hoped it would not come to that. "Protect your sister," he told Balien, but the man had already vanished into the night.

Illyria cheered with the rest of the town as the wooden likenesses of Anshara's historical enemies were burned for the enjoyment of the crowd. Effigies of Djido, A'Cha, dragons and demons were held up and pelted with stones, paint filled eggs and over-ripe fruit before being cast them into the blazing bonfire.

"Seregil!" everyone shouted as they bombarded a particularly brutish looking demon. She doubted anyone outside Ilthanara even knew the true story. It was an ancient tale, even older than the Noss, and she didn't know it well, but she did know that High King's champion had been a man. Or, at least, he had started out as one.

The energy of the crowd was infectious and she cheered as wildly as anyone else as the wood and straw effigy caught fire. The burnings marked the climax of the evening. There would be more food and drink next, and then the couples dance. The couple's dance was all about courting: a chance for young men and women to seek out potential mates and partners. Many marriages occurred on the second day of SummersEnd and for those lucky couples—often the Lord and Lady of Summer—this dance was extra special. It was both their last time together as an unmarried couple, and a celebration of their upcoming marriage.

The best last dances end the morning after. She hadn't asked Gennald if there was a similar expression here, but the look in his eyes told her that there was.

The man in question stood behind her with his strong arms wrapped around her chest. She leaned back against his chest, her own arms clasping his. It felt so good to be held like this, to feel the hard muscles of his chest press against her.

"I don't want this to end," he murmured.

Illyria nodded. She'd just been thinking the same thing.

"I'm not a yeoman, here, and you aren't a princess," he continued. "We're just a couple in love."

She turned in his arms. "Gennald, that doesn't mean anything to me. I ran away from my kingdom. You could be a slave or a peasant and I wouldn't care." She could see by his face that he didn't agree. Hoping that no one noticed them, but not really caring if they did, she pulled his face down to hers.

Their lips had barely touched when people began screaming. Illyria whirled in time to a group of rough looking men—at least ten, maybe more—entering the green. They all wore studded leather armour dyed in forest tones and carried bows and swords. Illyria looked around for something, anything, she could use as a weapon. Nothing presented itself.

"Nobody panic. We're not here for any of you," called out an older, bearded man with white streaks in his hair. "Nobody do anything stupid and nobody gets hurt. We're here for the elf."

Gennald stepped in front of her, blocking her from the bandit's view. His hand held her wrist hard.

"I know she's here, her and some knight," the leader continued. "Where are you, *Illyria?* I don't want to hurt these fine Karalmen, but I will if you don't step forward."

She tugged at Gennald's hand, but his grip was unyielding.

"What do want with her?" asked the village leader.

The bandit stepped up to the man and drew his sword. "You should be more worried about what I'll do to you if you don't tell me where she is."

Eldoth swung his arm out even as he focussed his mind on the metal of the arrow head. It was a futile gesture but an instinctive one, as it was his magic that deflected the arrow away from him but he made it nonetheless. Even as he turned to face his attacker—it was a man wearing some sort of concealing cloak—he could hear other people moving through the underbrush.

I am not suited for this kind of battle! Where the others? Theramus and his towering profile would have been ideal, but he would have appreciated the company of any of his fellow knights right then. Even Sephana. Especially her.

The archer reached to draw another arrow and Eldoth gestured again, even as his mind reached out to the ring of hot stones lining the camp fire. The one nearest to his opponent flew towards the man, making him drop his weapon and scream in pain. He turned to run when he felt someone grab his sleeve and suddenly he was hurtling through the air.

He hit the ground hard enough to knock out his breath. Fear inspired him to turn onto his back and scramble to his feet but he was too slow. Something struck his arm out from under him and then hit him in the chest—someone's foot, he thought—while he was still reeling.

He was going to lose. More likely as not, he was going to be captured.

Oh, no. Not again.

An angry, inhumanly loud yell sounded from beyond the clearing. Eldoth heard a sickening crunch from above him and then people started to scream.

Gennald and Illyria stuck out. There was no way anyone would mistake them for villagers, even by firelight. Gennald had to do something soon. He felt Illyria tugging at her wrist but refused to let go. She was defenceless here and, if the only protection he could give her was concealment, then he would do so.

Half the outlaws were surrounding everyone with their weapons drawn while the rest pushed through the crowd searching. Gennald didn't know how they had heard about Illyria—a spy in the village maybe?—but surely they had been given a description along with her name. There weren't many blonde women in New Wighton and fewer still under the age of thirty. As for young, golden haired women so beautiful as to make your heart stop: there was only one.

He gasped in pain as strong fingers dug into the tendons of his wrist and he was forced to release her hand. *Damn it, Illyria. Stay still and let me rescue you!* Illyria, being Illyria, was having none of that. Darting with the speed of a cat she snatched up a burning brand from the bonfire. Striking before anyone could react— including Gennald—she smashed the burning log into an outlaw's face. The blow wasn't hard enough to knock him out, but it did stun him long enough for her to snatch his dagger.

"Don't harm these people," she declared loudly, steeped in every damned bit of pride and majesty that she possessed. "If you want me, come and claim me." She turned and ran.

She might have made it if she had been wearing her normal clothing.

The man she'd disarmed, still reeling and clutching at his face, was nonetheless able to reach out and blindly grab the hem of her dress. There was a sound of cloth ripping and she fell to the ground.

Everyone began to move at once. Outlaws drew weapons and tried to surround them. Illyria struggled to regain her footing but the outlaw grabbed her ankle. Gennald didn't think. He was unarmed but far from harmless. He threw himself on Illyria's captor with a fierce growl and clamped both hands around the arm that held her.

"Run!" he yelled as he forced his opponent to free her.

Illyria, bless her, chose not to be contrary, and ran.

Half of these men have bows, he realized. *She'll never make it out of the clearing unless I act.*

Somehow he managed to subdue his opponent and grab the man's sword, just in time to cross steel with three other outlaws. He had no armour other than his honour and was outnumbered. Unless he fought his very, very best, he knew that the next few moment would be his last.

It would not happen. *This* was why he lived. "I swear by Emuranna's name that you will not harm her," he declared. "Face me and die."

The bearded leader smiled wolfishly. "Get him, boys!"

CHAPTER SEVENTEEN

"And when Darius beheld the depravity and debauchery before him, he had to turn away. 'Such behaviour is beneath the lowest standards of men. As the king of a civilized land, and the final heir of lost Anduilon, I will cleanse you of this sin and show you proper behaviour.'

"And so Darius, king of Akkilon, sent ambassadors and teachers into foreign lands to teach them proper behaviour and to rid them of sin. And when his outstretched hand was spat upon, and his ambassadors slain, he did raise an army, and the Crusade Against Sin began."

—*excerpt from* A King's Folly: The Reign of Darius the Mad

By the time Eldoth regained his senses, it was over. Three men lay crushed to death while at least two more fled through the darkness. If he had faced a huge, staff-wielding embodiment of destruction like Theramus, he would have run as well. Only one of the outlaws that tried to capture him had even gotten within striking range.

The horses snorted and neighed in fear, but remained in their traces. "Your timing could have been better," Eldoth groused, still coughing. He clutched his side and grimaced as he got to his feet. "I thought you would have left me to be captured."

"We are both knights. Of course I came for you," Theramus said. "Have you seen Sephana? Has she returned since I left?"

"No." It hadn't occurred to him that anyone else had been a target. "Do you think she is in danger?"

"We are all in danger. There are dozens of outlaws, all armed."

Spikes of fear assaulted him, though he could not fathom why. "I-I am sure she is fine. I have seen her defend herself against ten times her number." He meant his words to be reassuring, but they came out tentative.

"It is possible she is in the village with Illyria. Come."

Nodding, trying to keep a growing sense of panic at bay, Eldoth gathered his coat and followed Theramus's large silhouette through the darkness. They hadn't even made it half way to the village before finding Balien and Illyria. Only Balien and Illyria; no one else.

"They've captured Gennald," Illyria said. "We have to rescue him."

Eldoth didn't care about the Karalinian boor. "Is Sephana with you?"

The brother and sister exchanged glances. "No. We thought she was with you. We have to assume that they have her as well."

"Have her? They can't have her." Eldoth shouted, his voice shrill. "She's Reshai. They'll kill her on sight!"

Theramus looked at him sidelong. "What do you care? You do nothing but berate her at every opportunity. I would think that you would be glad."

Eldoth stared. "Glad? Why would I be glad? She's my wife!"

They all stared at him and he realized what he had just said.

"Ex-wife," he amended. "As well as our fellow knight and your friend. Of course her fate concerns me." They all continued to look at him. "Also, she carries a magical treasure beyond value. I cannot permit it to go missing."

"You insult both her and yourself," Theramus said. "You cannot be this blind. Admit that you are still in love with her. There is no shame in it."

Eldoth stared. The words hit him like a blow to the stomach. *In love...* "That's preposterous. She betrayed and abandoned me. I hate her. I..."

"That is not hate. That is hurt, but it changes nothing." Theramus's voice was as gentle as Eldoth had ever heard it. Certainly more gentle than had ever been directed at him before. "It is obvious to everyone, Eldoth. Admit it to yourself."

It was all he could do to whisper. "Can-can you love someone and hate them at the same time?" It wasn't an admission.

The giant smiled. "It is surprisingly easy."

Images of hazel eyes, teak coloured hair, impish smiles and glimpses of brown scales flashed through his mind. He remembered how she had looked in her borrowed wedding dress when they were married, the fire in her eyes when she argued with him. It was easy to recall the grace and perfection she displayed when she wielded her newfound dagger with supernatural skill. The gentle innocence only visible on her features when she slept.

A face that he might never see again if she had, in fact, been captured. A fury as great as his fear consumed him.

"I will not dispute your words." It was as close to an admission as he was capable of. "But they are meaningless at this juncture. If she has been captured, then she is in great danger. We must find her before she can be harmed."

Why? Why reveal this truth to me now, when it is entirely possible that I never see her again?

Illyria's guilt denied her any enjoyment that she may have otherwise derived from witnessing Eldoth's revelation. Gennald had availed himself bravely, allowing her time to escape, but had been beaten rather brutally for his courage. She had seen the outlaws drag him away—unconscious, she thought, but not dead—but that didn't mean that they wouldn't kill him later.

He had taken those blows because of her. More precisely, because of her stupidity. He wouldn't have been in that village at all except for her. Gennald may have been the one who had first suggested Joining the festival, but she had agreed to it. They had been expecting the outlaws to arrive—albeit not like this—and while every other member of the Knights of Anduilon had been ready and waiting for something to happen, she had been wearing a dress and sharing kisses.

She could feel Balien's eyes boring into her and was unable to meet them. He had endured the most because of her selfish decision, other than Gennald. And Sephana, if she had indeed been captured. "I'm sorry," she said to her brother.

Balien, damn him, didn't get angry. "I'm not the one you need to apologise to."

"I was stupid, and selfish."

"Yes, you were." She winced, but appreciated his honesty. "This is not the time for placing blame. We need to plan and then act. If they are alive, we need to rescue them." He paused. "If not, avenge them."

She closed her eyes in an attempt to fend off the mental image his words provoked. She failed. "It was an attack. They knew we were here."

He nodded. "We weren't being that secret. Anyone could have followed them back from the road, or learned that you were in the village."

"They wanted to capture me," she said. "They knew me by name. Did they come after you, too?"

"No. I saw them come down the path from the mountain and followed them. I did catch one."

"You have a prisoner?" Theramus, who had been conversing with Eldoth, looked over. His eyes were bright. "I would like to have words with him."

Their prisoner, bruised and shaken but intact, had required some persuasion but had ultimately proved cooperative. Appropriately terrified, he had led them through the dark forest. They travelled slowly, wary of ambush, but it seemed that they were the only people left in the forest.

"It was a raid!" 'Jax' had squealed after watching Theramus rend a six inch thick log into splinters. "We were supposed to capture as many of you as we could and take you back to be questioned by the Lady."

"Who is the 'Lady?' " Balien had asked.

"We call her the 'Black Lady.' None of us know who she is, but Manson and all of his men obey her."

"Manson?"

"He's our leader; our new one, I mean. He and his men came out of nowhere a few years ago and took over. He does what the Black Lady does, so the rest of us do, too."

"Where have they taken them?" Theramus had roared. As important as this information was, Sephana had been taken (and Gennald, too) and was in jeopardy. As Eldoth had pointed out, her Reshai nature put her in greater risk than a normal human would have been.

Jax had almost soiled himself in the face of Theramus's rage. "In the cave. They're in the cave!"

"Where is this cave?" Illyria had asked. He had only laughed when they had asked him how well it was guarded and now Theramus saw why. The 'cave' was inside the nearest of the Silverhearts and its only entrance was a collapsed mineshaft. There were hundreds upon hundreds of tonnes of stone between the Knights of Anduilon and their quarry. It would take Theramus days with a pick-axe to clear it away, if not weeks.

"We were right here, three different times," Illyria said with disgust, examining the surrounding area. "The trail led here every time, and every time we dismissed it as impossible."

Balien had been examining the collapsed stone. "It *is* impossible. This isn't a trick or a false front: all of this stone is real."

Theramus glared at their prisoner. "If you have played us falsely it shall be the last mistake you ever make."

Jax cringed. "I haven't! I didn't! I swear!"

"Then tell us how you get into your cave?"

"Magic!" he cried. "One of Manson's men knows magic. He opens the door for us."

All eyes turned to Eldoth. "It's impossible," he said. He looked more frantic than Theramus had ever seen him. "This is hundreds of tonnes of rock. It would take a fourth ring orange wizard to move or shape this." He frowned. "Even if such a wizard did exist—which he doesn't—it is still beyond my abilities."

Theramus lifted Jax from the ground. "Do not lie. Where is the entrance?"

"It's here, I swear, and we do use magic. Jaden—he's the guy who opens it—he doesn't make the rocks move. He just stares at it and then we have to push it open. I don't know how he does it."

Theramus dropped him and went to Eldoth. "I believe him. Is it possible?"

Eldoth had never been so confused, frightened, or angry in his entire life. *I'm in love with Sephana.* It was both the most ridiculous thing he had ever heard and the most glaringly obvious. *What do I do about it? How do I act around her?* Then there was the question that frightened him most of all: how did she feel about him? What would he do if she did not reciprocate his feelings?

Just two days ago he had listened to her tell the story about how the man she loved had heroically died while saving her life. He had heard the pain in her voice and knew her feelings to be true. What was he compared to that? How did the man who antagonized and insulted her compare to the memory of the knight who died for her?

Damn Theramus. This revelation did not grant him any peace. It only opened entirely new doors of torment.

"Eldoth." Strong, heavy hands fell on his shoulders. He looked up into the gentle eyes of the being who had inflicted this upon him. "I understand your pain, but, if we are to rescue her, then we must first get through this door. You must focus."

Focus. That was a laugh. His focus was gone; shattered. He opened his mouth to make some cutting comment but an image of Sephana in danger stopped him. He could hear voice her in his mind, insulting him for his inability, and somehow it calmed him.

"I will try," he said, his voice thick, and turned to the mine entrance. It wasn't a main entrance, that was obvious. Based on the sediment lines on the stone as well as the dried stream bed below them he guessed that this was some kind of drainage shaft, an adit. He knelt and pressed his hands against the stone. Closing his eyes, he concentrated beyond his normal senses. He felt the stone before him, sensed its immense weight.

Something was wrong.

"This stone is fused," he said aloud. "It looks like a collection of fallen rocks, but that is an illusion. It is one piece. I see how it was joined. It was done deliberately."

"Can you move it?" Theramus's voice asked.

"No. It is far too large, but there is something more. It has been shaped and fitted to this entrance. It fills it completely, like a plug."

He was vaguely aware of something pushing against the stone. "I cannot budge it."

Eldoth sensed something else. "No, you wouldn't. You were right before, to call this a door. I sense hinges, shaped out of stone. It would turn, if it were free to do so." He 'felt' along the rear of the stone door. "Like any door set to keep out intruders, this one is locked. I can feel it. It is a separate stone, moveable."

He reached out with his mind and mimed the same action with his hands. He grasped at nothing and twisted while his magic imitated the motion through five feet of solid stone. Beyond him, in the darkness, he sensed something move.

He opened his eyes and took a deep breath. It was dark still, only the small glimpses of the full moon through the clouds giving any illumination. Three silhouettes watched him. "It is done," he said. "All that is needed now is the strength to push it open."

Theramus smiled and stretched out his fingers. "Strength I have in abundance. Stand aside."

Gennald slowly regained his senses. His head throbbed from where a sword hilt had struck it, there were some shallow cuts along his arms as well as several boot shaped bruises on his ribs, but he was otherwise unharmed. He'd cut two of them, one fatally, before being overwhelmed. He'd honestly thought that he would die there.

His hands were bound behind him. He tried to look around, but almost everything was hidden by darkness. There were a few flickering yellow patches of light, torches and campfires that revealed at least thirty silhouettes. He was in some sort of cavern.

A female voice rose angrily. "Just one? That's all?" There was a reply but Gennald couldn't make it out. The woman's voice was heard again, quieter and barely audible. "Fine. Let me see him."

Gennald rolled over. There were two men watching him by the light of a small fire. He saw a slender shadow walk towards him. She was slender but by no means weak and wore an outfit made entirely of black. Twin sword handles crossed her chest and a tight hood hung off of her head, revealing dark hair.

The mystery woman knelt before him. Gennald could not help but compare her to Illyria. She was very pretty, but in a different way. There were small differences: this woman's jaw was more square, her eyes darker and nose slightly more upturned, but mainly she was...*hard* in a way that Illyria was not. Certainly her eyes had none of the same warmth. When this woman looked at him, it was with the same dispassion that he might have examining a horse's hooves.

"This isn't even one of them," she said with a curse, surging to her feet. "It's just that idiot knight that accompanied them."

"What do we do with him then, My Lady?"

"I don't care." She turned to leave, then stopped. "No, wait." She looked at Gennald and smiled. It only made her look more frightening. "I can use you. Who are you scowling at now, my handsome Karalinian knight?"

"What will you do now, My Lady?" asked someone else.

"I'll take this one as well as the prisoner I *did* get. She at least, might know something. There isn't anything else planned until after the holiday, so all of you just relax and enjoy SummersEnd."

Take her? Had Illyria not escaped after all?

"Let her go, you evil witch!" Gennald shouted, rolling to keep her in sight. "If you harm Illyria, I swear that I won't rest until you're dead."

The woman turned. "Knights and their oaths," he heard her mutter. "Gag him and beat him, but not so much that he can't walk." Someone kicked Gennald's back and he cried out in pain. Without another look at him, she walked into the darkness.

A second man's foot joined in until, mercifully, he passed out.

The tunnel fit Theramus so long as he stooped. He was in the lead, his 'owl's eyes' allowing him to see somewhat in the near pitch blackness. The rest followed, hands holding the belts of the person in front of them. Illyria couldn't see a thing.

Eldoth had offered to create one of his mage lights, but Illyria had refused. They knew nothing about where they were sneaking into and needed every edge that they could get. That edge right now was surprise, and even the smallest of lights could betray that.

It was hard moving so slowly and carefully. Gennald and Sephana were within, or so they hoped. Were they being imprisoned? Tortured? Executed? She didn't know, and that lack of knowledge ate at her like a disease festering beneath her skin. She wanted to charge into battle like a rampaging giant, slaying enemies right and left to enable the rescue of her friends, but did not. It was a foolish, impulsive lack of planning that had gotten her into this mess, just as an impulse had led her to attack that Dragonfleet ship.

It was practical, well-thought action that would win this battle, if victory was possible. She was a knight, and she had to start acting the part.

Dammit, though, but it was *hard*.

She felt more than saw Theramus stop. They had been travelling for a few hundred yards through the water smoothed tunnel, always at a steady upward angle. "We have arrived at an opening," Theramus whispered into her ear. "There is a large, central cavern surrounding a pit. Beyond it are men and lights."

"How many?"

"Twenty that I see," he reported. "They are not on alert and I see no guards."

There was a pause while Illyria passed Theramus's information back to Eldoth, who in turn passed it to Balien. "Let me see," she whispered, and the invisible Noss led her forward.

Even with her eyes accustomed to the darkness, the outlaw camp was only visible as a series of distant fires. The pit Theramus had described was only visible by its absence; torches illuminated its perimeter about a quarter of the way around an unfathomable black centre.

"This was the main entrance to the mines," Theramus told her. "They used water wheels to drain the shafts below and this cavern was used for separating ore. The water wheels are destroyed. I imagine that without them the shafts became submerged and impossible to mine."

Trust Theramus to turn her attack plan into a history lesson.

"They have made their camp in the old smelting area, amidst the furnaces. I think that they are celebrating." Illyria could hear the sounds of talking and laughing from across the cavern and had to agree.

"That will make this easier." Balien and Eldoth had moved up to join them. It took a moment, but soon all four of them had their heads together. "This is what we'll do..."

Eldoth could feel Balien's eyes on him, and found it both calming and frustrating. He didn't want to skulk and hide right now. Sephana was in danger. He wanted to bathe the cavern in fire. He wanted every man here to die horribly, writhing in agony for what they had done to her. If Balien hadn't been with him, he would have done so ten times by now.

He hadn't wanted to listen to logic—ironically—but Balien's patient, understanding voice had somehow talked him back from the brink. When he truly felt he was losing control, the man's hand on his shoulder allowed him to keep it. With the enigmatic swordsman accompanying him, Eldoth had somehow managed to cross the dark cavern's perimeter without detection.

The place reeked of mildew, male sweat, and wood smoke. These outlaws had been living here for months at least, possibly years, safe from discovery behind the ingenious 'magic' door in the hillside. He understood why they had not set a guard. He was quite possibly the only person in Karalon capable of opening it.

Other than the wizard who had created it, of course.

The idea was both nerve wracking and exciting. He was more prepared now and doubted that another wizard would beat him as soundly as Veeshar had five weeks previously, and yet this new wizard represented an unknown quantity. He should not exist, any more than Eldoth should. The teaching of the High Wizards were too arcane and too rare for more than one person to have pierced them. He had never dreamed of actually encountering a living, human spellcaster, and yet there was one living among these outlaws. Had he learned as much as Eldoth? More? Less?

Balien squeezed his foot and Eldoth nodded. It was time.

The red college of magic, his college of mastery, was the college of energy. There were other forms besides the fire and lightning that Eldoth had mastered, but he was unable to summon them with any consistency. He had only managed to create Essential Fire the one time—it had been what had killed Draxul so horribly—and was unwilling to experiment further.

The exception to that was light.

It was the most basic of energy forms, used as a utility and in practice. He could create and manipulate balls of light with little diminishment to the rest of his abilities. If he chose to put all of his strength into making a light source as large and bright as possible—something he had never seen any reason for—it would likely be brighter than the noonday sun. If cast inside a darkened cavern against unsuspecting foes it would blind them completely, or so it was hoped.

Eldoth focussed his will, formed his hands into joined fists, clenched his eyes shut, and cast.

Theramus did more than shut his eyes, he hid them behind his arm. He was very sensitive to bright light and could not afford to be disabled.

He could not see Eldoth's distraction, but he heard its effect on the relaxed and semi-drunken outlaws. There were a few moments of confusion followed by a chorus of screams. Theramus counted to three before lowering his arm.

Men were writhing on the cavern floor, their hands over their eyes. Some drew weapons to defend against foes that they could not see, but most were completely insensate. It was child's play to stride among them, staff at the ready, and rapping as many as possible about their heads and shoulders.

His eyes interrogated the darkness, looking for curly hair and patterns of scales. He found nothing.

Enough of Eldoth's light globes remained to dimly illuminate the cavern. Balien and Illyria were likewise making short work of the opposition, using their Ilthanaran fencing to disarm and subdue with impunity. Despite being outnumbered by a factor of almost six to one, they were destroying the outlaws quite handily.

Eldoth was wielding a fist sized rock without even touching it. It connected painfully with faces and bodies with only the slightest flick of his hand. The few men slowly coming to their senses and beginning to resist were unable to see the small dark object and were defenceless against it.

It was over almost as soon as it had begun. It didn't take long to rouse the captured outlaws enough to gather them in the remains of an old fuel bin. Neither Gennald or Sephana were anywhere to be seen. Eldoth, who could not be described as *calm*, given his circumstances, had at least kept himself controlled. Now that he was knew that Sephana was not present, that control was slipping.

"Tell me where she is!" The anguish in his voice broke Illyria's heart. She doubted that he had known, before this moment, how much Sephana meant to him. A person experiencing that depth of emotion was capable of anything.

It was a kind of reaction that she was *not* experiencing. Gennald, the man she had professed her love to, had been captured ensuring her escape and was equally unaccounted for. She was concerned, yes, and guilty, that was all. What did that say about her?

Eldoth repeated his question and, when he still did not receive the answer he wanted, raised both his hands, which promptly burst into flame. "Tell me, or I'll burn the flesh from your bones."

He would too. Illyria motioned for Balien to watch the prisoners and quickly stepped close to the wizard. She didn't want to surprise him, not when he was like this and armed (if that was the appropriate term) as he was.

"Eldoth!" He glanced at her, annoyed. Flickering, frightening shadows writhed across his face. "Eldoth, you need to stop."

"Not until they tell me what I need to know." His voice, in contrast to his hands, was chilling.

She hesitated before placing a hand on his shoulder. She could feel the heat from his flames against her arm. "Eldoth, listen to me. Put your...hands out."

"Why?"

Why, indeed. There was only one thing motivating him now. She had to appeal to what little reason he possessed. *Ah! I have it.* "Because Sephana wouldn't want you to."

It worked. The flames vanished as suddenly as they had appeared. "You're right. She thinks it's cruel."

Illyria made sure not to voice her own opinion on the subject. This was not the time for lectures. "Come." She led him away from the cowed prisoners. "You've frightened them. Balien and Theramus can get the answers we need now. You've done all you need to." Her kept her voice calm and soothing.

Thankfully, his other lights were still...lit, and the outlaws campfires were burning also. The cavern was dim, but navigable.

"Its...I'm...she...it's not fair," he was finally able to say, while Illyria rubbed his shoulder consolingly. "I've just discovered this. Us. She cannot be gone now. It would be so wasteful."

The Bear and the Thistle

"We didn't find any bodies. She could still be alive." As could Gennald. She said it for her own benefit as much as his.

"Or they could have pitched her down the mineshaft," he countered. "They've been using it as their refuse pit. There are any number of things they could have done to her in the time they had. I can give you a list, of you'd like."

No, she did not like. "Or, they could have taken her for questioning. We can't lose hope, Eldoth."

Balien walked over. "They talked. Sephana and Gennald are both alive. The 'Black Lady' took them both with her when she left an hour ago."

Both of them pretended not to notice as Eldoth burst into relieved tears.

CHAPTER EIGHTEEN

" 'Do you think the woman you know as Sephana was born with that name? You are a fool if you do. It is not an Akkilinian name, nor a Karalinian one. She gave it to herself upon her rebirth, and once the stories began no one ever called her by anything else. 'Azavana' was what I knew her by when I married her, and she shall always be 'Zavi' to me.' "

—Eldoth

Sephana had no idea where she was.

Her hands were bound in front of her and she had a sack over her head, but at least her legs were free. She was ready to make the dash for freedom if the opportunity ever presented itself, but so far it hadn't. The rope that bound her hands was being held by someone who seemed to enjoy jerking her whenever her balance was off. Between him and the person behind her—who seemed to take some sick pleasure in shoving her randomly—she had lost count of the number of times she had fallen against the cold, stone ground.

That was the other reason she hadn't run: she was in some sort of cave. It had spread into some kind of cavern a while ago and had been full of men. She thought she'd heard Gennald's voice among them but wasn't sure. Since then, she'd been taken through a narrow corridor that had gone up and then down. She'd 'fallen' a lot more on the downward part than the upper.

There was another sadistic push followed by the customary jerk against her bonds and Sephana fell painfully onto her hands and knees. The ground had levelled out, but something was different. It was the sound, she realized. It wasn't echoing in the same way. Were they coming into another big cave?

No, that wasn't it. All the sounds from the front weren't echoing the same way. The tunnel had come to a dead end. She heard a woman's voice give orders in a tone that said she was used to being obeyed. "Indush, Edjeet, come help with this. Adaram, stay with the prisoners."

It was easy for Sephana to hide her surprise, what with her head being in a sack and all. Those weren't Karalinian names; they were from Akkilon. She hadn't heard them spoken aloud in years. Most refugees that she had known had changed them to something less foreign sounding to local ears.

She had no idea what that meant.

There was a sound of laboured grunting and then she was bathed in cool, fresh air. She hadn't appreciated how much she had missed it until it had returned.

The people in front of her groaned and panted. Whatever door they had opened must have been heavy. She heard the tired shuffling of feet and then a jerk on her hands as her captor—Adaram?—led her forward. *This is my chance.* The man behind her hadn't returned to his position yet and, for the first time in hours, sge had something other than confining walls surrounding her.

It wasn't hard to fake a stumble as she passed through the door and she fell forward against Adaram, who shoved her off of him with disgust. *Good. Now I know where he is and he's off balance.* She grabbed her rope as tightly as she could and brought her knee up to where she thought his crotch was.

She was rewarded by a gasping, choking (and satisfying) sound. She pulled the rope out of Adaram's hands at the same time as she shoved him as hard as she could. Not checking if he fell or not, she turned sideways and ran as fast as she could.

Almost immediately, there was a cry of alarm from behind her, followed by the sensation of branches hitting her body. She pushed at the bag over her head as best as she could, but she didn't need to see to know where she was. The distant stink of sweat, human waste and rotting fish wafting up from below made it obvious: she was in the hills above New Aukaster.

Sephana stumbled into a gulley that she couldn't see and fell painfully to the ground. Hearing cries of alarm and running footsteps from behind her, she didn't even try getting back to her feet. Instead she rolled down the gulley, hoping that the darkness would cover her escape.

She managed to get her head free of her sack by the time she reached the bottom. The sky was mostly overcast but glimpses of the full moon let her see where she was. She stopped to listen as she tried to undo her hands with her teeth. People were stomping around the bushes and yelling, but not near her.

I might just get out of this.

She froze when she felt cold steel against her throat. She didn't have to turn to know it was the dark haired witch who had caught her outside New Wighton. "You're pretty good at sneaking up on people," Sephana growled, raising her hands in surrender and doing her best not to move her head. "But I bet things would be pretty different in a straight fight."

"Perhaps," the woman replied. Something about her voice was familiar. "But you'll never know."

"Why are we wasting time here?" Eldoth demanded. "They have Sephana! We should be going after her!"

Illyria sighed. She hadn't been able to keep the wizard calm for very long and, truthfully, she agreed with him. The two of them were somewhere in the outlaw's camp, in sight of Theramus and the bound prisoners but far enough away to not be overheard.

"I know. They have Gennald, too, but we can't leave the prisoners unguarded."

"Zulum take them," he spat. "Rescuing her is much more important."

A large part of her was in agreement. Her friend and her...the man she loved...were in danger. This 'black lady' was somehow able to cow a group of three dozen dangerous outlaws and had a wizard of unknown power in her service. She didn't want to think about what horrors the pair of them might inflict upon their prisoners given enough time. Every moment that Illyria and the others were forced to wait was one more that Gennald or Sephana could be tortured.

"To us perhaps, but not Karalon. We're knights, and we have to place our duty first. We can't kill them now that they are our prisoners, and we can't let them go." That was where Balien was: going to New Wighton to organize a militia capable of holding the outlaws until the group of knights from up the road could take possession of them. It meant that she and Eldoth had nothing to do except wait.

She didn't normally socialize with him. She was self-aware enough to admit that she found his intelligence intimidating and his arrogance unpleasant, but, somehow, knowing that they had both lost someone made him easier to tolerate.

"We should kill them, then," he said dully, referring to the prisoners. He'd tried this argument before.

"We can't," she said. Again. "They're our prisoners. We safeguard the helpless, Eldoth. It's in our oath."

"I disagree with your interpretation," he said. "Anyone who tries to kill us is, by definition, not helpless."

"They become helpless once they surrender," she countered. "Slaying prisoners without trial is murder, not when there are no other options available. 'Do no wrong' is also in our oath."

"I...perhaps you are right." He punched his thigh. "I am sure there is a counterargument to that, but I can't concentrate enough to find it. I *miss* her. I want her to insult me right now; the most horrid, scathing insult that she can generate, which as you know is quite awful." He gave a short laugh. "I sound insane."

She rubbed his shoulder, taking comfort in his touch as much as giving it. "No, you sound worried." It made it easier for her to forget that Gennald was also missing.

He stood. "I cannot wait here doing nothing." He looked around the cave. "Theramus has the prisoners contained and Balien will not return for a while." He looked at her and opened his mouth to speak, but hesitated. "There are numerous side caves here that we could examine. Would..." he hesitated. "Would you like to explore them with me?"

Illyria smiled. "Yes, I would."

Eldoth didn't want to think. Thinking led to too many questions with answers he did not like, and, for the first time, he found himself envious of all the other idiots in the world. For them, life was about *doing;* experiencing. They drifted through their lives without ever having contemplated anything deeper than their next meal, and Eldoth was fairly certain that they were happy in their ignorance.

His mind, however, would not stop turning. It continued to spin faster and faster, like a rock rolling down a hill until it struck the cliff face at the bottom and shattered. He had contemplated leaving Illyria and the others, but concluded that he had better chances of success with them. He'd pondered killing the prisoners and forcing their hands—with no one to guard, there was no reason for them to remain—but doubted that the others would co-operate. As an addendum to that, it was all too easy to imagine Sephana berating him for being 'cruel' if he did so. His wife was frustrating that way.

Ex-wife. Whatever.

Instead, he was exploring caves with Illyria. It was frustrating and tedious, but better than doing nothing, if only slightly.

"Most of this interior stone is soft—well, soft for stone—and has been carved out by water," He explained. He was finding it hard to stay silent. "Most of these caves were made by running water. It is what accounts for their strange shape."

"You know a great deal about stonework."

"I read a book on it once," he said. "It was one of the few ancient texts I discovered, gathering dust in some senator's library. A firm of knowledge of the different states of matter is essential to grasping the essentials of orange magic."

"When did you meet a senator?"

He hesitated. It was not a subject he wanted to discuss right now. "I have spent some time in Tirim."

She seemed to sense his reluctance. "What is down here?" she asked instead, turning down an unexplored branch.

Eldoth sent a light ball down the length of the tunnel. The other ball he had created remained over their heads, illuminating their surroundings. The tunnel in question was long and straight, with squared corners.

"This tunnel is man made," he noted. "You can see the chisel marks."

"Then it seems obvious that it was made to go somewhere. Come on." She smiled and beckoned him. Eldoth followed, finding himself taken in by her charm.

Any other time, the layout and construction of these mines would have interested him. The choices the designers had made concerning adapting natural caverns and cutting out artificial ones with regards to the obvious challenges of drainage and access looked to be fascinating, but not right now. Now they were just bits of tedium placed one after the other.

The tunnel turned sharply and ended in a pair of large, impressive looking double-doors. Riveted iron bands criss-crossed their lengths and, as if that was not enough to ensure their security, numerous door bolts, locks and chains fastened them shut.

"These doors are new," Eldoth said. He pointed to the metal-work. "This is made of iron, and only partly rusted. Anything from the same era as the mine would have disintegrated centuries ago."

"It makes you wonder what's on the other side, doesn't it?" Illyria asked. "I don't remember seeing any keys on any of the outlaws."

"Keys will not be necessary," Eldoth said with a grim smile, examining the door and its fasteners. It was impressive looking to be sure, but designed to keep out mundane intruders. He took the nearest lock in his hands and closed his eyes. It was as he expected: rudimentary, and made wholly of metal. It was simple for him to simulate the entry of a key with magic and cause it to disengage.

The next four locks met the same fate within a minute, and he was self aware enough to admit he was just showing off as he made the various bars and chains retract seemingly on their own. He gave Illyria a self-satisfied smirk before stepping away and gesturing for her to open the door.

She took a grip on one side and gestured for him to join her. "You're stronger than I am."

If he had to. "It's too bad Gennald isn't here," Eldoth muttered as he prepared to pull. "Acts like this are all people like him are good for."

Illyria straightened and looked at him with hurt eyes. "That was very rude."

Eldoth realized the extent of his gaffe. "I'm sorry."

"Saying 'people like him' is offensive and derogatory," she scolded. "Gennald is brave, intelligent and capable. Implying that he is only suited for manual labour is insulting. He's a knight." She hugged her arms to herself, looking suddenly very vulnerable. "He's missing, too, and in just as much danger as Sephana."

"I'm sorry," he repeated. "I speak without thinking sometimes." She just glared at him, her fascinating eyes so pale as to almost be without colour. He resumed his grip on the side of the door. "Would you care to help me open this door? I think it will take both of us."

She didn't reply, but after a long moment took her own hold on the thick door. It was heavy, and the hinges stiff from disuse, but, between the two of them, they managed to pull it open enough to squeeze through. Eldoth was pained and sweaty from the exertion, but chose to make no complaint. Illyria was his only sympathetic ear at the moment and he didn't want to offend her further.

Neither could see what lay beyond. Eldoth summoned more mage-light and directed it into the darkness. Almost immediately he was able to see many objects within, giving off metallic reflections.

Illyria gasped and Eldoth recognised the yellowish glitter right away. The room was filled with gold.

"This is more than a single lord's tax money," Illyria said, wandering between the various chests and sacks littering the floor. "This is enough to pay the entire tribute."

Eldoth guessed that the room had been a vault in the days of the High Kingdom, likely for the namesake silver that filled these hills. The current residents had only needed to replace the door to allow them to continue using it for its original purpose.

"This much gold must have taken years to gather," Illyria said. "To what end? Why collect all this and do nothing with it?"

Balien arrived in the room before Eldoth could answer (assuming that her question wasn't entirely rhetorical). Other than a slight widening of his eyes, he gave no reaction to the sight of the gold. "We can go now."

"Can you re-secure this room?" Illyria asked. "This much treasure is too great a temptation to leave unguarded." She didn't say what they were all thinking: that neither the villagers or the knights that would replace them could be entrusted with its care.

"I can do more than that," he said, using his meagre skills in yellow magic to remove a square of cloth from a nearby coin sack. He withdrew his stele—an Ansharite stylus that he used to scribe runes—and drove it into the flesh of his forearm with a pained hiss. "Shut the door and I will spell it closed."

Runecasting was elementary magic, at least in theory. Any spell a wizard could cast he could also scribe, if he had the right tools. Eldoth had read references to the magical ink that ancient wizards has used to inscribe their spells into mundane objects, but had never found the recipe itself. It was on his mental list of things to research if he ever had the time and resources to devote to it.

There was, however, a substitute for rune-ink for the strong of heart: a wizard's blood. It was painful and draining, but also the only way to scribe a spell without sealing it off for an indefinite period and hampering any subsequent spellcasting.

His hand was shaking as he scribed the spell that would bind the two doors together with ten times the strength of any chain or bar. He knew that it had taken successfully when the Renfel characters began to glow. Well, not 'glow'. It did not emit visible light that everyone could see; rather, it was a kind of extra sensory perception usable only to wizards. He would be able to sense the runes even if his eyes were closed.

"It would take a team of elephants to open it now," Eldoth announced, wavering slightly.

"What about the other wizard?" Illyria asked. "Won't he just be able to counter it?"

"Possibly, but if he was capable of casting this magic, I think he would have done so." Eldoth shrugged. "Besides, we are not keeping him out as much as we are our untrustworthy allies." He squared his shoulders. "Have we finished wasting time on this? Are we now free to follow Sephana's abductors?"

Balien nodded.

"Then let's go," Illyria said.

Gennald should have, at this very moment, been laying with Illyria in his arms. The last dance would have ended hours ago, and Gennald had arranged with the village leader for the use of an unoccupied cottage. It had been equipped with comfortable beddings, sweet meats and honeyberry wine. It would have been perfect, if only...

If only everything that had happened in the last two months had gone completely differently.

If Lord Jannery had left the Northmarch a day later, he would not have left his son in charge and Gennald would not have been imprisoned for his 'treasonous' Golden Bear plotting. He would have been the hero of 'Dragonhead Keep' and he would have been able to court Illyria properly. If they had not arrived at Westbridge at the precise moment of the Dragonfleet attack, he would not have had to break a century old royal commandment for her sake and this whole chain of events would never have happened. If he had kept his mouth shut the night of the Blackshield attack, or if the outlaws had not come when they had tonight, he and Illyria wouldn't have been knight and elf with conflicting opinions regarding the role of women in combat; just the King and Queen of Summer sharing one final, beautiful dance.

If...if...if...

Instead, he was bound and chained, stumbling over terrain that he could not see because of the sack covering his head. They had left the caves half an hour ago and were walking steadily downhill. There had been some problem just after they left the cave, but he had been too well guarded to take advantage of it (a heavyset man had literally knocked him over and *sat on him* until order had been restored), and there had been no opportunities since then.

He knew by smell and the sound of merriment that they were approaching New Aukaster. There was no point asking how—these tunnels obviously ran the length and width of the Silverhearts, however they managed to conceal them—but why here? Why now? Did the outlaws have some sort of noble patron or mastermind? He supposed he'd have to wait until they arrived at their destination.

Gennald knew his mission: discover who the outlaws were allied with and the extent of their patron's treachery, escape, and do as much damage as he could in the process. Finally, if he survived, report his findings to Lord Jannery. It would not be easy, he knew, but he welcomed the challenge. He had just been denied the perfect night in the arms of the woman of his dreams. He would return payment for the misery and frustration he had be given, with ruinous interest.

They were not moving fast enough for Theramus's liking. While he understood and agreed with the reasons that had prevented them from giving immediate pursuit to Sephana's abductors, that did not mean that he was happy with them. Given that, he also understood the need for prudence now that they had begun their pursuit—the outlaws had proved themselves adept in their trap use—but it did not mean he did not want to break into a run.

The tunnels had been made by, and scaled for, men. Theramus had spent the last few hours stooped over painfully, with only the occasional respite in the form of natural formed galleries. They had travelled for several miles in an approximate north-easterly direction and had descended roughly one hundred yards while doing so. If he was correct in his estimations, they would emerge somewhere around the shore level of Lake Vinander.

Before them, the tunnel ended abruptly in a wall of stone.

"Eldoth, is this..." Illyria began to ask, but was cut off.

"Yes," the wizard answered. Eldoth's mood, apparently, had improved no more than his own had. "Physical force will not avail you here. Let me." He half closed his eyes and made a grabbing gesture with one hand. There was a deep, heavy knocking sound from deep within the stone and Theramus saw the door shift slightly.

Even the fetid air of New Aukaster was welcome after being in the stifling tunnels for several hours. It was dark, cold and overcast. It being the first night of SummersEnd, Theramus knew that Nashith was at full blossom and hanging in the centre of the sky, where it would remain for all of the night and tomorrow as well. The fact that it was not visible tonight of all nights was yet another reminder of the sad state of this land, and the urgency of their quest.

"All right, we're here," Eldoth announced impatiently once they had exited the tunnel. "What are we waiting for?" he asked, desperation and frustration lacing his voice.

"We need to find their tracks, first," Illyria said. "Some light, please. Something dim that will not reveal us." The wizard waved negligently and a pale blue light formed on the ground in front of her. She picked it up—he had cast his spell on a small stone—and she cupped it in her hand as she held it over the ground. Beside them, Balien led Eldoth off and spoke to him quietly.

"There are plenty of tracks here. They aren't even trying to hide them." She continued to look at the signs that only she could see. "There was some sort of struggle, but then they all went down there." She pointed towards New Aukaster, below them. "We'll follow them, of course, but we'll lose their trail once we enter the city."

Theramus recalled Sephana's tragic story of herself and her slain knightly lover. "Count Attenham has been in league with the outlaws for years," he declared. "Sephana has been taken there, I am sure of it."

"And Gennald," Illyria reminded him. "We have no evidence. Even with our letter from Lionar, we can't assault a noble's residence—especially one so powerful—without something more concrete."

"Evidence be damned!" Theramus thundered. "We know him to be guilty. He has her, and we shall free her from his clutches."

"Then we need to get proof," Balien said.

"Attacking a count in his own home is a prickly thorn bush," Illyria mused aloud. "It can be passed through, but not without care and caution. If Attenham does have her, the whole of the Dragonfleet will not be able to stop us from rescuing her, but, if we charge through blindly, we'll find ourselves shredded. We need council."

"Council?" Eldoth repeated, incredulous. "Advice is useless here, as are laws. In fact..." Balien gave him a pointed look and, to Theramus's surprise, he subsided. "...but perhaps your strategy also has merit."

"We should seek out Lord Jannery," Balien said. "He is staying with Duke Raebyrne. They will be able to advise us."

Yet another delay. Theramus did not like it, but he was the first to admit that his judgement was lacking in matters such as this. He had decided long ago to follow the path of his younger, cannier, companions. Noss followed, it was their way, and he would: to the feet of Zulum himself if need be.

CHAPTER NINETEEN

"And then Anur beheld Imusasus and the waters of the Lifestream that flowed from it to create a mighty lake. Anur then created several large ewers which he gave to Nasha and her children. 'Use these, my daughter, and see to it that the waters of the Lifestream fall only onto the hearts of sleeping titans. This is your task for as long as it puts forth water.' Nasha, ever the dutiful daughter, agreed, and it was so.

"Anur then used his titan magic upon a handful of unborn souls. 'I hereby name you Imvir,' he said to them. 'The Lifestream is now be your home, and it shall ever be your task to traverse its length, betwixt beginning and end. You are the wardens of the unborn, and under your watchful eyes, none will ever fail in their purpose of creating life. This is a good life, a good purpose, that I give to you. Be happy in what you do, for you spread joy.'

"Being so purposed, the quicklings leapt from his hands with happy cries and dove into the waters of the Lifestream, and from that day forevermore was that lake known as the Lake of Joy."

—Ancient Histories of the Middle Waters

Redding was getting tired of making excuses for the whereabouts of his mistress. It was well known that there was no love lost between himself and his wife, who never left her estate in Deremshire. She had no issue with his public dalliance with Myria, so long as they did not appear at formal functions together and that any bastards he had by her would not endanger the legitimacy of his legal offspring. The former was not a problem since Myria was usually busy during formal occasions, and the latter would never, ever be a factor.

There were, however, many *informal* occasions when he and his 'mistress' appeared together and, after a short period of moral outrage at court, it had become common and accepted for him to be seen at social gatherings with her on his arm. While it was not yet fashionable for married men to parade in public with young, beautiful women on their arms, Redding was fairly certain that trend would change once he officially became Ander's royal councillor.

The court's familiarity with Myria, and their like of her appealing contrast of refinement and coarseness, made it difficult for him the few times that her 'business' kept her occupied. The Duke of Stollerton's SummersEnd ball was *the* social event of the season, and there was no reason why Myria should not have been present and displaying the cutting edge fashion that she had become known for. There were only so many ways that Redding could explain that she wasn't feeling well and might arrive later before he grew sick of it.

He would have rather not attended tonight, everything being as close to the cusp as it was, but that would have been disastrous. As the leader of the Anderites and confidant of the crown prince, it was essential, not just for his supporters but also his enemies, that he be seen in public strong and confident.

For one of the first times, the luxury of his station meant nothing to him. He didn't care about the fit and expensive embroidery that went into his jacket, the exotic flavours and rich textures of the food and drink or the obvious wealth displayed in the room and on the guests. At first, after being named Count, that had been all that mattered to him. As the fourth son of the younger brother of the previous Lord of Deremshire, he had thought himself doomed to knighthood or, worse, civil service. When Myria had first arrived and dangled his wildest dreams before him, he had revelled in the pleasures given to Peers of the Realm. Now, less than a day before that dream's fruition, he found that he really didn't give a damn.

Tomorrow, he would be the crown councillor to a king. He would be the third most powerful man in Karalon, behind only Ander (who he would control) and the knight-grandmaster (who Myria had taken care of). The fripperies in this room were the *trappings* of power. They were nothing next to power itself.

Everyone in the room knew it, too. His star, already level with the heads of dukes and princes, was about to fly higher than the Karnems, and they all wanted to rise along with him. Myria's absence had been noted by many of the pretty young women in the room to whom social climbing was a necessary tool in life. He was both flattered and tempted by their thinly veiled offers (divorce *was* possible for a Peer of the Realm, just difficult), but regretted that he could not accept any, or at least, not now. His star was too firmly tied to Myria's, and he could not risk upsetting her plans at this point. She needed to be his mistress as much as he needed her unique services. He couldn't be seen to be disloyal to her.

Everything would change tomorrow, though. Once Ander was crowned and Redding was named his councillor, he would be free to share the company of women who would be mistresses in deed as well as name. Until then, he would have to wait.

He'd gotten used to it.

The truly well-endowed woman currently flirting with him abruptly cut off whatever she had been saying. Eyes wide and face suddenly pale, she gave a quick curtsy and mumbled excuse before leaving. Redding had just begun to turn to see what nightmarish vision could have inspired such a panicked flight when he felt small feminine hands encircle his waist. Despite their size and gentle appearance, they were very strong and he understood.

"Act pleasantly surprised. People are watching," Myria whispered into his ear. No doubt it looked like she was whispering endearments to him.

"It's about damn time you got here," he whispered. The entire damn room was indeed watching. Having Redding's mistress sneak up and surprise him while he flirted with another woman would undoubtedly be the height of tonight's entertainment.

"And who was she?" she asked accusingly, loud enough to be heard by those around them.

He spun to face her and took her hands in his own, his face a mask of apology. "She was nothing. Nobody. A pale shadow compared to you."

Her finger dug into his wrist, a silent signal that she needed to see him alone. He bent in to kiss her but she turned her head in the classic female rebuttal.

So that is how she wants to play this.

They proceeded to have a polite public squabble. It was a tired, predictable dance by now. He knew her act well enough to recognise when she was giving him an opening to apologise, which would be followed by her wanting to return home with him so that she could accept his apology in private.

Instead, he plucked a goblet of wine off a passing steward and struck up a conversation with the Duchess of Stollerton. He didn't need to hear the surprised murmuring of the other guests to know that his move had caught his mistress off guard.

He knew it was petty and foolish. He knew that he would pay for it later, but it was the only real power he had. In public, Myria was his mistress. In public, she had to do what *he* said.

"If you wanted to make her angry, Redding, I dare say you've succeeded," the duchess told him, watching over his shoulder.

Redding smiled. "Have I told you lately how beautiful you are, Addie?"

She laughed. "You'll be sleeping with the dogs for a week if she hears you say that."

His face hardened. "Not if she wants to share the company of the royal advisor, she won't."

The duchess's eyes widened. "You're not thinking of changing mistresses, are you, Redding? After all that woman has done for you?"

"After what *she* has done for *me?*" he could not help but snarl, realizing after he said it that he had potentially revealed too much.

The Duchess took his arm and led him across the room to where Myria was flirting with a handsome young knight more heavily and blatantly than Redding had been. "Myria, dear, take this one home before he makes an even larger fool of himself." The two women embraced and the duchess murmured something into Myria's ear.

Redding's 'mistress' took both of his hands in her own and gave him an inviting smile. "Come, my love. It is bad form to disobey a duchess at her own party."

He couldn't rebel anymore without making even more of a scene. Reluctantly, he allowed himself to be pulled from the hall and into his carriage. She dropped his hands like he was a plague carrier the moment they were hidden from view.

"What was that?"

Redding shrugged carelessly. "It is the night before our victory. I wanted to celebrate."

"It's too early for celebration, *My Lord*," she said with long suffering patience.

Redding grinned, knowing that he had gotten to her. Why shouldn't he be free of her strings, even if just for one night? "Well, it's not like you'll celebrate with me," he goaded, the honeywine he had drunk giving him courage.

For a moment she made no attempt to hide the dislike he knew she felt for him. "I have prisoners," she said a moment later, softening. "Would you like to see them before they die?"

It had worked. He had gotten her to back down, even if it was just over a small point. Redding smiled. He was going to enjoy this. "I would like that very much."

It was getting hard for Gennald to keep his focus. His captors hadn't been gentle outside the city gates, when they'd bound, gagged, and trussed him before throwing him into the back of a cart and hauling him through New Aukaster. They'd been even less gentle unloading him once they'd arrived at their destination (somewhere in the noble quarter, he thought), thrown him to the ground and carried him to wherever he was now. They had deliberately knocked him into every door frame and corner they could as they had hauled him down some stairs into a basement. He hadn't been so beaten so badly since his hazing before taking his oaths of knighthood.

There was someone else there with him. He'd heard them fighting outside the city and had felt them bump into him during the trip in the cart. Whoever it was, they were smaller than him, which meant little since the only one larger than him in Illyria's merry band was Theramus. He hoped it wasn't Illyria, after all he had done for her freedom. Was it Balien, perhaps? He hoped so. A hot flame burned inside Illyria's soft-spoken brother, though he seldom allowed others to see it.

He didn't know how long he lay on the floor of wherever he was, bruised and in pain. Certainly long enough to realize that it stank horribly. If he had to describe it, he'd say that someone had poured curdled milk over a week-old body, dumped it into a vat of sour beer and left it all in the hot sun. Whatever it was, it reeked. There were several men in the room with him, and they weren't afraid to kick him when he moved. It didn't take long for him to learn to remain still. He soon came to deeply appreciate just how much pain he was in.

After a long, painful eternity, he heard two sets of footsteps coming down the stairs.

"I want to speak to them," he heard a familiar male voice say.

"I had intended to handle the interrogation personally, My Lord," a female voice—the soft footed brunette from the cave, no doubt—replied. "You are welcome to watch, but I expect it to take a while."

"So long as I can see her face when you do," the first voice said. "You should untie them, Myria. Make it sporting."

"No names," the woman—Myria—hissed. "This is no sport. He's a knight and you heard what the girl did in Westbridge. She's dangerous."

Gennald froze. They did have Illyria.

"I'm sure that was exaggerated," the still unnamed man scoffed. "Look at her: she's tiny. Besides, she's unarmed. I have her 'amazing magic dagger' that our guest went on about. Are you saying that you can't handle one little snake girl?"

No, it wasn't Illyria here with him at all, it was Sephana. Gennald didn't know how he felt about that.

Myria made no reply. "At least remove their hoods," the male voice suggested.

Gennald heard soft footsteps approach from behind him and then someone crouching. The noose around his neck loosened and then fell away, followed by the lengths around his arms and ankles. Another, separate, rope still bound his wrists behind his back. Two sets of strong hands hauled him to his feet and only then was the sack pulled off his head and his gag removed.

He took in as much as he could. It was indeed Sephana standing next to him, just as bound as he was, her hair rumpled, and her eyes spitting flame. He couldn't see any bruises on her, but that didn't mean much with her dark skin. The room was medium sized and obviously some kind of store room. Various sundries lay in stacks and piles along the walls and a large, cloth covered crate occupied the far side of the room. Directly in front of him was indeed the dark haired woman from the cave—Myria—as well as the source of the voice he thought he had recognised.

"Attenham," he spat. "You're committing treason. Your head will roll for this."

The traitorous noble was holding Sephana's dagger by its scabbard and absently slapped the pommel into the palm of his free hand. "*Count* Attenham," he corrected absently, "and soon to be much, much more." He turned to Myria. "I understand the snake girl: she suits our purposes, but aren't there supposed to be five? And why Jannery's knight? He's useless to us."

Myria was visibly annoyed. "There were complications. I lost five men. The elves escaped into the forest."

Illyria was safe. That was all that mattered.

"And what is the knight, then? A consolation prize? I'm not consoled."

Myria smiled thinly. "He's bait. I heard it from her own lips: the elf girl is in love with him."

"Is she now?"Attenham looked down his nose at Gennald. "You'd think she'd set her sights somewhat higher."

"Zulum take you!" Gennald spat, but Attenham had already turned away. He turned his scrutiny to Sephana, who squirmed under his gaze. He looked at her like she was a bug, and he had bad breath.

"By Emuranna, but you're even more hideous close up." He brushed her hair back and leaned in to examine her ear pit. "How can any of the Reshai been allowed to live? I will rectify that error once Lionar does us all the favour of dying tomorrow."

Veiled stares on the street were one thing, but blatant death threats were something else. Eyes narrowing to slits, she lunged forward and slammed her forehead into his face. She would have preferred to break his nose but was content to hit him in the mouth and bloody his lip.

"Ghaa, she's a beast!" he spat, retreating even the guard holding her jerked her backwards. "Even dogmen have better manners," He raised Dawn's First Crescent to examine. In spite of the pain she knew was coming, it heartened her to see that her weapon was here and not back in New Wighton. He struck her across her cheek with it, the unbreakable Ansharite pommel cutting into her skin.

"Beast?" she snapped, her cheek throbbing. She could not help but think about Edrik. "I'm not the one who ordered me tied to a stake and ordered the execution of an innocent man!"

Attenham dabbed at his bleeding lip with a cloth. "Ah, yes: the fugitive snake girl from last year. I thought that might be you. There can't be too many hideous things wandering about with snake tails." He looked down at her tail in revulsion. "Why weren't you drowned in a sack at birth? Isn't that you do with freaks of nature?"

She should have been frightened. After what had happened to her, where she was, and what she knew was going to happen to her; she should have been terrified. To her surprise, while she did feel that fear stirring somewhere beneath the surface of her mind, it was dwarfed by her immense anger. Even Eldoth at his worst had never made her quite this mad before.

"My friends are going to find me, expose you, and make sure you never get appointed advisor to anything," she growled.

Attenham laughed. He laughed! "Oh, I don't think so. My Lady here—" He nodded smugly at Myria. "—travels routes that no one can follow. Even if they do know to come here—which I doubt—they will never arrive before Lionar kills himself and then it will be far too late for you."

"My Lord!" Myria said sharply. "Perhaps it would be best if you retired and allowed me to complete this."

Sephana watched as he looked pointedly at the guards in the room and then back at Myria. He smiled. "Oh, please. Our victory is assured at this point and so is the very convenient, incriminating death of this wretched mongrel." He turned back to Sephana, his eyes gleaming with hate. "You and your circus band of friends are known allies of the Golden Bears. It would have been nice having more of them here to paint the picture I wanted, but you and your snake scales will do, I think."

Sephana could see Myria fuming—although she was trying to hide it—but Attenham seemed intent to gloat. Goading him was easy. "You couldn't paint a picture even if someone sketched it out for you," Sephana said with a sneer. She put just the right amount of arrogance—learned from Eldoth—into her words. "No one is going to believe your pathetic fabrication."

"Oh, but I will!" he replied, furious. "An ally of the Golden Bears, secretly working in league with the Dragonfleet? Their power block within the Council of Peers will be destroyed, and I will be the most powerful man in Karalon."

"You're doing all of this for political leverage?" Gennald asked, aghast.

"Hey, wait a minute," Sephana said. "What's all this about allying with the Dragonfleet? No one's going to believe that."

He grinned evilly. "Oh, they will. You see, there will be a witness!" He strode over to a cloth covered crate.

"My Lord, no!" Myria yelled.

He ignored her and pulled on the cloth. It covered a cage, in which crouched a small, dirty rat-like creature covered in coarse, black fur. There was a bandage on its back. Sephana stared. She'd seen this creature before. In fact, she had fought it in Westbridge.

"Meet Kaystan," Attenham said theatrically. "Your band of circus freaks were quite thorough removing all evidence of the Dragonfleet raid, and in ensuring the villager's silence." He glowered. "I tried threats and bribery against them, but nothing worked. I was about to give up entirely when Myria found our new friend here." He laid a hand on the top of the cage. The rat-man glared up at him with intelligent, hate-filled eyes. "It told us quite an interesting story about what had happened there, and it will tell another one when my knights come across your treasonous corpse next to all of the stolen tribute money. Obviously, you were cutting a deal with the Dragonfleet on behalf of your Golden Bear masters."

"No one will believe that!"

"Ander will, if Attenham is the one to tell him," Gennald said dully. "If he becomes the new crown councillor, he controls what information the king receives and from whom. A young king, his father still fresh in his grave. I imagine he'd believe anything he's told." Gennald nodded. "It's brilliant."

"Hey! Who's side are you on?"

"I'm so glad you approve." Attenham said to him. "You're not entirely stupid, are you?"

Sephana thought back over the last few weeks. "So that was why you had the blackshields try and capture us after our audience?"

He shook his head. "Sadly, no. If that had been my intent, I would have succeeded." He glanced at Myria. "Or perhaps not."

So who did order that attack then? The answer to that question would have to wait.

Sephana wracked her brain. There was still something that didn't make sense. Hopefully she could manage to goad Attenham in to revealing the rest of her plan. Of course, after that, she still had to escape...

"This whole stupid plan of yours only works if Lionar doesn't Join with the Land. You're just an ordinary count," she told him, her voice dripping with enough disdain to be worthy of Eldoth. "There is no way you could manage that."

"Trust me: that conclusion is all but guaranteed." He looked at her with knowing eyes. "Perhaps I have said too much. Bind her," he ordered, "and put her somewhere that I don't have to look at her. She pains my eyes."

This was her chance. She had to act now, before they locked her up like that rat-man. "You made one mistake, Attenham," Sephana taunted.

He turned. "Oh, and what is that?"

"You took my dagger from me," she said levelly.

He glanced down at Dawn's First Crescent, still held in both his hands. "I did, didn't I? It will make a fine coronation gift for my new king, I think."

Sephana made no reply, just flexed her hand, the one that still wore her controlling glove, in just the right way. The hidden pommel blades, each of them razor sharp, completely unbreakable, and more than an inch long snapped out and bit into Attenham's hand, which was wrapped around the pommel.

Gennald knew the capabilities of Sephana's dagger well enough to know what would happen next. Attenham, fool that he was, did not, and his hand paid the price for it. He shrieked in pain and threw the weapon from him. Myria was either more prepared for danger than her master, or she had the reflexes of a cat, because she had darted in and hurried him from the room before Sephana's dagger had stopped rolling. In less than a heartbeat, there was just Gennald, Sephana and four guards in the room, along with a bared dagger on the floor.

"Secure them!" Myria ordered as she disappeared, but Gennald and Sephana were already moving.

Gennald did not have time to be angry at the strange twist of fate that had placed him in this predicament with the one Knight of Anduilon that he disliked above all others. That didn't matter now. He had many issues with the classless Reshai girl, but her ability to act quickly was not among them. She wanted the same as he did, and that made her his ally, albeit a reluctant one.

The first thing he had to do was get free. Free of ropes that bound him would have been ideal, but he would settle for simply escaping the grip of his captors. He had very little time to act before they stopped being startled by the sudden violence against Attenham. He twisted with his body, using all of his weight to try and wrench himself out of the grip of the two men. It worked with the one on his left, but the other man's grip was too firm. Gennald pushed towards the man, bent his knees and then drove his head upward into the man's jaw.

It hurt, but he was braced for it (and had nothing to lose), while his captor was not. He felt the impact though his skull at the same time he heard a hollow knocking sound and felt the grip on his arm loosen.

Across from him, Sephana had freed herself with her tail somehow and was scrambling towards her fallen dagger. One of her captors had been upended onto the floor while the second just looked angry and was not even a step behind her. Gennald knew that, tied up as she was, there was no way she could get to her knife and free herself with it before he caught her.

As much as he would rather hold the strange dagger himself, better she have it than one of the guards. Not allowing himself to ponder the wisdom of his act, Gennald hurled himself at the guard that was so close to catching Sephana. He did his best to drive his shoulder into the man's spine, and they both fell in a heap in the corner. Sephana skidded to a halt in front of her dagger, felt around her with hands still tied behind her back, and managed to grab it.

Her original captor, the one she had knocked over, had gotten to his feet and had pulled a truncheon off of his belt. Gennald, from his place on the ground and still struggling with the one he had knocked over, kicked out with his foot and caused him to trip. Then the last man was on him and he could do no more.

As much as it galled him, it was all up to Sephana now.

Ross D Jenkins

● ∪ ■ ✕ ▼ ★

Unless she was flying through the air, Sephana normally thought of her tail as more than a hindrance then a benefit. It got her a lot of unwanted attention, made getting clothes really difficult, and got really cold in the winter; but it could be really handy when fighting men who had no experience against people who had them. They hadn't realized that, even as tied and bound as she was, she still had one limb free. She didn't have fingers or toes on the end, and it wasn't flexible enough to grab a weapon or a stick, but it could wrap around a leg easy enough and it was *strong*, as strong as her leg at least. She had knocked the guard on her left onto his butt before he had even known that she was trying to escape, and smacked the other one on the back of his head with the tip before the first had hit the ground. It wasn't enough to really hurt him, but it had startled enough that he had loosened his grip, and then she was gone.

Dawn's First Crescent was laying on the floor, surrounded by Attenham's blood (it was too bad that he hadn't been holding it against his crotch!). She ran towards it, knowing that the man she'd tail-swatted in the head was right behind her. She hadn't gotten five steps towards it before Gennald—Gennald, who hated her—had crashed into him and cleared her path.

Dammit. Now I can't hate him.

She squatted overtop her dagger and tried to find it by feel. The nearest guard to her fell when Gennald kicked out his ankle—now she *really* couldn't hate him— and one of the others tried to recapture him, which left one other. He was bleeding fairly badly from his mouth, but he had his truncheon out and, from the look in his eye, wanted to spread some of his pain around. Sephana, lucky her, seemed to be the one he wanted to share it with.

Her dagger continued to elude her, and the guy with the bloody mouth was getting closer. Just before thought she might have to flee without it, she felt it with one of her fingers. She grabbed it and leapt out of the way of the heavy wooden club, which missed her by inches.

Okay, what do I do now? She backed warily away from the guard, looking for something—anything—she could use to her advantage. Turning Dawn's First Crescent in her hands and cutting her bonds would take her too long, and she didn't want to risk it while fighting. What else was there? She could run, but there were only two ways out of the room. One was the door that Attenham and Myria had escaped through and the other was right behind the guard and his truncheon.

Gennald and the three men subduing him with their boots were between her and the stairs. That left her with door number two, and the faint hope that there was something in there that could help her escape. In any other city, she'd search for a sewer escape, but that was pointless here. The best she could hope for was...she had no idea, but it couldn't be worse than staying here.

The Bear and the Thistle

Bloody Mouth advanced towards her, weapon swinging. Sephana feinted left and ran right, towards where the rat-man was still trapped in his cage. She threw herself onto the cage's top, rolling over it with her shoulder and barely keeping grip on her dagger. She landed on the floor on the opposite end of the cage—tail making sure she didn't over balance and fall—just as the guard slammed into it, his weapon striking only air.

The rat-man hissed and gibbered at both of them while Sephana got to her feet and ran for the now clear door. It was closed, of course, and she turned and slammed into it with her back. The guard ran around the cage with its angry occupant and rushed towards her. Her tail fumbled with the door latch—luckily it was a simple lifting bar and not a knob—and she fell back across the threshold just underneath his grabbing hands.

She scrambled backwards into the room. It was going to be hard to escape the guard on the ground the way she was, but he didn't follow her inside. Instead, face white with fear, he reached in just far enough to grab the door handle, and slammed it shut it.

Oh, this is not good.

Gennald stopped fighting once he saw Sephana escape through the far door. He was still tied up and outnumbered three to one. Further resistance now would just get him even more injured. She'd be fine on her own. She would have to be, because Gennald didn't think he had much fight left in him.

A man could only take so many kicks to the ribs.

They struck him a few more times with their boots before they realized that he wasn't struggling. When they hauled him (roughly) to his feet, he noticed that all four men were still in the room with him. Even the one he'd struck in the jaw, who'd been chasing Sephana.

"Well that's that, then," the man on Gennald's right said.

"She's as good as dead, going in there," the one he'd shoulder-checked agreed.

The bloody-mouthed one said nothing and instead punched Gennald painfully in the stomach.

"What...is...in...that...room?" Gennald gasped out when he finally righted himself.

"We don't know. Lady Myria brought it, and no one who's gone into that room has ever come out alive."

"We call it 'The Thing'," the second guard said.

Gennald's hope vanished. He couldn't escape now—that horse had left the stable—and, unless some unseen opportunity presented itself, there was nothing he could do to prevent being used as a hostage against Illyria. He was doomed.

Sephana looked around her but couldn't see anything. The only light in the room came from the crack under the now closed door and all it revealed was a dusty, web strewn floor. What she did notice was that the awful smell that had made the previous room stink so badly was even worse in here.

She turned and lay her back against the door. She didn't know what was in here, but the fact that whatever it was could frighten an armed man made her cautious. Eyes vainly searching the darkness, she fumbled with Dawn's First Crescent until she was finally able to cut herself free. She clutched the dagger defensively in front of her. Of course, it was hard to defend against something when she didn't know where or what it was. Maybe the guard just didn't like the smell.

Slowly and cautiously, she got to her feet. Her eyes were slowly becoming accustomed to the dark and she was barely able to make out the layout of the room. It was mostly clear. There was a lump of something in the middle and what looked like another door on the other end. She began to cautiously edge around the room, keeping her back to the wall the entire time.

She kicked an empty crate and the sound seemed unnaturally loud in the darkness. She cursed, ignored the pain in her toe, and continued. She made it to the first corner without further incident and had edged maybe five feet beyond it when she felt something un-wall-like beneath her hand. It was coarse and fibrous, almost like a vine, but sticky. She shook her hand free and reached beyond it but felt only more thick, sticky strands.

Something above her moved. Something big.

She didn't wait to find out what it was. Pushing away from the wall, she ran across the room towards the far door. She tripped over something in the darkness and fell headlong onto the floor. Whatever it was she had run into had shifted when she kicked it and now lay alongside her. The light from under the door fell squarely onto it, and Sephana now saw that she was looking into the face of a dead man.

A *very* dead man. Oddly, his body hadn't rotted as much as it had...dried up. Its skin was withered and leathery, its eyes sunk in, and it had an expression of extreme pain on what was left of its face.

In the split second before she scrambled to her feet, Sephana realized that she had seen that face before. Five days ago. It had been on top of a horse and wearing a steel helmet, but she had met this person. How could she forget? He'd called her a snakespawn.

The Bear and the Thistle

That's impossible. How can the High Priest of Karalon be both alive there and dead here at the same time?

Whatever she had heard above her moved again. It was a heavier sound, almost like...skittering, and Sephana wasted no more time on thought. All the fear that she had pushed down came and she ran across the darkened room, terrified. She tripped on something, recovered, slipped on something else and then fell bodily against the door. There was more skittering behind her and Sephana fumbled with her hands, looking for some kind of latch or handle.

The sound in the darkness became impossibly loud and she almost gave up in her search but then she found a deadbolt at head height. It was stiff and coated in some sort of viscous liquid, but her fright gave her strength. Jerking the bolt back, she flung the door open and ran through. On the other side she hurriedly slammed it shut, and apparently just in time, because a moment later something large and heavy imbedded itself on the far side.

Wherever she was now, it was just as dark as the last room but somehow so much less creepy. The door bucked against her hands and she leaned against it, holding it shut with her back and legs. *I have to find some way to shut it.* Whatever it was slammed into the door again and again she barely managed to keep it shut. There was a moment of frightening silence and then it struck again, harder. Knowing that she wouldn't be able to hold back many more of those, she knelt and pressed Dawn's First Crescent into the crack at the bottom of the door. The pommel spikes extended, their Ansharite blades biting into both the stone floor and wooden door as easily as they had into Attenham's fingers. Whatever it was on the other side would have to break the door off its hinges to get through now. Dawn's First Crescent wasn't going anywhere.

She took her dagger and released the chain that connected it to the pommel. Now she could use her dagger against anything else that might be in here as well as keep the whatever-it-was entrapped on the other side, as long as was within thirty feet of the pommel.

It wouldn't do her any good if she couldn't find a source of light. The room was as black as Attenham's soul, without the benefit of even a crack of light. Her nose and the tip of her tail both told her that it was quite dusty; a good sign, as it meant that nothing had walked on these floors in weeks. So long as the door held, she was safe...or, at least, that was what she hoped.

Of course, that thing had *crawled down the wall* towards her. It didn't need a floor...

The banging against the door stopped, leaving only ominous silence and the rapid beating of Sephana's heart. Her breaths came fast and heavy and seemed unnaturally loud to her own ears. She held her breath, straining even harder to detect any sound, but heard nothing. *I liked it better when it was trying to break down the door. It least then I knew where it was.*

She crept along one side, keeping one hand on the wall and using the other to clutch Dawn's First Crescent. She found some furniture along one wall—some sort of workbench—but other than that the room seemed to be empty. There wasn't even a door.

The only way out seemed to be the way she came, past that...thing.

"Gha! Damn that snakespawn bitch. She maimed me!"

The voice was obviously Attenham's. It was distant and muffled, like she was hearing it through something, but what?

Attenham cried out in pain and Sephana smiled. *Serves you right, too! I hope it gets possessed by a disease spirit.*

She turned her head rapidly from side to side, trying to hear where his voice was coming from, but her earpits made it hard. Unlike human ears, which stuck out from the sides of their heads, her earpits were basically holes in her skull. Despite what some stupid people thought, she could hear just fine. In fact, she could make out some sounds—low ones, like hoof beats or war drums—even better than men. What she had trouble with was figuring out where sounds came from. What took someone like Eldoth less than a second to determine could take her five times as long, if she figured it out at all.

"Augh! Gently, woman," she heard, barely. "I have already lost two fingers to that Zulum-cursed blade! Do you seek to tear the others off as well?"

Someone—Myria?—made an unintelligible murmur and then there was another cry of pain.

She found it! There was a fireplace against the far wall and Attenham's cries of agony were coming down its chimney. Sephana ducked her head into the cold, dry hearth and looked up. There was light! It wasn't much, just a faint square against the one side of the chimney, but, as the first thing she'd seen in minutes that wasn't trying to kill her, she thought it was beautiful. What was more, while the chimney was pretty narrow, it wasn't so much so that she couldn't climb it. The insides were rough enough to act as finger and toe holds, and she was pretty sure that she could brace herself against the sides even if they smoothed out. She was a good free climber; she could make it.

As long as the shaft didn't narrow as it went up, or it wasn't too tall, or nobody lit a fire beneath her as she climbed...

Stop that! Anything is better than where you are. Climb!

She ducked into the narrow stone shaft but had to stop for a moment before she began climbing. It was narrower than she had first thought. She might get really stuck in here, and no one knew where she was except for the mysterious skittering monster. Somehow she doubted that it would tell anyone.

Sephana crept up the narrow chimney. Her hand was still on Dawn's First Crescent, which made climbing harder, but she wasn't letting go. If she let go that would mean that she'd have to retract the pommel, which would let...*it*...into the room. Just the chimney itself was a big enough challenge; there was no point adding to her problems. Instead, she climbed.

Finally, when she was fully inside the shaft and nearing the end of the chain's length, she retracted the dagger's pommel blades and retracted the chain. Then and only then did she tuck the weapon into her belt and begin to climb in earnest. She heard the door creak open below her and then more of that spine-chilling skittering. It got closer to the fireplace and then stopped.

Sephana could either try to be as silent as possible or do her best to climb even faster. Freezing might have made more sense, but there was no way she was going to manage to keep still and silent while the creepy, mysterious *thing* was right below her. Sephana climbed faster.

She was nearing the square of light when she heard more talking.

Redding still didn't understand what had happened. One second he had been taunting the hideous snake-scaled bitch and the next something had happened to his hand. It hadn't really hurt, not at first. It had been too sudden and he had been more shocked by the sight of the bloody ruin of his hand than anything else. Myria had rushed him up the stairs to his library before he been able to think and pressed a cloth into his profusely bleeding extremity. He had still been taking in what had happened when she had vanished back into the basement.

He wasn't drunk anymore. The injury and the excitement had exorcised any final traces of honeywine from his system, leaving him sober, bleeding, and in pain. It had happened too suddenly for him to feel it at first, just a sense of unreality and numbness, but now it hurt: a sharp, deep pain that throbbed up his arm into his chest as if pressed by a titan. He'd lost two fingers, he knew that much, and couldn't move the other two. Only his thumb was still capable of movement, but every time he tried it sent out piercing shots of agony and he'd soon stopped trying.

He'd been stupid. He shouldn't have drunk as much as he did, and he shouldn't have tried to get a rise out of Myria in front of his men, where she had to defer to him.

And now, the day before his victory, he had been maimed.

How would he sell this? A wound of this type would be impossible to conceal, not at court where his every move and aspect of his appearance was scrutinized and gossiped about. The leader of the Anderites had to be seen as being strong. It was part of his job to appear vital and unconcerned.

Myria came back a few minutes later. Her face was as blank as always but he could see that under her mask, she was shaking with rage. She knelt in front of him—wearing her nurses uniform, ironically—and gently pulled the cloth away from his wound.

It was too red, too much like a piece of meat, for his stomach to handle and he had to look away. A moment later he could feel her beginning to stitch up his wound. "You have to punish her for this," he ordered with a hiss. "I know you can't kill her, not yet, but you can maim her like she did me. I want to watch."

"I told you not to say anything," she said neutrally.

"That doesn't matter now!" He cried out as she did something particularly painful. "She'll be dead in two days, anyway. She can't tell anyone. She's a prisoner."

"Not anymore. She escaped."

Redding blinked. He must have heard that wrong, what with the life threatening wound he had just received. "What? Escape where? Escape how? There's no other way out."

"She ran into the store room."

"The—" He paused and grimaced. That was that, then. "Oh. What about the plan then? Are you going to try to lure the she-elf out with that knight? Is there still time for that?"

She made no reply and he gritted his teeth as she tied off the thread on his first wound. "No need. There should still be enough of the Reshai girl to identify if we get the body back soon enough. Her tail is easy to identify. We can say she was burned by fire, maybe."

He had to laugh. It was either that or cry. "Burned to death," he chuckled. "It's appropriate, for her."

Myria said nothing.

"I can't believe that she was the only one of them you captured," he snapped, not thinking to filter his words through his pain. "We wouldn't be having this problem if you had done what you had said and—aieee!!!"

Agony; intense, blinding, body-wracking agony consumed Redding's body and he realized to late who he had been speaking to and in what manner. He had fallen to his knees before her and was cringing in pain before he realized it. Anything to make the pain stop.

"Do not presume, *My Lord*, that you can order me around like one of your knights," she hissed. "I made you who you are, Redding. I chose you, out of all your relatives, because I knew that you were the easiest to control. *I* put you in power. *I* made you the leader of the Anderites, and *I* gave you control of the outlaws that manufactured this crisis. You are nothing."

"In two days I will be Ander's royal advisor," he gasped. "You can't kill me, not now."

She tightened her grip and he cried out, his wordless cry high and shrill. "Don't think that your new position will protect you from me, *Count*. I know your every sin and your every secret, things that not even a king can protect you from." She released her grip on his hand and the pain stopped. The underlying throbbing agony was still there, but Redding found that he welcomed it. That pain was bearable. "You are my creature," she continued, "and you will do what I say, when I say."

He knew when he was beat. There was nothing he could do, not now. Redding grovelled before her, his bloody (and still dripping) hand cradled to his chest. "Forgive me, My Lady. What do you wish of me?"

"Get the snake girl's body back, if she's actually dead."

He cringed. "Yes, My Lady, as you wish, but how could she be alive? No one has survived against that thing."

"The girl is resourceful." Myria's voice said in a more conversational tone, content in her dominance. "I'm not going to truly believe her dead until I see her body. Things are too delicate now to take any chances."

Redding didn't move. "Yes, My Lady. What else would you have of me?"

"I must leave. It is up to you to keep your Anderites wound up and maintain control of the crown prince.

"Where are you going, My Lady, if I may ask?"

Ice was warmer than her eyes. "To the palace, to tend to the king, and then to fix your mess. The girl's fellow knights are still at large, and you told her almost our entire plan. We still have Illyria's lover, as you say. Perhaps we can use him to control her. I will take him with me along with the outlaws to guard the vale until the end of the king's Joining. All our work will be for naught if that does not go as we wish it."

"Emuranna's Grace, My Lady," Attenham grovelled.

Myria strode from the room but stopped on its threshold. "This could be your finest moment, Redding, if you do what you're told." She paused and smiled. It made her look both beautiful and cruel. "You should probably see to that hand; it's bleeding."

Redding didn't dare say the curse he wanted to aloud, not when she was within earshot.

Gennald lay in a corner of the secret basement room, too tired to move even if he had the will to do so. They had beaten him again, on Myria's order. She wanted him too wounded to run, but not so much that he couldn't walk. They had performed their jobs with enthusiasm.

He had heard some banging from the room Sephana had run into, but nothing more. Certainly no screams or cries for help. Perhaps whatever was in there had slain her so quickly that she had been unable, but the sounds from within suggested a struggle of some kind, and she hadn't said a word. He hated to admit it, but that kind of bravery was very knightly. Despite everything she was and everything he had said to her, she had died in a way that any knight in Karalon would have to respect.

He didn't know if he would face his end so well. It was coming, he was sure of that. He had seen the face of the conspiracy against his king. They had to kill him. He was alive now, he knew, only because they planned to use him against Illyria. If he could have killed himself to stop it from happening, he would, but even that ability had been taken from him.

Further contemplation was interrupted by the sound of someone coming down the stairs. It wasn't Myria's tread, but someone else's. Gennald looked up to see Redding Attenham, most of him at least, coming towards him. A red tinged bandage swaddled his left hand.

"Leave us," he ordered the guards. Attenham, his face pale, stared at Gennald. Gennald, lacking the energy to look away, returned it.

"I find myself in need of a new lieutenant," Attenham said without preamble. "Lady Myria has reached the end of her usefulness to me."

It took Gennald a moment to realize what was being said. "And you want *me* to replace her?"

"You impress me. You are intelligent, skilled, and capable of thinking for yourself. A man in my service with those attributes could go far."

Gennald eyed him warily. "I am loyal to my lord."

Attenham's eyes lit and Gennald realized that he had been outmanoeuvred somehow. "Are you really that loyal? Then why are you in the company of a group of foreigners who profane everything that knighthood represents? A group, I might add, who left you to die."

"I—" Gennald began to protest out of reflex but stopped. To counter Attenham's argument would mean defending Illyria's ludicrous and offensive claims and he couldn't do it, not even to the slime currently standing in front of him. "You have, by your own admission, conspired against the crown," he said instead. "I will not aid a traitor."

Attenham smiled wolfishly. "You only say that because I have not yet named your payment."

The Bear and the Thistle

"There is nothing you could offer me that I would want," Gennald spat.

Attenham didn't acknowledge his protest. "Your father is a burgess, is he not?" They both knew that he was. Gennald declined to answer. "He has given a lifetime of service to Jannery and commands the most important castle in all of Karalon, and his only reward is the right to administrate some tiny little croft in the Northmarch. And, when he dies, he can't even pass it on to you. He's just a *yeoman*."

Gennald just glared.

"Your great-grandfather was knighted in the Year of Broken Lances, and given land and title for his brave actions?"

"Which *your* great-grandfather forced the king to revoke," Gennald snapped. "I know my family's history."

Attenham's smile widened. "When this is over, I will have the ear of the king and control of the Council. I can make you a landed noble, Gennald: a baron, or even a count. What do you think? Is that price enough to give me your loyalty?"

Gennald was struck dumb.

CHAPTER TWENTY

" 'As your vassal, I give my life into your service. I promise, with Emuranna as my witness, to be faithful to you, never cause you harm, execute your service, to act in good faith towards you, and always be without deceit.'

" 'As your liege lord, I accept you into my service. I will protect you and your family and provide for their well being in times of need. I will treat you justly and with honour. I swear this in Emuranna's name.' "

—Karalinian Oath of Commendation and Fealty

Sephana was covered from head to toe in soot by the time she finally crawled out of the top of the chimney. It was probably just as well, given how poorly people would react if they saw her. Blackened the way she was, and, with the aid of Dawn's First Crescent, she was able to pass along the city's rooftops like a silent shadow.

She was still in shock about what she had just seen and heard. Myria wasn't his servant, but rather he was hers. It kind of made sense: Sephana had always thought him too stupid to do all of the things that he had been credited for. It meant, though, that Myria even more dangerous than Sephana had first thought.

She had Gennald. She was taking him to 'the vale', wherever that was, and now, however much Sephana didn't want to, she had to rescue him. She couldn't have escaped without his aid, which meant that, no matter how big a jerk he was, she was honour-bound as a knight to get him back.

First, though, she had to find help. Alone in New Aukaster as she was, the only person that came to mind was Willem Jannery, who, after the still mysterious blackshield attack, was staying with Duke Raebyrne.

Damn.

She recognised his blue, red and yellow coat of arms flying over a particularly large manor near the edge of the city. All the doors and windows were locked. While she was happy to see that Duke Raebyrne was taking security seriously, it made her getting in a lot harder. Should she just knock on the front door? She didn't think anyone would let her in as dirty as she was, no matter what story she told.

That left breaking in. Maybe—*maybe*—if she could get to Lord Jannery and explain everything to him, he could speak to the duke on her behalf. Hopefully His Grace would be able to look past her appearance and help her.

She found a third floor window that was only partly secured and opened it with minimal difficulty. It was very obvious that the duke was rich. She hadn't seen any place so opulent since she had been a child, before the coup in Akkilon that had banished her into slavery. She padded down the hall and couldn't help but feel guilty at her sooty footprints marring the lush carpet.

The house was huge and, as best she could tell, the entire third floor was empty. She would have loved to sink into any of the empty beds and sleep—it had been a *really* long day—but too much was at stake. She crept down the stairway to the second floor and saw that the halls were lit with lanterns. It was a good sign.

The first room was unoccupied and the second was a withdrawing room. The third one was more promising: its door was thicker, iron banded and had decorative carvings. It was just the kind of room an important guest might stay in.

Sephana was just reaching for the brass door handle when it opened from the inside. She must have been more tired than she had thought because she didn't even try to run; she just stared dumbly while the door opened to reveal Hadran Raebyrne, the duke of Chasselford himself.

He turned and fled. "Guards! To me! Guards!" Sephana looked around her, trying to see who he was running from before realizing that he meant her.

She followed him. "Wait! Don't run from me. I'm not attacking you. I swear I'm not."

The duke was somewhere between the ages of Eldoth and Lord Jannery: old enough to have gray in his beard but young enough that there wasn't too much of it. Certainly he was fit enough to still be dangerous with his broadsword, which he had drawn and was pointing towards her. "Stay back. You'll not find me easy meat!"

"I won't find you any kind of meat! I don't want to eat you." Sephana's hand lashed out on its own, hurling Dawn's First Crescent's pommel towards his sword blade. She wasn't even thinking as she entangled it with her Ansharite chain and jerked it from his hand. It was her strange instinct, closer to the surface now because she was so tired. "Look, I'm sorry about that, but will you please listen to me?"

He stared at his now empty hand. "What other Djido magic will you do now?"

"I'm not a Djido!" she yelled louder than she needed to. "I am *so* tired of having everyone think that. I'm a knight!"

"Then why do you threaten me?" he asked, his back to a wall.

Sephana looked down at her hand dumbly, surprised to see her dagger pointed towards his heart. She hadn't even known that was holding it. "Sorry." She sheathed it hastily, fighting against her instinct's urging, and held up both of her hands in a gesture of peace. "Look: I'm not dangerous. Really."

"Forgive me if I don't take your word for that," Raebyrne said. "Seize her!"

She looked around behind her and saw two knights. Her hand hadn't even reached her belt before strong hands grabbed her by her arms and shoulders and immobilized her. "Let me go! I'm not your enemy. Please, I have important news. The king is in danger and you need to warn him."

One of Raebyrne's knights took Dawn's First Crescent from her belt and handed it to the duke. He cupped its pommel in his palm and she had to stop herself from triggering its hidden blades. Unlike Attenham, he wasn't her enemy; he was just confused. She had, after all, just broken into his manor and threatened him at knifepoint.

He regarded the dagger a moment before laying it on the table behind him. "You have important news, do you?" he asked coldly. "Let me guess: it is a matter of life and death and you need to speak to the king right away. Is that how you lure in your victims? Get them to them trust you before you stab them in the back?"

She gaped. "What? No."

"Hadran!" came a yell from the hallway just before Lord Jannery rushed into the room, sword in hand. "I heard yelling. Are we under attack? What is—" He stopped short. "—Oh. Sephana. What is...why is she being held?"

Raebyrne continued to stare at her. "She is a spy, or an assassin; I haven't determined which. She is an accessory to murder, that much I do know, and I will see justice done for it."

Understanding struck Sephana like a bolt of Eldoth's lightning. A lot of what had happened in the last two weeks suddenly made sense.

"You are in error, your Grace," Lord Jannery said, confusion obvious on his face. "I know this woman, and I assure you that she is no criminal. Given who she shares company with, I have no doubt her story sounds fantastic, but also that it is true. You must listen to her."

Sephana smiled at him. "Thank you. You've always believed in us and I thank you for that, but I don't think he's going to listen to you. Not with this and not about me." She turned to Duke Raebyrne. "Will you, your Grace?"

"I will not! You are in league with the outlaws, which means that you are allied with the Anderites and seek the death of my king. I cannot allow that."

"Your Grace. Hadran." Lord Jannery: older, greyer and lower in station, stepped closer to his younger, and more vital social better. "I do not know what you think her guilty of, but you are mistaken. You must release her."

Duke Raebyrne ignored him.

"I killed your brother," Sephana said. Lord Jannery looked at her in surprise and The duke's face became even darker.

"That's what you think, right? That I was part of some conspiracy to frame him and get him executed?"

"Do you admit it?"

Sephana shook her head sadly. "No. I didn't kill Edrik and I had nothing to do with his becoming a blackshield. I loved him."

The duke's face was red with rage. "My brother would never become involved with a snakespawn. I will not have you insult his memory after what you did to him in life."

It was hard, but she ignored the insult. "You sent the blackshields that attacked Lord Jannery's house, didn't you, with orders to capture me? That's why no one else was hurt?"

Jannery stared at Raebyrne in shock. "Is that true, My Lord?"

Raebyrne shook his head dismissively. "They would never have hurt you, Willem. My orders were quite specific."

Jannery's face lit in comprehension. "Yes, I remember. One of them suffered broken ribs rather than strike me." He scowled. "You attacked my house. You bribed and subverted my servants."

"It was necessary, Willem. I'm sorry."

Jannery was furious. "You cause me to flee my own home after an attack you ordered, and you're *sorry?*"

Duke Raebyrne sighed. "Willem, please: I have wronged you and I know it. I will make amends for what I have done, but not now." He glared at Sephana, who still being held by his knights. "There are more pressing matters."

"What pressing matters? Beating what you think is the truth from a woman whose loyalty and sincerity I have vouched for to the king himself?" He raised his sword. "I will not let you touch her, Hadran. If you want vengeance for your brother then you will do so through me."

Sephana looked at Jannery with new respect. He knew what she was and heard what she was accused of, and he still defied his lord for her, even though he was severely outmatched.

"Stand aside, Willem," Raebyrne warned. "I will not be denied on this matter."

Several more knights entered. Two of them placed themselves between the duke and Lord Jannery. "I don't want to hurt you, Willem," Raebyrne said. "Stand aside."

Lord Jannery remained undeterred. "I will not! Act like the nobleman I know you to be, Hadran, and release this woman. She says that she has important news. Listen to her and heed her warning."

"Remove him," Raebyrne ordered, "but do as little harm as possible. He *is* my guest." The two knights advanced warily, their swords turned. Jannery had no such compunction and attacked the nearest knight with lethal intent. He was a veteran warrior, but far beyond his prime and was wearing only bedclothes. He drew blood against one knight but was soon overpowered. Sephana could only watch sadly as a mailed fist to his stomach took his air and a sword pommel to his skull took his senses. Within a minute of the fight's start he was being dragged limply from the chamber.

"Wow: beating up old men; that's real honourable."

"You're a snakespawn," Raebyrne replied darkly. "Your kind knows nothing of honour."

"My *kind,* huh?" She took a deep breath to try and calm herself. It didn't work. "It's just as well that Edrik is dead; if he saw you acting like this, it would have killed him."

He struck her. If she hadn't been held by his knights, it would have sent her reeling. Instead, she just bent backwards and came back up like a reed in a windstorm. "Don't you dare say his name! You will confess to your crimes so that I may pass judgement upon you. That is all you are permitted to say."

I climbed up a chimney and almost got eaten by...something...for this?

"He talked about you all the time," she said, tasting blood. "You were his big brother, his hero, and he wanted to prove his innocence so that you wouldn't think of him as a criminal." She saw him waver momentarily, but then the moment passed. "He said that you were the bravest and most noble man in all of Karalon." She ignored the pain in her jaw and spat bloody saliva at his feet. "All he ever wanted was to be a worthy knight for you. But I see now that you aren't worthy of *him.*"

Had she gone too far, or not far enough? She still didn't know when Raebyrne snarled and struck her in the stomach.

She was tired. In the last month she had put up with crappy food, no sleep, public ridicule, jackass ex-husbands, and scary, mysterious women. For what? Being killed by a man she had been told to trust over a crime that she hadn't committed? If it was just about her, if the only thing that mattered was her life and Edrik's honour, she would have argued against the duke until he beat her to death, but it was more than that. She was a knight sworn to a cause, even if no one acknowledged it. *She* knew what she was, and what was important. As Balien had told her: it was about being noble, not being right.

She sagged in the grip of her captors and coughed as she tried to regain her breath. She raised her head and glared at the face of her dead lover's brother. "If you want to kill me, then I can't stop you. It would be wrong, and a betrayal of everything Edrik believed in, but you have all the power here. I'm sorry I couldn't save him. I tried, I really did, but Count Attenham wanted him dead and there wasn't anything I could do about it. He gave his life to save mine and I didn't want his sacrifice to be for nothing."

"Shut your lying mouth before I do it for you."

She squared her shoulders and looked the duke in the eye. "I won't because that's not important now. You need to put that aside and listen to me: the king is in danger." She put every ounce of sincerity she had into her words. This was quite possibly the most important thing she had ever said in her life. "Count Attenham is in league with the outlaws, and he has some plan to make sure that the king doesn't join with the land. He is going to frame the Golden Bears with the stolen tribute money and convince Ander that you're in league with the Dragonfleet. You need to warn the king and let me go so that I can find my friends and stop him, and you need to do it now."

"Let you go? I think not." She could see that he didn't believe her. "Everyone knows that snake tongues only speak lies. If anyone is in league with the outlaws, it is you."

"I suggest you reconsider that decision, Your Grace," came a stern, angry voice from somewhere behind her. Sephana couldn't see the speaker, but she'd know that voice anywhere.

Illyria.

The festival had been dying down when Illyria and her fellow knights made their way through New Aukaster. The full moon hid behind thick clouds and most street lanterns had disappeared along with the revellers. The city felt like it was under a funeral pall, choking and drowning in its despair. Their steps had been oddly hushed as they navigated the empty city streets into the noble quarter and Duke Raebyrne's mansion.

Illyria had hesitated when the building came into sight. They were within their rights to be here, on the business of the king and in possession of a letter that allowed them to do basically anything. She could break down the Duke's door and loot his house if she wanted; certainly marching up to its front door and demanding entry was within her rights, too; and yet she had not.

Balien had shared her unease. One shared glance had been agreement enough for them to approach with caution. Theramus had obeyed their non-verbal order without question and Eldoth had done likewise, though he had given them a look of impatience and confusion first.

They had observed the house, trying to determine what it was that seemed off, but found nothing. Finally, they entered through a side door, its lock and crossbar barely even slowing them down thanks to Eldoth's magic. The house had been dark and quiet, but the narrow servant's entrance had been too small for Theramus to enter. He had remained outside, which was just as well. If he had seen Lord Jannery dragged half-conscious through a hallway his anger might have destroyed the building.

She could not help but think of what Gennald would have done, had he witnessed this. She felt ashamed a moment later, for it had been the first time she had thought of him in over an hour. He was the man she loved; it seemed a dishonour not to have him weigh on her thoughts.

Eldoth was proving quite adept at using magically flung stones as weapons. He and Illyria, working together, had quietly and efficiently subdued the two knights holding Lord Jannery. All it had taken was a weak whisper about Sephana being held captive to justify their need for caution. She lay Lord Jannery in a vacant bed, assured herself of his health, and then proceeded silently and quickly to Duke Raebyrne's quarters.

Illyria had never been more proud of Sephana as she had been listening to her lecturing the duke, nor had she been so disappointed when she had heard his response. A quick glance into the room told her that there were four men present besides the duke and Sephana. She had quickly given her commands to Balien and Eldoth, then stepped into the doorway to catch everyone's attention.

"I suggest that you reconsider that decision, your Grace," she said loudly and clearly, then squeezed her eyes shut and hid them behind her arms.

Not a foot in front of her, a light as bright as Nuran itself burst into being.

It felt good to act. Once Eldoth had discovered that Sephana was being held captive, he had wanted nothing other than to burn the whole house down to ensure her safety. (Yes, he was aware that burning down the very house that she was imprisoned in was an incredibly stupid thing to do, but that made his urge no less compelling). Creating a light flash similar to the one he had employed in the Silverheart Mines was nowhere as satisfying, but better than nothing.

He did a good job of it. Once everyone was focussed on Illyria, he gave them a second sun. The three of them stormed the room less than a second later. Illyria made short work of one of Sephana's captors. Sephana herself (who had been held facing the other direction, and had thus avoided the worst of the light's effects) seemed to have freed herself from the other, and Balien had disabled the other two knights. That left Duke Raebyrne: the man who had imprisoned Sephana and delivered the worst of insults to her face. Eldoth would have happily cooked the man's flesh for what he had done, but Sephana was right there, and he would never have heard the end of it. He settled for magically hurling the fist-sized rock he had taken to carrying into the man's face. He hadn't conducted any experiments to determine just how hard his blow struck, but he estimated it to he twice as hard and fast as a man's fist, if that fist happened to be made of stone. However much it hurt, it was less than the man deserved.

Raebyrne was completely oblivious in the aftermath of flash of light and was completely unaware of the coming blow. He fell to the floor without a sound, and it was only the sight of Sephana barely able to stand upright that prevented Eldoth from pummelling the duke on the ground where he lay.

The cuts and bruises on Sephana's face mad him wince. The knight she had freed herself from had still gotten in a few good blows before Illyria had struck him senseless. Sephana's eyes were glazed over as she rested her hands on her knees and tried to recover. Eldoth brushed her hair away from her face. The cut on her cheek was deep and would likely leave a scar, even if stitched properly

Eldoth couldn't have that.

His proficiency in yellow magic—body magic—was rudimentary at best, but he could heal minor wounds and, better, he could do so without scarring. He visualised her cheek, smooth and perfect, with the flesh beneath it healed and whole. The wound began to mend as he watched.

"Ghaa!!" Sephana flinched and slapped his hand away. Before he could understand what had happened, she had turned, grabbed her dagger from a nearby table and pointed it towards him. "What in—Eldoth?" Her eyes took in everything in the room at once before returning to him. She put her hand up to her now unmarked cheek. "What did you do to me?"

He had spent a great deal of time trying to decide what his first words to her would be. It would start with an apology, he had thought, followed by a declaration of some sort. Instead, he replied automatically and caustically to her outburst.

"I was rescuing you and healing your wounds. You should be thanking me, not holding me at knifepoint."

He could tell by the look on her face that his words had not been well received.

Illyria heard the sound of many feet approaching. Raebyrne's knights, no doubt, coming to rescue their lord...who they had just kidnapped.

Things had just become complicated.

She looked around. With Theramus outside and Sephana recovered, they were all within the duke's chambers. Built to house a high ranking noble, his mansion was designed for defence, both within and without. The doors and windows of this room were made from thick wood and banded iron, and, more importantly, could be barred from the inside.

The sound of approaching boots became louder. Illyria shut the door and dropped the bar in place only moment before urgent fists began to pound on it. "My Lord Duke!" Someone called from the other side. "Are you all right?"

She exchanged a glance with Balien. Raebyrne was unconscious and showed no signs of waking after being brained so thoroughly by Eldoth. The four knights they had disabled were just beginning to stir.

Balien motioned to the door with his eyes and she rolled hers in reply.

"The duke is alive but unconscious," she called through the door. "I give you my word that we mean him no harm."

"You'll rue the day you ever set foot in this house, Anderite scum," she was warned. "Open this door now and let me see his grace if you want to leave alive."

"We are not Anderites," Illyria said, "but we cannot open the door to you at this time."

"Blackshields," the knight spat. "Are you in it for money then, holding him for ransom? You won't get a copper from us if he's dead."

She looked back at Balien. */What do we do now?/*

/We came here for council/ he reminded her.

It was a good idea. "I'll only speak to March-Lord Jannery," she announced to the door.

There was some quiet talking from the other side, a few more back and forths, and then she heard Lord Jannery's voice.

"I'm here, Illyria."

It was a few more minutes before they considered it safe for him to enter the room, lock it after and then explain the situation. By then the duke was just regaining consciousness. His knights had already been restrained.

"You can arrest him," Jannery said. "You have the kings writ; it gives you that power."

"Arrest him for what? And to who?"

"It's not like being an ass is a crime," Sephana added. "If it was, Eldoth would have been locked up years ago."

"And if pigheadedness was criminal you'd be in the cell right next to me," he responded without heat, the curve of his lips barely visible through his beard.

Ah, love.

Lord Jannery gave the couple an odd look before answering Illyria. "He has broken the rules of hospitality and attacked one of his vassals. These are both serious crimes for a nobleman."

"What is the sentence for this, and how would it be done?"

"Any accusations would have to be made to the king, in the Peer's Court. As to the sentence, it would depend on the wishes of those he offended, in this case myself and Sephana." His face was grim. "For myself, I would seek a public apology, five years of him paying my taxes, and a commitment of men to help me defend the Northmarch. Sephana's restitution would be more difficult."

"And you will not be seek this?"

He hesitated. "I will not, and I suggest, My Lady," he nodded to Sephana, "that you do not either. These are difficult times, and the nobility cannot be seen fighting itself." By 'nobility', she knew he meant the Golden Bears. "What the duke did was wrong, and he knows it. Better to have him in your debt."

Illyria frowned. "I dislike my order's foundation being based on lies and omissions."

He shrugged. "We have been lying since this adventure's very beginning. Such is the nature of politics."

Sephana scowled.

"Is that agreeable to you?" Illyria asked.

Sephana turned and looked at Edrik's brother. He was awake, though he had a bloody bruise on his cheek (thank you, Illyria!). "I don't think I can get what I want. I want an apology, and I want to hear him say that he doesn't blame me for Edrik's death." She glared. "And I want him to mean it."

"I will not."

She bit back on her anger. It wouldn't help things now, no matter how good it would have felt to yell at him now. This wasn't about her.

"I'll settle for an oath, given in front of his knights, that we'll have his hospitality and political favour."

The duke looked like he wanted to be sick, but eventually nodded.

Illyria nodded towards the still barred door. "Then please, Your Grace, admit your knights and give your oath."

CHAPTER TWENTY-ONE

" 'There are fewer figures in recent history as simultaneously worshipped and reviled as Myria Tydris, or as speculated about. The number of verifiable facts about her that survived the Crown War could fit inside a thimble.' "

—Introduction to The Black Lady: Villain, Whore, Queen

Theramus did not need more reminding that he was a giant living in a man's world. It was simply too impractical for him to manoeuvre within Duke Raebyrne's fortified manor. As their initial plan had just been to meet and confer with Willem Jannery, this had not seemed a significant complication. Once their plan had changed into a covert entry, the complication became larger.

He did not doubt their abilities, of course, but the fortunes of war made anything possible, especially in dealings with one's allies. He had sworn—to himself, though Emuranna had witnessed it, of course—to keep his fellow knights safe, and he could not do so from without.

From the sights and sounds within, matters had indeed turned violent. He had been ready to smash his way inside, consequences be damned, when Sephana— Sephana!—had come outside to update him. She had been imprisoned by Count Attenham but had escaped. She had then made her way here, where she had once again been captured before being rescued by her fellow knights. He was very proud of all of them.

He had asked her cautiously about Eldoth, but she had only responded with annoyance and distain. Clearly she knew nothing of the anguish the wizard had undergone during her abduction, and it was not Theramus's place to inform her.

With Sephana freed and the Duke of Chasselford's oath secured, it was now time for them to plan their next move, and the best place for that (in which Theramus could conveniently fit) was the kitchen. The proximity to hot, fresh food was in the room's favour as well.

They all listened while Sephana told her story. When Illyria learned that Sir Gennald was still in Attenham's custody, she insisted on marching there and freeing him.

"You cannot," Duke Raebyrne insisted. They had allowed him to be present during their council, though his knights had not been. He had remained silent up until this point. "Any overt move against the leader of the Anderites right now will spark a civil war."

"Then we will be *covert*," she replied. "We snuck in here easily enough."

"I wasn't expecting any of you. Attenham will be on alert after Sephana's escape. In addition, he *does* have secrets to keep and will have higher security because of it. If Lady Myria is, in fact, the spymaster you claim her to be—which I find hard to believe—she will not allow you simple access." Illyria began to look pensive; Raebyrne pressed his point. "Any sign of you attempting to force entry and both Anderite and Golden Bear knights will appear. It will be open combat on the streets of New Aukaster and we *cannot* have that, not with the king's position as precarious as it is."

"Gennald is strong," Balien assured his sister. "He can hold out until we think of with something."

"Who is this Myria?" Theramus asked from his place on the floor near the head of the table. He held a large bowl within his cupped hands. "Or the 'Black Lady', as the outlaws call her. She is more than his mistress, obviously."

"She's not from any Karalinian noble family," the duke said. "I have had her thoroughly researched. Popular rumour says that she is exiled Akkilinian royalty, fled here after their coup."

"Her name isn't Akkilinian," Sephana said.

"It is an old Anduili name," Theramus replied. "Used in the days of the High Kingdom,"

"It's not uncommon for royalty to have Anduili names," Illyria said. "Both my name and my mother's are from that era."

"The outlaws who took me were all Akkilmen, if that helps any," Sephana said, "or at least they answered to Akkilinian names."

"We can determine the truth of her identity later," Illyria interrupted. "What is more important now is what she is doing. We need to work out the weak points of their plan." She began ticking points off on her fingers. "Using the outlaws, she's been selectively raiding tax caravans that travel through the Deremwood. She's been storing this money in the mines and plans to implicate us, and through us the Golden Bears, as working some secret deal with the Dragonfleet."

"That's preposterous!" Jannery protested. "Even Ander wouldn't believe such a ridiculous tale."

"One of the raiders from Westbridge survived," Sephana said, guilt tingeing her words. "Attenham has him."

"What raid on Westbridge?" Raebyrne asked. No one answered him.

"But that plot has already failed," Jannery pointed out. "None of you were captured and you have discovered the cache of stolen gold. If you remain visible here in New Aukaster there is no possible way he can implicate you."

"We don't have the gold," Balien said. "We know where it is and have made efforts to safeguard it, but that isn't the same as possession."

Eldoth, who had been staring at Sephana, spoke up. "My runeseal will not stop another wizard, which we know this Myria has. Both she and her wizard are unaccounted for. They could be taking possession of the gold as we speak."

"Then we need to secure it as soon as possible," Jannery said. "That gold is too important."

"There is the other matter," Illyria reminded him, "that of King Lionar's safety. Attenham said that he had a way of ensuring that Lionar failed in his Joining tomorrow evening." She paused. "Though I suppose it is this evening, isn't it? We've been awake through all of the night."

"How?" Duke Raebyrne demanded. "The covenant between king and land is ancient and unbreakable. How can anyone possess the power to interfere with that?"

Sephana snapped her fingers. "She's the nurse!"

"Who?" Theramus asked. "*Lionar's* nurse?"

"The one who gave us his note after our audience?" Illyria echoed.

Sephana nodded emphatically. "Yes. I knew I recognised her. She even said that she had to see Lionar before she went to meet her outlaws. She was wearing a nurse's clothing in her final meeting with Attenham."

"That's...hard to accept," Jannery said, frowning. "If that is true, and she is as dangerous as you say, she has unlimited access to him. She could have killed him at her leisure. Why go through this whole charade?"

"Are you sure you saw what you saw?" Balien asked. "You saw her through a flue grate."

"I saw her in the nurse's dress through the grate," she argued, "but she stood right beside me when Attenham was gloating at me. I know what I saw."

"I believe her," Eldoth said abruptly.

Sephana looked at him oddly. "...thanks."

"Whoever she is, she still claims to have a method of preventing the king from succeeding in his Joining," Illyria said. "We need to figure out what that is and stop it."

"It's a ridiculous claim!" Raebyrne insisted.

"The king *has* failed at his last four Joinings," Theramus pointed out. "If not for this Myria's interruptions, then how?"

The duke scowled, but gave no reply.

Eldoth found it difficult to contribute to the conversation. All he could do was look at Sephana: the teak curls of her hair, the curve of her neck and the glossy lines of scales that flowed from the collar of her shirt, up the side of her neck and into her hair. He was a fool to have missed it before.

She looked much better for having washed and eaten. She glanced at him from the corner of her eye and frowned.

"You're staring again," she said in a quiet voice. "It's still creepy."

'I wanted to make sure you are all right' was what he wanted to say, but that wasn't what came out. "I am merely ensuring that you don't attack me again." It was easier to argue with her. "You react unpredictably when people try to help you."

"I apologised for that already," she growled. "How was I supposed to know that you can heal with your magic? You've never done it before, and it hurt."

It was an aspect of yellow magic that he took for granted: the trauma it invoked. He was used to its effects and braced for it automatically. Even at his rudimentary level of mastery it hurt worse than a hornet's sting and became correspondingly worse with the degree of complexity of magic. When he had watched Veeshar the Djido merge the bodies of two creatures, the trauma of the act had almost killed the resultant creature.

"You can, and will, think what you want, when you want," he said. "You always have, and you need not concern about the future: I am unlikely to use my magic on you again, unless it is to defend myself."

"Like you could," she replied, but she smiled when she said it.

"There will be time for personal discussions later," Illyria said, interrupting them. "We have more pressing concerns. We need to rescue Sir Gennald."

"Let him rot in Attenham's basement," Eldoth sneered. He'd insulted Sephana almost to the point of tears, though Eldoth would never admit that to be the cause of his dislike for the man. "His sole tactical contribution to the mission was the 'reconnaissance' inside New Wighton that he coerced Illyria into joining. As plans go, it was idiotic."

Illyria coloured. "I wasn't coerced into anything. It may have been Gennald's idea, but I was an equal party to it. It was...a poor decision." She glanced around the table. "I'm sorry to all of you for the jeopardy I placed you in."

"Gennald may have been a jerk sometimes, but he gave up his chance at freedom so that I could escape," Sephana said.

"As he did with me," Illyria added. "Sir Gennald's wisdom may be lacking, but his courage and honour are not. If it is in our power to aid him, we should do so."

Eldoth's protest about the relative merits of courage and intelligence were overridden by Theramus. "I do not think that your presence in New Wighton would have changed anything greatly," he said. "None of us could have anticipated such a deliberate attack."

"Yeah," Sephana added. "They knew exactly where we were and when we'd be there." She paused and cocked her head in a way that Eldoth had always found adorable. "How did they know that, anyway?"

"No one passed between the village and the cave," Balien said with confidence. "If there were messages being sent, it was by some other method."

"How did we know we'd be there?" Sephana asked. "We were given specific information, weren't we?"

Illyria nodded. "Derra, the tavern owner's wife, contacted me when we first investigated the village." She paused. "It seems obvious that the information she gave us was planted, but I don't want to believe that she did it deliberately. She was...nice. I trusted her immediately."

"She could have been given false information to pass on," Eldoth thought aloud, "or others could have learned of what she had said afterwards, but it's unlikely. The simplest, most obvious answer to a question is very often the correct one."

"You're the only one who saw her, Lyri," Balien said. "What did she look like?"

"About my height," Illyria said after a moment's recall. "Red-brown hair. Older; in her late thirties, I would guess. Still very pretty, despite her age." She frowned. "I didn't see her at the festival, now that I think about it."

"What colour were her eyes?" Sephana asked.

"Brown, no: hazel. A little darker than yours."

"Myria has eyes that colour," Sephana said slowly. "And her height matches, too. She's a lot younger then Derra, though."

"The nurse who gave us the king's note in the palace was quite young," Balien pointed out. "Still in her teens."

"Such a level of disguise is not possible," Theramus declared.

"It is with magic," Eldoth said. "Changing hair colour and skin quality is quite a basic application of yellow magic. I could do it myself if I wished."

"*Another* wizard?" Sephana asked.

"Or the same one, using his magics to aid her," Eldoth countered. "I find that more likely."

"You could change my hair if you wanted?" Sephana asked, humour and interest lighting her eyes.

Having an excuse to run his fingers through her hair was very appealing, but it would not do to have her know that. "If I wished, which I do not. I am a wizard, not a stylist."

"If Myria can assume all these roles, it explains a great deal," Illyria said loudly, forcing the conversation back on topic.

Everyone stopped to ponder the implications.

"So we were having our strings pulled from the very beginning," Sephana said, indignant. No one disputed her.

Sephana may have said the words first, but Illyria had thought them at the same time. Anger welled within her, coupled with embarrassment and shame.

"We are done being anyone's plaything." She set her jaw. "Events are too far along for us to continue reacting. We need to take action. The critical event in all of this is the king's Joining. If he can perform the ritual successfully, then everything else falls apart: Attenham doesn't become the new royal advisor, the conspiracy to destroy the Golden Bears becomes meaningless and, of course, Lionar isn't forced to fall on his sword. The question, then, is: how does Myria— who I think we all agree is the main culprit behind all of this—intend to prevent the Joining from occurring? As has been pointed out, that is not a simple thing to do."

"She's posing as the king's nurse," Balien said. "Perhaps she's poisoning him?"

"Maybe. The act of Joining is very strenuous and could be fatal if the person attempting it is weak or injured." Illyria frowned. "But I don't think that she is. It's been bothering me from the very beginning: the king and the land are one. His soul is linked to the Lifestream. If he is ill, the land is ill. If he healthy, then so is the land."

"But they both are," Sephana said. "He's sick and there's that grain blight happening."

Illyria shook her head. "No, that's not enough. The grain blight and the bad rains, that's like...a cold, but Lionar isn't just a little sick, he's at Zulum's gate. If his condition was natural, then the land around us would be in much worse shape. There would be famine and pestilence across the kingdom. What's going on now, it's..." she gestured with her hands, trying to find the proper word. "...*wrong*. Something has made him this way."

"She's poisoning him," Sephana repeated.

"Maybe," Illyria repeated, "but my instincts say no." She threw her hands in the air. "I'm sorry I can't explain it better."

"Myria said that she was taking the outlaws to defend 'the vale,' " Sephana told them. "Do you think she meant Olsarum?"

"That's impossible," Duke Raebyrne snapped. "The valley itself would not allow them. Grandmaster Lanton would most certainly not do so."

"I saw a body in the dungeon under Attenham's manor, during my escape," Sephana said, her eyes not meeting anyone's. "I'm pretty sure it was the Grandmaster's, and that he'd been there for a while."

Duke Raebyrne's eyes narrowed. "Are you suggesting that the Knight-Grandmaster of Olsarum is an imposter?"

"Why don't you tell us what you saw, Sephana?"

Illyria listened with growing dismay as she heard Sephana's story of desiccated bodies and mysterious creatures in the dark. It was horrifying, if it was true, that someone or something had the ability to usurp the power of the high priest. She felt ill.

The duke, in contrast, grew angry. "You saw the body briefly, by the light of a door crack, while running in fear. You also admitted that the body had been dried into a husk." She nodded. "Then how can you try to claim what you saw with any certainty?"

"I saw what I saw."

"I refuse to believe it. Not him."

"If the grandmaster has been killed and impersonated, it does answer a great number of questions," Theramus rumbled.

"You did say that he has been acting strangely," Eldoth added.

"He is under stress," Duke Raebyrne argued. "Even if someone was found to impersonate him, how could he possibly deceive the other residents of the valley? What about the priests, and the wardens? That is the sort of thing that they are bred to detect."

"He ordered the priests away from the valley," Theramus pointed out. "And the one hound warden we saw treated him like an enemy."

The duke only spluttered in reply.

"If there is a way to disrupt the king's Joining, the High Priest would have to be complicit in it for it to succeed," Balien said.

"Your arguments are not without their points," the duke admitted. "But your theories are based upon guesswork and unreliable evidence. May I ask, as your *host*," irony dripped from his voice, "what you intend to do with this information?"

Jannery turned to Illyria. "What is your intention, My Lady?"

She was reluctant to say it. It was sacrilegious, and yet it had to be done. "We need to go to Olsarum and investigate this, My Lord. We cannot forget that Myria has chosen to reinforce the valley, fearing our intervention. She seems to think that our presence can interfere with her plans."

Sephana grinned. "We'd better try our best to do that, then."

After that, it was just details. They stocked up on supplies from Duke Raebyrne's larder (Sephana was really, really tired of dried oatcakes) and prepared their gear. The plan was to rest until dawn—which was, sadly, only a few hours away—before leaving for the Sacred Valley by way of the secret mine tunnel. At that same time, Lord Jannery and Duke Raebyrne would seek out the king and attempt to warn him of Attenham's treachery.

It felt like Sephana had only just lay her head down before Balien was knocking on her door. Somehow resisting the urge to tell him her true opinion at being woken so early (she hated mornings at the best of times, and these weren't them), she dragged herself out of bed and got ready. It was too overcast to see anything outside, but she knew that, if she could, light would just be starting to crawl over the horizon. She also knew that Nasheeth, the moon, would be hanging high in the sky in full blossom.

Of course, the fact that they couldn't see it was part of the problem. On today of all days, it should have been visible in the highest point in the sky from before dawn (which was now; groan) through the day all the way to midnight. It was Anur's monument to his dead wife and was raised in her memory four times a year.

Sephana could relate.

She changed into some clean-ish clothes, belted Dawn's First Crescent onto her waist and stumbled downstairs. Her pack was already packed, her water skin was filled (seriously, when did Balien find the time to do all of this?) and hot porridge was waiting for her on the table. She slurped it down without ceremony, ignoring the sullen looks given to her by the duke's serving staff. When she looked up after finishing her last mouthful, Eldoth was standing over her and scowling.

"I've found a flaw in your logic," he said without any kind of greeting.

"I'm really not in the mood for this right now," she said, wiping her face clean and getting to her feet. If she was really lucky, she could slip out of the kitchen before he could say anything more.

He stepped in front of her planned escape route. There was no way she could get away now without being rude, and he *had* been part of her rescue party last night (although, she was sure, a very reluctant one). She supposed she could listen to whatever idiotic theory he had come up with this time. "Fine. What's the flaw in my logic?"

"Before, on the road, you stated that my feelings of anger and revenge were what motivated me to use overly painful means of attack."

"Yes, I remember."

"I am willing to concede that point."

"Really?"

"Yes. I have been practicing other methods of attack. More...humane methods."

"You have?" it came out as a surprised squeak. Eldoth had admitted to being wrong and had acted on her criticism, two things she had thought to be impossible. SummersEnd really was a day of miracles.

"It was for the sake of experimentation," he stressed, annoyance on his face. "That is the only reason."

"Uhh, ok."

He hesitated and refused to meet her eye: two more things that, while not miraculous, were more than a little strange. "My point, however, is that the presence of emotion when attacking is not always detrimental. *Passion*, as a motivator, can be beneficial. Would-would a mother—" he was starting to stumble over his words "—be criticised for wishing pain on those who threatened her children, or..." He swallowed. "A man avenging his lover, if he inflicted more pain than was necessary on the one who had harmed her? Would that person be blamed?"

She tried to make sense of what he was saying, or, rather, trying to say and bungling it. "Something that's wrong is still wrong no matter what the reason," she said slowly, still chewing on his words. "It would be more *understandable*, I guess. I mean, if it was someone you cared about..." She stopped, cocked her head, and glared. "Are you seriously telling me that I should forgive you for what you did to Draxul because you were in love? Eldoth, the only person you love is yourself."

His mouth opened to speak but nothing came out. Another first to add to the pile. His face went from white to red and every shade in between before he turned and stalked out of the room.

Sephana shook her head, gathered her pack, and went to rejoin the others. Compared to trying to figure out that conversation, saving Karalon would be easy.

The scowl on Eldoth's face was darker than the most violent of thunder clouds.

"You did not tell her," Theramus said by way of greeting.

"No, I did not, nor will I before WatersEnd," Eldoth spat. "That woman is impossible."

Humans.

Theramus said nothing. A moment later, Sephana came into the entrance chamber and it was time to leave.

The Bear and the Thistle

"I trust you, Illyria," Willem Jannery said gravely from just inside the door. "But, please, take no offense when I urge you to be very careful. Where you are going, any mistake could have dire consequences on my kingdom's future. I hesitate to think of what disasters may come if you are wrong."

"Thank you for your trust, My Lord," she answered. "I understand your concern and I share it. I will do nothing to endanger your kingdom. You have my word on this, as a knight and a carrier of the Mark of the Hawk."

He sighed heavily. "There is nothing left but to trust. Emuranna's Strength, My Lady." He glanced at the rest of them. "And to all of you as well."

"And to you, My Lord," Illyria answered. "Your task is equally important."

Jannery grunted. "I'd rather face down a whole pack of dogmen afoot than wrestle with the nest of weasels in that palace, but it must be done." He nodded to the doorman, who looked happy to be rid of all them. "Good journey."

"May the sun shine upon your road," she replied, and then they were off.

Outside, a drizzle had started.

CHAPTER TWENTY-TWO

" 'Whoever named them the 'Silverheart Hills' never had to climb over them. 'Silverheart Mountains', would be more like it. 'Silverheart Cliffs', even better.' "

—*Sephana, Lord Mayor of Daranduil, recalling days long past*

"If you make a sound, I'll personally slit your throat," growled a voice in Gennald's ear. It was Manson, the leader of the outlaws. If that man didn't have a history in the military, Gennald would beat his sword into a ploughshare.

Gennald's hands were bound again, but there was no point in blind-folding him anymore. He still had two of the outlaws guarding him, but they weren't going out of their way to be vicious. They were in too much of a hurry, and beating him for no reason would just slow them down.

They had re-entered the secret tunnels through the Silverhearts in the deep of the night and had been walking steadily through them for a few hours now. Gennald had no way to compare this trip through the heart of the mountain to the last one, but he figured that they had to be near the main chamber where the outlaws lived.

That had been when they had stopped and sent a man ahead to scout. That scout had returned and the news he had given had not been well received. Most of the outlaws had crept ahead on cat-feet, along with Myria, the 'Black Lady'. Only Gennald's two guards remained behind and Manson had felt the need to remind him that it was not in his best interest to alert whoever it was that the outlaws were off to ambush.

He waited almost half an hour in tense silence with only his two captors for company. He heard some kind of echoing animal call and was hauled to his feet. The main cavern was full of outlaws, most looking the worst for wear, and Gennald thought he saw some body-shaped lumps in the darkness. He didn't look any closer, and didn't want to know who they had been.

Illyria wasn't in there, and likely not any of her companions either. He only lived to be a bargaining piece against her, after all. If she had been killed, Gennald would have followed her to Zulanan.

She had been here, though; of that he had no doubt.

Manson beckoned to Gennald's 'escorts' and was led into a side chamber that ended in a large, thick door. Myria was there, looking frustrated, along with a burly man with reddish brown hair. "I don't know," he said. "I can't break it. I don't know what kind of magic he used."

'It' was a strip of cloth decorated with brown runes spanning both sides of the door. Based on the marks on the door surrounding it, they had tried to cut it, pry it, bash it and burn it away, all with no success. Presumably, with the cloth in place, whatever lay on the other side of the door was inaccessible.

"What kind of wizard are you?" she snapped. "It's just a piece of cloth."

"I'm a stone wizard," he said, his meek tone roughened by irritation. "I shape stone, it's what I was trained for." He shrugged. "This is cloth. I've never seen anything like it."

Myria turned to Gennald. "Tell me about Eldoth."

He didn't see the point in lying. Not anymore. "He's rude and arrogant. No one likes him much, but they can't do what he does either, so they put up with him."

"What about his magic? Have you ever seen him do anything like this?"

Gennald shook his head. "No. I've seen him use fire and lightning. He can throw stones and deflect arrows, and I've seen him mend cloth, but nothing like this."

"He knows three colleges?" the 'stone wizard' said with awe.

"Jaden: enough," Myria scolded. She stepped close and looked Gennald in the eye—she was shorter than Illyria, but no less imposing—before nodding and turning to Manson. "We can't waste any more time on this. We'll dismantle the door bolt by bolt if we have to, later. Get the men ready. Tell them that anyone not ready to march down the north tunnel in ten minutes will explain why to me personally."

Manson paled. "The north tunnel? All of us?"

"Do I need to repeat myself?"

"No, My Lady. At once." The outlaw captain's hand tightened in what Gennald thought would have been a salute if he had completed the gesture.

She turned to Jaden, the 'stone wizard'. "Collapse the entrance to the north tunnel behind us when we go."

"Yes My Lady."

It was mid afternoon before the Knights of Anduilon—whole in number, if not in spirit—were finally ready to begin their ascent of the Silverheart Hills. It was still overcast and gusty, which would not make their climb any easier.

Eight knights had been found dead in the mine cavern and their thirty prisoners vanished. They hadn't left through the New Wighton entrance, Illyria was sure of that. Theramus thought it most likely that they had departed through a recently collapsed tunnel on the north end of the cavern. The collapse had been deliberate and engineered, and neither Eldoth's magic or Theramus's strength would have been able to clear it any reasonable amount of time. Their only recourse was to make for Olsarum by the only route they knew: up and over the Silverhearts, but at twice the speed of their last attempt. It was going to be an arduous climb for all of them except Theramus, and they would likely be fighting a battle at the other end of it.

There were only two lights in this disaster of a situation: Gennald's body had not been found among the dead knights (which was a consolation only to her; the friends and families of the other knights would find no comfort in it), and the stolen gold remained secure behind Eldoth's 'runelock'. No matter what happened to them or king Lionar, Karalon would be able to pay the Dragonfleet their tribute this year.

It was a small comfort, but Illyria would take what she could.

They were taking a short break before their climb and discussing what they might face when they finally arrived in the Sacred Valley of Karalon.

"So at least thirty outlaws, armed and ready for us, plus Myria," Sephana summarized, "versus the five of us." She grinned. "So what are the rest of you going to do?"

They all smiled in reply except Eldoth, who Illyria was sure was scowling just to be contrary. "We've discussed what we'll likely be facing and what tactics to use against them," Illyria said, brushing pants that weren't dirty. "There is nothing more we can do here."

"Something's been bothering me," Sephana said. "The last time we were in Olsarum, you wouldn't let us kill one dog, because you said shedding any blood in there would upset the Lifestream so much that there was no way Lionar could complete his Joining. Now we're planning to fight off more than two dozen outlaws in that same place. What's changed?"

"Nothing's changed," Illyria said. "It's not the best comparison, but Joining with the Land is something like looking at a reflection in a pond. The smoother the water, the easier it is, and even a small pebble—injuring a hound warden—can cause ripples that obscure the water's surface."

"If one dog is like a pebble, then fighting thirty outlaws must be like throwing a bucket of rocks."

"But what a king does is not really like seeing a reflection, is it?" Eldoth asked, his eyes sharp. "From what I understand it is more similar to using his will to calm the water, correct?"

"It is a slightly better analogy," Illyria agreed. "The 'pond' of Olsarum is representative of all of Karalon. What happens there is mirrored to some degree to the rest of the kingdom. That is its magic. The smoothness of the water—really, the Lifestream—is what ensures prosperity in the kingdom. If the Lifestream flows smoothly, then the weather is calm, the sun shines nicely and the crops grow well. That's what Joining with the land *is,* what the king does."

"But we're going to be throwing a bucket of rocks," Sephana protested. "We're going to make it even worse than it is."

"Except that Myria and Grandmaster Lanton's imposter have already done that," Illyria argued. "Frankly, there is little more than can be done to make it worse. What most people *don't* know is that the king doesn't have to Join with the Land on this particular day. It is proscribed that he must Join with the Land eight times per year, and it is always done on the Holy Days, but it doesn't *have* to."

"*That* is what we are fighting for," Illyria concluded. "We go to Olsarum, clear it of filth, then find whatever it is that they've been doing to prevent the king from Joining. There is little more harm that can be done to the land this year—the wheat crop is already ruined, and the weather atrocious. But if we can cleanse Olsarum and prevent anything else happening to Lionar, hopefully he will be well enough to perform a real Joining later. Before Autumn's Heart, hopefully."

"And if we cannot find whatever has been causing this uncleanliness?" Theramus asked.

"We have to," Illyria said. "We will."

There was little else for them to say. They began climbing.

The climb up over the hillside (or mountainside, to hear Sephana tell it) and down to the Sacred Valley was tense and difficult. Even if they had the energy to spare—which they did not—it was unlikely that any of them would have spoken much.

Or, none of them save Theramus. Even carrying everyone's supplies for them, he found the climb untaxing. His giant blood thrived in this harsh land; in fact, he found himself reminiscing back to his younger days, more than a century in the past. Emilon—the secret haven of the Noss, given to his people by the High Kings countless centuries past—was nestled in the heart of the Darandy Mountains and filled with land similar to this. Was it wrong that, on the verge of a mission of the utmost importance, he felt young?

The sun was getting lower in the sky. He could have already completed the climb and subsequent descent if left on his own, but the Knights of Anduilon travelled at the pace of their slowest member. Eldoth, to his credit, was trying very hard and with minimal complaint. Even with Sephana and Balien giving him every assistance, though, their progress was slow. They would arrive in the valley before sunset—in Theramus's estimation—but only just. Certainly if they were wrong in their assessment there wouldn't be time for them to do anything else.

They stopped just short of the hill's peak and took a short break next to the tree that had been kissed by quicklings. They guzzled water from their skins and wolfed down the last of their oatcakes. The descent would be faster, but more dangerous. They would do what they could to not be seen from the valley floor, but complete invisibility was impossible.

It was entirely likely that they were walking into a trap, and there was nothing that they could do about it.

Gennald wanted to vomit. It wasn't anything physical that ailed him—he was sore and tired, but not ill—but rather his spirit. He had never known the outlaw's destination. He'd heard talk of a valley, but it had never occurred to him that it was *the* valley, the Sacred Valley of Karalon, Olsarum.

If they were here, then that meant that Sephana had been right: the grandmaster was an imposter, the sanctity of the valley had been broken and it was impossible for the king to complete his Joining. He would fail tonight and be dead by his own hand before morning. Ander would become king, and Attenham's agenda, whatever it was, would become law.

Everything Gennald had done had been for nothing. His last attempt at defiance: helping Sephana escape, had been fruitless. All he had accomplished had been sending her to her death and earning yet another beating.

He should have accepted Attenham's offer.

He had refused when it had been offered. He had transgressed against Emuranna during his headlong pursuit of Illyria, but he was still knight enough not to betray his king. But if his lord was doomed, anyway...

Why not survive? Why not right the wrong given to his great-grandfather whose lands and title—rightfully earned with Hanley blood and sweat—had been stripped from him by greedy and paranoid lordlings? Why not get rewarded for once, instead of having it always be just beyond his reach?

This was not the first time he had asked these questions, but the previous answer for them: 'because I am a knight', seemed so hollow now. If he wanted this reward, it was his for the earning. All he had to do was kill Myria. It would be difficult—she was fast and skilled—but he had both height and reach on her and was second only to Balien in his skill with a blade. All he needed to do, assuming he really *did* want Attenham's reward, was create an opportunity in which to confront her.

That opportunity had yet to present itself. He was locked in a room somewhere in the Campus of Ur, in one of the Templar's quarters. The Campus was the section of Olsarum given to the priests and their business. They lived here in these old, hallowed buildings, trained in its armsrooms and performed their sacred duties.

The Bear and the Thistle

These buildings and the streets between them should have been full and bustling. Even with all of its priests on quest to every corner of Karalon, there should have been squires, trainers and domestic staff and their families present. The Campus was a small but vital community whose existence centred around the maintenance and defence of Karalon's greatest treasure, and yet it sat empty.

Gennald didn't really want to know why it was empty. As foolish and naive as it was, so long as he did not know the truth, it was still possible that they were merely being held prisoner, or had been exiled.

The door to his cell opened and, for a brief moment, Gennald thought that he had been rescued. What he had initially thought to be a Templar, though, was only an outlaw wearing his armour. No real templar would ever allow himself to be seen with his surcoat in such disarray, or allow his armour to become so tarnished. "Come on," the imposter said. "Don't make me beat you."

Gennald was tempted. He was still bound, but, despite the many beatings he had been given, still had fight within him. Ultimately, he didn't care enough to fight right now. The heart of Karalon was being held by imposters and the actions of one knight mattered nothing at all. He followed the false templar out into the centre of the Campus.

There were more false templars there as well—all their equipment in equal levels of disarray—as well as Myria, two dozen outlaws, and another man in armour. Gennald's will to fight almost returned when he realized that it was whoever or whatever had replaced Grandmaster Lanton, and that he was deferring to Myria.

"And here comes the hostage now," not-Lanton said in greeting. The cruel smile that twisted his features jarred Gennald almost as much as his first sight of Olsarum had. That expression on that face was as wrong as taking dogwoman as a wife.

An outlaw came running into the square. "They're coming," he said. "They're making their way down the cliff. I can see them."

"Is it them?" Myria asked, her narrowed eyes the only change in her expression. "How many are there?"

He nodded. "it's the Knights of Anduilon, I'm sure of it. I saw the big blue one, and the one in the red coat. There are two or three more, I think."

Gennald couldn't breathe. Illyria was coming *here*. Sephana had survived somehow and warned her, and they had made their way either around or through the Silverhearts to get here. There was still hope.

Not-Lanton seemed to read his mind and slid a noose around Gennald's neck. "Don't you try anything, or I'll throttle you dead."

The lead outlaw, Manson—he was wearing templar's armour—strode up to Myria and bowed his head. "We're ready, My Lady, but you should know that the men and I are rusty. None of us have ridden horses into combat since, well, you know."

If she did know, she made no sign of it. "You'll be fine. It will be enough that you are there. They won't be expecting cavalry."

The false grandmaster jerked Gennald by his noose. "Come on, knight. You're with me now. Now we'll see if that elven princess really does love you."

Gennald's blood froze. He was being used as bait for Illyria. He had known this from the start, but had dismissed it as impossible. He should have known, though, that defying the possible was what Illyria and her knights did. Gennald found himself hoping, in the greatest of ironies, that she in fact did not return his feelings.

Eldoth was, strangely enough, getting used to feeling like he wanted to die. The climb and subsequent descent into the sacred valley had been brutal but, to his own surprise, tolerable. He wished that he could take credit for that, but his physical limits were just as pathetic now as when all of this mess had first started.

No, the credit for the difference between this wretched climb and its predecessor lay in his fellow knights. Theramus had carried his gear, Balien had steadied and supported him, and Sephana—who, on his personal scale of love and hate, was currently leaning far more to the latter—had used her unique ability to goad, anger, and cajole him into continuing.

They were at the bottom of the cliff-like hill now, the early evening sun shining the last of its rays upon them. Illyria and Theramus both had their weapons drawn and were watching the surrounding trees. Balien crouched next to Eldoth, ready to support him if he vomited again, while Sephana went to get him fresh, cool water.

"You did well," Balien said with what sounded suspiciously like sincerity. "You're getting stronger."

"I do not feel stronger," Eldoth replied, wiping his mouth and trying to ignore the taste within. "I feel like a burden."

Balien shrugged. "We all have our strengths and weaknesses. You may not be able to climb like Theramus, but only you can perform magic. The benefit of being in a group is that we share each other's burdens, as well as our strengths." He looked at Eldoth pointedly. "That is what having friends is about. We support each other."

"Friends," Eldoth scoffed. "I've heard what you all say when you think I can't hear you. We're not friends, just...useful to each other."

"You don't make it easy to like you, especially with how you treat Sephana," Balien admitted. "But I'd like to be your friend, if you'd let me."

He eyed Balien warily. "Everyone who has ever wanted to be my friend was either lied or wanted to use me."

"I'm sorry to hear that," Balien said. "But I'm not one of those people."

Eldoth wanted to believe him, but wasn't that exactly what someone who was trying to manipulate him would say?

Balien shrugged and braced his hands on his knees. "If you want to remain alone and untrusted, I can't stop you, but sooner or later we'll stop trying." He rose to his feet with enviable grace. "It's your choice."

"I don't know anything about you," Eldoth blurted out before Balien had even gone two steps.

He turned. "Ask me something."

"Perhaps I will, Eldoth said, "once this is all over and we both live."

Balien nodded. "I'll hold you to that. We're moving out soon. Be strong."

Eldoth found himself smiling. "I will."

Sephana returned with a dripping water skin. "You're smiling. What's wrong?"

He took the offered skin and took a small sip. "Nothing. You're too suspicious." Eldoth rinsed out his mouth. "Thank you for this, and for before, on the mountain."

"I liked you better when you were being creepy. What's wrong with you?"

"Nothing." Eldoth scowled. Trust her to ruin everything. "I was being delusional, obviously. We're going to be moving soon. You should make ready."

She cocked her head, confused. "I can't figure you out anymore. What happened when I was captured, anyway?"

He had to look away, his mood darkening even further. "Nothing important."

Illyria watched the wooded vale warily, alert for any sign of danger or that something was amiss. So far, she had seen nothing.

Gennald was out there, she hoped. She felt horrible for not making any attempt to liberate from Attenham's manor. Had she not tried hard enough? Part of her thought that her fellow knights were skilled enough that they should have at least made the attempt. It was entirely possible they could have entered it without being detected, but it was equally possible that they would have failed. If they resorted to force—between Eldoth and Theramus, she had few illusions about their succeeding—it would have brought both Anderites and Golden Bears into a bloody, vicious street battle.

Prudence had said not to do it. Logic told her that he was being kept him alive as a counter to her, and that he was strong enough to survive any torture they could inflict. Responsibility to her quest had said that the needs of King Lionar and all of Karalon outweighed her concern for one knight.

Prudence. Logic. Responsibility. They sounded so insignificant when weighed against the welfare of the man that she had given her heart and, almost, her body to. Surely he deserved more.

His attitudes still bothered her. He had said to her face that he didn't respect her. He and Sephana had almost come to blows over it. And yet, he had said that he loved her, and she had said those same words back to him. Surely, for love, there was some middle ground that could be reached. And, if there was, what would Illyria do when Myria inevitably used him against her? Would she lay down her arms if the price for not doing so was his death?

She didn't know, and she prayed to Emuranna that she wouldn't have to find out. They had prepared as much as possible, but there were too many unknowns. Illyria had no idea what would happen next.

There was no more time to waste with unanswerable questions. They had rested and recovered; even Eldoth's face had returned to its normal colour. To delay any further was pointless and self-indulgent. Either they were right and Myria's forces were here, or they were wrong and intruding into a holy place. She motioned in Forest Speech for them to move out.

They advanced slowly and quietly, or as much as they could with a giant and a heavy-footed wizard in their company. They passed where they had been intercepted by the false Grandmaster five days ago and had met the quietborn dog. Of course, in hindsight, if the grandmaster was an imposter, then most likely the dog had been a full-blooded hound warden.

But if the dog *was* a hound warden, why did it react that way to Balien? It was a mystery for another time.

There was a large clearing ahead. Illyria fox-crawled to its edge and peered beyond—she had no intention of crossing it and exposing herself to enemy fire— only to freeze.

A dozen armed and armoured horsemen stood in a line at the far edge of the clearing. The one in the centre wore the gold coloured tunic of the Grandmaster, but Illyria no longer had any doubt that he was the man he claimed.

Gennald stood before him, hands tied and with a noose around his neck. 'Lanton's' lance was pointed straight at his back.

CHAPTER TWENTY-THREE

*" 'To this day, there are fewer things I regret more about our earlier adventures than what
we were forced to do on that fateful SummersEnd in Olsarum.' "*

—The Private Journals of Illyria Exiprion

"So what do I call you?" Gennald asked. He would not call the imposter behind
him Lanton or Grandmaster—such a title was earned, not given blithely to anyone
wearing the golden surcoat—but he had to call him something. They'd been
standing in the clearing like targets for the last ten minutes, and for all of it he'd
had...*whoever's* lance pointed at his back. Bound and held by the noose around his
neck as he was, he knew that there was nothing he could do to avoid getting fatally
impaled should his captor want it.

It didn't seem to, not yet, and was instead content to let Gennald stand in place
before it.

"I am Lanton now," the imposter said with a bitter laugh. "I look like him, I
sound like him, I bathed in his thoughts for weeks on end, though doing so made
me nauseous."

"How? What foul magics did you use to accomplish this?"

Not-Lanton laughed. "Never question the might of the Djido, boy. They're not
as gone as you think."

Djido. Hearing that word, spoken in that way, froze Gennald's blood. "Then I
name you Snakespawn," he said hoarsely, "and so I shall call you until your
death." He saw now the true meaning of that word, and knew why Sephana had
tried to duel him after saying it. She had been right to take offence.

"Brave words for a man with a spear to his heart."

"A time will come when I am not at your mercy, Snakespawn," Gennald
swore, "and at that time we will have a very different conversation."

"You knights, always mistaking stupidity for bravery," it spat. "I've hated
being one of you." It shifted in its saddle, causing the horse to snort in annoyance.
Gennald could feel its hot, moist breath against his neck.

"They're here. I know they are," it muttered. "Come out, she-elf," it yelled at in
inhuman volume. "I have your lover. Come out and parlay, or I kill him."

There was only silence from the other end of the clearing and Gennald
wondered whether or not this was his end. As much as he hated the idea of dying

as a prisoner, it warmed him to know that, with him gone, there was nothing stopping Illyria and her knights from killing every single imposter in this valley.

Gennald tried not to think about how much the blow would hurt, how long he would linger after, or whether he would be able to see the lance jutting out from the front of his body before he died. Instead, he thought about Illyria, of how she had felt in his arms and tasted against his mouth. He thought about how good they would have been together, and how close he had come to realizing his dreams in New Wighton. He pictured her eyes, and the sigh of breath she always gave before he kissed her. He remembered...

She walked out of the forest, like the vision of a dream, alone.

"I'm here, imposter," she yelled across the empty field. "Release him and leave this valley, or you shall die here. This is your only warning."

The Illyria of Gennald's dreams would never have spoken so. She was definitely real.

Sephana had watched Illyria's face as she realized that Gennald was being held for ransom. She honestly didn't know what Illyria was going to do. What would *she* have done, if Edrik had been in Gennald's place?

The answer to that was easy: the same thing Edrik had done for her. He had braved impossible odds to free her, and Sephana knew that she would have done the same for him. Illyria, too, would surely do it for Gennald. What did that mean for the rest of them, then? For King Lionar and his Joining? Would they surrender?

"Balien, take Sephana and make your way around the clearing," Illyria said levelly. "Proceed with the plan." Balien nodded, but made no move to go. "Theramus, Eldoth: there are more men in the trees, I am sure of it. Find where they are and take them out on my signal."

"What of the cavalry?" Theramus asked. "They are templars."

"They're imposters. No priest would obey a command that incited violence in their valley, and no knight would let their grandmaster hold a knight hostage." Illyria's finger's twitched against her bow string. "Their armour isn't proof against my arrows. I'll handle them."

That made things easy, except for one thing...

Sephana made herself say it. "What about Gennald?"

"I'll not allow him to be a hostage, nor would he want himself to be used that way." Her face was as hard as a statue's.

She covered her mouth with her hand. "You mean you're going to..." She didn't care about Gennald—well, not much—but the choice Illyria was being forced to make was tragic.

"She'll do what she has to," Balien said. "We're ready Lyri. On your mark."

Illyria nodded and stepped into the clearing.

Balien touched Sephana's shoulder and gestured for them to go. Sephana followed and they ran through the forest as quiet as foxes. She didn't bother wiping away her tears.

Eldoth didn't like this plan. Logically, it was sound and there was no one else in the group who could perform his role, but it involved acting as a target for arrows *again*. Eldoth was forming new criteria for the evaluation of battle plans, and placed 'acting as a slow moving, red-jacketed target' as the exact definition of a bad plan.

He was sure that, if Sephana were to form her own list, such a factor would be placed in the opposite category. It was one of the things he loved about her.

He and Theramus crouched in the underbrush, waiting on Illyria's signal. He did not know what it was, but she had assured him that it would be impossible to miss. Theramus held a large, body length shield (body length for Eldoth, anyway) in his hands. It was constructed out of a wooden frame covered by a seamless sheet of lead and tin scavenged from the various pots and pans found in the Silverheart Mines. It was incredibly heavy for a man to carry, but Theramus had transported it up the Silverheart Hills and down the other side with no effort. It was completely impervious to arrow fire and Eldoth would come to no harm behind it, provided Theramus kept it aloft and Eldoth stayed behind him the entire time.

With Theramus acting as a target and forcing the enemy to reveal their locations, Eldoth *should* be able to wound them with fire or at least force them to leave their fortifications. At that point, Illyria would have been free to perforate them, but since she was now going to be occupied with the unanticipated horse warriors, Eldoth supposed he would have to deal with them as well.

Provided, of course, that she ever gave her 'impossible to miss' signal.

Upon further consideration, Eldoth was now positive: this was a bad plan.

Illyria had to give the imposter a chance to surrender, even though she doubted he would take it. This was the Sacred Valley of Karalon; if there was any chance to avoid bloodshed within it, she was honour-bound as a priestess to seek it. That it also meant safe-guarding Gennald from harm only made it more crucial.

He looked so *beaten* out there. Small. His hands were bound, his face bruised and his shirt dotted with too many dried bloodstains to count. Any of those would have made her falter, but the angry, stubborn expression on her face emboldened her. *This was what he would want.* If she continued to say that to herself enough times, it was possible that she might bring herself to believe it.

Illyria stepped into the clearing, Heartseeker in hand. She tried very hard not to think about the number of arrows trained upon her and failed. She could see a dozen expressions cross Gennald's face and steeled herself to act.

"I'm here, imposter," she yelled across the empty field. "Release him and leave this valley, or you shall die here. This is your only warning."

The Grandmaster's impersonator laughed.

"You are in no place to make demands, she-elf," he yelled back in a voice that was too loud to be human. "Drop your bow, and have your friends step into the open and *you* will live, along with your lover, the knight. This is *your* only warning."

She hadn't really expected it to go differently, despite what she may have hoped. There was no point in replying. She looked Gennald and mouthed 'I'm sorry', then raised her bow, aimed it at the man she had almost given herself to, and loosed.

Gennald had always known Illyria to be fast, both to decide and to act, but he had never seen her move this quickly. One moment her bow was by her side, and the next—before he could even register it—she had raised it, pulled back an arrow and loosed it. At him.

He felt a pain against his neck at the same time that he realized there was no pain in his chest. She could have struck him in the heart if she had felt merciful, but she had not. Instead she had struck his neck, and not even squarely.

She'd cut his noose; with an arrow. He was free.

Gennald came to this realization at the same time as Snakespawn, and he lunged away from the lance aimed at his heart at the same time that it stabbed down. He felt the heavy metal point snag his shirt and scrape against his leg, but it missed his heart and became embedded in the ground.

Gennald had never felt more alive. What matter exhaustion? What matter wounds? He was a knight on a field of battle, and the man who had slain the greatest knight in Karalon was within arms reach. If he fell, then he would rise again and again and again, and woe to the thing he had named Snakespawn, for, on his honour, he *would* avenge the great man whose face he now wore.

His hands were bound, but he was far from helpless. Snakespawn was trying to free its lance. Gennald turned, gripped the heavy spear in his hands, and pulled. Whatever Snakespawn had learned from the real Lanton, horsemanship had not been among them. The sudden move and shift of balance startled its mount, which, combined with Gennald's unbalancing jerk, sent it tumbling from his saddle.

The Bear and the Thistle

Illyria loosing her arrow at Gennald was undoubtedly her signal. (Had she struck him? No. That was good, for her sake). Theramus nodded at Eldoth, hefted his shield and stepped into the clearing. He had not even made it three steps before arrows began to pelt him harmlessly.

"Where are they?" Eldoth asked. "I can't see around you."

Theramus peeked around the side of the shield before advancing at a slow walk. "Thirty yards," he called back. "They are behind wooden barricades."

He heard Eldoth snort. "Wooden, eh? Their mistake."

Theramus was unable to see what the wizard did, but a moment later the ground in front of the outlaws burst into flame. They cried in alarm but continued to fire. More arrows embedded themselves into Theramus's shield.

"Close, but short," he called out. "They are three yards beyond you."

Eldoth grunted a wordless acknowledgement and this time the barricade erupted in flames. The archers—there were five of them—scattered. "They are running!" Theramus called and dropped his shield. "Follow me, quickly!" Brandishing his staff by one end and holding the other over his shoulder, he thundered towards the milling outlaws. Ten very long strides later he was among them and crushing bones with every swing.

Illyria didn't allow herself to breathe until after she saw Gennald evade the imposter's hovering lance tip and jerk him from his horse. She had freed him. It had been a difficult shot, and the thought of what she might have stuck if she had missed was horrifying.

He was on his own, now. Hopefully he was still hale enough that he could either defeat or evade the imposter without her assistance. She had other concerns.

She darted to the left, knowing that the archers she could not see had already loosed against her. Theramus and Eldoth would soon be drawing some of their arrows, but for now she was their only target. Their smaller, weaker bows were not as quick or as accurate as Heartseeker. They would need to arc their arrows, creating a short delay between their arrows leaving their bows and striking their targets. Therefore, if Illyria kept darting to and fro like a running deer, she was somewhat proof against them.

Until they began firing volleys, that is, or a lucky shaft happened to catch her. She was, ultimately, a single target in the middle of a clearing and there were too many arrows to avoid forever. Hopefully, between Theramus and Eldoth, as well as Sephana's and Balien's attempt at flanking, she could keep them occupied.

Her plans had not involved heavy cavalry. Moments after she had launched the shot that freed Gennald, they had lowered their lances and begun to charge. The face side of that coin was that meant she was unlikely to be targeted by the archers for much longer, since they wouldn't risk striking their own horsemen, but the capital side was that she was facing down ten armed and armoured horsemen, a prospect that would turn her insides to jelly if she allowed it.

Illyria pulled an arrow to her ear and loosed it against the nearest false templar. Such was the range between them and the magically enhanced strength of her weapon that the missile seemed to disappear from her hand and reappear in his chest. She ran another few steps, brought another arrow to bear and struck another target. This arrow pierced both his shield and armour and still retained enough force to strike his heart.

And then there were eight.

Sephana darted nimbly through the trees, Dawn's First Crescent in hand. Balien, she knew, was behind her. She had become very good at not thinking since finding the magical dagger she now used, but the image of the horrible situation Illyria was facing continued to linger. Her own brother trusted her enough to survive the situation—if he hadn't, Sephana was sure he wouldn't have left her side—so it behoved her to do the same.

She almost fell headlong into a steep ravine. Not thinking, just allowing her body to act, she swung the pommel chain outward, caught it on a tree branch and swung herself across the gap without breaking stride. Balien would have to take the longer way.

She found herself facing the rear of a group of outlaws, who clearly had not expected her to appear where she had. Still not thinking, she attacked them without pause.

It was like she was a passenger in her own body. There was no thought involved, none at all. She could feel her muscles bunching and feel the smooth, cool Ansharite of her dagger beneath her one bare hand. She was holding it by the middle of the chain, with the spiked pommel and unbreakable dagger each swinging like twin pendulums four feet from her hands.

She watched herself spin madly through the middle of the group of men, her Ansharite weapons acting as extensions of her arms. The swinging knife blade cut through armour like it was paper and the tearing blades of the weighted pommel bit at exposed flesh like a sculptor's chisel into stone. Within moments of the fight beginning, it was over and Sephana could only look down at the bodies of those she had killed.

A very small part of her acknowledged what Eldoth had said to her back in Jannery's manor, oh, so long ago. Maybe what she was doing wasn't wholly natural, but who cared so long as she could do things like this? As long as she held Dawn's First Crescent, she was invincible. And, more importantly she was *useful*.

Balien ran up, face flushed and breathing heavily. He looked at the bodies surrounding Sephana with obvious surprise. "Impressive."

"I know, isn't it?" Sephana smiled and twirled her pommel weight idly with her gloved hand.

Balien didn't reply. Instead, he leapt forward and thrust his sword behind her. Sephana was too startled to react. She knew that Balien wasn't striking at her—not only would he never do that, but if he did, he wouldn't have missed—and instead just stood and watched him.

She only turned when she heard the sharp, ringing sound of metal on metal. She looked to the ground and saw a strange, six pointed metal star and knew that it had would have struck her in the back without Balien's intervention. She turned to where the star must have come from.

All she saw was a slender shadow and a flash of dark hair. Sephana knew who had just attacked her.

I'm coming to get you, Myria, and this time my hands aren't tied!

Sephana ran into the forest, a grin on her face, leaving Balien no choice but to follow.

Gennald stabbed down with the lance against the now prone Snakespawn. The weapon was heavy, not made to be used in this manner or by someone whose hands were tied together. His target rolled away from Gennald's first, awkward strike and managed to avoid the follow-up as well.

The mounted outlaws were spurring their horses into action, some against him, but most against Illyria. He was dead on the ground, but Gennald knew, both by seeing them and by their own admission, that these were not true cavalrymen.

He hated doing it, but he abandoned his pursuit of Snakespawn and made for its horse. It was a true destrier, a warhorse—undoubtedly the real Lanton's mount—and would not shy in combat. More importantly, it was trained to be directed by a rider's feet and knees. Gennald's vaulted easily into its saddle, despite being bound, and knew that he was no longer helpless.

"Kill him!" Snakespawn ordered, on its feet now with its sword drawn and raised. Gennald spurred his borrowed mount and charged. The imposter was too startled to attack and was sent sprawling by the horse's barded chest. Gennald acted and managed to grab its sword by the blade before it hit the ground.

It was awkward and took longer than he would have liked, but Gennald was able to use the sword blade to cut the ropes on his wrists. Snakespawn used the time to climb, but the horse, in the mood for blood, reared back and lashed out with its forehooves. The imposter fell—its skull crushed, hopefully—and Gennald, finally unfettered, spun to face the first of the oncoming horsemen.

Eldoth crouched behind the immovable shield that, moments earlier, Theramus had hefted like a kite. He was still exposed in the middle of the clearing. Perhaps, in hindsight, it would have been better if he had followed the large blue giant on his mad charge into the trees, but it had all happened so suddenly and indecision had plagued him. By the time he had decided on a course of action, Theramus had left him, and he was alone.

He could hear violence from within the trees and see occasional flashes of blue skin. Eldoth's fire was still burning, though not horribly out of control. Illyria and Gennald (the ass) were engaged with the cavalry in the clearing, but Sephana and Balien were lost from sight. It was an aspect of their strategy that he did not agree with, but he had been unable to offer rational grounds for grouping him with his ex-wife. Also, she had started looking at him strangely when he had began pressing his argument, and he did not want to broach that subject yet. Later, when the battle was over; assuming that they both lived.

He sensed arrows flying towards him and deflected them easily. The location of the archers who had loosed them, however, remained unknown. If these were more controlled circumstances, perhaps he might have been able to examine their trajectories and determine their point of origin, but things had ceased to be controlled the moment his life had been placed in jeopardy. The irony of this did not escape him.

More arrows arced towards him and once again he nudged them aside. If his intention was to remain stationary in the middle of the clearing, undoubtedly he could have done so indefinitely. He was making no offensive moves and his fellow knights were much more inviting targets, Theramus especially. What few errant shots flew towards him could be deflected, and anyone foolish enough to approach him would find themselves turned into char. The most obvious and logical thing for him to do was remain exactly where he was.

And yet, he couldn't. Why did that idea rankle him so? Why did the idea of self preservation, up until now always his highest priority, suddenly seem so unappealing? Balien had offered him the hand of friendship, and, to the best of Eldoth's estimation, he had been sincere.

Friends. When had Eldoth ever had a friend? People had claimed to be his friend before, but they had lied to him every time. Sephana had only wanted freedom from slavery, Gerralt had used him as a weapon, and the less said about Mariska the better. Like any deal involving a woman, he had come out the loser in the end.

Were the Knights of Anduilon his friends? Balien and Illyria had only ever been courteous to him, unless he had done something especially obnoxious, and, even then, had never truly become angry with him. He and Theramus had reached an understanding and Sephana was...a very special case. He didn't object to their company and found their conversations interesting, but were they his friends?

Perhaps and perhaps not, but they were certainly his comrades; allies. He had entered into an association with them and had taken a oath of knighthood alongside them. Certainly he would have more access to hidden magical lore in their company then he would by himself. If they succeeded in their current mission, perhaps the king of Karalon would allow him to search his royal library. There had to be at least one volume of magic in there.

Well, that settled it, then. If only for the sake of his future magical research, Eldoth would aid his fellow knights in what he would normally consider an insane undertaking. To do that meant leaving his current place of safety and following Theramus into the trees. He could carry the large, heavy shield there, but it would be very slow. Better, perhaps, to move quickly and unburdened to the tree line while still keeping sufficient focus to deflect arrows.

His rational mind told him that it was a short run: not even one hundred feet. He could do it in less than ten seconds at a fast trot, but ten seconds could be a very long time, especially if an unknown number of archers tracking focused on his movement. A good archer could loose three times in that short period, and Eldoth doubted that he could detect and ward off that many arrows. Perhaps it was better to stay here after all...

Stop being a coward! Stand up and move. Now is as good a time as any other.

Eldoth stood on shaking legs, feeling like a giant arrow attracting beacon, and began to jog towards the trees. Sure enough, he was able to sense a number of swiftly flying arrowheads and was able to deflect them all. Subtle force was all that was needed, he had discovered. If caught early enough in its flight, even the smallest nudge was enough to alter its trajectory. It did not matter, after all, if the shot missed him by an inch, a foot or a yard. All that mattered was that it missed.

He had moved perhaps half the distance, nudging arrows as he went, when he felt a sharp, driving pain in his chest. Suddenly sitting even though he had no memory of getting into that position, Eldoth stared down at a feathered shaft rimed with his blood.

That's not fair! I didn't sense it coming at all!

Myria (or the 'Black Lady', or whatever other name she went by) was harder to catch than that last dream before waking. She was fast, nimble, and could climb faster than anyone Sephana had ever seen. Well, unless she was looking in a mirror.

Myria performed some neat trick that involved basically running up the space between an aspen and a short cliff face. It was amazing feat and something that Sephana knew that she could never duplicate. If the two of them had been in a foot race, Myria would have just won.

It wasn't just a race, and Sephana had more than her feet on her side. Far beyond the need to think about what she was doing, she swung out the pommel of Dawn's First Crescent, looped around a sturdy branch, and propelled herself into the air. Her path took her through the cloud of twigs and small branches, and she had to spit out a few leaves, but she still managed to land at the top of the bluff at the same time as Myria.

"Not so easy when I'm not tied up, is it?" Sephana taunted, snapping the pommel back into her dagger before casting it out again, this time with the blades extended. It was supposed to catch Myria's ankle, but she lifted her foot out of harm's way, drew a pair of short, heavy bladed swords from her belt and stepped into attack.

"Oh, that was a big mistake," Sephana said, readjusting the detached pommel so that it hung two feet from the end of her free hand. "You have no idea who you're fighting." Swirling the deadly pommel blades in a quick figure eight, she lunged in with her dagger.

Myria sidestepped the dagger strike and slid around the swirling chain like water. "Neither do you," she said; her first words of the battle so far. Her twin swords had thick hand guards with heavy pommels, one of which caught Sephana painfully across the jaw.

Sephana's powerful fighting instinct vanished. She was still trying to recover her senses when Myria struck her three more times; once in the stomach, once with her elbow and finally with a strong kick that hurled Sephana over the edge of the bluff and towards the ground below.

I think I'm in trouble, were Sephana's last thoughts before she struck the ground.

CHAPTER TWENTY-FOUR

"The Sacred Valley of Olsarum is the oldest, most sacred place in all of Karalon. The Circle of Joining was made by Emuranna herself, and the Temple of Ur is more than five thousand years old. Almost as sacred are the Line of Priests, whose bloodlines are as long and as respected as those of the royal family.

Even when the Great War was at its worst, the Sacred Valley was never defiled and the line of priests never broken. Any rumours about priests being impersonated by anti-monarchists, or the valley being used as a pitched battleground are offensive and completely untrue.

—A Line Unbroken: a History of the Priests of Karalon, *Simeon of Rath*

Despite everything else happening around her, Illyria could not help but admire Gennald's skill on a horse. He and his appropriated mount moved as one, weaving in and around the other more heavily armoured riders as if they were drunken revellers. He attacked with his broadsword both forehand and backhand on both sides of his body, attacking and defending against five times his number with effortless grace. He was by far the best rider on the field, though his opponents had the edge in both armour and weaponry.

Illyria was not just standing in place while Gennald battled the false priests, as much as part of her wanted to. Her arrows had found homes in the bodies of half the riders until an inadvertent roll had caused her to land on her quiver and break most of her remaining arrows. Perhaps one or two of them remained intact, but she didn't have the time to search through them. She carried Maiden's Fang now to fend off further attack, but the short blade will ill-suited against cavalry. Her opponents carried lances, broad swords and mace and chains. This battlefield was poorly suited to her talents. She would aid her comrades if she were able to locate them, but they, like their enemies, were hidden by the trees.

She spied movement near the tree line. Someone—he was wearing Karalinian armour, whoever he was—was staggering to his feet. She began jogging towards the fallen warrior, hoping perhaps to take him prisoner and get some answers, when he turned to look over the battlefield. It was Lanton, or at least the man who wore his face and used his name. The imposter priest gave the field one last glance before disappearing into the trees.

Illyria sprinted off in pursuit. One way or another she would get answers, and sunset was less than half an hour away.

Theramus turned, all foes near him vanquished, and looked for Eldoth. He had thought the wizard would follow him when he ran for the trees, but when he had entered battle he had found himself alone.

He looked back into the clearing in time to see Eldoth fall to the ground. There was not even time to curse. He was back to the wizard inside five strides but he had not even stopped before he saw Eldoth slowly clambering to his feet. He did not even have to pull the arrow from his chest; the act of standing dislodged it.

"The head must have fallen off in flight," Eldoth grimaced. "The blunt shaft barely penetrated the skin." He stood, leaning on Theramus for support. "Still hurts like the blazes, though."

"I am glad to see that your wound is—*uughh*" He broke off as he felt a decidedly *not* blunted arrow shaft penetrate his back. His giant's skin lessened the wound, but Theramus could still only take so many of them. "—not debilitating," he continued with a growl. "Come, we must get to cover before anyone else—" As if on cue, another shaft dug into his arm. "—chooses to attack us."

Eldoth looked up at Theramus sharply. "Am I one of your primes now?" He flicked his finger and Theramus heard an arrow fall at their feet.

"You are a fellow knight," Theramus corrected, leading the two of them to the tree line. "I would do the same for any of the others."

"How touching." They made it to cover without sustaining further injury. "Hold still," the wizard instructed and a moment later both arrows in Theramus's back jerked free painfully. Theramus could not help but hiss in pain. "Sorry." He lay his hand on Theramus's bare arm and Theramus experienced a sensation quite unlike anything he had ever felt.

It was as if unseen hands had grabbed onto all sides of his wounds and pinched them together, then applied a burning brand to cauterize it all. It was painful, yes, but mostly...*unsettling*. Unnatural.

"This is no substitution for a proper physician's care," the wizard said, "but it will stop them from bleeding."

Theramus moved his arm experimentally, feeling how the magically repaired muscle behaved. They felt like they were a week old: tender, but functional. "Thank you."

Eldoth's eyes narrowed. "It wouldn't have been needed if you had not abandoned me."

"There they are!" A voice called. Theramus turned to see a large group of archers—a dozen? fifteen?—twenty yards off with their bows raised. "Loose!"

Sephana's instinct had vanished. When she rolled away from Myria's attack—a blades-down leap off the top of the ten foot bluff—it was solely by her own agility and speed. When she scrambled gracelessly to her feet and gave a panicked, wildly off-target slash, it was without her accustomed otherworldly awareness. She was just herself for this fight, and she was in trouble.

The black clad woman attacked mercilessly, raining down blow after blow with her short, wide-bladed swords that Sephana barely managed to dodge. Myria's face was blank and expressionless as she fought, though after a while a frown began to form.

"After all that talk you gave, I'm frankly disappointed." She said it casually, like they were chatting over tea at the fireside. "After all the time I have spent in this awful kingdom, I was hoping for a challenge."

Sephana ducked one slash and dodged another by darting behind a tree. "So where did you come from, then?"

Myria just smirked. "My lips aren't as loose as some people's."

Sephana dodged another sword stroke, only to realize that it had been a feint. She tried to avoid the follow-up blow but was too late. She caught a knee to her chin and, as she tried to stagger away, felt Myria's foot stomp down painfully on her tail.

She sprawled onto the ground and managed to roll onto her back. She lashed out desperately with Dawn's First Crescent, only to have Myria blocked her wrist effortlessly with her foot before kicking the dagger out of Sephana's hand.

"No challenge at all," Myria said, sounding almost bored, as she drew back one of her swords for a killing blow.

Gennald had tried to grab an upended lance off one of the slain imposters, but hadn't been able. Instead, he had been forced to confront one of the three remaining horseman—this one with a lance—with only his broadsword. He had expected his opponent to strike at him and had prepared for that, but found his horse lanced through the heart instead. The poor, noble animal had been dead before it struck the ground.

His brave words earlier about pushing on despite his wounds or fatigue were getting harder to live up to. He was long past the point of feeling the pain of individual wounds, but they had all combined into a communal ache that pressed upon his spirit like a titan pressing down on his shoulders.

And yet, he could not allow himself to stop. Olsarum was still defiled, Illyria still in jeopardy (wherever she had run off to, he doubted that it was *away* from danger), and, more, he was furious. He had been insulted, captured, pulled on a rope like some kind of pet and unmanned in the eyes of the woman he loved. He would get his vengeance, no matter how what he had to endure.

The idiot who had attacked him wasn't an experienced lancer. The impact of landing had sent him hurtling from his saddle and he actually struck the ground before Gennald did. Certainly Gennald was on his feet first, his side on fire from the impact, but still in a better state than his opponent. Ankle twisted from the fall and his arm obviously broken from holding the lance incorrectly, he was weaving on his feet and still trying to draw his sword with the opposite arm it was intended for.

Another horseman charged Gennald, not even bothering with his lance. Instead he unfurled a mace and chain and swung the heavy, deadly iron ball what would have been lethal force. Barring the lance, it was a horseman's most dangerous weapon versus footmen, and Gennald had used his own to deadly effect countless times against dogmen in the march. The disadvantage of a mace was that it was almost impossible to defend with and, while a trained knight could make up for that with his shield, these horsemen were not knights. They needed one hand on the reins at all times to keep control of their mounts, which meant that the man facing him had no defence when Gennald hurled his sword and struck him in the chest.

After that it was almost comically easy to drag the dying man from his horse, rid him of his weapons, and take his place in the saddle. He was properly mounted now, and armed, too. This battle would be over soon.

There was no way Eldoth could deflect so many arrows, not when shot at the same time and from so close. His decision to leave the cover of the shield behind was seeming less and less wise.

He gestured with his hands and a bright, noisy wall of flames came into being between himself, Theramus, and the line of archers. It was a comparatively cool flame, little warmer than a torch, and would have no effect on any arrows launched through it, but it would hopefully give the archers pause enough for him and Theramus to seek cover.

They scrambled through the underbrush, arrows raining around them as they fled. Eldoth's poor, abused coat snagged at least one of them and, based on the sounds Theramus made, one of them had found him as well.

They came to rest, ironically, behind the barricade Eldoth had set on fire, which was mostly unharmed, if somewhat charred. Broken, dead bodies of fallen outlaws surrounded them.

"So what do we do now?" Eldoth asked, his nose filled with the reek of burnt wood.

Theramus was crouched comically low in order to avail himself of the barricade's protection. "I am open to suggestions, but we should act soon. They are undoubtedly flanking us."

"I'm a wizard, not a strategist," Eldoth protested. "Shouldn't you know what to do?" He glanced over side the barricade and immediately sensed half a dozen arrows hurtle towards him. He deflected two of them and ducked the others.

"This is beyond my experience," Theramus said. "In my last encounter with large numbers of men, my armour was proof against arrows and I had no one to safeguard."

Eldoth was sure that he heard people moving in the forest around them. Theramus was right: they had little time. He sensed arrows moving and heard them impact against the barricade a moment later. Obviously, the outlaws wanted to keep them in place. It was the same strategy that Illyria liked to use, and he knew from experience how that usually ended.

He knew roughly were the outlaws were but couldn't do anything about it. The trees were too green to burn well. He could not pinpoint their locations enough to try combusting them. He would have to expose himself in order to hurl fire or lightning with any accuracy and would likely find himself riddled with arrows if he tried. Eldoth glanced around him, trying to find something he could use to aid him. His eyes settled on the body of the nearest body. It had a full quiver of arrows.

I wonder...

He grabbed the sheaf of arrows and held them in front of him. The steel arrowheads were pointed over his shoulder, vaguely towards the enemy. He closed his eyes, concentrating on his magical senses and not wanting any distractions.

All he needed to know was where they were. He could not detect them by their flesh, not with only one ring of mastery in the yellow college, but he could sense the movement of their arrows.

"You will need to attack the ones in front of us on my signal," he said to Theramus. "This will only distract them momentarily. You will have to move quickly."

"Will you follow me this time?" the giant asked. "I cannot protect you if you stay here."

Eldoth nodded. "I will. Be ready."

He sensed an arrow begin it flight towards him, followed by another from nearby. He flung the arrows in his hands over his head and then, once they were in mid-air and generally pointed in the direction he wanted them to go, used his magic to hurl them towards their unseen foes.

"Now!" he yelled, scrambling to his feet even as he heard screams of pain from behind him. Beside him, Theramus exploded into action.

The blow never fell.

Not even a second before Myria would have killed Sephana dead, Balien slammed into Myria with his shoulder and sent her sprawling. Sephana could only watch, stunned, as Myria rolled to her feet and held her swords defensively in front of her.

Both Myria and Balien squared off. Their eyes seemed to widen in mutual recognition before they began to circle each other warily.

"Are you all right?" Balien asked Sephana. His eyes never left Myria.

Sephana nodded before realizing that Balien couldn't see her. "I'm fine." She gave Myria a smug grin. "I think you're going to get your challenge now. Balien is the best."

"Is that so?" Myria asked, her face expressionless. She switched both swords to one hand and threw something to the ground at Balien's feet. He stepped away before it landed, but was still blinded by the black cloud of smoke that erupted. Myria was already moving, snatching star shaped blades from her belt and throwing them as she advanced. Balien dodged one, deflected another, and caught a third across his leg but did not let it slow him as he closed with Myria and engaged her blade to blade (to blade: Myria had two, after all).

Sephana scrambled to find Dawn's First Crescent, all too aware of how badly Myria's various punches, kicks and elbows had hurt her. Myria, on the other hand, didn't look slowed down even little a bit and was holding her own against Balien handily.

Sephana found her dagger at the same time that Myria used the hook-like tines on the guards of her swords to bind Balien's sword. He gave her a brief, curious look before shifting his grip and levering the cross-guard into her stomach. Myria grunted, released his weapon, and backed away warily.

Sephana did her best to clear her mind and allow her instinct to take over, but nothing happened. She was too panicked. *I've scaled castle walls and fought off Djido sorcerers*, she scolded herself. *She's just one person. I can do this.*

In front of her, Myria performed some kind of rolling, flying kick that caught Balien high in the chest. He changed his grip so that he held his sword like a staff and stepped in close to engage her with both tip and pommel.

Sephana gave up. *I'm going to have to do this anyway. Balien needs me.* She released six feet of pommel chain and began to swing it around her head while trying to get behind Myria. She saw her opportunity a few seconds later and lashed out with her weapon, but Balien and Myria shifted positions even as she released it. She was barely able to pull her weapon back without striking her friend, but she still distracted Balien enough that Myria got a slash past his guard and into his forearm.

Balien retreated, switching to a conventional sword grip and keeping Myria at bay with three feet of steel. "Go help the others," he told Sephana, his voice tight.

"Are you sure?" What he really meant was 'all you're doing is getting in my way' but, being Balien, he'd never say it so cruelly.

"I'm sure. Remember: this isn't about you getting any revenge, it's about the king. Be noble, Sephana."

Right. She was a knight now; she had friends that she could rely on and that relied on her. She nodded. "Ok, I'm going, but you'd better win."

Myria launched into another flurry of sword strikes that put Balien on the defensive. Sephana watched for a few seconds, torn, before turning and running towards the last place she'd seen anyone.

'Lanton' was running, as far as Illyria could tell, to the valley's campus. Beyond it, undoubtedly, was the Circle of Joining where King Lionar was waiting. While he didn't require assistance to begin Joining, it was customary; or, at least, it was in Ilthanara. All of the priests within the valley were imposters, though, as was Lanton. Since the intent seemed to be to get Lionar to fail in his Joining and not simply kill him, she wondered what excuse the imposter would give the ailing king.

He had shed his armour in pieces as he ran and now wore only pants and a shirt. Despite his lack of encumbrance, though, Illyria was still gaining. They were in the campus proper now. The buildings they were running between now were made of grey, weathered granite but were no less ancient for their mundane construction. She could see green Heartstone walls in the distance: undoubtedly the Great Temple.

Illyria increased her pace, determined to intercept 'Lanton' before he reached the Circle of Joining and, presumably, the king. If she had Heartseeker, she could have ended all of this minutes ago. The imposter would not even have left the field, to say nothing of reaching the campus, but there was no point in lamenting what could have been. She was a realist and did not have time for fancy.

She was close now. Her quarry entered the doors of the main temple, dimly lit from within by countless candles, torches and braziers. Second only to the circle itself, this was the most holy place in Karalon and it sickened her that her confrontation with the man who had killed and replaced the high priest would be within these walls. She entered the building warily.

The entryway was lined with statues of High Priests of days gone by. Their helms and armour were carved out of stone but their swords, she saw, were real. Carved stone hands held real gold chased leather scabbards and steel blades...except for the nearest one, which clutched only air. An empty scabbard lay at its feet.

She stepped into the inner temple, its interior flickering orange. Bas-reliefs depicting Emuranna and the first kings of Anshara lined the walls, their shadows sinister in the half light. It looked like beautiful work and she would have liked to admire it in any other circumstance, but now was not the time. Now she had to find and kill the man who wore the skin of its high priest.

There was a sound from above her. Illyria turned and raised her sword just in time to block an attack from the impersonator, who had leapt off of a tall plinth behind her.

For the moment, all Illyria could do was defend. Whoever the impersonator was, he was strong and skilled. He attacked with savage fury, lashing out with blow after blow from his stolen sword. It was a heavy weapon made in the Karalinian style, about the same length as Balien's, but with a much wider and heavier blade. It did not have the speed and versatility of her brother's sword but made up for it with weight. She had no doubt that it could decapitate a horse in a single blow.

Her hands stung from her few attempts at parrying it. Her sword weighed less than half that of the imposter's blade, and Illyria herself, while tall and muscular for a woman, was still far weaker than her opponent. If she continued to try and meet strength with strength, she would lose.

She would have to play to her strengths. She was still fleeter and more agile than her opponent, not to mention—she liked to think—smarter. She began stepping farther back with each defence and circling around him. The farther he had to reach with his heavy sword and the more he had to move, the more of his wind he used. Despite his size and strength, wielding that heavy weapon had to be hard work. Sooner or later, he would begin to tire and make mistakes, and Illyria would be there to take advantage of them when it happened.

Assuming she lived that long.

Theramus charged ahead of Eldoth, readying his staff against any and everything that might threaten him or the wizard. Of the seven men before him, two were reeling from arrow wounds, three others were just peeking their heads out from behind trees, one was seeing to his injured comrade, and the last was drawing his sword. They would be no challenge at all to dispatch.

Grudgingly, Theramus had to admit that he had begun to like the stubborn, brilliant and sharp-tongued man. He knew of no one else who could take such a desperate situation and reverse it completely in so short a time. If Eldoth could perform such an act in the heat of combat, what kind of grand work could he create given time, resources, and loyal, unflagging support? What miracles could he perform?

The archers were dispatched quickly and without incident. Two men tried to flee, but Eldoth proved that his trick of hurling arrows was no fluke. He only had to hold it in his hand, point it towards its target and it would leap forth to do his bidding.

The second group of outlaws, the ones who had tried to surround them, attempted to come up on his and Eldoth's flank to no avail. After the wizard killed three of them with their own arrows, the rest fled or surrendered.

"Please, have mercy us," the lead one said, kneeling with his hands behind his head.

"If you wish mercy, you will tell me everything you know about this plot," Theramus demanded

Gennald dispatched the last of the false priests with a mace blow to the chest. He was alone in the clearing. He had caught sight of Illyria's golden hair running towards the campus, and there were sounds of mayhem coming from the trees. He briefly considered stopping, but rejected it. Despite the weight of fatigue and injury upon him, Snakespawn still lived, and Illyria was no doubt pursuing him. That was his path, then, and he could rest when it was over, or when he was dead.

He was about to spur his horse into action when he saw something running across the field. He steered his mount towards it and readied his mace. He had not even closed half the distance when the cloud of hair and narrow frame made it obvious that it was Sephana. He almost turned away and left her. Of all of Illyria's companions, she was the one he got along with the least (although, to be fair, he had treated her very badly). In the end, one thing stopped him: she had been right. She had accused Lanton of being an imposter from the beginning and had remained steadfast even in the face of his derision.

She slowed and her face closed off when she realized just who was riding towards her. He saw her raise her dagger in a defensive position before stopping and lowering to her side.

"I am glad to see you are alive," he said in greeting. "Attenham thought whatever was in that room had killed you."

"It almost did." She squinted up at him, the last rays of the setting sun shining into her eyes. Such was the way the light shone off her skin that her scales were made invisible. She could have been any Karalinian woman, except for her tail. "Thank you for helping me escape."

He nodded. It was apology enough for both of them.

"Do you know where everyone else is?" she asked.

269

"I think Eldoth and Theramus are in the trees. I heard fighting there. Illyria is chasing down Lanton. I was about to pursue them." He hesitated, then held out his hand. "Join me."

She looked up at him and his outstretched hand, her expression unreadable, before reaching out and taking it. Her grip was strong. 'Illyria needs me more,' he thought he heard her mutter as she settled behind him.

"I wronged you," he blurted. He had intended to ride in silence but fatigue seemed to have loosened his tongue. "I insulted both your nature and your character, but you have proved me wrong at every turn. I apologise."

She didn't say anything for a moment. "I still think you're a jerk," she finally murmured, but without anger in her voice.

It was a start.

I can't believe that worked. Eldoth's plan had been desperate and foolish. He had charged down a half dozen archers at ranges so close that he could not have deflected any arrows shot at him. By rights he should have been killed, but found himself standing over a group of five prisoners instead.

Theramus was an effective interrogator. It had mostly to do with his being an eight foot wall of muscle, but he knew also to ask the proper questions.

They spoke at length, but most of their information was either out of date, irrelevant, or so vague as to be useless. Eldoth already knew that the Black Lady ruled them, that there were factions within their ranks, and the location of their secret cave. "The wizard," Eldoth interrupted. "Where is this wizard that accompanies you, and what powers does he possess?"

Apparently, Eldoth did not have the same ability to intimidate as Theramus, for none of them said anything. Eldoth glowered, then slowly began to wreathe his body in flames. "Where is the wizard?" He liked to believe that he was sufficiently intimidating, and that they would have answered him shortly, had the tree not fallen.

It had been a healthy tree. There was no reason for it to fall, and yet it did, and it did so right on top of Theramus. Suddenly Eldoth found himself alone with five desperate criminals, all of whom were larger and stronger than him.

Luckily, he was still on fire. Evidently the prospect of assaulting a man covered in flames was less inviting than flight, for they all turned and ran. He was still watching them go when he sensed something being hurled at him. He turned to see a jagged, head sized rock speeding towards its face. It was moving too fast to have been thrown. Something else had moved it and when he saw the cloaked man standing next to the tree stump that he had undoubtedly broken, Eldoth understood.

He had found their wizard.

The Bear and the Thistle

Illyria finally got her chance. She ducked behind a statue and the imposter's sword caught in the stonework. He was exposed, and she wasted no time driving her sword into his side.

He did not fall as she expected him to.

She was getting tired. There was no other reason for her to just stand and watch her opponent after she struck what should have been his deathblow. She should have withdrawn her blade and either struck him again or taken a defensive posture, but she did neither of those things. Instead she stood and waited to see what his reaction would be. She did not expect him to let go of his sword, ignore the one sticking out of his chest and instead grab Illyria's wrist in a steel-like grip.

"Now I have you," he growled in a voice that both was and was not the one he had spoken with earlier. It was different somehow; not human.

Illyria tugged at her wrist but found his grip unyielding. Trying a different strategy, she drew her dagger with her free hand and stabbed his face. He was ready for her, though, and grabbed that wrist as well. Dagger-like fingers dug into her tendons and she cried out in pain before dropping the weapon. She was now both weaponless and helpless in his grip.

"How can one woman cause me this much trouble?" Lanton/not Lanton said. He stepped back and pulled Illyria with him. His face slipped into a ray of light brought in by the setting sun. Illyria gasped.

"What are you? Why are you doing this?" He had a huge gash on the side of his head. She had not struck him there, so either Gennald had delivered it, or he had received it falling from his horse. The gash itself was not unusual, but what lay underneath it was.

There were scales. They were partly covered in blood, but she recognised them clearly beneath that, and their colour as well. It was a dusky mustard yellow, the same as Veeshar's lizardman bodyguards. Tsrinn, they had been called. Whatever this thing impersonating Lanton was, it was scalykind, which meant that, one way or another, it was in league with the Djido.

"I am Zipulk, and I serve the Order," it said as it pulled her in close to it. It wanted to *bite* her. Illyria wasn't having that. She pulled back as hard as she could. She couldn't break its grip— it was still stronger than her, even injured as it was— but it did allow her to slam into the sword hilt still embedded in its side.

The creature, the Zipulk (was that its name, or the name of its race?) groaned and loosed its grip. Illyria yanked one hand free, brought her leg up to its chest and *pushed*. It was enough to pull free, though her wrist felt like it had been stamped on by a horse. She fell sprawling onto the floor.

It growled at her and drew Maiden's Fang from its own body. Now armed, it moved in to attack. Illyria was being threatened by her own weapon.

Eldoth smiled even as he raised his hand and exerted his magical will against the incoming rock. A wizard duel. He was finally getting to participate in a wizard duel. This one would hopefully go better then the last.

The rock slowed to a halt five feet from Eldoth and hung there. He and the other wizard—did he have a name? Would it be considered rude to ask, since he had not volunteered it?—stared at one another for a moment before releasing control of the rock. It fell harmlessly on the ground between them.

The tree pinning down Theramus began to move. It was appropriate—the Noss was far too annoying to die so easily—but Eldoth did not have the time or energy to spare freeing him. There were other, more pressing, concerns.

More to test his mettle then out of an attempt to harm him, Eldoth glanced at two arrows on the ground and with a twitch of his fingers, sent them towards his opponent. As expected, partway during their flight they veered aside as if struck by a fierce wind.

So, he has two rings in the matter college, then. What level of mastery does he have with red magic?

Eldoth didn't make any gestures with his hands this time. He had learned that error fighting Draxul in the controlling room in Durnshold. Instead he just looked at the other wizard and gave no indicator of what he was doing next. The bolt of lightning burst from the middle of his chest and struck the other wizard squarely. The man cried out in pain and fell to his knees.

As much as Eldoth was thrilled by his success, he was also disappointed. *He has no facility with red magic at all? Really?*

He waited for a counter attack, curious as to what form it would take. His opponent had at least one ring in yellow magic? Would he give Eldoth uncontrollable painful spasms? Perhaps he was also a mentalist. Would he try to influence Eldoth's mind?

The wizard, still on his knees, made a broad gesture with his arms and a cloud of pebbles flew towards Eldoth. So they were back to orange magic, were they? How disappointing. He didn't even stop their flight, just deflected an Eldoth-sized hole out of their centre and stood in place as they flew harmlessly by.

"I was hoping for something more," he said to the other man who was just now getting to his feet. "I imagine, then, that you won't be able to counter this either." He made a pinching motion, although it was just for theatrical effect.

From the very beginning, Eldoth had been able to feel, for lack of a better term, the other wizard's magic gathering within him. It was the indigo college of magic—the one that dealt with the manipulation of magic itself—that allowed this. He hadn't had any training in this college before a month ago. He hadn't even been aware that it existed and it had taken a humiliating defeat by Veeshar the Djido sorcerer to fill that hole. His training had been entirely theoretical, but now that the wizard was near, it was time to put theory into practice. Eldoth extended his will into the cloud of unformed magic—it was a terrible way to describe it, but no other term came to mind right now—within the opposing caster and *blocked* it.

There was no other description for it. Eldoth used his own will and knowledge of indigo magic and placed it like a barrier between the other caster and his magic. He cut him off.

Eldoth crossed his arms over his chest and smiled as he watched the other wizard—really, was it so hard not to give even a basic introduction?—come to the same realization. "I think you will find that I have just won," he said. "You are a decently skilled beginner, but your abilities are lacking against a wizard of my character. I am Eldoth, by the way, Eldoth the Red. May I ask who you—hurkk!"

Thrilled with his victory, Eldoth hadn't paid too much attention to the man himself. He was defeated, after all, and no threat, but the other man apparently didn't see it that way. Instead he had ran towards Eldoth and given him a very strong punch in the stomach.

"Now, really, is this necessary?" Eldoth gasped, bent over. "There's no need for violence now...gakk!" The still unnamed wizard grabbed Eldoth by his neck and began choking him.

Eldoth was suddenly reminded of his last wizard's duel, the one he had lost so ignobly. Veeshar was a Djido, slender of build and barely more than five feet tall. Physically he was no threat to anyone, though his magic gave him a most formidable defence. When he was blocking another wizard, though, he could perform no other magical act. He was vulnerable. The Djido had, most wisely, taken on a trio of bodyguards: strong, vicious and exquisitely trained lizardmen called Tsrinn. While Veeshar had countered Eldoth's magic (with, as much as he hated to admit it, embarrassing ease), it had been the three Tsrinn who had actually captured him.

Without their magic, Eldoth and the other wizard were just men, and this other man was apparently built like a stone mason.

This is entirely unfair, Eldoth thought to himself as began to blackout.

CHAPTER TWENTY-FIVE

" 'I learned in our first year of being knights that if we ever had time to prepare for a battle, it meant that we'd been tricked or figured something out wrong. I'm pretty sure that all of our really important fights caught us totally by surprise.' "

—*Sephana, recalling her years as a Knight of Anduilon*

Illyria needed to regain the upper hand. The Zipulk (she'd decided that it was its race, not its name) had slowed after the wound she'd given it, but not fallen. If she'd still had her sword, or even her dagger, maybe she could have matched it, but her dagger was lost and it was using Maiden's Fang to hunt her. All she could do was continue to guard herself and hope for an opening.

None were presenting themselves, and she was running short on time. They were in the gallery overlooking the temple floor. Light from the setting sun bathed both of them in angry red light and almost made the Zipulk's scales invisible. Illyria leapt over a low slash onto a balustrade, giving the false priest a solid kick in its head as she did so. It reeled slightly and she used the opportunity to leap over its head, twisting in mid air as she did so that she landed facing its back. Using a move she'd learned from Balien, she kicked out the back of its hamstrings and, once it had fallen to its knees, stomped on the wrist holding her sword.

Not only did it not drop her weapon, it lashed out and struck her in the chest with her own sword hilt. She staggered back and barely managed to catch onto a column to avoid falling. By the time she'd righted herself, the Zipulk had stood and turned to face her, completely negating any fleeting advantage she may have once had.

She was tired. This had lasted far longer than she had expected, and had come on the heels of an extended sprint through the entirety of the Sacred Valley after a long, arduous climb over the Silverheart Hills and two long marches *though* those same hills. Just once, she'd like for a critical battle to not happen when she was dead on her feet from lack of sleep.

Her fatigue was costing her, both in speed and judgement. She tripped over a raised step that would never have bothered her otherwise and, when scrambling to recover, ran through a wooden door which led to only Emuranna knew where. It was a some sort of withdrawing room, and had no windows or other exits. She whirled to face the Zipulk, but, to her surprise, it did not follow her in. Instead, it stared at her, said 'I'll finish you later,' and slammed the door shut. When she tried to open it a moment later, it was, to no surprise, barred shut.

Illyria pounded futilely against the effectively unbreakable wooden barrier. There was nothing she could do now, other than hope that her fellow knights managed to stop the Zipulk and save king Lionar. She had failed.

Theramus gave the heavy trunk one final shove and pushed it off his body. Enough of its branches had absorbed its impact or, giant or no, it would have crushed him to death. Wrestling his way out from underneath its enormous weight was still an ordeal, and took a frustrating amount of time; time in which Eldoth was alone against at least five outlaws.

He crawled through the cloud of branches and leaves towards where he had last heard the wizard. He had caught snippets of sound and conversation that had ended with a pained whoop, followed by sounds of gagging and choking. He feared the worst.

He finally cleared the fallen tree and saw Eldoth on his knees, his face unhealthily purple, while another, much larger man, throttled him. He was very focused on his task and did not notice Theramus coming up behind him. When Theramus brought his fist heavily down upon the man's head, he fell without a sound.

Eldoth collapsed to the ground, holding his throat and coughing. He looked awful. After a moment, he glared up at Theramus. "You couldn't have arrived earlier?" It barely came out as a rasp. "You're a terrible warden."

"I'm sorry." Theramus knelt and gently helped Eldoth to his feet. His guilt was overwhelming. He opened his mouth to speak, but hesitated. Eldoth deserved the truth. "I am no longer a warden, nor are any of you my primes." He looked away. "A warden who loses his prime can never receive another."

"How did your prime die?"

"He did not die; I *lost* him," Theramus corrected. "There was a war. We were fighting together and became separated."

Eldoth said nothing and Theramus continued. "This was long ago, by your standards. I do not even know if you were alive during the Akkilinian Crusade."

"I was very young," Eldoth rasped. "My father died in it."

"I'm sorry." Theramus did not ask if he had died as a soldier or a victim; there had been little difference in that pointless conflict. "Then you know of the war's final days?"

Eldoth just nodded. The Akkilinian king—later deposed in a coup de tat—had engaged in a 'war against sin' against two neighbouring kingdoms simultaneously. When things had begun to go badly, he had ordered mass conscriptions and fielded the largest army Anshara had seen since the end of the Great War. His strategy had failed spectacularly, and both his armies had ended up slaughtered.

"It was horrible and chaotic. We were alone against hundreds, and I fought a holding action to give him time to escape. I searched for him after the battle's end, but never found any trace of him, alive or dead. I lost him."

"This is when you were the Steel Colossus and wore the armour you spoke of earlier." Eldoth must have used his magic on his throat, for his voice already sounded better.

Theramus wasn't surprised that the wizard had made the connection. "Yes, that is the name they called me afterwards. I will never forget the blood I was forced to spill that day."

"Who was he, your prime?"

Theramus paused. He had never said it aloud, not outside of Emilon. "He was the last High King of Anduilon. His name was Baldwin."

Eldoth gaped. "The High King still lives? It has been centuries."

"I was not lying before when I said that my people served the high kingdom still," Theramus said. "They have lived in Emilon since Daranduil's fall, waiting for a day they could reclaim their birthright."

"But you left your city, and you lost him. Why would you do that?" There was no accusation, just curiosity.

"There was an incident," Theramus said. "His family were all killed, and it became unsafe for him to remain. We fled and travelled the world in secret. I would never have left if there had been alternative, believe me."

"I do." Theramus could see Eldoth's mind at work, processing this new information. "What became of your search? What are the Knights of Anduilon to you then?"

"My search continues still, but it has been more than a generation. I have lost hope that I will ever find Baldwin now. I can only hope that he passed his crownmark down to an heir, and that his line has not been severed. As for all of you," he shrugged. "You are an old giant's hope. Baldwin has been missing for decades, and I had lost my direction. With Sephana, Balien, Illyria and now you," he looked Eldoth in the eyes, "I have dared to believe that there is hope for the future, even if another High King is never crowned."

"You include me in your list now," Eldoth said. "Whereas before you did not."

Theramus heard his unspoken question quite clearly. "You offended me, with your demands for information." Plus, of course, his rude treatment of Sephana, but that had been before. "I did not deem you wise enough to be worthy of it."

Eldoth bristled. "I see. And that has changed?"

"You were quite correct before: there are many volumes of knowledge within Emilon that could be used to improve the quality of life in Anshara, but the Wise Elders of my people decided not to share it until mankind was ready to receive it." He lifted a finger to hold off the tirade that Eldoth was about to begin. "You are also correct when you say that knowledge is power, but that power can be abused. It can be used to oppress. Knowledge of sanitation, irrigation and metallurgy, if not applied universally and well, can create horrible differences in class and culture. We saw it in the days after the Great War, when we tried to do exactly as you suggested."

"But you could police it," Eldoth argued, "ensure that such abuses did not occur."

Theramus shook his head. "No, if we did that then mankind would be serving us, not we them. The Noss cannot be mankind's saviours. It is against our very nature. It has been agreed for centuries that we will impart this knowledge to man only when they are worthy of it, and not before."

"That's asinine and horribly insulting," Eldoth argued. "Who are you to decide what we are worthy of, and how can we know if never given the opportunity? Not only that, but how many generations must live in illness and squalor while you stay hidden within your mountain and sit in judgement over us?"

"Perhaps you are right," Theramus admitted. "The Wise Elders are very removed from the plights of the outside world. No Noss has travelled beyond Emilon's borders for as long as I have for many, many decades. They do not have my perspective."

Eldoth's eyes were still narrow and distrusting, but less so than before. "I see."

Theramus stood and offered Eldoth his hand. "Come, we must go if you are rested enough. The others need us."

Eldoth accepted the offer of assistance. "This conversation is not over."

Theramus had assumed as much. In fact, he was sure that it had just begun.

Illyria gained more respect for Sephana. Not that she had ever *not* respected her, but her ability to wriggle through any hole just big enough to fit her body was something that Illyria wished she possessed right now.

Illyria had not thought herself afraid of enclosed spaces before. She had, after all, just spent three days within a space the size of a cart bed with her brother and it had not bothered her at all. Her hide outside New Wighton, though, had been open to the sky and she could have stepped outside it anytime she wished. She never would have, of course, for anything less than a forest fire or a cattle stampede, but she *could have*. She had the option.

Here, there was no option. She had been incorrect in her earlier assumption that there was no way out of the withdrawing room, and obviously so had the Zipulk. If it had known that there was a narrow chute in the rear of the chamber (meant for trash, if the smell was any indicator), it might have stayed to finish her off instead of just locking her inside.

Unless, of course, it knew that the shaft was impassable, or led to nowhere. Illyria had her doubts regarding both. She had gotten in easily enough once she had discovered it (courtesy of her sensitive nose and the distinctive scent of rotting food) and managed to descend eight or ten feet, but now there was a projection blocking her way downward and, worse, she doubted that she would be able to climb back up. She was trapped worse than she had been before.

She couldn't lift her arms over her head; the chute was too narrow, and every attempt to lift her legs ended with her banging her knee against the wall.

Her breathing began to speed up. She tried to fight against her rising panic and only partly succeeded. She didn't slow her breathing, but she did manage to swallow back the scream that fought to escape her throat.

Stop. Relax. Panicking will get you nowhere. Picture yourself somewhere— anywhere—else.

She wasn't inside a garbage chute inside a defiled temple. She was in the Ilthwood Forest at the beginning of summer, moments before sunrise. The forest was still, the air cool and heavy with mist. It was magical and perfect: her favourite memory from before she and Balien had left Ilthanara.

She closed her eyes even though she couldn't see anything. She could almost taste the mist. *That's not mist; it's rotting food.* The sharp tang of decay almost broke her concentration but she fought it back. She was in the forest, tracking a buck for her farewell dinner with her family. Slowly, slowly Illyria's breathing returned to normal.

You're not trapped. You can still move. Find out what you can about where you are.

She could do this. She was standing on a projection: a piece of stonework that stuck out of the wall for some reason. She felt it with her foot and found that there was a gap, albeit a small one, where she could get through. It was small. It was *very* small, but not so much that she couldn't slip through.

Not for the first time, she wished for Sephana's slender build. Illyria was descended from warriors and had trained hard all of her life. She had a wide carriage and hard muscles; attributes almost always to her benefit, but not right now. Right now she'd give all of that up for weighing thirty pounds less.

No matter how badly the roast is burned, you still have to serve the meal. It didn't matter how much she wanted to be different; she was what she was. She'd have to make due.

The Bear and the Thistle

Taking a deep breath (and ignoring how shaky it sounded coming out), Illyria lowered first one foot and then the other past the stone she stood on. She tried to hold her weight up with her arms, but not only did she not have a good angle for that, but the chute was slick with moisture and other things she didn't want to think about. She fell through the hole until her hips caught.

It was getting harder not to panic. She couldn't move her arms enough to do anything, it was pitch black, and the temple had her in its unbreaking stone grip. A whimper escaped her lips, and no amount of imagining was able to calm her.

She wiggled her hips and shook her body. Inch by slow inch she felt her body slipping further down. As to whether it held her possible freedom or was just the chute tightening its grip upon her changed from moment to moment. She was whimpering and moaning continuously now.

One final twist of her hips and she fell downward, only for the stone to catch painfully at her bust. She was able to twist her hips and swing her legs to gain momentum and that, combined with working her chest back and forth allowed her to work herself still lower.

Again, she had no warning. One moment her bust was stuck between the protruding stone and the side of the chute and the next she was falling. She felt the bottom of her chin impact painfully with the stone, and then she was sprawled on a pile of filth.

She knew she had to get up. The sun had surely set by now. If Lionar had not begun his Joining yet, he would soon, and the Zipulk was with him. It was imperative that she find her way out of the temple and do what she could (which was what, exactly?) to stop him. She knew she had to get to her feet, she *wanted* to get to her feet, and yet she couldn't.

All she could do was pull her knees up to her chest and tremble. She had almost been permanently trapped inside a narrow, stone prison. She would have died slowly and horribly, unable to move, in the dark. The enormity of it, of what had almost been, hit her like a hammer. She couldn't breathe. No matter how large a gulp of air she took, it wasn't enough. She could feel tears stinging her eyes and couldn't control the huge sobs that burst from her chest. It had been one of the most horrible experiences of her life.

No.

She couldn't do this, not now. Later, when the king had been saved and civil war averted, she would collapse in her brother's arms (yes: Balien and not Gennald; not for this) and soak his shirt with her tears. She would not allow a king to die because she had been too busy crying. Not her. She was Illyria Exiprion, descendant of Illystil, possessor of the Mark of the Hawk and member of the Knights of Anduilon. She made no claims at being perfect or above human frailties, but neither did she use them as excuses for failure. She was a child of

279

royalty, from an ancient line of kings. She did not wallow in her problems. She overcame them.

Squaring her shoulders and pushing herself to her feet, Illyria spit out some blood and grimaced at her latest bruises and scrapes. She was free of her imprisonment, hale (well, hale enough), and short on time.

Now all she had to do was determine where she was and then how to escape it. Then she would save the king.

Gennald reined his horse outside what could only be the Great Temple of Ur. He had never been worthy enough to set foot in Olsarum, but he had minded his lessons as a child. The tall, green building could be nothing else.

"I saw him come out of there, and he was wounded," Sephana insisted from behind him. "It has to be Illyria who hurt him, and she's not with him, so she's probably inside."

He didn't doubt what she claimed to have seen; not this time. She said that Illyria was either injured or in danger within and that was enough for him. Gennald leapt clear of his borrowed mount and rushed inside. He was vaguely aware of Sephana following him.

The temple was eerily silent. What was supposed to be pristine beauty had been marred by violence. Furniture was knocked over, there were gouges missing from stonework and a greatsword had somehow become embedded within the base of a statue.

"I hear something," Sephana announced and ran to one of the doors. Gennald followed and could soon make out a knocking sound. He lifted the bar and then Illyria was there, dishevelled and bleeding. He couldn't see what colour her eyes were, but he could see where streaks of tears scored into the grime on her face.

The sight of her hit like a punch to the stomach. During his abduction, thoughts and memories of Illyria had been almost all that had sustained him. Yes, he had seen her across the clearing when she had freed (and almost killed) him, but that hadn't been as close and intimate as this. She had looked so strong before, and now she did...not.

She had fought and travelled her way across forest, city and mountain, though whether it had been for him or despite him, Gennald did not know. Of course her journey and battles had worn on her, and yet he could not stand seeing her weak. He did not know this Illyria, this wan and defeated woman and did not know what to do with her, or how to approach her.

Her eyes met his, and in an instant, she had assessed the situation and transformed. Between one blink and the next her tears disappeared and she appeared as strong as any knight he had ever met. Had that woman he had just seen been a phantom? Which was real, and which did he love?

The strong Illyria wasted no time on such contemplations. "We have to stop the imposter. He will have reached the king by now."

Gennald could only stare at she rushed past him and out of the temple. He rushed to catch up.

"Illyria," Sephana called out. When she turned, Sephana presented her with Heartseeker, which she had found in the clearing, and two arrows. "They were the only ones I could find that weren't broken."

Illyria smiled widely (it said something that not even her smile could save her from looking truly terrible) and took the weapon. "Thank you."

"We will ride. It is faster," Gennald announced, then looked at both women.

There was no way the horse would fit all three of them. Sephana gestured for the two of them to get on. "Go. I'll catch up." They nodded and a moment later were gone. Sephana watched them leave and followed at a jog.

The Karalinian Circle of Joining was identical to the Nemoran one that Illyria was familiar with. Green pillars of Heartstone surrounded a raised, inscribed disk. All of the pillars were inscribed with characters of Anfel, the language of the gods, and spoke of mysteries than mortals would never know. Two of the nearest pillars were thicker and joined together overheard to form an arch. There were carrels in the arch that she knew held a crown, rod and shield: the Holy Regalia of Karalon.

King Lionar stood alone before the arch, dressed simply as the ritual dictated. Free of the trappings of his royal robes, he looked truly awful. His skin was pasty and hung off him unhealthily. His face was haggard and lined with fatigue, even more so than the last time Illyria had seen him. It was entirely possible that the act of Joining might kill him, even if nothing else went wrong.

He was speaking to the Zipulk wearing the form of Grandmaster Lanton. The scalykind imposter was obviously wounded. It had wrapped a bandage over the damning gash in its head and had another over the wound she had put into its side. When it caught sight of Illyria and Gennald, it placed itself between them and Lionar.

"Stay back, traitors," it snarled. "I will not let you harm my king." It was a very good actor. If Illyria hadn't seen its true nature for herself, she might have believed it. She *had* believed it, last week.

She slipped off of Gennald's horse with as much grace as she could currently muster. One of her arrows she placed in the ground before her, while the other was nocked into Heartseeker and pointed at false-Lanton's heart. She looked over its shoulder at Lionar, whose expression she could not read. "The man before you is an imposter, sire," she called out. "The real Grandmaster has been dead for weeks. He is why you have not been able to Join with the Land."

"She's a liar! She and her band of criminals slaughtered my priests. They have defiled this valley by shedding blood."

Gennald climbed down from his saddle and fell to one knee. "My king, I swear by Emuranna that I am loyal to My Lord, March-Lord Jannery, and to you. Everything this woman says is true."

"You are no knight," not-Lanton sneered. "He is the one who struck me," he said over his shoulder to king Lionar. "He is an honourless blackshield seduced by this foreigner. They are in league with the Dragonfleet."

"You are a liar and I will have your head," Gennald snarled, drawing his sword.

"That is enough!" Lionar's voice had more power than Illyria had thought he could manage. Even wracked with disease and two feet from death, he was still a king and was descended from kings. When he raised his voice, people listened. Gennald was stopped in his tracks and Illyria lowered her bow.

"There will be no more bloodshed in this valley, not today." He stopped to cough into a bloody handkerchief. It lessened his spell, but only barely. "I do not have time to referee arguing children. My kingdom needs me." He turned and made to pass through the heartstone archway.

"Sire, if you attempt to Join with the Land, you will fail and die," Illyria announced. "That is his goal here: to discredit you and see your son ascend the throne."

"She lies," Lanton countered. "I care only for your health and the good of your kingdom."

King Lionar have Illyria a long, even look. "And how is he doing this, lady?"

Illyria faltered. "I...don't know exactly, but I know that he has. How else do you explain your last five failed Joinings?"

Lionar scowled. "The land is out of balance. There is evil out there, corrupting it."

"Sire, no. Your priests scour your kingdom, searching for evil, but have they found anything? Have your seekers?" He gave no answer. "The sickness in Karalon lies here. With him." She pointed to the Zipulk.

"This woman is a liar and a murderer, your majesty. She slew my templars when they tried to stop her."

"I will not listen to this." Lionar turned away. "Kill me or do not; I am too weak to stop you. If you do not, then leave me to my responsibilities."

"There is one way to tell who is lying, sire," Illyria called.

He stopped, but did not turn. "How?"

"Have the Grandmaster remove his bandage. You will have your proof." She swallowed. "If I am wrong, I will accept any justice you see fit to give me."

The king turned and looked at the Zipulk. "She lies, my king," it replied. "This is a meaningless trick."

"Then there is no harm in seeing the falsehood revealed," Lionar said coolly, barely able to keep his feet. "While I draw breath, I remain your king. Remove your bandage." The air rang with his command.

'Lanton' hesitated, then grabbed Lionar by the throat. "All that matters is that you die," it snarled. "I am the Grandmaster; your sheep will believe any tale I tell them, especially with such convenient scapegoats here." He held the king before him like a shield.

Illyria did not consciously choose to loose her arrow. One moment her bow was lowered in her arms, the next she was holding it before her, and her arrow was embedded in the imposter's skull.

Lionar looked at the body at his feet. "Remove the bandage."

Illyria approached and knelt over the dead Zipulk, but nausea overcame her before she touched it.

Gennald was at her side immediately. "Illyria, are you all right?"

Despite what had passed between them, she was happy for his strength and support. Leaning heavily on his arm, she removed the concealing bandage and slowly got to her feet. Her head was swimming. "How can you not feel that, sire?"

Lionar looked at her oddly. "I feel nothing."

Gennald, too, looked at her like she was crazy, but she didn't hold that against him. He didn't have a crownmark and wasn't attuned to the land.

"The Circle of Joining, its...perverted; corrupted." She swallowed hard, trying to keep her gorge down. "It's like bathing in filth. It's hideous. You really don't sense it?"

He shook his head.

"I think Sephana was right," Illyria said. "I think you have been poisoned, but not to kill you; just to dull your senses."

"But why?" Lionar rasped. "Why not just kill me? If Lanton is an imposter then he has had countless opportunities."

"I think..." Illyria looked around her, looking for anything that might be out of the ordinary (other than a dead lizardman wearing human skin). "I think that the Djido want the kingdom to burn. They want it weak. If they kill you, everyone is outraged, but if all they think is that you aren't strong enough to rule..."

"Civil war." Gennald finished grimly. "Or, if that doesn't work, then war with the Dragonfleet. Either would benefit them. What are you looking for?"

She began walking down the length of the Circle, paying close attention to the sense of *wrongness* that threatened to overwhelm her. She saw a mound of freshly turned soil. She knelt in front of it and almost vomited. She had never known you could *feel* evil, but whatever was buried there crawled along her skin like the tiny feet of a thousand plague-ridden ants. "I wonder..."

Gennald supported her. "What is it?"

"I think...I think that it is a Stone of Seregil." She just stared at the mound. She knew that she had to dig it up, but didn't think that she could bear to touch it.

Lionar had followed them. "Seregil? The demon?"

She remembered that no one here knew the story. "He was a man once. Seregil was one of the High King's Champions as well as his closest friend. They shared everything, including a love of the High Queen. Seregil loved his king like a brother and would never dream of betraying him, but his love for the queen was all consuming." She swallowed. "To love so strongly, and never being able to touch, it drove Seregil mad. It twisted his love into hate and made him into a demon. He vowed to destroy the High King and so he created these," she gestured at the mound that she could not bring herself to touch, "cut from his own body, so that the High King could never Join with the Land. I thought the stones were myth, but I can think of nothing else that could create this effect."

"What happened to him? To Seregil?" Gennald asked, his voice subdued.

"He was defeated, but, despite everything he did, the High King could not bear to kill him. He was banished and forbidden from ever setting foot on Anshara again."

Illyria surged to her feet, barely able to keep control of her stomach. "I cannot touch this. Can you, Gennald?"

He did, and moments later held a irregular purple/black lump in his hands the size of a head. It was hard for her to look at. "Take it away," she hissed. "Far from here."

Both she and Lionar watched as Gennald carried it off. It felt to Illyria as if a great wind had sprung up and swept everything toxic away from her. "So that is the thing that has been poisoning my kingdom?" Lionar said sourly. "An ancient relic born from hate?"

Illyria could not help but think of Myria, Attenham, the outlaws, the stolen tribute money and the dead Zipulk lying at her feet. "It was only part, sire. A great conspiracy was created to get to this point."

"So I'm told." His voice was anguished. "What can anyone, even a king, do when so much evil stands against him?"

"Stand fast, sire," she answered without hesitation. "Stand fast and have faith in those who are loyal to you."

"Such as you."

She bowed her head. "Yes, My Lord, but there are others."

His steps were heavy. "I can put this off no longer. I owe you a great debt, lady."

She looked in his eyes. He knew what would happen and was resigned to it, but she had to try anyway. "Sire, please. Wait until you have recovered. It is not necessary to do this today, not with everything we have accomplished. The Stone has been removed and the traitors near you exposed. This Joining can wait until you are well."

His smile held little humour. "Oh, but I do. I promised my kingdom that I would do this. Even now they are looking to the sky and waiting to see the moon."

She could feel tears falling down her cheeks. "Sire, you will die. Your health is too far gone, and too much blood has been spilled. We both know that these holy days are guidelines. You can Join with the Land later, when the currents of the Lifestream have calmed. I beg you."

"If I betray my word to my people, I will have died anyway. People need their symbols, Illyria. After this last year, they need to see that full moon. If you take nothing else from this meeting, take that."

"I will." It was barely a whisper.

He grunted and knelt at the edge if the circle. There, in their customary places, lay the High Regalia of Karalon. A sword, crown, and shield all made of pure Ansharite; they were as old as Karalon itself, and required to be worn by the ruing monarch before each Joining. Lionar tried to place the crown on his head with shaking, palsied fingers.

"Let me, sire, please." Illyria knelt and placed the pale green circlet on his sweating brow. It was the duty of the High Priest to perform this act, but there was no other. A moment later the king bore his regalia. It looked superficially absurd, the man so unhealthy wearing clothes unsuited to his body and clutching priceless artefacts in shaking hands. Yet, despite all that, the strength in his eyes, and the determination with which he held the regalia were incredibly kingly. Illyria had never seen anything so courageous.

The sun was fully set now, and the daylight fading fast. If the sky had been clear, Illyria knew, Nasheeth would have been hanging full in the sky. The Harvest Moon, as the farmers called it, but it was hidden behind cloud and remain so unless Lionar was able to achieve the impossible.

Gennald felt as if he had washed his hands in lye. That thing, that evil stone, had looked unassuming but its touch had made his flesh crawl. Illyria had said to take it 'far away'. He did not know how far that was, but hoped a few hundred yards was enough. He wasn't touching it again without blacksmith's tongs and a large sack, tied to the end of a very long pole.

He saw Sephana and Balien walking towards the Circle of Joining where Illyria and King Lionar were talking. He watched as the king walked alone into the circle's centre. He looked very small and frail within it.

He walked up behind Illyria, who looked over at him when he neared. Her eyes were hazel and tears streaked openly down her face. Without thinking, he wrapped his arms around her from behind and held her body against his. At her touch, his pain and fatigue vanished as if they had never been.

In the circle, King Lionar fell to his knees and gasped. Gennald made to go aid him, but Illyria held him back. "No. No one can enter the circle now that the Joining has begun. He must to this alone."

Gennald watched, horrified, as Lionar began to tremble uncontrollably. "Then what can we do?"

"Wait," she said grimly. "And watch."

They did so, in silence that soon became oppressive. Gennald opened his mouth to speak three separate times but closed it silently each time. So much had happened between them, all of it beyond his experience. No other woman had excited him so much or frustrated him so greatly. At times, she was everything he wanted, and, at others, what she did drove him mad.

"I never thought I'd see you again," he said finally. Both were still watching Lionar's struggling.

"I hoped," Illyria relied, "but never really thought it would happen."

Gennald turned her in his arms. "You came for me, through mountains and valleys. Thank you doesn't seem enough."

She looked away. "You were captured while defending me and you've suffered horribly for it. Thank you doesn't seem enough for that either."

He turned her chin until she faced him, but couldn't tell the colour of her eyes in the fading dusk. "The words don't matter, Illyria, not for us." He stepped closer. "I love you."

He kissed her, but she didn't respond. "Illyria?"

She turned away from him and hugged her arms to her chest. "Eldoth is in love with Sephana."

He blinked at the sudden change of subject, unable to ignore the growing pit of fear in his stomach. He tried to think of a response to her odd statement. "I wondered about those two."

"He didn't realize it until she'd been captured," she continued, eyes fixed somewhere off in the twilight. "He went insane. He was frantic. He had to be physically restrained from chasing after her, and he would have done *anything* to get her back."

Gennald couldn't really picture that, and right now he didn't want to. "As you did for me."

She looked at him then, her face bleak. "I did it for the mission, Gennald. I did it for Lionar and Karalon."

He shrugged with false casualness. "We're knights. Of course our duties come first."

"It didn't for Eldoth."

"You're not Eldoth." He turned her and held her by her upper arms. "You *did* come for me. We've won, and we're together." He tried very hard to keep the desperation out of his voice and didn't know how successful he had been. "Illyria, I love you and I want to be with you. I don't know how yet; I am certain that will be complicated, but we will find a way." She didn't meet his eyes and Gennald felt like he'd been punched in the gut. "Do you want to find a way? Do you want any of this, Illyria?" She made no reply. "Do you want me?"

"You were being held hostage," she replied without answering. "Lanton's imposter held a lance against your heart."

"And you freed me."

"The opportunity was right for me to do so, but surrendering never occurred to me." She glanced up at him, her expression sad. "I was never frantic."

"There are different kinds of love." He could hear the desperation in his voice. "That doesn't mean anything. I feel our love: right here, between us." It was, too, like the heat of a banked fire: hidden but always present and only needing fresh tinder to ignite anew. "And I know you feel it, too." He pulled her to him, and leaned down to kiss her.

She turned her head and his lips touched her jaw. "I feel it, too," she whispered into his ear, "but it isn't love, Gennald." She pushed herself away. "It's a Quickling's Kiss, and it's not enough."

Snakespawn's lance couldn't have slain him more thoroughly. "It's because I'm a yeoman, isn't it?" he heard himself asking in a cold voice. "Because I don't own land?"

She stared. "What? No, of course not."

He didn't know what to say. He didn't even know if he could form words right now. After all he had suffered through, all that he had fought for, *this* was his reward? He wanted to hit her; he wanted to pull her to him and kiss her until she acknowledged what he knew she felt for him; he wanted to cry; he wanted to collapse.

He did none of those things. What remained of his dignity would not allow it. Instead, he just walked away.

Sephana was tail-dragging tired. She looked over as she walked and saw Balien behind her. It was hard to tell in the dimming light, but he looked pretty roughed over. Still, that was a lot better than dead. She rushed over to him.

"Did you get her?"

He shook his head. "She escaped."

She stared. "She got away? From *you*?"

He glanced at her and gave a small, Balien-like smile. "I'm just an ordinary man. I'm not perfect and I make mistakes. She's very, very good."

There was something about how he said that that made her eyes narrow. "But you hurt her, right? Painfully?"

"You shouldn't delight in the pain of others," he chided. "It's beneath you."

She brushed aside his criticism. "Yeah, yeah. I'll be noble later. She *stepped on my tail*. I just want to know that she suffered for it."

He looked at her crossly, but a chuckle escaped his lips, seemingly of its own volition. "You're pride will have to heal on its own. I can't help you there."

Illyria waited in silence. She felt awful for what she had said, but she hadn't been able remain silent. She wasn't sure when she had realized that she didn't love Gennald. Part of her had always known, but she hadn't wanted to admit it to herself. Being with him, stealing kisses and exploring what it was really like to be with a man had been *fun*. Exhilarating. It had been so easy to deceive herself. Part of her, she knew, would always regret that she would never be able to finish what they had started in New Wighton.

Gennald had been right in that respect: she still felt that incredible, passionate—and, she suspected, supernatural—connection that joined them. Even now, she wanted to chase after him, throw herself into his arms and do her utmost to slake this sharp, all-consuming hunger that consumed her. It would be wrong of her and horribly irresponsible (and more than a little bit sacrilegious), but she also knew that it would be *good*.

She didn't. She wanted to, badly, but she didn't. King Lionar still struggled bravely to perform the impossible task he had set himself, and someone had to witness his futile, brave struggle. She had watched her uncle perform this rite countless times. In Ilthanara, all of the priests and Children of the Mark observed and attended the reigning monarch as he performed his ancient responsibility. It was an ordeal at the best of times that took several days for a healthy man to recover from, and these circumstances were far from ideal.

Lionar's whole body trembled. He was down on its hands and knees, his arms locked to prevent him from falling down completely. His breathing was laboured and was accompanied by constant whimpering. If there was anything she could have done to ease his burden, she would have, but, as king, this was something he had to do alone. Such was his role in Emuranna's covenant and the price of kingship.

She felt tears running down her face and didn't know if they flowed because of Gennald or Lionar. *Does it really matter which?* There was a flicker of movement from the west. For a brief, pathetic moment she thought it might be Gennald returning (what would she do if he did? Could she deny him a second time?) but whoever it was was too slender. Illyria drew her last arrow and sighted on the unknown person's heart, but lowered it as he drew near.

Whoever he was, he was dressed nobly in the blue and gold colours of the Usard family. He was somewhere around Balien's age and handsome enough. He carried a broadsword in front of him with confidence. He was a younger, finer version of the man who even now fought the Lifestream itself for the sake of his kingdom.

"Prince Ander?"

He nodded. "And you are Illyria? The elf princess?"

She was too tired to be annoyed. "I safeguard your father as he undergoes his Joining. May I ask your intentions?"

He sheathed his sword and looked into the circle, where Lionar continued to struggle. Illyria unnocked her last arrow. "I do not want my father to die here. It is not how I want to gain my throne."

She searched his face. He seemed sincere. "I believe you. His task is very difficult, and he is very weak from his illness. He may still fail." It was an exaggeration, but a kind one.

"I pray to Emuranna that he does not." For a moment they both watched Lionar struggle to perform his task. "I learned this morning that the man I thought to be my greatest ally is a traitor to the throne. I'm told that you exposed him."

Illyria nodded. "One of my knights did, yes. It is never easy to learn that you have been betrayed. I am sorry."

"Half the kingdom thinks I want my father dead," he said. "They spit on me in the street."

"I'm sorry," she repeated.

"Is my father's condition part of this conspiracy?" he asked, "or has he truly lost his connection to the land?"

Illyria quickly summarized the extent of Attenham's treachery.

Ander's brow furrowed. "Where did they get a Stone of Seregil?"

"They have been lost since before the Great War," Illyria said. "I can only guess that the Djido found them during their occupation."

"Djido." He shuddered. "It sounds childish, but I had always hoped that they didn't really exist, that they were in stories."

"Were that it were true, but you have seen the face of the creature impersonating Lanton with your own eyes, and all my knights and I saw a Djido and his bodyguards in Durnshold."

"Oh, 'Dragonhead Keep.' " He coloured and turned away. "There's a song about that that, but I was told that it was Golden Bear propaganda. I mean no offence, lady."

They're singing songs *about us?* "None taken."

Sephana and Balien walked up to them. Illyria was thrilled to see her brother—he looked beaten up, but fine otherwise—and greeted him with a smile. */Where are the others?/*

/I don't know. I'll go check now that I know you are safe./

She nodded her acknowledgement, but then Sephana gasped. She was looking at the sky.

The clouds had parted, and the light of the full moon shone down upon them all. Inside the Circle of Joining, Lionar gasped and fell onto his side.

Illyria and Ander both raced to his side.

CHAPTER TWENTY-SIX

There remains debate to this day about the Zipulk. Were they a true mongrel race, like the Reshai, able to breed true generations after their creation, or simply an altered form of Hrallar? There is no doubt that they began as Hrallar ('lizardmen', as they are commonly called on Anshara) and that they were changed through the use of Djido magic to be able to wear human skin. Their classification is made more difficult in that they were 'native' to Anshara, being created by the Djido that remained there following Anshara's so-called 'Great War.' Unfortunately, with the Zipulk's apparent eradication during Anshara's Crown War, their true classification remains lost to history.

—Cyclopaedia of the Ensouled, *Winnus of Alashadimm*

When Redding saw the sky clear and the moon appear, he knew that he had lost. Myria had failed in her task and the symbol of that failure hung brightly in the sky. The king had just laid all debates over his fitness to rest, which meant that the Anderite movement had just been neutered. He was still a peer of the realm and able to live in luxury, but it was a poor consolation prize compared to what he had just lost.

"My Lord, soldiers are approaching," a guard told him.

"Whose?" Redding asked without looking away from the celestial body that had doomed him.

"The royal guard, and they come in force."

That made him look away. "Are they accompanying Prince Ander?" It was unlikely. The snivelling princeling usually only travelled with a few guards within the city.

"No, My Lord. It is March-Lord Jannery."

A sick fear began to infect him. "See what they want. Do not allow them entrance." It was immensely rude: no one denied the king's royal guard, but if Redding was right, it was preferable to the alternative.

He was in his study, gathering enough coin to ensure him safe passage to his estate, when he heard Jannery's rude shout echo through the house. "He's a damned traitor to the crown and he's under arrest. Now let me in!"

Redding rushed to the servant's entrance but it, too, was guarded. His knights could only deny Jannery for so long before letting him in—their chivalric oaths gave higher loyalty to the crown than him—and, once they were in the house, he was a dead man. The only leniency possible for cases of high treason dealt with the method of execution.

Something touched his neck and Redding froze. Something was moving behind him.

"Do you wish escape, nobleman?" came an inhuman hiss.

He was afraid to move. Whatever the thing behind him was, it stunk. Horribly. There was only one place that reeked quite like that...

It's the thing from the room. The thing from the darkness that slew anyone that entered its lair had crept out from Redding's basement and was now talking to him.

"Do you wish escape?" it hissed again.

He nodded, not letting any other part of him move. "Yes." As frightening as a creature he had never seen was, he still preferred its mystery to the certainty of a hangman's noose.

"Come with me."

Sephana could get used to working for royalty. The food was good, the sleeping accommodations even better, and, while people still stared at her tail and said unkind things about her heritage, at least they did them in the form of sidelong glances and barely heard whispers. No one dared get caught badmouthing the Prince Regent's personal bodyguards and advisors, not after they had saved the kingdom from a treasonous plot and ensured another year of protection from the Dragonfleet.

It was only the appearance of respect and not respect itself, but it was still a whole lot better than having disgusting things thrown at her, or being almost burned to death. She knew that it would disappear in a heartbeat if they lost Ander's favour, but it was the closest she had ever come to being openly accepted by everyone around her.

It felt *good.*

It was four days after the Battle of New Wighton (officially, they had never entered the Sacred Valley or killed two dozen outlaws inside it; it had all happened at New Wighton); four days since King Lionar had collapsed and refused to wake, forcing his eldest son to become regent. It was only three days since the sacred valley had been (secretly) purged of the filth that defiled it and two days after Eldoth had unlocked Myria's treasure vault. It had taken thirty men to carry out the truly ridiculous amount of gold within, and another hundred men to guard it. At Illyria's suggestion, it had all been placed before the gates of the palace so that everyone could see with their own eyes that Karalon's annual tribute would be met. The eight foot mound of gold was under very close watch. Every noble family in the kingdom had provided men to guard it, and they spent as much time watching each other as the treasure.

The Bear and the Thistle

The Knights of Anduilon were all taking turns watching over Not-Quite-King Ander. Sephana was pretty sure that he was hoping that his father woke before the next Joining happened, before he was forced to do something unspeakable.

At the moment, she and Theramus were Ander-sitting. Illyria was doing something all courtly and political with Balien, while Eldoth was off muttering to himself somewhere. The Prince Regent had spent a tedious morning in on his father's throne, receiving audiences. Golden Bears were trying very hard to get into Ander's good graces. With all the praise and promises of friendship they heaped upon him, you'd never know that, only a week ago, they'd denounced him as an unstable man-child unfit to rule.

The Anderites (who needed a new name, now) were no better. They were busy distancing themselves from (former) Count Attenham, and making up any number of excuses to say why they had put their support behind a man who had been declared a traitor to the throne.

They were a bunch of bald-faced liars, all of them.

Ander was spending the afternoon in his official office, which really meant that the most powerful of the nobles (counts and dukes only; barons and march-lords need not apply) were seeking him out for extra special one-on-one sucking up. Sephana didn't know why she and Theramus needed to be there for it, other than to maybe make sure that Ander didn't drown in all the slobber from everyone kissing his feet, hands and other body parts.

The Crown Prince of Karalon was cute, in a stuffed shirt kind of way. He was a little shorter than Gennald, with light brown hair cut shorter than most Karalinian noblemen, and while not very muscular, still attractive. Sephana could see his head being on a coin one day. He was doing okay, as far as she could tell. He'd made some wrong choices—trusting and believing the Count Attenham, for example— and spent a little too much time overthinking his problems, but he was getting better by the day. This afternoon of private audiences without Illyria to advise him was a test, and he was doing fine.

The latest noble in the ongoing parade of overstuffed shirts was her least favourite: Duke Raebyrne. He didn't look too thrilled to see Sephana and Theramus, but hid it well. He was an experienced politician, which meant that he was a veteran liar.

Was thwarted political ambition the only reason for his resentment, or did he still hold her to blame for Edrik's death? Sephana had made her peace with it all, but had he? His granting her absolution had been an nonnegotiable part of their deal, and he had said the words, but she had no idea if he had really meant them. Could she, if it had been her brother that had been killed? Okay, so she didn't have a brother. Theramus, she supposed, was the closest. Could she forgive someone involved with his death...to which the obvious answer was 'no'. She'd want that person to suffer, horribly and painfully, for a very long time. She'd want them to burn...

Wait. Something about that was wrong. Burning and suffering, because someone she loved had been hurt...

Damn. I have to forgive Eldoth now.

Oblivious to her unpleasant revelation, Duke Raebyrne bowed low before Prince Ander. "Your Majesty, I have done as you requested. The Golden Bears are no more, and all of its members swear their loyalty to you."

Sephana pulled her mind back to the present. For reasons that completely baffled her, both factions were still bitterly feuding. Both had kind of won but also kind of lost. Lionar had proven his fitness to rule by succeeding in his Joining, but had fallen into a coma and wasn't expected to live. Ander currently sat on the Throne of Ur, but still wasn't king. Ander, acting on Illyria's advice, had officially disbanded both parties yesterday and had gone so far as to rearrange the furniture in the Hall of Peers to reflect it. This had succeeded in angering the entire council against Ander —which, as far as Sephana was concerned, was a sign that he had done the right thing—but he had stuck with his decision, and now everyone was trying to get back in his graces.

"I am glad to hear it, Hadran," Ander replied, hesitating only briefly his use of the duke's first name. Kings—and regents—called people whatever they wanted. "Now, perhaps, we can all work together to repair the damage that unpleasant disagreement has caused."

"I couldn't agree more, your highness." He took a breath. "I am hoping, perhaps, that you might reconsider your choice of escort to the tribute presentation next week. Surely a delegation of the finest Karalinian knights would be more befitting your status as the leader of a united kingdom."

Ander had declared that The Knights of Anduilon would form his personal bodyguard for the trip, something that the Golden Bears and Anderites had both disagreed with. Ander hadn't officially recognised them as knights yet, but this honour was the next best thing. Raebyrne's attempt to dissuade him marked the fifth time today that someone had tried to do so. Ander, bless him, had not.

"I am content with my decision," Ander said in an even voice. "The Knights of Anduilon have earned this reward, and deserve this symbol of my gratitude. I thank you, however, for your sharing this opinion with me."

"They aren't even Karalmen!" Raebyrne hissed, his pretence of calm slipping.

Sephana cleared her throat. Raebyrne gave her an angry glare before plastering his smile back onto his face.

That answers that question.

"Of course," he slimed. "The Knights of Anduilon deserve all our thanks."

"Is there anything else you wanted, Hadran?"

"None that cannot wait until after the tribute has been delivered." The duke bowed again. "Emuranna's Grace, My Liege."

Ander nodded both in acknowledgement and in permission for Duke Raebyrne to leave. "Emuranna's Grace." He glanced over at Sephana once the duke had departed. "I've never seen Hadran give up on a subject that easily. What secret do you have on him?"

"If I told you, then it wouldn't be a secret, Your Highness" Sephana said, making sure that her face was a blank mask. She couldn't call him 'Your Majesty' or 'Sire' so long as his father lived.

He slouched back in his chair. "How do you think I did?"

"You were very good, Your Highness. It is so," Theramus said. "You were strong and conceded nothing. Those are good traits in a king."

"I'm glad you think so. Thank you both for being here."

"It's our pleasure."

A pair of tailors carrying bolts of cloth and a measuring rope approached, bowing and scraping the whole while. "Pardon me, Sire, but I must measure your escorts for their new livery."

"Of course. Spare no effort. They have to look like worthy escorts of a king."

"Sir Theramus, Lady Sephana, if you will follow me please?" They were led to a withdrawing room, where a ladder had been brought to help them with Theramus.

"My Lady, if you will stand and lift your arms, please?"

Sephana stood as directed and smiled when the second tailor, confronted with the task of measuring Sephana's tail, gave an involuntary squeak. She had made enough of her own clothes over the years to have some idea what was happening.

"Hold on: stop." The tailor stood, confused. "You're fitting me for a dress, aren't you?"

"Of course. A lady accompanying royalty must have an appropriate gown."

Sephana ground her teeth. "I'm not a lady." She glared at everyone's incredulous looks. "What I mean is that I'm not *accompanying* the king, I'm protecting him, and I'm not a lady: I'm a knight."

"But, My Lady, how—"

"In fact, don't even call me 'My Lady'" she continued, speaking over the confused tailor. "Ladies wear dresses and ride in carriages; knight's fight and wear armour. Call me *Sir*."

She looked scandalized. "But..."

"No buts. Make me some clothes—real clothes, like you would for a man, but with a hole for *this*—" she pointed to her tail "—or I'll go out dressed like I am now."

That threat obviously was sufficient (and she wasn't sure if she should have been insulted by that or not), for she was refitted and promised a rough, working outfit before the end of the day.

"*Sir* Sephana?" Theramus asked, amused.

She shrugged. "Why not? I'm a fighting free Reshai with a tail. I make my own rules."

He smiled widely. "And I would have it no other way."

Lord Jannery shook his head. "I'm sorry, My Lady, I have not seen him."

Illyria hid her disappointment. Lord Jannery had returned to his own residence after the unpleasant business with Duke Raebyrne. Prince Ander had graciously ordered him his own royal knights to protect him. At the moment, she, Balien, and Lord Jannery were seated in his private sitting room. She had been nervous at the idea of seeing Gennald again, apparently for naught.

"Not recently, My Lord, or not at all?" she asked, trying to keep her voice even.

"Not at all, not since I gave him leave to join you." He frowned. "I was rather hoping that he was still sharing your company."

"Alas, no, My Lord. I have not seen him since SummersEnd. I had hoped that he had returned to your service."

Lord Jannery hesitated before speaking. "It is not my business, but he is my man and I care for him, so I must ask: how did matters fare between you?" He grimaced, his embarrassment obvious on his face. "I will confess that I had hopes that you would find happiness together."

It took Illyria a moment to find her voice. She had kept herself busy these last five days so as not to dwell on the stabbing pain that was her relationship with Gennald. Their last words to each other and the anguish on his face haunted her dreams. Had she made the right decision? Should she have stayed with him anyway, despite the disparity in their feelings for each other? She changed her mind as to what was right countless times per day. Finally, unable to purge herself of him, she had come to visit Lord Jannery. Allegedly she was here on the Prince Regent's business, but it was a lie. She had wanted to see him again. To know.

She had heard songs and poems about the Imvir and their particular style of humour, about how complete enemies would fall into each other's arms because those magical, invisible beings had chosen for them to be together. She'd never really understood. Seregil's obsessive desire for his queen had almost destroyed a kingdom. Illyria had never been able to comprehend why two people would destroy themselves and everyone around them for the sake of selfish passion...until now.

"My Lady?" Lord Jannery asked, concern in his eyes.

Illyria blinked, refusing to acknowledge the tears welling in her eyes. "Sadly, My Lord, what we wish seldom means anything in the face of the cruelty of the world."

"I'm sorry."

It was his gentleness that undid her. Illyria stood abruptly, needing very much to be elsewhere. "Thank you for your hospitality, My Lord. I will mention your concerns to Prince Ander."

He stood as well. "Thank you, My Lady, and mention to him also my apologies for not being able to capture that lying snake, Attenham."

"He is aware. Until later, My Lord." Without even waiting for Balien and the comfort she knew he would give her, Illyria fled.

Eldoth grimaced and examined himself in the mirror. He looked ridiculous. He had tolerated being poked and measured earlier by a pair of clucky tailors and had promptly forgotten about them until now, when they had suddenly returned bearing useless clothing and looking very pleased with themselves. He had told them that he would try the new garb on later (which was to say: never), but they had been annoyingly insistent until, if only to shut them up, he had acquiesced.

The shirt was fine white linen and the pants dark grey wool, over which he wore a surcoat with matching cloak. It was all very...blue, and was accented with golden bears and thistles. Oh, yes: he and the others were supposed to be part of some royal entourage in a few days. They had to dress to match, he supposed.

"They're fine," he said, reaching for the cloak-tie. His work was waiting him. He had almost completed cataloguing the different instances in which he had used his orange magic to deflect, catch, or hurl arrows during the final battle, and he wanted to get back to it.

"Just one moment, Sir Eldoth, please. We must check the fit. Please lift your arms."

"I'm a wizard, not a dress-up doll," he grumbled, but did as they asked nonetheless. This was not the first time he'd been accosted by clothiers on behalf of a rich patron wanting to show him off. He had tolerated it in Tirim and he'd do so again here. This time, unlike before, the rewards were well worth the inconvenience. Ander had promised him unrestricted access to the royal archives once the tribute had been presented. For that, Eldoth would wear a frilly dress in front of the whole Council of Peers.

The tailors were still fussing over him when Sephana and Theramus entered the common room of the suite they shared. As always, his heart beat faster at the sight of her.

"You're wearing your hood backwards," she called out as she crossed to her private quarters. "I can still see your face."

"You think you are being funny, but you are not."

She stopped and smiled. "No, I'm pretty sure that I am. You just can't take a joke."

He was unable to come up with a rejoinder that was appropriately scathing without being cruel before she left the room. He cursed under his breath and the tailors, wisely, said nothing.

"You have not told her yet," Theramus said from his place on the floor.

"That is surely sufficient for now," he said, shucking his unwanted finery. "You can complete this elsewhere." It was a command, not a suggestion. They bowed, his clothing bundled in their arms, and left.

"What I tell her and when is my business, and certainly not for palace gossip."

Theramus was not dissuaded. "In small groups such as ours, these matters become everyone's business."

"What's everyone's business?" Sephana asked, returning to the room.

"Nothing at all," Eldoth said, perhaps just a bit too hurriedly.

Sephana's eyes narrowed for a moment before she shrugged. "Like I care."

There was a moment of uncomfortable silence, broken by Theramus standing up. "I feel the need for some air. I will leave you two alone." He gave Eldoth a significant glance before leaving.

Sephana did not miss it, as she was not a fool—Theramus and subtlety were not good friends—and watched him as he retreated. "That was weird."

Eldoth opened his mouth to speak but no sound came out. He did not know if he could do this. It was three words: *I love you.* It should have been easy to say them. Certainly he wanted to; at times it was as if they were ready to leap out of his throat, and yet at others—like now—facing a dozen archers at close range would have been easier.

What would happen if he did? Laughter, without a doubt. Mockery until WatersEnd was another distinct possibility. What was the ideal outcome? A reciprocal confession, followed by an embrace and, possibly, an adjournment to the bedroom. Yes, it was the best foreseeable outcome, and yet it also seemed so unlikely. Her heart belonged to a man who, if he had not been a hero in life, had certainly become one in death. Eldoth could not compete with such a hallowed memory.

The worst outcome? The laughter and mockery detailed above, making his life a greater endless torment than it already was. More likely it would be something in between, but much more awkward than either.

The silence between them grew. She looked strangely ill at-ease herself, which was odd. He opened his mouth to speak, still unsure of what his words would be, when she started to talk as well. They both stopped and laughed nervously.

What is concerning her? Does she know? That would make things more complicated. She gestured for him to speak but he demurred and motioned for her to begin. He would base his words on whatever hers would be. It was *not* a coward's move; it was prudence.

"So, uhh, I was thinking about something you said the other day, after you guys saved me at Duke Raebyrne's."

"I see. Go on." It was inane, but he had to say *something*.

"You were talking about rage and hurting people, and how sometimes it was forgivable."

That was not really what he had said. Normally, he would have corrected her on that subject, but at the moment it was easier to just let her continue.

"You rejected my theory, as I recall." She had, in fact, accused him of only being in love with himself, something he knew to be utterly untrue.

"I may have been wrong."

It was a huge admission for her. Sephana was never in error, or at least not according to her. He couldn't help it: he smiled.

"So there was *not* an error in my logic?"

"Maybe not."

"So I was, in fact, *right*?"

"Do you have to be such a jerk about it?"

"I'm sorry," he said, not sorry at all. "It is just that this sort of thing happens so rarely. It must be savoured." He was smiling openly now, and stroked his beard dramatically. In his mind, though, it was her chin that his fingers caressed. "Please, please, go on about my logic, which was not flawed."

She rolled her eyes. "Never mind."

She couldn't leave, not yet. He put his hand on her arm before she made it more than a step. "Wait, please. I'm sorry."

Her eyes narrowed again, but she did turn back to him. "You're sorry? You?"

"I apologise for being rude," he continued. "Please, continue. You were considering our conversation in the Raebyrne manor?"

"I was thinking about love, and I realized that you were right: a person can sometimes do bad things, horrible things in the name of love. It doesn't make it less wrong, but it does make it...forgivable."

He smiled. "Thank you for saying it. May I ask what inspired that thought?"

"No." Annoyance flickered across her face. "I still think it's a bad argument for what you did to Draxul. I've never seen you love anything more than your books and your magic. You burned him to death because you were angry, but you also helped rescue me, so I guess I kind of forgive you."

"You say that with such confidence," his mouth said with a sneer before his brain could stop it. "How can I not accept an apology so sincerely given?"

"You are such an ass!" she growled and left the room.

Eldoth's eyes lingered on the empty door she had just passed through. That had not gone the way he had intended. '*You're wrong. I love* you. *I always have*'. He had taken the coward's way and he knew it, but Eldoth was under no misconceptions about himself as far as that went.

When Theramus re-entered the suite, Eldoth was still seated at the table, but his journal lay closed before him. His expression, combined with Sephana's angry exit, told the story of what—or, in this case, what had *not*—transpired. *Why must humans make simple things so difficult?*

Eldoth looked up as he neared. "I know what you are going to say. Don't."

He tried to not sound accusing. "You are obviously unhappy, and will continue to be so until you tell her how you feel."

"I think I won't."

"And why not?" If Theramus had eyebrows he would have raised them.

"I enjoy arguing with her." A wistful smile appeared on his face. "It's...fun."

Theramus sat. "I do not think that she enjoys your conversations together to the same degree that you do." He stopped himself from raising a warning finger against the wizard. One did not threaten one's ward. "I understand that there will always be pain between you, but I would consider it a favour to me as your fellow knight and, I would like to think, as your friend: do not hurt her unduly."

It took Eldoth a moment to answer. His face was grave. "I won't. Not unduly, anyway." He returned to his books.

It would have to be enough.

"Feeling better, Lyri?"

Illyria nodded wordlessly, too winded to speak without effort. She and her brother were near the entrance to the Golden Palace, where they had briskly walked (well, closer to a run, really) since leaving Lord Jannery's manor. Such had been her mood that she had feared bursting into tears as she had spoke to anyone. She had chosen instead not to speak, and to walk the twisty, hilly route to her new residence at as fast a rate as she could sustain. She wanted to blame Gennald for this—she'd never felt herself continually on the verge of crying before she had met him—but her actions and reactions were her own.

Balien had kept by her side the entire way. If there was anyone who understood not wanting to talk, it was him. She loosened the neck of her tunic, letting the autumn breeze cool her. She hadn't thought to bring water with her, not a simple errand, and was thirsty. Something to drink when she returned to the suite would be ideal. Water, or wine. No, definitely wine. Ander had given them unlimited access to the royal cellars, and he swore that the honeyberry wine there was the finest in the kingdom.

Men dancing by firelight...the sharp smell of male sweat as he held her to him...the taste of honeyed wine on his tongue as he kissed her...

Maybe she'd have beer, instead.

"You made the right decision with Gennald," Balien continued when she didn't say anything. "I know it hurts, but it's for the best. You would have ended up more hurt than happy."

"I'm hurt anyway. Why can't I have had the happiness that goes along with it?"

He made no reply, just rubbed his hand along her back. She appreciated his company and the effort he was making, but this was a conversation she'd rather have had with Sephana. And she would, too, if Sephana was willing. Tonight, with beer.

"You need to tell Ander about Westbridge," he said when she once again was silent.

They'd had this conversation before, also in private. Balien would argue against her in meetings to help strengthen her plans, but he never strongly disagreed with her near anyone else. For him to bring up a subject twice indicated that it was something he felt very strongly about.

She trusted his opinions and his instincts, but not this time. "It's too close to the tribute presentation," she said again. "Ander is too honest, and under too much strain right now. I don't trust him not to reveal his knowledge when he meets with the Dragonfleet admiral."

His angry frown looked unusual on his face. "We swore oaths, Lyri, to do no wrong. Lying to the Dragonfleet: fine; it serves a greater good. But not to a king; not when it is a truth he needs to know."

"He's not king yet, and we will tell him, just not now. His honesty is his greatest strength right now."

His jaw was set. "I won't undermine your authority in front of the others, but you're wrong, and ill will come of this."

She really needed that beer. Not wanting to argue, especially not with him, she starting walking back to the palace. She didn't know where Balien went to, but he didn't follow her. She had nodded her recognition to the gate guards and was making her way into the guest wing when a voice called her name.

She turned. A knight in a dusty white surcoat and a large, russet coloured dog approached her.

"How are you, Master Sheltan?"

The knight-master shrugged, his resplendent armour and surcoat dusty from travel. "Road weary. I have ridden three days to return here, only to hear an unbelievable story with you at the heart of it." He bowed his head. "I hear that you slew the thing that killed my master. The templars owe you a great debt, My Lady."

"I'm sorry for your loss," Illyria said. "I never met the true Lanton, but everyone says that he was a great man."

"He was. That Djido thing was nothing like him." He shook his head sadly. "His behaviour was strange, but we thought it was strain of our predicament. None of us imagined that he might be an imposter. None of us detected anything wrong."

Illyria did not tell him that he could not be blamed for this as she knew that he would not accept the answer. She would not have, had it been her. "I'm sorry," she said, though it seemed inadequate.

"It is I who am sorry. You and your knights did what my brethren could not, and for that you have the gratitude of the Knights of Olsarum. Any favour within our power will be granted, and you will always have our hospitality. I swear this as the next Knight Grandmaster."

"Congratulations, Wise Father, and I thank you on behalf of your fellows for your generous gift."

Master Sheltan smiled. " 'Wise Father.' It is a pleasant title. Lady Illyria, I bid you good evening."

She bowed. "May the sun shine on your road."

The Bear and the Thistle

CHAPTER TWENTY-SEVEN

"The Dragonfleet would never really have invaded. They were too used to using us as their breadbasket. All we've done is give them all of our money."

—*Anonymous*

We don't look like circus performers now, Illyria thought as she and her fellow knights rode alongside Prince Regent Ander at the head of a column of more than five hundred knights, squires, and labourers as well as countless horses and draft animals. It was as much a show of force and solidarity to any remaining doubters as for the protection of their precious cargo.

It was a sunny, crisp autumn afternoon twelve days after SummersEnd. All the Karalmen insisted that it was warm for this time of year, but she still felt cold and was thankful for the warm, woollen clothing she had been provided. She, like her friends, was dressed in a rich blue surcoat and cloak embroidered with the bear and the thistle. They looked impressive and very regal, even though Theramus's cloak looked large enough to serve as a medium-sized tent.

Apparently she and Sephana were causing a minor scandal, or they would have if they had not been so favoured by Ander right now. Women wearing the royal crest *did not wear pants*; only dresses. It had taken a royal directive from Ander for their clothing to be made, although it was whispered that Sephana had made some dire threat as well. Illyria didn't care that she was breaking social convention. Who she was had little to do with what people thought of her dress or how she acted. It was her deeds that mattered.

She could taste a slight salty tang in the air. They were near where, traditionally, the royal tribute caravan paid off their Dragonfleet extortionists (and how it saddened Illyria that it had been happening for so long that it was now a tradition). The location had once been known as Vauger Bay but had since been renamed Tribute Point. It was perhaps five miles away and hidden from them by some hills. The smell of the nearby ocean and their general downward travel were the only indicators that they were on the coast.

Ander was behind her, lost in his thoughts. They had ridden abreast and talked for much of the journey, but these last miles had driven the young regent—and, they all knew, soon to be king—deeply within himself. It was a harsh lot that his first real act as ruler was to face the gang of criminals and bullies that held his kingdom's safety for ransom, but Illyria was confident that he was up to the challenge. A great many people had misjudged him and mistaken his silence for weakness. She was looking forward to watching him prove them all wrong, and until he did she was happy to advise him.

A mounted scout crested the hill ahead and rode straight towards them. "They're here, Your Majesty," he announced breathlessly as he reined himself in next to Ander. "Twenty ships, at least, and hundreds of men. Their tents line the beaches."

Ander faltered. "So many?"

"Don't stop," Illyria warned him. "Surely they have spies watching us, and you can't be seen as weak or hesitant."

"That's twice the largest number they've ever sent before," he said, his face pale.

"Never mind that. Might I suggest that we send some men to find and secure a camp site within sight of the bay."

"Yes. Of course."

Illyria nodded to Balien, who gestured for the scout to confer with him. She trusted her brother to find a safe, secure location to camp free of any Dragonfleet surprises.

"It will be fine," she soothed. "They send more men to frighten you into compliance, but you are a king, Sire: you are not so easily bullied."

Ander nodded and straightened. "Yes. You are right. Let us continue."

Illyria exchanged a glance with Theramus. If the scout's numbers were anywhere near correct, they would be in trouble if events descended into violence. They only real edge they had were that most of their number were cavalry; if it came to battle, they would be able to manoeuvre around their enemy and safely retreat, though they would have to abandon their tribute and supplies to do so. The Dragonfleet raiders they had encountered in Westbridge hadn't had any horses of their own and hadn't seemed practiced at resisting them, but that meant little. They had been raiding before and expecting to encounter peasants; everyone knew that Karalon's military might lay in its cavalry, and only a fool would field an army into the kingdom without preparing for that.

She sincerely hoped that it did not come to combat. She had taken far too many lives in this last month.

Theramus came up behind Balien, who was standing at the edge of the tent line and looking down at the Dragonfleet encampment. They were on top of a small hill three miles from Tribute Point; close enough to observe, but far enough away that they could flee if needed. Ships and tents covered the bay and the lands around it like an angry blanket.

He made no attempt at stealth; there was no point given his size and Balien's hearing. "How many do you think there are?"

"Five hundred, maybe, and not all of them are fighters."

"A camp of that size could hold twice that."

"It's a ruse," Balien said. "That camp is spaced fairly widely, and I don't think all of those tents are occupied." He pointed to a single ship anchored in the middle of the bay. It was much longer than any vessel around it, with three masts. "What kind of ship is that?"

"It is a strand-ship," Theramus told him, "a deep ocean vessel. It can sail on the Maelstrom, between Titan-worlds. These other ships, they cannot leave sight of the shore when they travel, or the ocean will consume them."

"So the Dragonfleet is mostly based on Anshara," Balien concluded. "They have a port somewhere that we can find."

"They must," Theramus agreed, "but my road has taken me to all corners of Anshara, and in three decades of walking it I have yet to find such a place."

"We will," Balien said with confidence.

Of that Theramus had no doubt. "It shall be so."

"Have you talked to Ander's First Knight about patrols and staying close to camp?"

Theramus nodded. They had no real authority over the men in Ander's service, but their place as his advisors gave their words the weight of law. Balien had 'advised' the leader of Ander's forces that no one should stray beyond the camp's borders for any reason, especially after dark, and the guard should be tripled. "I have. Ander wishes another conference with you and Illyria before dinner. I believe that he wishes to finalize his negotiation points before the tribute is given tomorrow."

Balien just nodded.

It was time. The Dragonfleet honour guard were standing in loose formation at the edge of their camp. It was too far for Sephana to see what they were wearing, but she was sure that it was the same scaled vest with the dragon emblem that they had in Westbridge. Even from three miles away, a lot of them were obviously non-human. The biggest one stood almost twice as tall as everyone else and had red skin.

The Karalinian formation was much tighter and more precise. Everyone had stayed up late polishing their armour and cleaning their flags and standards. It wasn't like anyone could get any sleep, knowing how close the Dragonfleet was.

They hadn't—there had been some yelling and jeering from across the plain, but nothing more—but it had made for a tense night nonetheless.

Ander sat on his horse at the head of the delegation, and where he went the Knights of Anduilon were right there, too. Everyone else was back far enough to give them enough privacy to talk, but close enough to come to their aid if they had to. Twenty carts of wheat—sadly, almost all of the harvest this year—sat in a line as well as five more carts of gold. It was enough to pay for this year's tribute, the balance of last year's and a stiff penalty besides. It was more money than Sephana had ever seen in one place, and likely wouldn't again. And it was all going to pay off a bunch of bullies.

They were waiting for the command to leave, which would happen at the peak of noon and not one moment before. Never mind that they had all been standing here for almost half an hour; apparently it was bad form to start for the middle of the field early, and so they were waiting.

She hated waiting.

They'd leave when the flagpole's shadow crossed the top of the rock laying in front of them. Sephana had never tried it before to find out, but she had discovered that watching a shadow crawl across the ground was really, really boring.

It was almost there, and everyone was getting ready to go, when a voice that Sephana never expected to hear again broke the silence.

"There's one small order of business I'd like to bring before the council, if his majesty is willing to indulge me." He sounded horribly smug. It was Attenham, and with him, for no reason that she could tell, was Gennald.

Redding couldn't believe that he was here. Being here, a mere stone's throw from the Dragonfleet tribute presentation, was even more impossible than his escape from his manor. The *thing* that had rescued him—trussed up like a roast and ignobly hauled out a top floor window—had brought him to a rendezvous point with Myria deep in the forest. His intent had been escape, but she had other plans, and so he was here, between the hammer and the anvil. He would either succeed, and win everything, or fail, and lose...more than he was willing to contemplate.

He smiled at the shocked and angry looks of the various people facing him. Any one of them would have happily struck him dead, if not for when and where he was. There were many hands reaching for swords or tightening on lances, but Redding knew that they would not strike. Not here.

"We wouldn't want to give the impression of anything being amiss in sight of the Dragonfleet, would we, Prince Ander?" The elf witch, Illyria reached slowly for an arrow. "Don't, elf," he warned and raised his hand over his head. His good hand; his whole one. "If you look to the edge of the camp, you will see My Lady and a new friend." He knew what they would see: his smug bitch of a 'master', Myria, holding a chain that was looped around the neck of the foul tempered little rat-man from Westbridge.

"She will release the creature if my hand falls for any reason. They are very fast on their feet, rat-men. I'm sure that this one would be very eager to return to its Dragonfleet brethren, and oh, what stories it could tell." Redding smiled. "Stories that they would be very interested to hear."

Ander tried to keep his confusion off of his face, but Redding knew him too well. This was too good. "I'm sorry. Did the Knights of Anduilon not tell you of the little incident in the town of Westbridge, your majesty? Did your new advisors not share the tale of how they defied a royal order and slew a whole ship of Dragonfleet raiders?" Between Ander's shock and Illyria's grimace he knew that they had not.

"Is this true?" Ander asked, anger roughing his voice.

"It is, Your Highness. I'm sorry."

Traces of confusion and anger began to cross his face. "But...why?"

"I think you chose my replacements very poorly, Ander."

"I will explain later." Illyria told him, her voice deceptively calm. "It is more important that we deal with this situation."

"What do you want, Redding?" Ander asked.

"It's quite simple, Ander. I want back everything that was mine: my title, my house and my reputation. You will forgive me of everything I am accused of."

"Impossible!"

"If you do not, that talkative little monster runs back to its friends and tells them everything it saw. The Dragonfleet might not kill you, not the Prince Regent, but I don't doubt that everyone else here would be slain. It goes without saying that the treaty will be broken." He cocked his head. "I wonder if they will wait until spring before they resume raiding or get an early start of it before the snows fall. No matter; one restored title and a royal pardon are a small price for never having to find out."

Illyria couldn't contain her shock. Not at Attenham's sudden appearance—that was definitely within the realm of possibility—but at Gennald's. He was *not,* she noted, meeting her gaze.

Both he and Attenham were wearing non-descript common clothing. They had undoubtedly travelled with the caravan for the whole three day journey and been invisible the entire time. Who would think to look there for a traitorous nobleman and his mistress? And who would think to look for a knight who hadn't really been missing?

What could she do about this? What should she do? She'd gladly put an arrow through Attenham's eye. Myria was farther off, but Illyria was fairly sure she could hit her as long as she stood still. As for a running, dodging rat-man with a several hundred yard head start: that one would be more difficult.

The revelation of the lie of Westbridge was a larger problem. Ander had been repeatedly betrayed by those close to him, including the very man he was facing. She didn't want to think about how this harm the trust she had fostered. He was a king. He *needed* to be able to trust his advisors. The land would suffer if he did not.

Illyria kept her hand near her quiver. There was no point drawing until an opportunity came to act, and her bow was too large for her to use from horseback, anyway. She'd have to dismount before she could do anything.

She pictured the actions in her mind. Her left foot would kick over the saddle at the same time that her right hand began to draw an arrow. She'd fit the arrow into her bowstring as she slid across the saddle and fell to the ground. Once on the ground, she would draw back with her right hand as her left aimed the bow. If she did it properly it would take less than two seconds.

Even that was too long. She would have only have opportunity for one shot; it had to be perfect. *She* had to be perfect.

Illyria went over the motions she had to make, trying to imagine what might go wrong and what she could do to ensure that it did not. She forced all thoughts of Gennald from her mind.

"I can kill him if you'd like," Eldoth offered Balien, who rode the horse next to him. "But I'd most likely strike Gennald as well."

"Can you do it silently, without his arm falling?" Balien's eyes were on the edge of camp, where Attenham had said his accomplice was.

"No," Eldoth admitted. "I do not know enough yellow magic for that. To ensure his death I would have to use fire or lightning." He could hurl an arrow or a knife if there was one available, but did not think he could ensure a killing shot from this range.

"Then we can't risk it," Balien said. ""I need you to distract him for a second."

"How?"

"Shine a light in his eyes, but do it without moving. No one can know that you're doing this."

Eldoth cursed himself for his lack of imagination. It was a perfectly obvious solution. "And what will you be doing?"

Balien didn't answer. "Do it now."

It was a simple spell, even done silently. Eldoth pictured a bright light, of similar strength to the sun being reflected by a mirror, and shone it briefly at Attenham's face. As expected, he flinched and turned his face for a moment.

Eldoth turned to ask Balien if this had been sufficient to his needs, but he was already gone.

Sephana stared in shock. *What do we do now?* Myria and the little rat-man were just visible at the edge of the camp, and the Dragonfleet entourage were also visible, though distant, across the plain. There wasn't anything they could do without one or the other seeing them.

"Why did you raise arms against the Dragonfleet, Illyria?" Ander sounded angry, not that she blamed him.

"They were attacking the town and kidnapping children. My conscience would not allow me to do otherwise." Illyria looked and sounded distracted. Her thoughts were clearly elsewhere.

"Better to ask why the Dragonfleet were raiding on Karalinian soil," Theramus added quietly.

"And why did you lie to me about it?" From his tone, it was obvious which was the greater offence.

"We destroyed the evidence, or we thought we had. It was thought that you would be more convincing denying it if you didn't know about it," Illyria said. "I would have told you afterwards, I swear it."

"It's sad when you cannot trust your subordinates, isn't it?" Attenham taunted. "I would like an answer, Your Highness. My arm is getting tired."

"You were involved in my father's poisoning!" Ander snarled. "You conspired to steal the gold intended for this tribute, and you pretended to be my friend. There can be no pardon."

"I deny the first two," Attenham said. "Myria did all of that; I was merely her pawn. As for the third, there was no pretence."

Sephana saw Balien—off his horse, somehow—running through the camp in a path that kept him out of sight of both Attenham and Myria. He had stripped off his cloak and surcoat, probably so he didn't look quite so blue as he ran.

Balien will stop Myria. If anyone can, it will be him. Of course, he hadn't done that great a job last time...

They had to delay Attenham until Balien could secure the rat-man. The problem was that Sephana wasn't sure if anyone else had seen him leave, or even knew what he was up to. That meant that it was up to her.

And she knew just how to do it, too.

Theramus seethed with impotent rage. He would not allow the victory his companions had wrought to be undone by the self-serving machinations of a Djido collaborator. His greatest assets were his strength and his experience. The former availed him not a whit right now, while the latter told him that the Dragonfleet were fickle negotiators. They would use any excuse to claim insult and would demand steep reparations because of it. If they saw any sign of violence or dissent from across the plain, all of Karalon would pay for it.

Balien had already snuck away, presumably to confront Myria, and, from Illyria's expression, she was preparing for action of her own. He had no idea what it was, but he would be ready to support whatever they chose to do. There was a reason why he chose to follow instead of lead.

"I was never your friend, just an asset to be used." Ander accused. "You needed someone to sow discord and I was *available.*"

"I am ambitious, I do not deny it," Attenham said with a shrug. "You are the future of this kingdom and I created a friendship with you." He paused. "I am better as a friend than an enemy, Ander. I suggest you accept my offer."

"Should we even be talking to you?" Sephana asked, sounding bored. "I mean, Myria's the one in charge, right? You're just her lackey."

His face tightened in suppressed anger. "I don't talk to snakespawn."

"I watched you scream like a girl while she reminded you who was boss," she taunted. "How is your hand doing, anyway? Do you miss those fingers that I cut off?"

He quaked with anger. "I'll skin you alive when this over, snakespawn. You will suffer for what you did to me. I'll flay you in the largest public square until you're on the edge of death, and then burn you alive."

" 'Ieeee, make it stop, Myria,' " Sephana said in a high falsetto. She managed to sound both mocking and bored at the same time. " 'I'm your worthless servant. Tell me what to do because I'm too stupid to think of anything by myself.' "

Attenham was apoplectic with rage. He tried to speak, but only wordless splutters emerged.

"She raises a valid point, Redding," Ander said. "You are allied with a traitor and Djido collaborator. The Council of Peers would overrule me if I allowed that to pass."

Attenham visibly calmed himself. He smiled. "Then by all means, Your Majesty: arrest her and execute her for her crimes. Consider her my gift to you; a scapegoat to give to the Council. She used her magic and her wiles to manipulate a Peer of the Realm. I am merely her victim."

Standing next to him, his sword bared and shield raised stood Gennald, and Theramus could see that he was looking less and less comfortable.

Illyria looked good in blue.

She had not looked at him for more than a moment, but Gennald knew that she was aware of him. How could she not, with the bond that they shared?

What did it say of him that even now, with his sword raised against his king and holding a literal black shield, his first thought was still of Illyria? He had abandoned his Lord and joined ranks with this evil, evil man in a pique of anger (over *her*, naturally) and had dared to believe in Attenham's promises. Listening to him wheedle his freedom by blaming another for his actions made Gennald want to retch.

He was just so *angry*. He had been belittled and insulted, used as a hostage, and, ultimately, rejected by the woman he had risked everything for. It was more insult than any man and his honour could bear, so why not use this opportunity to grab at riches so far above his station that he had never even dared to dream of them?

He would become a peer. Attenham had promised it to him. If Gennald supported him in his bid for reinstatement (and helped to get rid of Myria afterward), Attenham would use his influence with the Anderites to support Gennald's ennobling. He would redress an ancient wrong done to his family and have a legacy to pass down to his children.

He would be worthy of Illyria.

Her protests of quickling's kisses and lack of being frantic were lies that she had told him to soften her rejection. He saw the truth in her eyes: that a mere knight-yeoman could never win the heart of a princess. To do so he would need a title, and if allying with this stinking turd of a traitor was the only way to get one, he would do so. She was worth it. He had already stained enough of his honour on her behalf; one more mark was of no matter, not if it gained him what he wanted.

Somewhere, deep within himself, his father's scolding voice told him that he was making a mistake, but Gennald ignored it. He was doing this for his father as much as himself.

He could see by the semi-vacant expression on Illyria's face and the curving of her first two fingers that she was envisioning an arrow shot. Theramus was primed for action and Sephana's tail was twitching, a sure sign that she was on the verge of action. Eldoth was as inscrutable as always and Balien...wasn't there. They had shuffled around on their horses so that his mount was concealed, but Gennald knew his horseflesh. Balien's horse stood riderless, and he wasn't here, he could only be in one place.

"We must act quickly, My Lord," he murmured to Attenham. "Time grows short."

"I need answer now, Your Majesty," Attenham barked. "One motion of my arm and the Dragonfleet learns everything. You know that they'll kill everyone here once they learn your own personal guard attacked and sank one of their ships."

Gennald's hand had been complicit in that. He had, in fact, struck the first blow.

"They weren't in my service then," Ander protested. "I hadn't even met them yet."

"The Dragonfleet won't care. They're wearing your colours. To an outsider, it will look as if their action was a royal order. Yours can be a very short reign, Ander, or a long one. Choose now."

Ander's face grew hard. "And what will prevent me from killing you once the tribute is given?"

Gennald heard Attenham's smile. "I know many secrets, your majesty, about you and many others. My Lady Myria is so very good at finding where the bodies are buried. The truth about Elisanna, among others. If I do not return, these secrets will be revealed and your life will be hell."

"I shall take my chances," Ander said, his voice cold. "Lady Illyria, kill this man."

For the briefest of moments, Gennald hesitated. That pronouncement had been very...kingly.

Gennald stepped in front of Attenham even as Illyria, with her customary elven grace, flowed from her horse as made of water and, between one blink and the next, nocked an arrow to her bow and raised it to his face.

He and Attenham had discussed this. Gennald had insisted that she would not be able to loose at him. Looking at her flat expression now, he was suddenly unsure.

Illyria didn't shoot. If even a sliver of Attenham's body had been visible behind Gennald's she could have stuck an arrow in it, but the height and broad chest she had appreciated so much at the SummersEnd festival blocked him completely.

She stared at the man whose eyes had once entrapped her soul. *Gennald, get out of my way,* she mentally commanded, but, if he heard her, he did not listen. He faltered slightly, then squared his jaw and raised his shield. He had seen her shoot. He had to know that his armour and shield would be no proof against Heartseeker.

I don't want to kill you. Please.

Ander spoke. "My father told me of something you said to him, My Lady. You said that two targets can be struck with one arrow if the archer is skilled enough. Are you as great as you say?"

Shoot *through* Gennald, he meant. Yes, she could do it. That was, her arrow was strong enough to pierce him and still strike Attenham fatally. She knew where to target so as to ensure that it did not hang up on bone or armour, but that did not mean that she would be able to release the bowstring.

She swallowed. "I am, Your Highness." She was partly proud, partly horrified to hear that her voice sounded steady.

She couldn't! She wouldn't! Sephana watched Illyria in horror. She could only see her in profile, but Illyria's face was set, though rather pale.

What could she do? There had to be something that Sephana could do to prevent Illyria from having to do this horrible, horrible thing. Sephana would kill Gennald herself she could. Not that she felt he deserved to die—a long, lonely, life filled with misery was much more just, for what he had done—but better it be her to do it then Illyria. She had done enough things that she needed to atone for, that adding one more to the list wouldn't cripple her. *No one* should have to kill their first real boyfriend. Even if he was a jackass.

He was just in range of the chain of Dawn's First Crescent. If she threw it really hard, she could probably hit him between the eyes. It wouldn't knock him out, but he'd have to flinch at least, and then Illyria could target Attenham.

Something caught her eye as she readied her throw. In the distance, at the edge of the camp, she saw Balien confront Myria. It was too far off to make out anything beyond general body position, but Balien's sword was out and Myria's wasn't.

Hurt her for real this time!

To her dismay, Myria just released the rat-man's leash. The creature immediately began to run off and Balien had to turn from her to catch it. As he did so Myria just...disappeared.

Gennald didn't have to die! She turned back to the scene in front of her, where Illyria and Gennald were standing like statues, their eyes locked. It wasn't easy to see, but Illyria's arm was trembling. Illyria *never* trembled when she had an arrow drawn.

"Kill him, Lady," Ander warned, "if you ever want my trust again."

Illyria wasn't faltering, except for her eyes. They were a pale grey, almost white. Gennald had never seen that colour before.

"Don't." His voice was quiet, but he knew she could hear him. "I'm doing this for us. I'll be a lord."

"What?" Disbelief flared in her eyes. "Don't commit treason for me. I told you that didn't matter. If you're going to betray everything you believe in, do it for any other reason, but *don't* do it for me."

"You have one more chance, Ander," Attenham called. "I'll order the creature's release if I don't get an answer."

"Kill him, lady," Ander ordered. "All your work is for naught if you do not."

Illyria's eyes were turning violet, a colour he knew well: it meant she was furious. She *would* kill him, and she didn't care why he had done what he did.

What had he done? He'd betrayed his lord. He'd betrayed his king. He'd chosen to side with a traitor and was party to his actions.

He was a blackshield.

Acting before he could think, praying that he still possessed even the smallest spark of Emuranna's Grace, Gennald turned and struck Attenham between the eyes with the pommel of his sword. Attenham didn't even have time to look surprised before crumpling to the ground, unconscious.

Gennald turned back to Illyria but found himself facing eight feet of very angry Noss instead. Illyria herself spun in place, no doubt to try and prevent Myria from releasing that dreadful little rat-man. Hopefully, Balien had dealt with that situation but if he had not, Gennald had no doubt that Illyria or her other companions would.

He was convinced at last: they *were* knights; more knightly than him, at least. Even as Theramus was pinioning him and Sephana was tying up Attenham with her dagger's chain, Ander—who had proved himself worthy of being king—was calling out to them.

"Get them behind the horses, quickly!" Ander ordered. "The Dragonfleet entourage is moving. We must ride."

CHAPTER TWENTY-EIGHT

> *"Ander fell to his knees in gratitude. 'You have saved my kingdom, Lady. Name your heart's desire, , and I shall labour to make it so.'*
>
> *"Then Illyria, elven princess and cousin of Lethia, whose beauty and grace transcended those of mortal men, smiled. 'My wish, majesty, cannot be granted by one man, even a king. I wish there to be peace across the land. I wish the High King restored, and all Djido slain for the evil they have done to our land. I wish the Dragonfleet driven from our shores, and for the Nintaran plague to end.'*
>
> *Ander wept. 'Alas, lady, I can give you none of those things, for I am just a man. Is there no gift, no boon I can grant you that will content you?'*
>
> *" 'Be a good king, your majesty. Rule your land justly and with kindness. Do these things for all your life and teach them to your children, and I will be content.'*
>
> *" 'I will,' Ander promised. In the years that followed, he was true to his word and for the rest of his days was Karalon known as the best of kingdoms. And Illyria was pleased."*
>
> — *'Bears and Thistles', from* The Crown Cycle, *Lord Florian*

It was much later in the day before anyone came to see Gennald. He had been bound and held alone in a guarded tent without word, food or water. He had no reason to complain, as there was only one fate for what he had done: execution. Traitors needed no amenities.

Two royal knights, their faces stern and wooden, entered the tent. "Is it time then?" Gennald asked. His voice was hoarse.

They pulled him to his feet and marched him outside. The sun was low in the sky. Off in the distance, the Dragonfleet were loading their ships. Looking around him, Gennald could see dozens of empty wagons.

"They accepted the tribute?" he asked, relief filling him. "There weren't any complications?"

They said nothing, but the lack of tension in the camp was answer enough. Gennald was glad, despite everything. He had betrayed many things in the last month, but through it all he had been a loyal Karalman. He understood, though, why his actions made that hard for others to accept.

He was led to Prince Ander. Two weeks ago, Gennald would have cringed at the idea of Ander representing the kingdom. The Golden Bears had done too good a job of painting the crown prince as too young, naive and innocent for the crown. The man before Gennald now was none of those things.

He needed no prompting to take his knee. "Your Majesty."

"You conspired with Redding Attenham, a known traitor, to usurp my power." Ander's voice was cold. "If his plot had succeeded and the Dragonfleet had learned of your actions in Westbridge, likely we would all be dead and our peace would have been broken. Thousands of Karalinians would have been captured or killed raiding had resumed, and it would have been on your head."

Gennald could deny none of it, and, so, said nothing.

"Have you anything to say for yourself?"

Not moving or even raising his eyes, Gennald spoke. "It was never my intention to endanger the kingdom or the crown. My alliance with Attenham was done for personal reasons, which I see now was wrong." He swallowed. "I would ask your majesty not to condemn my father or March-Lord Jannery for my actions. They had nothing to do with anything I did."

"I have yet to make a decision on that matter."

Gennald nodded. "I know I am in no place to ask for anything, Sire, but I would beg a service of you if I could."

"You struck the blow that felled Attenham. Ask, and I will consider."

"A soldier's death, Sire. Please." There were many unpleasant ways for traitors to die. Gennald had no wish to be eviscerated, torn to death by wild animals, or burned at the stake.

There was a pause. "Your sentence has already been determined."

Gennald nodded glumly. He was not a real noble and had no right to trial. The king could pass justice as he saw fit, when he saw fit. "What is my fate then, Sire?"

"Stand and receive your sentence."

Gennald stood, only to crash to the ground a moment later after being struck him in the face with a wooden rod. "I hereby strip you of your knighthood," Ander said, standing over top of him. "You are no longer worthy of Emuranna's Grace. Stand."

Gennald pushed himself once more to his feet, feeling the blood begin to drip down his cheek. He saw Ander rear back for another strike and faced it without flinching. It struck the other side of his face and, again, Gennald fell.

"I hereby banish you from this kingdom. Bans shall be read in every city on the second day of the new year, naming you a criminal who is to be arrested on sight. You have until then to flee by any means you see fit."

"Banished?" Not executed? Gennald didn't understand.

Ander's tone softened. "There were multiple requests for mercy on your behalf. They were quite persuasive." His voice regained its new hardness. "This matter is concluded. It would behove you to never find yourself in our presence again."

'*Our* presence,' He was sounding more like a king with every passing minute. "I'm sorry, Sire," he called out to Ander's retreating form. "For what it is worth, I am sorry for what I did. I was wrong, and you will be a good king." Ander paused for a moment but said nothing, and then kept walking. The two knights who had escorted him untied his bonds, turned their backs, and left him.

Gennald stood and wiped blood from his cheek. What were two more bruises, after all the beatings he had endured these last weeks? When he lowered his hand, Lord Jannery was standing before him, profound disappointment on his face. *Just Jannery, now*, Gennald realized. That knowledge stuck him harder than any blow.

"I know that you are no longer my lord," he said to...Willem, "but I name you that anyway, out of thanks and respect."

For the first time that Gennald had seen him, Willem looked old. "I do not know if I should condemn you or myself for failing you as a lord."

Gennald disliked the anguish on his face, and knowing that he had caused it. "My Lord, I swear by Emuranna that you did not."

Gennald's former liege continued as if he had not heard him. "I asked the prince for mercy for your father's sake. See him in Ruthcroft if you wish, but do not return to Northhaven." He pressed a small bag of coins into Gennald's hand. "My last gift to you. I do not know if I can bear to see you again, Gennald. Live as well as you are able."

With that, Willem left him. Gennald just stared at the bag in his hand, numb. When he turned, Balien was there.

"You threatened me, earlier," he said. It had been in Lord Ja...in *Willem's* manor, before all of Gennald's many problems had started. No, that was not true: the genesis of his woes had really been almost two months before, when he first laid eyes on Balien's sister. "Are you here to fulfil your promise?"

"No." His expression was even more inscrutable than usual. "You are wounded enough from that already."

That was true. "Then what do you want? I assume I owe you at least partly for my life."

He shook his head slightly. "I gave no council regarding your fate. I want you to stay away from Illyria."

"What?" Gennald's mind reeled from this final, unexpected blow. So much had happened to him these last few minutes.

He had heard Balien fine, and both of them knew it. "You hurt her, but she'd forgive you if you asked. I think she'd forgive you of anything." Gennald knew he was right. "Being free of your vows, it might seem a perfect opportunity to see her again, but it's not."

He hadn't had a chance to think about what his exile meant concerning Illyria, but Balien was right: there was nothing stopping them from being together. Despite everything that had happened; despite the pain she had caused him—as well as the pain he had caused himself, in her name—the idea of another chance made his heart beat faster. "Isn't that her decision?"

Balien hardened. "I may have said that before, but I was wrong. You're bad for her. I don't like who she is when she's with you. She needs to be great."

"She can make her own choices." He sounded sullen even to his own ears.

Balien gave a almost imperceptible shrug. "I'm her brother. Protecting her is my duty." He had given Gennald a threatening look before, back in Willem's manor, that had made Gennald step away from him in fear. That look had been a puppy's yapping. This one was the full-throated growl of a hound warden. "Don't see her again."

His message delivered, Balien turned to go. Somehow Gennald was able to find his voice. "How did Ander's negotiation fare?"

Balien turned. "It went well. They demanded a penalty for the missing ship, but Ander refused when he learned that Princess Elisanna hadn't been returned as they had promised."

It was all Gennald had ever wanted, before: to serve a good king; and now he would never be able to. "And Attenham?"

"In chains. He'll be hung if he confesses in front of the Council; drawn and quartered if not."

Gennald winced. It was a horrible and humiliating way to die. Attenham was a coward; he'd choose hanging, and his confession would destroy what little was left of the Anderite power block. "Thank you." He hesitated, then asked anyway. "How is Illyria?"

Balien just turned and left. Gennald hadn't really expected him to answer.

He stared at the bag of gold in his hand. It represented the sum total of his worth, for his honour had proved to be valueless. He had failed his lord and betrayed his king. He was a blackshield. Gennald felt truly alone for the first time in his life, despite being surrounded by Karalmen.

From the south, he heard sounds of yelling and smelled salt air. It was as good a direction as any.

Gennald began walking.

In her years away, Illyria had gotten out of the habit of having others do her work for her. In Ilthanara, as a member of the royal family, she had been forbidden from making her bed, packing her clothes or even putting them on. As Ander's escort and current advisor, she was permitted to dress herself, but that was all. A group of pages packed her belongings into trunks and took down her tent as she watched. Not wanting to give them further affront by offering to help, she began to wander through the disappearing camp.

She didn't want to think about what damage she had done to her relationship with Ander over both Attenham's revelation and her begging for mercy over Gennald. It was important for the Knights of Anduilon to be on good terms with the crown, and not just because they had not yet received royal recognition for their order. Much of what Illyria wanted to accomplish in the future—alliances between kingdoms, trade, cooperation—required her having ready access to the various throne rooms in Anshara. She was, by training and practice, a diplomat, and more experienced than most in dealing with royalty.

Ander had been distant and hard to read after the negotiation. He had retreated to his tent after returning from his meeting with the giant, red-skinned admiral. Other than giving the order to begin delivering the tribute, he had said nothing to Illyria or any of her knights. She had caught him just before he entered his tent but, instead of asking about his negotiation, had instead begged for Gennald's life.

Yes, she had begged, and likely burned any remaining traces of favour with the Prince Regent in doing so. In the long list of unwise decisions she had made involving Gennald, this was quite possibly the worst. She had risked the future of her order for the life of a traitor, and not only that, but a traitor that, half the time, she wasn't even sure she liked.

And yet, she couldn't *not* aid Gennald one last time. Yes, He had chosen to ally with Attenham and raised arms against Ander, but he had done so, at least partly, because of how bitterly they had parted. He had been promised land and title, which he would have used to bid for her hand. Never mind that he had been a fool to do it, and that she would not have wed him even if he been ennobled; he had committed treason *for her*. As much as, intellectually, she knew that he was responsible for his own actions and that his falling in love with her carried no obligation to him whatsoever, her heart found what he had done humbling, frightening, and more than a small bit flattering. Of course, she had begged for his life. As to whether he would see becoming a blackshield and living in exile as being better than death remained to be seen.

Maybe, now that he was free, he might...

One of Ander's pages found her. "My Lady, the prince asks to see you."

"Of course." She allowed herself a kernel of hope. Perhaps relations with Ander were more salvageable than she thought. She was led to his tent, in which only his field desk and two chairs remained unpacked. She bowed.

"Your Highness."

"Lady Illyria." The events of today had changed him. He looked more confident, more *regal*. She was happy for that, no matter how it had happened. Karalon needed a strong king.

"We are—" he began, and then stopped. "*I are...I mean am*." He paused, his face red. "I am pleased with how today ended. The tribute was accepted with no penalty, a known traitor was caught and his plot to extort me undone. This success was done in no small part to your actions, and of your comrades."

"Thank you for your praise, Highness." His words were kind, but his tone and face told her that he was polishing her up for something. She had no choice right now except to play along. "You are overly kind. Any success that was achieved today owes as much to your leadership as our actions."

Ander snorted. "Every noble in this kingdom has spent the last week gilding my bottom and insisting that they've always been my best friend. I think we are beyond that, you and I."

She would be direct, then. "Why did you ask for me, highness?"

Ander glared, any pretence at politeness disappearing. "You broke my trust today."

She wanted to recoil from the pain and anger in his voice. "I am sorry for how it was revealed," she said quietly, "but not for what I did, Highness."

"Do you think I care that you killed a ship of raiders? These parasites are sucking the life out of my kingdom, and they broke their own treaty to do it. No one is going to condemn you for killing them and getting away with it." He renewed his glare. "I am angry because you lied to me."

"You Highness, I—"

"I don't care what your excuse is! I trusted you." Before her eyes, the last traces of the kind young man she had been grooming for leadership vanished. "After a year of everyone spinning webs of lies around me, I thought I had finally found someone who could deal with me honestly, but your just as bad as the rest."

She kept her eyes firmly upon his desk. "If there is anything I can do to regain your trust, Ander, I beg you to tell me what it is."

"You want something from me."

She didn't like the tone that she heard in his voice. "I...yes, your Highness."

"You want recognition for your order," Ander continued. "You want to be a law unto yourselves, immune to prosecution."

"We serve a higher law."

"To restore the high kingdom, I know. I've heard your pitch." He stood and began pacing behind his desk. Illyria continued to kneel. "Sometimes I believe you intend to do it. Other times I think you and your knights are more dangerous than five Attenhams."

This was not going to end well. Based on his current mood, she and her companions were going to be lucky to escape Karalon without being branded as criminals. "Is there anything I can do to restore your confidence in me?"

"I will not be your weak, humble advisee again, Illyria. That horse has left the stable." He settled on the corner of the desk in front of her. "We shall do this in a more traditional way: I have something you want. You have something I want."

She wanted to weep at the bitterness behind his words. "And what is it that you want of me, Highness?"

"I want my cousin back," Ander hissed. "That Dragonfleet bastard laughed at me when I asked for Elisanna's return. He made me beg for her—beg!!—before revealing that his master, Loeking, had taken a fancy to her and that she would not be returning. When I asked what would happen if I tried to get her back, he invited me to try."

Illyria chose her words carefully. "There may be repercussions if she is taken, Highness—

"You do not get to advise me anymore." His voice was frigid. "If you want your recognition, then you will do this for me. There is no negotiation."

"If you will no longer accept my council then I will respect your wish, but please do not shut yourself off from other potential advisors." He glared at her, which Illyria took as assent to continue. "If you will accept one final suggestion from me, I have found March-Lord Jannery to be good and honourable, with a strong dislike towards courtly deception. I think that he would serve you well."

Ander's jaw unknotted slightly. "I will think on your council, but do not use it as an excuse to avoid the matter at hand. What is—"

His sentence was interrupted by the entrance of a knight. He was short of breath and stank of horse. From the dust on his surcoat, Illyria guessed that he had come here directly from the road. He knelt. "Your Majesty, I have urgent news from New Aukaster."

She saw the flare of fear in his eyes. "Rise and report."

"King Lionar is dead, Your Majesty. He passed on during the night."

Ander blinked, unable to speak. He was still a young man and a son, no matter how hard he wanted not to be. "He is with Anur, Your Majesty, in Eshumarum," she murmured. "I have never met a soul more worthy." She would have said it even if the future of her order did not rest on remaining in his good graces.

"Were there any last words?" Ander's voice was hoarse.

"I'm sorry, Your Majesty. He never woke."

"Leave us," Ander ordered with a shaky voice, "and summon Master Sheltan."

The knight nodded silently and left. Ander leaned against his desk, his body swaying and his face pale. Illyria knelt beside him.

"I'm sorry, Sire." She could call him that now. He was no longer the Prince Regent. "I knew him only briefly, but he was a good man."

He blinked away his tears. "I must make the announcement. Come with me." Not waiting for her reply, Ander strode out of the tent. Illyria could only follow.

What used to be the Karalinian camp was now just a bunch of loaded carts and waiting horses. Everyone except Illyria waited next to a wagon near Ander's tent. Criers had gone through the dissolving camp, calling for everyone to gather in front of the temporary royal residence. Obviously he was going to make some kind of speech. She wondered whether it would praise or condemn them. Her thoughts regarding Karalinian prison hadn't changed.

Until then, there was nothing to do except wait. She glared at Balien with mock severity. "You let Myria get away again."

The corner of his mouth quirked. "I had more pressing concerns."

Well, that was true. He had caught the rat-man (although Theramus said that they were called 'Dakeen', she still thought of them as rat-men; they just *looked* ratty) before it could escape, and had sat on it until after the tribute had been accepted. Sephana had been relieved to see it killed for real this time and it's body burned to cinders.

"You didn't even try to hurt her the second time!"

He gave another, private smile. "You'll have to avenge your own pride, I'm afraid."

Something was off. Sephana crossed her arms and glared at Balien, frowning.

He looked back and arched one eyebrow slightly. "What?"

"You don't seem too concerned that she got away from you...twice."

"She's very skilled."

"I'll bet she has skills," Sephana muttered. She stopped and stared at him, her jaw dropping. "You kissed her didn't you?"

For the slightest moment, Balien's mask dropped and she saw a mixture of surprise, embarrassment and longing cross his face.

"What makes you say that?"

It was just a moment, and then he was his usual, unrevealing self. She might of imagined it, but she was pretty sure that she hadn't. "You did, didn't you?"

"Who I may or may not have kissed isn't your business."

It wasn't a denial. "How could you kiss her? She threw me off a cliff!"

Balien made no reply, his mask fully replaced. A stone would have revealed more.

"This isn't over," she warned him, just as the criers called for silence. A moment later Prince Ander, Knight-Master Sheltan and Illyria walked out of the royal tent. They all looked very serious.

"My father, King Lionar Usard, died last night, in his sleep," Given his serious expression, no one was very surprised but there were still several moans and sighs of sadness. "Though his last few months were ignoble ones, I shall remember him as a valiant warrior who fought bravely for his kingdom, despite his many wounds, and who fell only after achieving victory over his enemies."

Knight-Master Sheltan stepped forward, his white surcoat orange in the setting sun's light. "Kneel," he informed the crowd. Without a word, everyone present, Sephana included, fell to their knees. At Sheltan's nod, even Ander dropped down. "In Emuranna's name and by the ancient, holy rights invested in me as her priest, I hereby name Ander Usard, first born son of Lionar, as King Designate of Karalon." He couldn't become king until he underwent the ceremony in Olsarum and woke his crownmark. Sheltan dipped his fingers into a jar of oil and smeared them across Ander's forehead. "Long live the King!"

"Long live the King!" the audience called out. "Long live King Ander."

Ander stood, his eyes visibly red and looked at his subjects. "Rise," he said quietly. He gave everyone a few moments to regain their feet before raising his hands for silence. "Our father's last words to us were to trust Illyria Exiprion. We heeded those words and found our faith well placed." Illyria's face was expressionless. "In the time we have known her, she and her companions have returned our stolen tribute to us and ensured another year free of Dragonfleet interference. She has given us wise council and delivered the traitor responsible for our late father's illness into our custody."

Something about Ander's speech was off. Sephana couldn't say for certain what it was, but there was more going on than she could see.

"We speak on behalf of ourselves and all of Karalon when we thank her and her companions for their brave actions. Three cheers for Illyria Exiprion and the Knights of Anduilon!" He raised his fist into the air and led the crowd in the three 'huzzah's' that Karalinians used when celebrating something.

"As thanks for the brave actions of the Knights of Anduilon," Ander continued, "it seems only right that our first act as king be to recognise them as knights." He raised his voice. "Let it be known, from this day forth, that The Knights of Anduilon be recognised as a knightly order by the kingdom of Karalon, with Lady Illyria Exiprion as their master. They are to given the rights and privileges in accordance with their station and are free to pursue their wishes and agendas with the full permission of the crown. He turned to Knight-Master Sheltan. "Do you recognise and acknowledge this proclamation, Knight-Master?"

"I do."

"Then it is so."

The crowd broke into spontaneous applause and cheers. People Sephana had never met were giving her congratulations. Sephana thanked everyone while glancing across the crowd to where Theramus was receiving the same honours. He looked just as surprised as she was.

"The Lady Illyria spoke to us earlier," Ander continued, and Sephana groaned. He had publically called Illyria a lady twice now. There was no way Sephana was going to get anyone to call her 'Sir' now. "She spoke of her outrage over the lack of honour possessed by the Dragonfleet involving the return of our royal cousin. She made a promise." He looked at Illyria, his eyes hard. "Would you mind repeating that promise, My Lady?"

Illyria's expression was that of polite pleasure, but Sephana knew her well enough to recognise that she was furious. "Of course, your majesty." She turned to address the crowd. "On behalf of my fellow knights, and in the name of Emuranna and the High King of Anduilon, we pledge to rescue the princess Elisanna from her unlawful confinement by the Dragonfleet and return her to her home here in Karalon. On our name and our honour, we will return with her within one year's time."

This time the cheering was much louder.

Eldoth made little effort to conceal how content he was to be back in his customary red coat. All of the Knights of Anduilon had changed out of their heavy woollen finery soon after leaving Ander's entourage. Theramus was very happy to be so unburdened. As a giant, he only wore clothing for the sake of other's propriety and found anything more than a sleeveless tunic too confining. He had no idea how the others tolerated wearing so many layers all the time.

Of course, being freed from uncomfortable clothing was the least of their concerns.

"So why did you make that promise?" Sephana asked Illyria. "I mean, he'd already made his big statement acknowledging us. We got what we wanted, didn't we?"

King Designate Ander had not invited them to accompany him back to New Aukaster, and they had agreed that there was no need for them to travel with the empty baggage train back up north. They had set out at their own pace and had made twenty miles before making camp. They had managed to shoot a pair of ducks to roast and accompanied them with barley mash and dried turnips (Sephana had declared her intention of never eating anything made from an oat, ever again, and no one had disputed her).

"He isn't king yet," Balien said from his place by the roasting spit. "His proclamation isn't binding."

"He isn't? What did we just see, then?"

"He's only the King Designate," Illyria told her from her place by the still-cooking pot of food. "Being king isn't about speeches and ceremonies. Ander has to undergo the Bonding ceremony in Olsarum and form his connection to the land. He's not anything until then, not in the eyes of Emuranna."

"Then why did he even declare us knights if it doesn't mean anything? It doesn't make any sense."

"It was a message, from Ander to us," Illyria said, stirring the barley. "We don't receive official recognition from him until we rescue Elisanna. If we do, he gets the credit for it because he asked us to. If we fail and enrage the Dragonfleet, he can deny being involved because his word wasn't binding, and we were never under his authority."

"That's really...calculating," Sephana said. "He seemed nicer than that, before."

Balien and Illyria held an entire conversation with their eyes that ended with her looking away, chastised. "He was just a regent before, standing in for his father." she said, her eyes fixed on the cookpot. "He's a ruler now; the ruler we made him."

"I don't think that we are the only people to have underestimated Ander," Balien said. "For better or worse, we are committed to rescuing Elisanna now." He looked at Theramus. "Where do you think the Dragonfleet port might be?"

"Not Karalon," Theramus said without hesitation. "And I have my doubts about Tirim. Kalumfar, perhaps. Vast stretches of it are unpopulated. Darandy, also, is possible, if they are brave."

Balien's frown told Theramus that he was aware of just how much coastline that encompassed, and how difficult it would be for them to search it. It also did not need to be said that locating the port would be only the first of their difficulties.

"We will find her," Theramus declared. "It shall be so."

"Do you still want me as your leader?" Illyria asked, setting her stirring spoon aside. Her eyes had turned a pale shade of turquoise. "Nothing was ever formally agreed on. It was just a habit we all fell into." She cast her eyes downward. "And I don't think I've done a very good job of it. I've made many poor choices these last few weeks, even before my decision not to tell Ander about Westbridge." She was referring, Theramus knew, to her relationship with Gennald. Theramus was pleased that it had ended. Eldoth and Sephana were more than enough romantic drama for their group.

"We all decided not to tell Ander," Sephana said to Illyria. "Well, almost all of us," she amended, glancing at Balien. "It looked like the best choice at the time. I thought it was, anyway."

"It was the easy choice, not the right one," Illyria said. "We're supposed to better than that."

"Pondering the effects of decisions you did not make is a waste of energy," Eldoth said, surprising Theramus. The wizard never contributed to conversations that did not directly involve him. "Better to learn from it then obsess on pointless speculation."

"Eldoth is right," Sephana said, her expression bewildered. "You can't play 'what if'."

"I can't help it," Illyria said, still staring fixedly into their dinner. "All I can think of is that we would have fared better if someone else had made the critical decisions."

"If not you, then who?" Theramus asked her.

"Anyone!"

He did not hold her indecision against her. All beings had moments of self-doubt. Certainly he had. She would be better in time.

Eldoth shook his head. "I have no interest in such a role."

"Me either," Sephana said. "Even Eldoth would be better than me."

He looked at her and frowned. "Did you just insult me, or yourself?"

"Umm...both?"

Theramus ignored them. "I am Noss. We do not lead."

Every eye turned to Balien. He thought a moment, then shook his head. "You're our leader, Illyria. We never said it formally because it didn't need to be said." He reached across and raised her chin with his fingers. "Lyri, look at me. You are a good knight. You made some mistakes, yes, but you were right when it mattered. Knighthood isn't about duty, or questing, or being brave in battle; it's about trust, trust in your friends. We trust you to lead us, and you have to trust that our faith in you in not misplaced."

Illyria closed her eyes and smiled, resting her cheek in her brother's hand. "I don't deserve you as a brother."

"You're right. You don't."

She punched him in the chest and they both laughed.

"Hey, I just thought of something," Sephana said. "When Ander named us, he named Illyria as the master of our order." She turned to Illyria. "Does that mean we have to call you Knight-Master now?"

Illyria grimaced. "Please don't. That's worse than being called an elf."

END

Did you enjoy this novel?
There is more at www.titanheart.ca.

Read novels, download podcasts and check out exclusive on-line content including:

- *Additional and deleted scenes*
- *Previews of upcoming work*
- *The Titanheart database (The 'Library of Alashadimm')*
- *Character Profiles & More*

Why Titanheart?

- *~~Weekly~~ Semi-Regular Updates*
- *On-line content is always free*
- *Two complete novels published per year*
- *Your choice of format: Novels, PDFs, Kindle, iPad, MP3s, Podcasts*

About this book: This novel was written in Microsoft Word 2007 on a HP netbook PC running Win7 Starter. It uses the Americana BT, Stoertebeker, and Times New Roman fonts and uses a customized formatting template created by the author. All significant editing and formatting was done by the author (though he'd be happy to pawn the job off on someone else if they offered).

About the Author: Ross is an intellectual, creative geek and proud of it. He has had many jobs but in his heart he has always been a writer. It took twenty years of frustration and a world-wide recession before he finally found the courage to become a full-time novelist. His education, like his career, is widely varied. Notable among his many literary influences are Jacqueline Carey, web author Minisinoo, Andy McNabb and Suzanne Brockmann.

Ross currently resides in Edmonton, Alberta where, when not writing, he spends his free time kayaking, trying to create the perfect bottle of mead, and torturing others by means of karaoke.

8099665R0

Made in the USA
Charleston, SC
08 May 2011